WIND
FROM THE
WILDERNESS

BOOKS BY GILBERT MORRIS

THE HOUSE OF WINSLOW SERIES

1. The Honorable Imposter
2. The Captive Bride
3. The Indentured Heart
4. The Gentle Rebel
5. The Saintly Buccaneer
6. The Holy Warrior
7. The Reluctant Bridegroom
8. The Last Confederate
9. The Dixie Widow
10. The Wounded Yankee
11. The Union Belle
12. The Final Adversary
13. The Crossed Sabres
14. The Valiant Gunman
15. The Gallant Outlaw
16. The Jeweled Spur
17. The Yukon Queen
18. The Rough Rider
19. The Iron Lady
20. The Silver Star
21. Shadow Portrait

THE LIBERTY BELL

1. Sound the Trumpet
2. Song in a Strange Land
3. Tread Upon the Lion
4. Arrow of the Almighty
5. Wind From the Wilderness

CHENEY DUVALL, M.D.
(with Lynn Morris)

1. The Stars for a Light
2. Shadow of the Mountains
3. A City Not Forsaken
4. Toward the Sunrising
5. Secret Place of Thunder
6. In the Twilight, in the Evening
7. Island of the Innocent

THE SPIRIT OF APPALACHIA
(with Aaron McCarver)

1. Over the Misty Mountains
2. Beyond the Quiet Hills
3. Among the King's Soldiers

TIME NAVIGATORS
(for Young Teens)

1. Dangerous Voyage
2. Vanishing Clues
3. Race Against Time

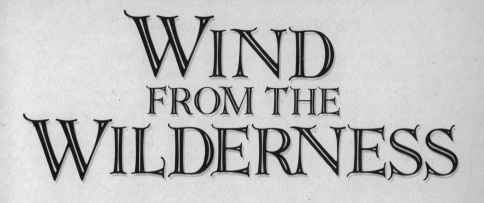

WIND
FROM THE
WILDERNESS

GILBERT MORRIS

BETHANY HOUSE PUBLISHERS
MINNEAPOLIS, MINNESOTA 55438

Wind From the Wilderness
Copyright © 1998
Gilbert Morris

Cover illustration by Chris Ellison
Cover design by the Lookout Design Group

Published by Bethany House Publishers
A Ministry of Bethany Fellowship International
11300 Hampshire Avenue South
Minneapolis, Minnesota 55438
www.bethanyhouse.com

Printed in the United States of America by
Bethany Press International, Minneapolis, Minnesota 55438

Library of Congress Cataloging-in-Publication Data

CIP data applied for

ISBN 1–55661–569–8   CIP

To Johnnie

Thanks for fifty wonderful years.
I've enjoyed every second of every year!

GILBERT MORRIS spent ten years as a pastor before becoming Professor of English at Ouachita Baptist University in Arkansas and earning a Ph.D. at the University of Arkansas. During the summers of 1984 and 1985, he did postgraduate work at the University of London. A prolific writer, he has had over 25 scholarly articles and 200 poems published in various periodicals, and over the past years has had more than 100 novels published. His family includes three grown children, and he and his wife live in Texas.

CONTENTS

PART FOUR
The Gypsy
Fall 1777

THE LIBERTY BELL

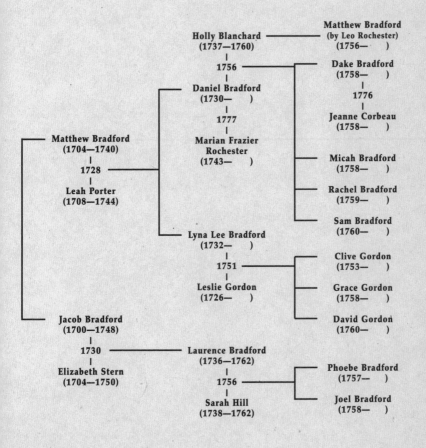

Matthew Bradford
(by Leo Rochester)
(1756—   )

Holly Blanchard
(1737—1760)

1756

Dake Bradford
(1758—   )

Daniel Bradford
(1730—   )

1776

1777

Jeanne Corbeau
(1758—   )

Marian Frazier
Rochester
(1743—   )

Micah Bradford
(1758—   )

Matthew Bradford
(1704—1740)

1728

Rachel Bradford
(1759—   )

Leah Porter
(1708—1744)

Sam Bradford
(1760—   )

Lyna Lee Bradford
(1732—   )

1751

Clive Gordon
(1753—   )

Leslie Gordon
(1726—   )

Grace Gordon
(1758—   )

Jacob Bradford
(1700—1748)

David Gordon
(1760—   )

1730

Laurence Bradford
(1736—1762)

Elizabeth Stern
(1704—1750)

1756

Phoebe Bradford
(1757—   )

Sarah Hill
(1738—1762)

Joel Bradford
(1758—   )

PART ONE

—

BOSTON

Spring 1777

1

An Affair of Honor

PHOEBE BRADFORD OPENED HER EYES slowly, blinking sleepily as the morning light entered from the mullioned window on her left. She burrowed down luxuriously into the deep softness of the featherbed, and the sweet smell of clean linen was a distinct pleasure to her. She was not quite fully awakened, but as the bright sunlight beat persistently against her eyelids, she stretched and yawned hugely. Throwing the multicolored quilt back, she sat up in bed and looked around with satisfaction.

"This is the finest room in the world," she whispered. "And it's all mine!"

Phoebe was a tall young woman of twenty. She was short-waisted with long legs but had a very attractive figure. Her ash blond hair was curly, especially during rainy weather, and she had very dark blue eyes with light brown brows arched over them. She had an oval face, a short nose, and prominent cheekbones, and on her right cheek a dimple would appear when she smiled.

The bedroom was of medium size with warmly stained oak flooring covered with light blue area rugs. The walls were papered in a bold design with peacocks and trees on a blue background, and two small windows were covered with thin white linen curtains. Sunlight streamed through the windows, bathing the large oak tester bed in its warmth, and its beams made a reflection from a small hanging mirror and seemed to dance on the walls on the other side of the room. A mahogany wardrobe and washstand gleamed from their highly polished surfaces, and a glass lamp on a dressing table beside the bed flickered a rainbow of light on her face.

A thought came to Phoebe and her eyes lit up. "I'm going to have me a bath," she announced. Then leaping out of bed she rummaged

13

through the drawers and walked barefooted down the hall with an armful of clothes. She entered the room that contained the copper bathtub that Mrs. Marian Bradford had showed her the day before, and after closing the door, she stood staring at it. It was a wonder to her, for she had never seen a bathtub in her life, nor had she ever had a complete bath except in the creek, but that had been years ago when she was but a child.

Placing her clothes on a small wooden table, she moved across and tested the mechanics of the thing. As Mrs. Bradford had showed her, the plumbing was attached to a wood furnace outside the house that had a boiler. The water was pumped up so that it ran down into the kitchen and into the bathroom. Gingerly she turned the handle and at first was disappointed, for the water was cold. But she held it there for a moment, and to her delight it became warm and then got warmer still. She watched as the tub filled up with eight inches of water, then she turned it off. Hesitant just for a moment, she slipped out of her gown and then picked up a washcloth from a rack on the wall. Stepping into the tub, she sat down. The water was not hot but pleasantly warm as she lay down in it, delighted at the luxury it afforded.

For a few moments she simply enjoyed the new pleasure. Then seeing a bar of white soap, she picked it up and lathered her body thoroughly. She had forgotten to tie her hair up and it got wet, but it did not matter. Finally she lay down and soaked for a while, and then when a voice called outside the door, she sat up.

"Yes, ma'am?"

"You'd better hurry up, Phoebe. You can have breakfast with Joel if you hurry."

"Yes, Mrs. Bradford. I'll be right down."

Yanking the plug from the tub, Phoebe got out with alacrity, dried off on a fluffy white towel, and then began to dress. She slipped into a pair of white cotton drawers and chemise, then laced up the heavy linen corset with difficulty. Turning around she picked up two quilted petticoats, slipped them on, and tied them around her waist. Then she slipped into a simple brown dress made of heavy cotton. The dress had a low bodice, but it was covered with a white linen handkerchief tucked into the bosom, with pagoda sleeves flowing down past her elbows.

She marveled at the softness of the clothes. They were all new. Mrs. Bradford had purchased them for her, and she felt like a princess as she ran back to her room, pulled on her stockings and shoes, then quickly brushed her hair.

Leaving the room, she stopped for one moment and looked around at it. "Lord, I'm thankful to be in a place like this! It's like a palace after what I grew up in. . . ."

✢   ✢   ✢

Joel Bradford had arisen at approximately the same time as his sister, Phoebe. The sound of horses stomping and whickering below his window brought him out of a deep sleep. With a startled motion, he sat up and looked around rather wildly. He was in a new land now, and it all seemed strange to him.

Stepping off the rope bed with the cotton mattress, he looked around the small room Daniel Bradford had taken him to the night before. It was rather rough, not at all like the fancy room Phoebe had, but that was only fitting, since he was a man and she was going to be Mrs. Bradford's personal maid. Quickly he moved over to the washstand, poured out a basin full of water into a pewter bowl, and washed his face, splashing and sputtering.

Joel was a young man, lean and muscular, and stood almost six feet tall. He weighed a hundred and sixty pounds, ten pounds less than he had weighed when he had first arrived in America. He had lost weight during the time spent in a debtors' prison in England, but the three months under Daniel Bradford's roof had caused him to fill out and had hardened muscles from the work he had done all of his life. He quickly worked up a lather and, looking into the mirror, studied his face for a moment—the blue-gray eyes deep set in a lean face, the prominent nose that he did not like, and the thin and mobile lips. A pale scar ran down his right cheek to his chin, the relic of a fight where he had gotten hit by a piece of wood. He shaved quickly, and although his hands were very large-boned and strong, they were able to do the delicate work. He ran his fingers through his thick blond hair, noting that it was too long and needed a haircut, and then he turned and began to dress. His upper body was very strong, since he had done some prizefighting in England. He had been good at it, too, and he wondered if he would ever enter any pugilistic competitions here in America.

For one moment he stood quite still, his mind running over the past few months of his life. *Hard to believe I was in debtors' prison back in England only a few months ago. I'd still be there if Matthew Bradford hadn't come to see Phoebe and me.* A quick rush of gratitude filled him as he remembered how Matthew had set the wheels in motion to free them and bring the two of them to live at the Bradfords' house in America. *We're only distant relations, but they treat us like family!*

He quickly put on his underwear, then donned the snuff-colored trousers and the maroon wool shirt, the finest he had ever had. It had belonged to Daniel Bradford at one time and had scarcely been worn. It was a little large for him, but still he was proud of it. Quickly he slipped on the black leather shoes with the brass buckles and then moved to the ladder and agilely slipped down.

The smell of hay and horses and leather filled the air, and as a movement caught his eye, he turned to see a young man dumping feed into a trough.

"Hello, Patrick," he said. "Let me help you with that."

"Almost done. You can go get some water, though, and fill the bucket." Patrick Mears, the Bradfords' stablehand, was a short, muscular young man with a thatch of red hair and a pair of bright green eyes. He cocked his head and grinned. "I guess if you're kin to the master, I can't be givin' you any orders."

Shifting his feet uncomfortably, Joel shook his head. "No, it's not like that, Patrick."

"But you are kin. That's what the word I heard is."

"That's true enough in a way. My grandfather Jacob was his grandfather's brother."

The two young men stood there and Mears asked, "Did you hate to leave England?"

"No, I was glad to get away. My sister and I were just at the rope's end when Mr. Daniel's son, Matthew, found us. I think we might have starved if he hadn't come and helped us."

"Things are tough in England, are they?"

"Oh, like everywhere, I guess. Some people are rich and well fed, and others are starving."

"Well, you've come to a fine place here. The master, he's got a good business. Find you a good wife, get married, and have a lot of kids."

Joel grinned suddenly, a crooked grin that made him look younger than his nineteen years. "Well, I'm not thinking about that right now. I'm just glad Phoebe and I have a good place to stay."

At that moment Daniel Bradford, the master of the house, entered the barn. He was an inch over six feet and weighed a solid one hundred and eighty-five pounds. He had a heavy and strong upper body from years of blacksmithing. He had wheat-colored hair and eyebrows, and hazel eyes with just a touch of green. His wife, Marian, always insisted he looked a little like a Viking with his thin face and high cheekbones and broad forehead. His chin was cleft and there was a scar on the bridge of his nose.

"Better come in, Joel. Phoebe's just come down to breakfast. I expect you're hungry."

"Yes, sir. I was just going to help Patrick with the horses."

"You can do that later."

"Yes, sir." Moving quickly to match Daniel Bradford's footsteps, Joel said, "That's a fine room over the stable, sir. I slept like a rock last night on that good mattress."

"I'm glad you like it, Joel. Not anything fancy like Phoebe's room, but women need a little pampering, I suppose." Bradford stepped inside the back door and stood in front of the fireplace to the right of the large kitchen.

Hattie, the black cook, said with rebuke, "This food's gonna burn up if you don't sit down and eat it!"

"All right, Hattie, don't shoot us." Bradford laughed at her, then turned as Marian and Phoebe entered from the inner door. "Better sit down," he said. "Hattie's getting upset, and you know what that means."

"Never mind what that means! Just sit down and eat!" Hattie said. She had been a slave but was now a free woman. Her husband, Josh, had worked for the Fraziers, Marian's family, for years. She now scurried around, and as soon as the four sat down, she began piling the food on the table.

Breakfast consisted of johnnycakes made on the griddle, with freshly made apple butter, breakfast puffs, fried ham with gravy, and dressed eggs. Large glasses of cold milk were served along with steaming mugs of coffee or tea.

"Well, I don't know about all this food," Bradford said, winking at Joel. "If I say a grace long enough to take it all in, we might not get started until dinner."

"Just make it short and sweet, Daniel," Marian said. "We'll hear long prayers when we get to church tomorrow."

Daniel nodded, bowed his head, then said briefly, "Lord, we thank thee for this food. You have provided it all and everything we have. We thank thee for our young relatives who have come to stay in this country, and we pray your blessings will fall on them. And I ask this in the name of Jesus. Amen."

Marian and Daniel watched with concealed amusement as Joel and Phoebe both ate like hungry sharks. They were pleased at the way the matter had turned out for their young relatives. Daniel had discovered that he had relatives in England, and Matthew, who was there on a visit, had found them in rather destitute conditions. Daniel had written him

17

to bring them home, and that he would find a place for them. As he sat there looking at them he was content. They both were fine-looking young people, and as far as he could tell, they both had good qualities.

Joel took an enormous bite out of a biscuit and said around it, "Mr. Bradford, would you—"

"Don't talk with your mouth full, Joel!" Phoebe scolded.

Joel swallowed the biscuit and said, "I'm sorry, Mr. Bradford—Mrs. Bradford. I guess my manners aren't much."

"They're as good as mine, Joel. Now, what were you going to ask?" Daniel smiled.

"Well, we've heard a lot in England about the war over here, but I don't rightly understand it."

"It's very simple, Joel. We're fighting over here to decide who will rule over us—a king in England three thousand miles away or a Congress composed of men that we elect ourselves."

Joel considered that for a moment, then nodded. "I guess I'd like that second one best—but who's going to win?"

Daniel looked quickly at Marian and shrugged. "Why, that's yet to be decided, I suppose. Briefly, the war's been going on about two years. It started in April of seventy-five at Lexington and Concord, and then we had a battle at Bunker Hill that we won. Right after that George Washington took command of the army."

"We've heard quite a lot about him, Mr. Bradford," Phoebe said. "Everybody in England knows about General Washington."

"He's just about the best man I know of," Daniel agreed. "General Gage had Boston under his command, but General Washington, with the help of some cannon that one of his officers delivered from Ticonderoga, blasted them out. So we won the Battle of Boston, and I'm glad of it," he said fervently. "It was pretty bad while the British were here."

"That sounds wonderful," Phoebe said. "So you won."

"Well, not really." A grim look came to Daniel Bradford's eyes, and he leaned back and sipped his mug of coffee. "Washington went to New York, and the British brought a big army over and ran him out. They forced him to retreat all the way through New Jersey and across the Delaware River. It looked like everything was lost. The Revolution was falling apart. I've got a son in that army. His name is Dake Bradford, and my son Micah was there at the time. You ought to hear them tell about what happened last Christmas."

"What was that, Mr. Bradford?" Joel asked eagerly.

"Washington took what little army he had across the Delaware in boats through the ice, and he whipped the British at Trenton and then again at Princeton."

"That was a good thing, too," Marian said. She herself was drinking tea out of a fragile, beautiful china cup that had come all the way from Holland. She added, "If Washington hadn't had those two victories, I think the cause for liberty from the Crown would have been all over."

"Well, you're right about that, Marian. Right after that Washington took his army into winter quarters, but now that spring's come, we're all waiting to see what he'll do." Daniel got up from the table abruptly. "There's hope, that's all I can say." Then he turned and said, "Come along, Joel. We'll go down to the foundry and see if we can find something for you."

🛎   🛎   🛎

Albert Blevins was a tall, sour man with a cadaverous face. Although he was only fifty-six, he looked older, and he had been a faithful servant to John Frazier, owner of the foundry, since it had opened its door. Later when Daniel Bradford had become a partner, he had been suspicious and jealous of his position. But when John Frazier became ill and was unable to take any active part in the work, Blevins quickly recognized the skills Daniel possessed, for he had saved the foundry with his hard work and leadership.

Still, Blevins somehow acted as though the business belonged to him, and when Daniel walked in and introduced his young relative, he grunted, "What can you do, boy?"

Somewhat put off by Blevins' cold manner, Joel said, "I don't know much about the foundry business, but I'm used to hard work if that means anything."

"Of course it does," Daniel grinned. "Don't be such a grump, Albert. We can always use another pair of good hands around here."

"We need to make money, that's what we need!"

Daniel shook his head with mock sadness. "You're a miser, Albert. How does the payroll look?"

"How do you expect it to look when you keep doing free work for the army?" Blevins snapped. "We've got to get paid for what we do! That's the first rule of a business!"

"The Congress will vote the funds soon. General Washington promised me."

"And if they do pay us it'll be in Continental notes. What good are they? They're just good for papering the walls, nothing more!"

Gaining financial support and supplies was the eternal problem of

George Washington's Continental Army. The Congress itself had had one bad experience with the king and were apprehensive that a strong military commander might become an American Caesar. Leary of such oppression happening again, they paid the bills slowly and with great reluctance. In fact, there was not a great deal they could do, for the various Colonies preferred to invest their money into their own militia rather than in a national army.

"Come along, Joel. I'll introduce you to some of the men, and you can try your hand at it."

Moving down out of the offices located upstairs, Joel was confused by the clanging sounds and the strident ring of steel on steel. Men were working everywhere and he could hardly hear Daniel when he spoke.

"This is my son, Micah. I'm turning you over to him."

The young man reached out his hand. "I'm glad to know you, Joel. Follow me and I'll show you what we're doing around here."

Micah Bradford was very much like his father in appearance. He had the same straw-colored hair and hazel eyes, but there was a slowness in his mannerisms and a gentleness that was lacking in his father.

"Micah's not himself, Joel," Daniel grinned. "He's just gotten engaged, and his bride-to-be has fled."

Joel shot an astonished glance toward Micah, who merely shrugged and smiled briefly. "Don't listen to Pa, Joel," he said. "She's just gone for a visit to her sister who lives in Baltimore."

Micah, indeed, had been somewhat disturbed when his fiancée, Sarah Dennison, had left Boston. Their courtship had been rocky, but she had explained, "After we marry I won't be able to visit Mary. I'll only be gone for a few weeks." Micah had growled and complained, but finally gave in. He was so in love with Sarah that he would have granted her anything.

Turning toward Joel, Micah said, "The worst thing about Sarah's going is I have to put up with a lot of ribbing from my family—especially Mr. Daniel Bradford."

"A prospective bridegroom is fair game, son," Daniel laughed. "Just hope this is the worst you have to endure. Now, take your cousin for a tour of the foundry."

As he took Joel all over the foundry, Micah was very careful to explain all the procedures involved in what they were doing. Even during that brief tour Joel heard several things Micah Bradford said that gave indication of the young man's strong Christian beliefs and his desire to be a minister.

Micah put Joel to work right away shifting heavy metal from one shed to another. Thankful for a job, Joel eagerly went at it with all his might.

From time to time Micah came back to check on the young man and gave him an encouraging word. Finally at four o'clock Daniel Bradford stopped by to say, "Well, I've got a good report on you, Joel. Micah says you can work hard enough to put a horse to shame."

"I don't mind it. I'm used to hard work," Joel said as he wiped his brow.

"Are your hands cut up much from handling the steel?"

"Oh no. I've got fairly tough hands and I wore the gloves that Micah gave me." Joel stretched out his hands palm upward and said, "See, they're fine."

Daniel stared at the young man's hands and suddenly put out his own. "Let's see what kind of grip you have."

Startled, Joel stuck his hand out and it was enveloped by Daniel Bradford's large hand. He felt his employer begin to close his grip and tightened his own to meet it. The grip became tighter and tighter, for Daniel Bradford was a tremendously strong man.

Finally Daniel said with some surprise, "Your grip is as good as mine. For a young man that's very good."

"Well, as I said, sir, I've done a lot of work."

"Your sister tells me you did some prizefighting back in England."

"Oh, just a little, Mr. Bradford. It's not anything I'd want to do for a living. I find it rather brutal."

"Your face isn't scarred."

"No." Joel suddenly grinned. "I spent most of my time running away from some of the bruisers there. I finally quit. Didn't like it."

"Well," Daniel said, "it doesn't hurt a young man to be able to defend himself. Now, Joel, I want you to go down to the farrier and pick up a horse and take him home. Here, I've written down how to get to the farrier; then he'll tell you how to find your way to the house, in case you're confused."

"Yes, sir, I'll do that."

"Don't tarry. You know how upset Hattie gets when we're late for a meal!"

🚩   🚩   🚩

The sun was going down as Phoebe stepped into the drawing room. Quickly she moved around dusting and cleaning and admiring the elegant furnishings. She had always loved fine things but had no hope of ever having any of her own. Now, of course, these were not her things, but still the warm sense of something very like possession came to her. After all, she *was* a Bradford and this was the Bradford house.

Once she paused before a painting and studied it carefully. It was a picture of a cottage somewhere in the distance, and in the foreground a group of men on beautiful horses were racing across the green grass. A number of hunting dogs were scattered in front of the horses, and far off to one side, barely in the picture, was a red fox running for cover. The picture was so realistic and well done that Phoebe stood lost in admiration for some time. Once she thought, *It must be wonderful to be able to ride and hunt like that. I don't suppose I ever shall, but maybe Joel can someday.*

The sound of a bird's song penetrated her concentration, and turning, she walked over to the window. It was closed, and she raised it and leaned out, for the sound came from a cherry tree to her right. Looking in that direction, she saw a small brown bird with a yellow breast that she could not identify. *It's probably an American bird, not an English one*, she thought as she leaned out farther to get a better look.

A sound behind and above her caught her attention, but she had no time to move. The heavy window suddenly descended and struck her across the shoulder blades. It was so heavy that it forced her down, and she uttered a small cry of distress as it pinioned her. Her arms dangled out of the house, and she was unable to shove the window up. Although she was not hurt, the breath had been knocked out of her for a moment. She struggled in vain but could not manage to move the window even an inch.

"Well, what have we here?"

Pinioned as she was, Phoebe could only turn her head upward. She saw a young man standing there regarding her with a twinkle in his eyes and a rash grin on his broad lips. He came closer and stooped a little bit. The window was so high that her face was almost on a level with his as he shook his head. "I don't believe I've had the pleasure of meeting you."

Phoebe's face turned a dull red. She was embarrassed and humiliated, and now bit her lip as she struggled vainly to free herself.

The young man stepped even closer and studied her carefully. "It seems you have quite a problem here."

"Please, sir, could you lift the window and help me get loose?"

"Well now, that would require some thought."

The speaker was young Sam Bradford, the youngest son of Daniel. He was seventeen and had auburn hair and electric blue eyes. He was not tall but was strongly built. As he stood there smiling, he was very amused by the plight of the young woman whom he had never seen before. He lived in his father's old house, for after his father's marriage to Marian Rochester, they had of necessity come to live at the home of her father, John Frazier. He was failing in health, and Marian could not leave him.

"I'll tell you what," Sam said, nodding thoughtfully. "I'll be glad to help you out, and all it will cost you will be one little kiss."

Furiously Phoebe tried to free herself, but her hand slipped off the windowsill and she struggled in vain. "Don't you touch me!" she warned.

"Why, somebody's got to help you! You might stay trapped there until you starve to death." Impudently Sam reached forward, put his hand under Phoebe's chin and kissed her right on the lips.

"You . . . you get away from me!" she cried out.

"Well, you paid the price, so I'll gladly help you now." He reached forward and with one effortless motion raised the window. He had no sooner done so when a rough hand on his shoulder turned him around. Sam was shocked and off balance at the sight of a young man he had never seen before.

"I'll teach you to insult my sister!" the young man yelled.

The next thing Sam knew, a fist had caught him in the face and knocked him so hard that he sprawled backward on the fresh green grass. For a moment his head swam and he saw what seemed to be green and purple stars. Then his vision cleared and anger swept over him.

Leaping to his feet, Sam lunged forward and threw a mighty blow at his assailant. The blow missed and he was caught in the stomach by a hard fist that drove most of his wind out. Sam, however, was tough and moved forward throwing blows from every direction.

Phoebe had raced outside and stood there horrified, watching the two men fighting. At the same time Marian Bradford arrived. Joel was thoroughly angry, for he had seen and heard what had taken place, and now he simply shook off the young man's blows and proceeded to punch him at will in the face. He got in several strong blows that bloodied the young man's nose and one that closed an eye at once. Then he threw a roundhouse-right that caught Sam squarely in the jaw and knocked him down flat on his back.

"Joel, stop fighting," Phoebe pleaded and ran to him, grabbing his arm.

"I'll teach the fellow to insult my sister!"

Marian ran over to where Sam was lying flat on his back. She lifted his head, and taking her handkerchief, she began to wipe the blood from his face. "Sam, are you all right?"

Sam was struggling to get his senses back. One eye was already swollen shut, and he peered out of the other one at the young man who had soundly bested him in seconds. He stumbled to his feet and said, "Who do you think you are?"

"My name's Joel Bradford! Who are you?"

"This is my stepson Sam," Marian said quickly. "What's this all about?" she demanded.

Sam then remembered vaguely that two of his cousins were coming from England, but he had not expected one of them to be such a pretty woman. However, he was still angry. "Let me go, Mother. I'll teach that fellow a lesson!"

"No, there'll be no more fighting," Marian said.

"I'm so sorry, Mrs. Bradford," Phoebe said. "It . . . it was all my fault."

"It wasn't your fault!" Joel said grimly. He stepped forward to Sam. "I don't care if you are Mr. Bradford's son! You had no business insulting a young woman like that!"

"Why, I'll break your head!" Sam struggled to free himself from Marian's grasp.

"Did you insult her, Sam?" Marian demanded.

"No, I didn't insult her. I just—" Sam looked around guiltily and wiped more of the blood from his bleeding lip and nose. "I just gave her a kiss, that was all."

"I'm ashamed of you, Sam Bradford!" Marian scolded. "You've been brought up better than that."

"Well, this fellow didn't have any business hitting me!"

"I'll fight for my sister's honor, Mr. Sam Bradford, the same as you'd fight for yours!" Joel said hotly.

Sam then blinked his one good eye and Marian whispered, "What would you do if you caught a man insulting Rachel?"

Sam Bradford was an impulsive young fellow but good-hearted and fair-minded. He realized that Joel had done exactly what he would have done. Now as he looked at Phoebe and saw tears in her eyes, he felt a wave of shame.

Looking at Joel, Sam said, "Well . . . all right. I'll forgive you this time, sir, but you be more careful, or I'll have to give you another thrashing." He stepped forward and asked anxiously, "I didn't hurt you, did I?"

The remark suddenly struck the others as hilarious. Sam's eye was closed, his nose was bleeding, and he had a bruise on his left cheek.

There was not a mark on Joel Bradford, for he had taken no blows what-soever, but there was something so ridiculous and yet at the same time good-natured in the expression of the battered young man that Joel at once put his hand out and said, "I believe I'll survive, sir, and I appreciate your not wanting to harm me any longer."

"Come inside and let's get you cleaned up," Marian commanded.

Soon Sam was sitting in the kitchen and his stepmother was mopping his face and giving him a cold press to put over his swollen eye. She was also delivering a lecture. "Sam, sometimes I think you're nothing but a foolish and impetuous boy. The idea of doing such a thing to a young woman in this house!"

"Well, I couldn't help it."

"Couldn't help it!" Marian snapped. "Of course you could help it!"

"Well, maybe I could have helped it," Sam admitted, "but I didn't want to. She looked so innocent and pretty there, and what's so wrong with a little kiss?"

Marian grabbed a handful of Sam's hair and held his battered face upward. "Listen to me!" she said. "These young people have been taken abruptly out of their home, the only home they've ever known. They're strangers, and they're working for us, but they're kinsfolk and they need friends. I want you to be nice to them."

"Why, I was just trying to be nice, wasn't I?" Sam retorted, and his one good eye glinted. "Doesn't the Bible say, 'greet one another with a holy kiss'?"

Marian could never remain angry with Sam for very long. She laughed abruptly and shook her head. "You're impossible, but here's your kiss." She kissed his bruised face and then shook her finger at him. "You be sure that you treat them nice from now on. I won't stand for any more of your foolishness."

2

"I Don't Have Anything to Offer a Woman"

MARIAN BRADFORD WAS SITTING at the dressing table brushing her hair. She was very proud of the dressing table, for it had been a special wedding gift from her husband. Made of fine rosewood imported from across the ocean all the way from Africa, it had been crafted by the finest furniture maker in Boston. With one small drawer in the center and two on each side—all that worked noiselessly and with perfect ease—it was beautifully carved and inlaid with mother-of-pearl in a fanciful design. The frame around the mirror that matched the table was crafted from the same wood, an intricately designed oval with the finest glass that could be bought. Now the pieces glowed with a rich gleam, and the mirror reflected the image of the woman who sat stroking her dark auburn hair. She glanced at the reflection of Daniel, who was sitting in bed waiting for her and watching. "What did you say to Sam about the fight?" she asked.

"From what I understand it wasn't much of a fight. Joel just cleaned his plow." He grinned slightly. "I think it's good for Sam to have someone take him down a peg or two. He's too ambitious and a little over-enthusiastic about his own talents. I don't think he'll be taking on Joel anymore."

Marian's eyes danced as she smiled back at Daniel. She took another stroke on her hair, then put the brush down and rose from the table. She was wearing a pink and blue striped satin negligee with self ruching. The gown was long, low-cut and short sleeved, and had a small lace

27

ruffle ending at the elbows, and the robe came to about mid-thigh and had lace sleeve ruffles that ended at her wrists. Discarding the robe, she placed it on a chair and slipped into bed, turned out the lamp, and faced Daniel as she pulled up the covers. It was a warm April night, so it was only a single sheet.

"He was so funny, Daniel," she said. "Forgiving *Joel!*—as if Joel had done anything—and then asking if he had hurt him when he hadn't laid a hand on him!"

"It didn't do him any harm, not permanently. His face was kind of a mess, but actually, it wasn't Joel's fault. He was a boxer over in England. The average man wouldn't have much chance against a trained pugilist."

"Was he really? He doesn't look like a boxer. I always think of them as huge, bulky creatures, somewhat like gorillas."

"And how many gorillas have you seen?" he teased her. Putting his arm under her, he pulled her close and ran his hand down the silky skin of her back, causing her to shiver a little, for she was very ticklish.

"None, but I've seen pictures of them."

"I've seen pictures of dragons, too, but I don't expect to see one."

The house was quiet now, for they had stayed up late. From the window that reached almost to the floor, the light from a large, brilliant moon filtered through, shedding silver beams across the floor and on the faces of the two who lay in bed. It was their favorite time together. During the day, Marian stayed occupied caring for her father and seeing to the running of the house, and she also was quite busy with church affairs. Daniel, of course, was gone all day, working hard at the foundry sometimes until late at night. Bedtime was the one chance they had to be together and talk without distractions.

For a while they lay quietly, discussing the affairs of the day, and then they fell silent.

Daniel had grown highly sensitive to the moods of this woman he had married. She was still a new bride, for they had not been married long. Daniel's first wife had died years before, and he and Marian had fallen in love after Holly had died. By that time, however, Marian was married to Sir Leo Rochester. He was a cruel and heartless man, and the marriage was devoid of any love for Marian. Leo had remained married to her in name only, for his affections were given to others in drunken and riotous living. After Leo's death and Daniel's proposal, she had come into this second marriage with the passion and love of a young woman.

Now Daniel was aware that something was troubling her. "What's wrong, Marian?" he inquired gently. "You're not really bothering your-self over that scuffle between Sam and Joel, are you?"

"No, it's not that."

"Well, what is it, then? It's not like you to be so quiet. Can't you tell me?"

For a time Marian did not answer. She felt secure in his embrace, with his strong arms holding her close, and she thought about all the years she had lain cold and unwanted in a bed. She was suddenly grate-ful that she had a husband, one whom she loved with all of her heart and deeply respected. Still, she could not speak for a time. He urged her again, and finally she said, "Daniel, I've never had a child of my own."

Daniel was surprised, and yet not greatly so. Although Marian had never spoken of her childlessness, Daniel was convinced that every woman wanted a child to love and nurture. Because she had not spoken about it before, he had assumed she had overcome her grief, however deep it might have been, and now was content. Cautiously, he said, "I didn't know you ever thought about that."

"I'm forty-four years old and really too old to be having babies, and I suppose I'm barren anyway."

For once Daniel had no answer to give her. He knew that Leo had been capable of producing a child, for he was the biological father of Matthew. Daniel had married Holly after Leo had forced himself on her and gotten her pregnant. When the child was born, it was soon obvious that the boy had none of the physical characteristics of the Bradford family. In fact, he had been the exact image of Sir Leo Rochester. Since Leo had fathered a son, it was in Daniel's mind that Marian was inca-pable of conceiving.

"Does it trouble you a great deal?"

In order to assure Daniel, Marian quickly said, "Oh, I can't com-plain. I've got a wonderful husband, a nice house, and a comfortable life. So many things that other women don't have. Just forget that I said anything about it."

Daniel held her tightly, for he knew this was not her heart speaking but her head. *She doesn't want to trouble me*, he thought. *I didn't know how much this meant to her.* After a while, he whispered, "We'll ask God to give us a child."

"Oh, Daniel, I can't have children!"

"Neither could Hannah, the mother of Samuel, but she had a fine boy. Don't forget," he said, "with God anything is possible."

"I love you when you talk like that," she whispered. She put her arms around his neck and pulled his head closer. Her kiss was soft but passionate and demanding, and he held her tighter and knew that he had found a love that few men ever had for a woman.

☩　　　☩　　　☩

For several days after Joel's so-called fight with Sam, Joel was worried. He said to his sister, "I sure made a mess out of things, Phoebe. Imagine beating up our employer's youngest son."

"It wasn't your fault, Joel," Phoebe assured him. Actually she had been very proud of her brother for defending her. She had since learned that Sam was absolutely harmless, just filled with high spirit, and there was no ill feeling between the two.

Sam had shown no grudge toward Joel, but Joel could not help being apprehensive about it. For nearly a week Joel had worked hard at the foundry.

Micah had come by more than once to slap him on the shoulder and say, "You don't have to work so hard, Joel. You're going to kill yourself."

"No, I don't reckon hard work ever killed anybody."

Micah grinned. "I suppose that's right, but I just want you to know that you're doing very well—better than any young fellow we've ever had come to work here."

Joel was wearing his oldest clothes, for he was stoking the furnace where one of the forges was operating. His face was smudged and he had taken off his shirt. The muscles of his upper body stood out clearly. He reached up and pulled down on the bellows, and the flame caught at once. Wiping his brow, he glanced at the blacksmith, who was heating a piece of iron until it was red-hot. Suddenly he turned to catch up with Micah, who had walked away. "Mr. Bradford," he said, then waited until Micah had stopped and turned around. "I'm worried about that fight I had with Sam."

Micah was surprised. "Why, there was nothing to that. It was all Sam's fault."

"I know, but—"

"Look, Joel," Micah interrupted. "I know you're a little bit apprehensive being in a new place with a new job, but if you're worried about any of the family feeling hard at you for punching Sam, forget it." He grinned and shook his head. "Sam's always getting into fights. As a matter of fact, he wins most of them. He's not tall but he's strong. I think it was good for him to get his comeuppance. Where did you ever learn to fight like that?"

"Oh, I fought a little bare-knuckle for a while in England, but I didn't like it."

"Well, you learned well, but don't you worry about Sam. He hasn't said anything about it, has he?"

"No, he just grins and keeps saying he hopes he didn't hurt me." Joel suddenly smiled himself and shook his head. "He's a good-natured young fellow, isn't he?"

"Yes, he is. The finest in the world. Just don't worry about it. It didn't mean a thing. Besides, you're family."

"Well, thank you, Mr. Bradford."

"Tomorrow's Sunday. I'd like for you and Phoebe to go to church with us."

"Yes, sir, we'd be glad to."

☥   ☥   ☥

Joel and Phoebe attended church the next day with the Bradfords, and to Joel's surprise, he enjoyed it tremendously. The pastor, Reverend Asa Carrington, was a fine preacher. He had direct black eyes that sometimes rested on Joel and made him take the remarks personally. Joel said nothing to Phoebe, but the sermon made him think about his soul, which was something he had rarely done before.

The following Monday he got up and ate breakfast with Phoebe and the rest of the servants in the kitchen. Hattie had fixed battered eggs, buckwheat cakes, and biscuits, and as usual he piled his plate with a generous portion of each. He got into an argument with Oleander Smart, the gardener. Smart, a tall, gangling man of sixty, was much involved in the study of prophecy, especially in the books of Revelation and Daniel. He was arguing that George III was the anti-Christ, and his talk grew rather salty the more he talked about his favorite subject.

"He's the spawn of Satan, that's what he is!" Oleander declared, stabbing another buckwheat cake and baptizing it in molasses and then chewing it thoroughly. "Straight out of the pit! The right-hand man of the devil!"

"Oh, come now, Oleander!" Joel said quickly. "George III is not a bad fellow. He's a good family man with a whole house full of children, and he treats them all well."

"He's a red-handed murderer! For every American that dies, their blood's on his hand. I'm surprised, young man, that you'd take up for such a beast!"

The argument had gone on for some time, and finally Patrick Mears shook his head and said, "You see the anti-Christ behind every tree,

Oleander. Well, I can remember when you thought it was some sultan over in Egypt, but he died and you had to have another one, so you elected King George."

Cato, the butler, was enjoying the argument. He himself was a devout Christian and had his own ideas about the book of Revelation, but he had learned the futility of arguing with Oleander. He smiled now, his white teeth gleaming against the blackness of his face, and said, "Don't argue with Oleander, Joel. It don't pay."

After breakfast was over, Daniel wandered into the kitchen and said, "Joel, Mrs. Bradford has some work for you."

"You don't want me to go to the foundry?"

"If you finish in time, you can come on down." He smiled and said, "If you were Sam, you'd be sure it lasted all day. Then you could loaf a lot. Sam's that way. He's the busiest young fellow you ever saw when he's working on one of his inventions, but otherwise he's as lazy as a slug. But I know you're not like that. Mrs. Bradford will show you what there is to do."

Joel left immediately to go find the mistress of the house, and after the others had left, Daniel said, "Cato, what do you make of my young relative?"

"Mighty fine young man, sir, mighty fine indeed." Again his smile brightened his face, and he said, "Did you know he's a mimic?"

"A mimic? What do you mean by that?"

"I mean, sir, he can imitate anybody." Cato shook his head. "I never seen nothin' like it. You oughta hear him sound like Oleander. If I wasn't lookin' right at him, I'd swear Oleander was there, and he can sound just like Patrick, too, and walks like him. It is a sight to behold."

"Does he do an imitation of me, Cato?" Daniel asked and grinned at the guilt that washed across Cato's face. "I see he does. Well, I won't give you away. He's a bright young man, though. You tell him something once, and that's all that's necessary. Got a phenomenal memory, apparently."

"Yes, sir, I think he's mighty fine. And Miss Phoebe, she brightens up the whole house. She sure is company for Miss Marian. Why, them two talks all the day long just like a bunch of parrots."

"I'm glad they're both here," Daniel said. He turned and left the kitchen and found Joel listening to Marian. "I've got to go to the foundry. Good-bye." As he kissed her she put her arms around him and pulled him down for a longer kiss.

She held him so long that Daniel laughed. "You've got to try to get over being so shy. Especially in front of company, Mrs. Bradford."

32

Marian simply laughed back and said, "Try to get home early, Daniel."

"As early as I can. Good-bye."

As soon as the door closed, Marian said, "Joel, I have a job for you, but not here at the house. I have some friends who need help and no man to do it."

"What sort of work, Mrs. Bradford?"

"I don't know exactly, except that the roof leaks. Do you think you can fix that?"

"Yes, ma'am, I expect so."

"Well, take care of that and then ask Mrs. Denham what other work needs to be done."

"Mrs. Denham? That's the lady who owns the house?"

"Yes, Mrs. Esther Denham. She's an elderly woman and not in very good health. She had a fine home in New York, Joel, but when the city half burned down, her home went with it, so she left and is living in a house she owns here in Boston. She has a young lady living with her—her niece, Miss Abigail Howland—and I'm afraid the two have had a difficult time of it. Stay as long as you need to get the house in first-class shape."

"Yes, ma'am, I'll do that." He hesitated, then asked, "Relatives of yours, Mrs. Bradford?" A troubled light came into Marian's eyes that Joel did not miss.

"No, not really. My husband's oldest son, Matthew, was once engaged to marry Abigail." Again she hesitated, then said, "There was some difficulty and they broke it off, but I've wished that they would patch it up. I like Abigail a great deal. She's had an unfortunate life, and of course her aunt lost practically everything in New York, so they're really in need of help. I want to do all I can."

"Yes, ma'am. I'll do the best I know how."

After getting directions from Marian, Joel made his way across the city. He found the house without any trouble in a run-down section of Boston. He stood looking at the white frame structure with the name *Denham* painted on a sagging fence post. It was a larger home than he had expected, but it had certainly seen better days. He took in the dilapidated fence, the broken stones in the front walk, and the shakes that were missing from the sharply slanted roof; then he glanced at the stable in the back. The doors were twisted from their hinges, and almost all the paint had been turned to a silver-gray by sun and rain. Stepping up on the porch, he knocked briskly, and almost at once a young woman opened the door.

"Yes?" she asked pleasantly.

"I'm Joel Bradford, ma'am. Mrs. Marian Bradford sent me over to help with some repairs."

"Oh, how thoughtful of her! Just like Marian. Please come in."

As Joel stepped in he saw that the woman was very attractive, a little older than himself. She had an oval face, hazel eyes, and rich brown hair.

"I'm Abigail Howland," she said. "Come along. My aunt will want to speak to you."

Joel followed the young woman out of the foyer and turned off into a sitting room on the west side. An older woman was sitting by the fireplace, and she looked up with interest as Abigail said, "This is Joel Bradford, Aunt Esther. Marian sent him over to help with the repairs."

"Why, Marian didn't have to do that." Esther Denham had silver hair and mild brown eyes. She was very frail and small boned, but she still had traces of a youthful beauty. "Your name is Bradford? Are you related to Daniel Bradford?"

"Yes, ma'am. My sister, Phoebe, and I just came from England. We're distant relations of Mr. Daniel Bradford. He was kind enough to bring us over and give us both work."

"Well, that's just like Daniel. I don't know of a better man anywhere."

"I think you're right, ma'am. I understand your roof is leaking."

"Indeed it is," Abigail said quickly. "It's leaking in the dining room, too. The last rain we had did some damage. The water poured down right in the middle of the mashed potatoes. It just about ruined the table. And the wind pulled the doors of the stable loose."

"Well, I think maybe I can fix that, ma'am, if you can show me where the leak is."

Joel followed the young woman into the dining room, fixed the location of the leak in his mind, then said, "I'll see what I can do." He left the house and went out at once to the stable. There were no horses there nor any evidence of any having been there recently. He did find, however, three large bundles of shakes evidently left over from a roof job. He also managed to locate a blunt-handled hatchet and enough nails for the job.

He spent the morning patching the roof, and by eleven-thirty he came down, carrying the remaining shakes and the hatchet, which he put in the stable. As he was turning to leave, he became curious when he saw a set of wooden stairs leading upstairs. He mounted them quickly, opened the door, and found himself in a large room, apparently used at one time as housing for a coachman. The furniture was old and not much to look at, but structurally it was still solid. He turned, closed the door, and descended the narrow stairs. Leaving the stable, he went to the back door of the house. He knocked and when Abigail opened it, he said, "That job's all done, miss."

"Oh, that's wonderful, Joel! You must be starved. You've been working so hard. You must come in and have lunch with my aunt and me."

Joel was very hungry and thanked them for the invitation as he followed the two ladies to a formal dining room. The meal was well prepared. It consisted of steaming hot mutton, freshly baked wheat bread with whipped butter, green beans, and fresh fruit and cheeses. Abigail kept his glass filled with milk, and when he had finished, she brought in slices of cake on thin saucers.

Joel ate the cake and said, "Ma'am, you're a fine cook."

"It's good to see a man eat so heartily," Mrs. Denham said as she sipped tea from a dainty cup. "We two women just rattle around in this place. Daniel had it fixed up when we first came from New York. We were like a pair of refugees, weren't we, Abigail?"

"Indeed we were, but God was good to prepare a place like this for us. I know you hated to lose your fine things and your home in New York, though."

"Well, the Lord giveth and the Lord taketh away. Don't you agree, Joel?"

"Yes, ma'am, I certainly do."

"If you haven't found a church, there's a very fine one right down the street from us. It's the Congregational church. We'd be happy to have you visit," Abigail said.

"Yes, ma'am, I'll try to do that." Quickly he added, "Now, Mrs. Bradford told me to fix anything that needed fixing, so if you'll just show me anything that doesn't work, I'll do my best."

"That will be wonderful!" Abigail said fervently. "I can't fix anything myself."

"Well, I'm no genius, but if I can find the tools here, I can do the best I know how." A thought came to him, and he said, "I noticed the stable doors are falling off. I could put those back on."

"Oh well, we don't keep any animals now. There's little need for it."

"Yes, ma'am, but there's a nice room upstairs. You might want to use it someday. The building seems to be in good shape otherwise, and it wouldn't take much work to fix the doors. Mostly just reset the hinges, I think."

35

"Well, it would be nice. They look awful hanging loose like that," Mrs. Denham said mildly.

Joel thanked them again for the meal and then went back to work. By five o'clock that afternoon he had fixed everything that either of the two women could think of. As he left, both of them thanked him fervently and he smiled at them.

He is very good-looking, Abigail thought. She admired his tall stature and his blue-gray eyes. She wondered where he got the pale scar on his right cheek but did not dare ask. "We'll be looking for you to visit us at church, Joel."

"Yes, ma'am, I'll try to do that."

Joel left the house whistling, and when he got back to the Bradford house, he went at once to see Marian to give her a full report of his activities.

"That sounds like you did a good day's work. What did you think of Mrs. Denham and Miss Howland?"

"The younger one—Miss Abigail—she's a very attractive young woman. You say she was engaged once to one of your kinfolk?"

"Yes, to my husband's oldest son, Matthew."

"Well, he won't find one much finer looking than that." He saw that something about the situation between Abigail and Matthew troubled his employer, so he quickly changed the subject. "I guess I'd better go get ready to eat."

"Yes, you do that. Hattie's fixing a good supper for you."

As soon as Joel left, Marian walked slowly around the drawing room. She was thinking mostly of the strange relationship Matthew Bradford and Abigail Howland had had. Abigail had been a wild young woman in her day, having had an affair with Paul Winslow. She had, however, been converted and had dramatically changed her ways. Marian knew that Matthew had been in love with Abigail, but something had come between them and he had broken it off. She also knew that Abigail was still in love with Matthew, no matter what others said.

"I wonder if they'll ever make it up," she murmured. "Matthew's too hard. He's a little bit like his father." By "father" she meant Leo Rochester, for Matthew had Leo's blood in his veins, and Leo had been a hard man.

T   T   T

The house the younger Bradfords had grown up in was now occupied by Jeanne Bradford, Dake's wife. Dake, Micah's twin brother, was away on active duty in the army. Rachel, Daniel's only daughter, still lived there, and Micah was staying there as well, at least temporarily.

Both Jeanne and Rachel had been anxious to show some interest in the new arrivals from England and had planned a dinner party. Phoebe and Joel were taken aback but pleasantly surprised when Marian told them of the plan.

"You mean they want to have a party for us?" Phoebe exclaimed.

"Well, not a party. Just a family supper. You'll get to meet the rest of the young people—all except Dake, who's serving with General Washington."

When the evening for the party finally arrived, Phoebe and Joel went in the carriage along with Daniel and Marian. Both of them were nervous, and Marian leaned forward and patted Phoebe's knee. "Don't worry. You shouldn't be nervous. They're all very anxious to meet you."

"I think Matthew will be there," Daniel said.

"Oh, that's wonderful! He was so kind to us in England," Phoebe said.

"Yes, indeed, he was. We were really at rock bottom when Mr. Matthew came and bailed us out of prison. I guess we'd still be there if it wasn't for him, and you too, of course, sir," said Joel as the carriage moved along.

"Well, he'll be glad to see you again."

The carriage pulled up in front of the house, and Daniel jumped out to help the women disembark. When they approached the door, which opened without a knock, Rachel Bradford greeted them with a warm smile. "We're so glad you could come!"

Marian said, "This is Phoebe and this is Joel."

Rachel shook hands with both of them. She was a very beautiful woman, with red hair, green eyes, and a heart-shaped face.

Phoebe felt drawn to her at once, and as for Joel, he thought she was truly a fine-looking woman.

"Come in," Rachel said. "Matthew's already here. And Micah says he's starving to death."

They entered the house and followed Rachel into the dining room. It was not an ornate room such as the Fraziers had, but it was more than adequate and nicely furnished. The table was set and a young woman came in with a pewter bowl, steam rising from the top.

"This is my daughter-in-law, Jeanne Bradford," Daniel said.

Jeanne smiled and spoke. She was a striking young woman with very curly black hair and beautiful violet eyes. "I'm happy to know both of you. Please sit down."

"No time for talk," Micah grinned. "Just sit down and eat—just like the hogs in the lot."

Jeanne was standing close to Micah, and she reached out and slapped him hard on the chest. She liked her brother-in-law very much. He was the exact replica of her husband, Dake, and it always made her a little lonely to see Micah. "You can go eat with the hogs if you please, Micah, if that's the way you're going to talk!"

"No, I'll behave. Don't whip me anymore."

Matthew Bradford had come at once to shake hands with the pair, saying with a smile, "You look very well. It appears that America agrees with you."

"Oh, Mr. Matthew, I can't tell you how happy we are," Phoebe said, "and how much we have to thank you for!"

"That's right, sir. I still remember the day you came to that prison and you didn't know us from anyone, but you got us out."

"Well, it only cost ten pounds. I guess my generosity's good up to that point," Matthew said.

Seeing Matthew with the rest of the family, Joel noticed just how different Matthew looked from the other Bradford men. He was slender, with brown hair and blue eyes, and something about his manner was unique. Now that Joel and Phoebe knew he was not Daniel Bradford's real son, this explained a great deal.

"Well, here she is. Come in, Keturah."

They both turned to see a young woman enter from the kitchen bearing a bowl of bread. She appeared no more than sixteen at most. She had large, rather startling light blue eyes, very widely spaced, thick dark lashes, and arched black brows.

"I'm glad to know you," she said shyly, setting the bread down, and then she said breathlessly, "I'll wait the table, Rachel, if you want."

"We'll all do it," Rachel said. "You men sit down and we'll have the blessing."

They all sat down and bowed their heads, and right in the middle of Micah's blessing came the sound of a door slamming loudly and someone bellowing, "Where is everybody?"

The voice continued until it entered the dining room. "Oh, you're already eating!"

Micah looked up with an irritated expression. "No, we're trying to have the blessing, if you'll sit down, Sam!"

"Go right ahead," Sam said. "Don't mind me." He grinned over the table at the two guests. "Well, hello, Joel. Did you get over that thrashing I gave you yet?"

"Just about," Joel said solemnly.

All eyes turned to look at Joel. All evidence of the beating Sam had received was gone, and he seemed genuinely to have forgotten it.

Sam took his seat and said, "Amen." He laughed aloud at the expression on Micah's face. "I guess Micah was off on one of his long prayers again. It takes him longer to thank God for food than any man I ever saw. Pass the potatoes."

Rachel reached over and grabbed a generous handful of his auburn hair and pulled his head over. "You behave yourself, Sam. We have guests!"

"Ow—let go of me, Rachel!" Sam gave her an offended look, then said, "Well, go on, Micah. If you've got to preach, go right at it."

Micah laughed, for he could not remain angry at Sam for long. "I guess it's blessed enough. Pass Sam the potatoes before he starves."

At first, both Joel and Phoebe were tremendously shy and didn't enter into much of the conversation. But Daniel and Marian soon had them feeling welcome and enjoying their meal thoroughly. After the meal was over, the men rose to go into the parlor while the women gathered the dishes together. When the men were settled inside the rather snug room, the talk turned at once to Washington and his Continental Army. Joel had nothing at all to say, but he did notice that Matthew was not as enthusiastic for the revolutionary cause as the other Bradford men. Sam, he saw, was all ready to join up as a soldier, but at one point in the conversation, his father replied sharply, "You're too young, Sam!"

"I'm seventeen! There's plenty in the army no older than me!"

"I thought you were going to save the world with your privateering ship," Micah inquired, lifting his eyebrow with mock surprise. "Haven't you and Jubal got that thing working yet?"

"Of course it's working. We've just got to make the finishing adjustments." Sam saw that Joel was listening intently and said, "I'm going to be a privateer, me and my partner, Jubal Morrison. You oughta come and help us, Joel."

"I don't know the first thing about ships," Joel confessed.

"You don't have to know anything. All you have to do is row a little bit. I'm going to fire the cannon. We just need strong backs and weak minds."

"Well, I qualify, then," Joel smiled.

"Don't pay any attention to him," Matthew said. "Sam is just going to get himself killed. Why, if one of those little craft that you call a 'spider catcher' ever got close to a British ship of war, it'd be blown right out of the water."

"You don't know anything, Matthew. I'm surprised a man as educated as you can be so dumb," Sam said airily. "We don't fight warships; we find fat, happy, dumb merchant ships. Most of them don't even have cannons. They either pull up and we take over, or we blow them clean out of the water."

A long argument ensued about the wisdom and feasibility of all this, of which Matthew took almost no part.

Finally Daniel said, "I give up on you, Sam." He turned to Joel and said, "I understand you went over to help Mrs. Denham out again, Joel."

"Yes, sir, I did."

"How is she getting along?"

"Oh, very well, apparently. She's a little frail, but Miss Abigail is healthy enough." Even as he spoke the name, Joel suddenly remembered that Matthew Bradford had been engaged to this woman. He lifted his eyes and met those of Matthew, who stared at him with an unreadable expression. Joel stammered, "They . . . they're very nice ladies. Very nice indeed."

Daniel and Micah exchanged glances, for they were also aware of the sudden flush in Matthew's cheeks. Micah said quickly, "It was a shame she had to lose her home in New York."

"Yes, she had some very fine paintings in it," Matthew said, glad to change the subject. He had been in New York at the time and had helped her mother and her aunt make her escape. Abigail had been there too, and he still had unpleasant memories of what had transpired between the two of them.

The ladies soon entered and the small parlor was crowded. Phoebe and Joel, of course, were in a sense outside of much of the talk, for it was of family matters. They did notice, however, that young Sam Bradford took every opportunity to sit close to Keturah.

When they left, after having been warmly invited back by Rachel and Jeanne, Joel asked as the carriage rattled along, "Is Miss Keturah a member of the family?"

"No, not really," Daniel said. He did not know how much to tell of Keturah Burns' history. He thought for a moment, for the truth might shock the two, although he doubted it. Keturah was the daughter of one of the camp followers, little more than a prostitute, who had died following the army. Micah had found Keturah after her mother's death and saved her from a brutal member of the militia. He had watched after her, and when she had gotten terribly sick, he had brought her home where she could be cared for properly. Daniel merely said, "She has both lost her mother recently and suffered a difficult illness. Jeanne and Rachel have nursed her back to health. She's been a great help around the house ever since."

Phoebe knew there was more to it than this, for she was very perceptive. She asked no more questions, however, but determined that she would find out more about Miss Keturah Burns and Mr. Sam Bradford somehow.

It was two days later before she had a chance. She was polishing the silver when Marian came to help. As Marian sat down beside her Phoebe cautiously asked, "Miss Keturah, is she going to stay there for long at the other house?"

"I expect she will. She has no place else to go."

"Sam likes her, doesn't he?"

"Yes, he does. You saw that, did you?"

"Oh yes, ma'am. He didn't get very far away from her. She didn't seem to pay much attention to him, though."

"Well, the truth is," Marian said slowly, "Micah saved her life at least twice. Once when she was attacked by a soldier and again when she was very sick. She grew extremely fond of him as she was recovering."

"You mean she's in love with him?"

"Well, she's young—seventeen, I think, and she has a strong attachment. But Micah's engaged now to Miss Sarah Dennison, so Keturah has got to learn to get over it."

Phoebe thought about that for a moment, then shook her head. "How do you do that, Miss Marian?"

"How do you do what?"

"How do you not love somebody after you once loved them?"

Marian stared at the young woman. It was an innocent question, and she suddenly found she had no answer. "I think it has to be a matter of time. Keturah will find a young man, but for a while, I suppose, she's grieving a little bit. You must have had attachments when you were younger, Phoebe."

"I don't know as I ever had."

"Didn't you ever have a sweetheart?"

"No, I never did, not a real one anyway."

"Well, you're young, too. You have plenty of time."

3

OUT OF THE STORM

FOR THE FIRST FEW WEEKS that followed Joel Bradford's introduction into work at the foundry, he learned the fundamentals. He quickly became accustomed to all the loud sounds—the screeching of the steel-wheeled carts dragging their loads and heavy objects crashing to the ground. These he soon learned to filter out as he threw himself into the process of learning. His first job was tending the fire for the forges. Most of them were square and made of stone or brick. They had fire beds hooded to carry smoke and fumes to the chimney, and a set of bellows to direct a blast of air onto the hot coals. It was Joel's job to add fuel when needed, using a long-handled, lightweight shovel called a *slice*. He learned that hot coals packed around the outside of the fire kept the heat from escaping, and he used a rake called a *fire hook* to remove the burnt fuel from the forge.

Regulating a fire, he learned, was essential. It had to be large enough to accommodate the work being done, yet a fire that was too large wasted fuel. Micah taught him that the hot spot of the fire had to be close to the draft of the bellows, but if it was too close, it would be scattered by a powerful blast.

"When I first came," Micah said one morning as the two were engaged in something new, "all we made were things like bayonets and scythes. But General Washington needs cannons desperately, so we're in the process of learning how to make them."

"Making a cannon!" Joel shook his head. "That's really something, Mr. Bradford."

Micah, who was wearing a leather apron over his linsey shirt and cotton trousers, nodded. His eyes gleamed as he said, "It's been quite a challenge. We call this a foundry, and a founder is a person who makes metal castings—not like what you've been seeing for the past few days."

"I don't understand any of this. Why is there so much wood here, Mr. Bradford?"

"It's all part of making a cannon. Strangely enough, it takes wood to make a casting out of metal. We've had to become our own pattern makers. What we do is make an exact pattern of the object we want to cast in metal. First, we do a lot of carving and chipping away and planing. And let me tell you something—if you think it's easy to make a wooden cannon that's exactly the right dimensions, you'll learn differently."

Joel was fascinated by any new process, and the idea of making a cannon engrossed him. He stayed right on Micah's heels, learning that those who work in metal had to be skilled carpenters as well. Micah showed him how metal that was liquid enough to pour would shrink when it set in a mold; therefore, the pattern had to be larger than the end product.

Micah said once, "We've made five cannons and something's been wrong with every one of the patterns." He nodded at the round object up on a table. "This one's about ready. If it doesn't work, I'm tempted to give up."

"What do we do now?" Joel asked.

"Well, we make a sand mold first," Micah said. "In this box over here we pack the finest sand. It has to be specially shipped in. I'll let you do that. Make it up even with the top."

Carefully Joel filled the box with sand and packed it down, wetting it slightly from time to time. When he had finally filled the box, he fetched Micah, who nodded with satisfaction. "All right. Now we take out enough so that exactly half of this cannon fits right down inside of it. Don't be in a hurry, Joel. Just take it out a spoonful at a time."

It was a painstaking task. Joel and Micah worked slowly until finally the wooden pattern fit down exactly. "Now the trunnion will have to be done very carefully. That's the part of the cannon that swivels to give you height and elevation."

Late in the afternoon the job was done, and Micah stood back looking at the mold with satisfaction. "I think that'll do it," he said. "Now we have to add the sprews."

"What's a *sprew?*" Joel asked.

"We have to have some way to pour the hot metal into this mold. So we put tapered tubes into the wet sand. When the tubes are finally pulled out, it leaves a hole that we pour the metal into."

"Can we pour the metal today?" Joel asked eagerly.

"No, it takes a while to get that metal at just the right temperature. We'll do that tomorrow, though. You've done a good job, Joel. You've made a good hand."

That afternoon when Joel got home he found Phoebe outside hanging clothes on a line to dry. "Phoebe, let me tell you what I've been doing." The two stood there under the bright April sun, the breeze blowing and the clothes flapping on the line as he spoke excitedly about his day at the foundry.

"Do you think you might like to do that? I mean for a living, Joel."

"I like it right well," he nodded. "But what I'd really like to do is join the army. Maybe I could get in the same outfit that Dake's in."

A touch of fear came to Phoebe then. She knew that if Joel left she would be alone, a stranger, although the Bradfords were distant kin. She had never been separated from Joel all of her life, and quickly she said, "I don't think that's a good idea. You need to wait awhile and get settled. We haven't been here very long."

Joel shrugged and said, "I think it's a good cause, Phoebe. This isn't like England. If the Colonists win this war, a man will be free over here. That's something worth fighting for."

Phoebe started to speak, but even as she did so a voice sounded.

"Well, Miss Phoebe."

They both turned and Phoebe said with surprise, "Well, hello, Mr. Bickerson."

"A beautiful day, isn't it?"

"Yes, it is," Phoebe said. "I don't believe you've met my brother, Joel."

"How do you do, sir?" Bickerson was a tall, massive man with black hair and brown eyes set a little too close together. He had a strong lantern jaw and a broad smile. "I understand you are working with Mr. Bradford at the foundry."

"Yes, sir, that's right."

"Well, let me welcome you to Boston. I've already done so to your sister. We met at the church last Sabbath Day."

Bickerson stood there talking for a moment, and then after a time he said, "There's a service at the church this evening. I'd be pleased to have you accompany me, Miss Bradford." As an afterthought, he said, "And you, of course, would be welcome, sir."

Phoebe colored slightly and hesitated. Finally, however, she could think of no excuse and said, "We would be happy to come."

"Yes, we'll be very happy," Joel said. He saw a light of displeasure flicker in Bickerson's eyes. Joel recognized instantly that Bickerson was accustomed to having his own way, but the man recovered quickly.

"Fine. I will be here with my carriage about six. Good day to you, then."

"Who's that?" Joel demanded. He watched Bickerson move away and shook his head. "Not the sort of man I'd think you'd care for."

"I don't care for him." Phoebe did not mention that Bickerson had already pressured her several times to attend various social events around the city. He was a persistent man, and she was too inexperienced to know how to avoid his advances.

"Well, I suppose we'll have to go, but I'll sit between the two of you in the carriage," he said, grinning. "That ought to dampen his ardor a little bit."

The church service was a disappointment to Silas Bickerson. Joel did exactly what he had told Phoebe. When Bickerson arrived he helped Phoebe into the carriage, jumped in beside her, leaving the place on his right for Bickerson. Bickerson said nothing, but the muscles of his jaw tightened, and he said little during the ride. When they reached the church Joel did exactly the same. He arranged it so that he sat between the two for the entire service. On the way home he repeated the same maneuver. Getting out of the carriage at the house, he said, "Don't bother to get out, Mr. Bickerson. It was a fine service. We must do it again sometime."

Bickerson stared at Joel, appeared about to say something, then nodded and said, "Good day, Mr. Bradford, and to you, Miss Bradford."

As soon as his carriage pulled away, Joel took Phoebe's arm and marched toward the door. He imitated Bickerson's swaggering walk and nasal tone perfectly, saying, "And now, Miss Bradford, suppose we go over the sixteen points of the sermon that we just heard."

Despite herself Phoebe laughed. She could never resist Joel's mimicking ways, although she rebuked him for them. "I hope he never asks me to anything else."

"If he does, just invite me. You two can be like a pair of bookends and I'll be the book in the middle."

❦　　　❦　　　❦

"Joel, I'd like for you to go pick up some supplies over at Pineville."
"Pineville. Where's that, Mr. Bradford?"

"It's about ten miles from here over to the east. It's right on the main road, so you can't miss it. Nothing much there but a couple of stores and a church, but there's a sawmill. I bought some timber for making cannon patterns. Take a wagon and go over and pick it up. You have driven before, haven't you?"

Actually Joel had never driven a team before, but he said quickly, "Not a great deal, but I can handle it, sir."

Micah helped Joel hitch up the team to a heavy wagon and said as Joel climbed onto the seat, "You don't have to worry about this team running away. They're slow and faithful. Just don't get lost." He looked up at the sky and shook his head. "I think you're going to run into rain. You'd better take something to cover yourself up with. Here." He found a piece of canvas and returned with it, tossing it up to Joel. "You can get under that if you get caught in a downpour."

"Yes, sir, I will."

After the long days of hard work at the foundry, the trip to Pineville was a pleasure for Joel. He had not been outdoors a great deal, and he found the countryside outside Boston beautiful. The rolling hills and the tall trees pleased him, and he kept a sharp eye out for native American birds, most of which he did not recognize at all. He arrived at Pineville by ten o'clock, found the sawmill, and walked around studying the mill itself while the owner had the timber loaded. By the time they had finished, rain had begun to fall.

"You're going to get drenched," the tall, dour man with a pair of steady gray eyes said. "You'd better stay here until it passes over."

"I guess I'll take my chances. Thanks a lot."

Joel drove the team out. By this time he had confidence in his driving, and the horses, a pair of matched bays, plodded along. The rain began to fall lightly at first, and then it came down harder. Joel reached down, got the canvas, and shook it out. It was very large and he had to struggle to get it unfolded. Finally, he draped it around himself and made a canopy with which he could be sheltered from the worst of it.

He was only two or three miles outside of Boston when a movement caught his eye. The skies were overcast and it was dark, and the rain came down in slanting lines, drenching the earth. The patter of the rain on the canvas was pleasant enough, but when he saw a man and a woman moving slowly along the side path, he pulled up beside them and lifted the canvas enough to say, "If you need a ride, I'd be glad to help you out."

The couple turned and looked at him. They were a miserable sight.

They both carried some sort of brown cloth bag, which evidently contained the only clothes they owned. By the time Joel pulled the wagon alongside them, they were soaked into sodden masses. The woman's gray dress was completely saturated, and the water ran down her face as she looked up. She was young, and fatigue had made her features tense. The man appeared much older. His clothes were as poor and thoroughly drenched as the young woman walking beside him. The water ran down off of his hat onto his clothes. It had crushed the felt into a shapeless mass, and now he reached up, lifted it, and said in what was almost a gasp, "We'd be most grateful, sir."

"Come ahead. Get on the seat, then," Joel said. He watched and saw that the young woman had more strength than the man. He helped her on first, and then it took two tries before the man could hoist himself up. When he settled into the seat, he let out a gasp from the effort. "Here," Joel said, "spread this canvas over you. It'll help a little bit."

"I'm afraid we're too gone for that." The man turned and said, "We are much obliged to you, sir. I don't think we could have gotten on much farther." He seemed to gather strength to say more, and then added, "My name is Ezra Tyrone and this is my wife, Leah."

"I'm glad to know you, Mr. and Mrs. Tyrone. I'm Joel Bradford."

The young woman seated between the two men turned a wan face to him. She was rather plain but had clear blue eyes. Her hair was blond and would be bright had it not been soaked as it was now. A travesty of a hat covered her head, but her long hair strayed out from underneath it. "I thank you very much. My husband is not well," she said breathlessly.

Joel almost said, "Then he shouldn't be out in this weather," but he caught himself in time. Anyone out in this inclement weather could claim only necessity as a reason, so he spoke to the horses and the wagon moved ahead again. His passengers seemed to be too tired and weary to say anymore. The man slumped and closed his eyes.

"This is mighty bad weather to be out, Mrs. Tyrone. I suppose you are headed for Boston."

"Yes." The single word was all she could manage. She seemed to be very shy, but finally she said, "My husband has been there before, but I never have."

"You have no family there?"

"No, and we don't know anyone."

"Well, I'm sure you'll like it. I'm new there myself. Just came from England a few weeks ago."

As the wagon rolled on, splashing through the mud, the horses pulling against their collars, Joel managed to break through the reticence of the young woman. He discovered that her husband was an actor, which interested him. *Acting must not be very prosperous*, he thought, but he asked only, "Is he joining some sort of troupe in Boston?"

"He's . . . hoping to find something."

This did not sound very propitious to Joel, and by the time they had reached the city limits, he had decided the two were destitute. The man began coughing as they drove down the streets, and Mrs. Tyrone reached over and put her arm around him and drew his head down.

"He's been sick for several weeks." Then she said under her breath, "I don't know what we're going to do."

Joel Bradford was a compassionate young man. He had been through hard times himself, and now his heart went out to this vulnerable couple as he said quietly, "I don't mean to pry, but do you have any idea at all where you would like to stay?"

Ezra Tyrone roused himself and said, "Sir, I must confess we have no plans and almost no money."

Quickly Joel thought of their dilemma. He knew that he could not simply let the pair out in this driving rain with no place to take shelter. The man's cough was indicative of a serious illness, and his young wife needed to be out of the weather herself.

What can I do to help them? he thought. *Maybe I could take them to the Bradfords'. They'd help.* He played with this idea for a moment, and then suddenly he looked up and saw that he was directly on the road that passed by the home of Esther Denham and her niece, Abigail. A thought came to him and he instantly seized on it. *That room up over the stable would be a good place for them to stay. Perhaps I could offer to pay Mrs. Denham a little for the two of them. Just till they get on their feet and find a place of their own.*

When they arrived in front of the Denham house, he drew up on the reins and said, "If you'd wait out here for just a minute, I have to go inside." He wrapped the lines tightly, knowing that the horses would not bolt, jumped into the mud, and moved quickly up to the house. He was dripping wet himself when the door opened, and Abigail stood there. He pulled off his hat, and the water ran down his face. "Miss Howland."

"Why, Joel, come in. You're soaked!"

Joel stepped inside and said, "I don't want to make a mess. My feet are muddy and I'm dripping wet. The fact is, Miss Howland—" He stopped, not knowing exactly how to make his request. He did not like to ask favors and could not think of what to say.

"What is it, Joel? Is there a problem?" Abigail was concerned and she glanced out at the wagon. "Who's that on your wagon?"

"Well, that's it, Miss Howland. I've been over to Pineville to pick up some lumber, and I came on these poor folks just outside of Boston. They were caught in the storm and soaked to the bone. The man's sick and his wife's very young. They have no place to go."

"How terrible to be out in weather like this," Abigail said. She bit her lip and shook her head, adding, "Something has to be done for them."

"Well, I've got an idea, Miss Howland, but I don't know if I should ask."

"What is it, Joel?"

"Well, when I was here working the other day, I saw that room over the old stable. It's got a bed in it, and it's warm and dry. I know you don't know these folks and I don't either, but if I could put them up there until I do something better for them—"

"Why, I think that's a wonderful idea!"

"But we'll have to ask your aunt."

"Oh, of course, but she's very considerate. You wait right here. She's in her room right now, but I'll go ask her."

Joel stood there, trying to make no more of a puddle than he could help. Abigail was not gone long. When she returned there was a smile on her face. "Aunt Esther says you put those folks right in there, and I have some food cooked. If they have wet things, we can dry them out in front of the fire."

"That's mighty generous of you, Miss Abigail," Joel said gratefully and felt a rush of relief. "I'll go get them settled, and I'm sure they need something to eat."

Moving back outside, Joel climbed onto the wagon and picked up the lines. He turned the horses into the drive and then stopped and got out. As he opened the doors of the stable, he thought, *I'm glad I fixed these doors. It will make it a little better.* After walking the horses into the stable, he turned to the Tyrones and pulled the canvas back. "I've got a place for you to stay if you'd like." He motioned to the room. "There's a nice room up there, warm and dry. Mrs. Esther Denham and her niece, Abigail, own the place."

Ezra Tyrone sat up straighter. He coughed harshly and then said with some hoarseness, "My dear young man, how kind of you to be so thoughtful."

"Why, it's nothing," Joel said. "Here, let's get you upstairs, and we'll dry some clothes out and get some hot food down you."

For the next two hours Joel worked with Abigail to get the Tyrones settled. Abigail came out to the stables, bearing blankets and some of her own clothing. She spoke, saying, "My name is Abigail Howland."

"This is Mr. and Mrs. Tyrone, Miss Abigail," Joel said.

"I'm so sorry you got caught out in the rain. I've brought some blankets and one of my old dresses and a robe if you'd like it, Mrs. Tyrone. I'm sorry we don't have any men's clothes. We'll just have to dry some of yours out, Mr. Tyrone."

The young woman stood there in the middle of the room, and suddenly tears ran down her cheeks. She could not restrain a sob, and she bowed her head, saying, "Thank you so much. It's so good to be out of the rain."

She took off her coat and stood holding it. The rain had plastered her thin dress to her body, and it was obvious she was expecting a child. Abigail and Joel exchanged glances, and Abigail said quickly, "You get into those dry things and let me have some of your wet clothes, Mr. Tyrone. I'll dry them out and bring them back to you."

An hour later the Tyrones were sitting in front of a fire in the kitchen of the house. Esther Denham was up and had met them, and they were eating hot soup and fresh mutton that Abigail had set before them. Joel and the two women saw how they tried not to show how hungry they were, but it was obvious they were half starved.

Finally Ezra shook his head at the offer of another helping and said, "No, ma'am, that's plenty." His voice suddenly seemed stronger and more resonant. His face was pale and he had the look of a chronically sick person. He had brown hair streaked with silver, and gray eyes that were large and expressive. His face was drawn, however, and he was lean to the point of emaciation. Now he looked at his wife, then back to the three, and said, "I'm especially grateful for your care of Leah. I don't know what we would have done if it hadn't been for you."

"Why, it's fortunate that Joel picked you up," Abigail said. "I think the Lord must have directed you, Joel."

"I don't know about that," Joel said. He stood up and said, "I'll tell you what. I need to be getting my load back to the foundry, but I'll come and check on you later."

"I'll go with you to the door." Abigail accompanied Joel to the door.

When he put on his coat to go, he said, "I'll try to make some arrangements for these people, Miss Abigail."

"They can stay here as long as they need to." Abigail bit her lower lip and shook her head despondently. "They're a sad couple, aren't they? He's older than she is. He must be over fifty, and she's just a child, really—and expecting a child."

"I'll see what I can do to help."

Abigail suddenly reached out her hand. Joel took it in surprise and she squeezed it firmly. "You're a generous-hearted young man, Joel Bradford, just like the rest of the Bradfords I've met."

Joel ducked his head and gave a half smile. "It's you two ladies who are generous. I just gave them a ride."

☨   ☨   ☨

Joel felt good as he approached the Denham home several days later. He thought of how the Tyrones had become an important part in his life since he had rescued them that day on the road from Pineville. It was fortunate that Mrs. Denham and Abigail had taken them in, for Ezra Tyrone had grown worse from the chill he'd caught in the rain that day. When Ezra did not improve, the doctor was summoned. His name was Claude Bates. He was a short, round man with gray hair, sharp black eyes, and a thunderous voice. He was the family doctor of the Bradfords and the Fraziers, and he had come at Daniel's request. Daniel was interested in the pair and was proud of his young kinsman for taking the initiative to see that they were well cared for. After examining him, the doctor spoke words that were not encouraging.

"You won't be doing anything for a while, sir," he said.

Joel was in the room as the doctor made the examination, and when they were outside he asked, "What's wrong with him?"

"Is he a relative of yours?" the doctor asked.

"No, doctor, he's no relation. I just found them on the road."

"Well, the prognosis isn't good," Bates said. He modulated his usually loud voice so that the couple inside the room could not hear. They descended the stairs from the room over the stable, and the doctor stood beside his buggy shaking his head. "I'm afraid it's consumption."

"That's bad, isn't it?" Joel said.

"Yes, he's a very sick man," Dr. Bates replied. "And that young woman is not in good enough health for bearing a child." He had examined Leah Tyrone earlier, and now he said rather sharply, "They both need care, and I don't know how they're going to get it."

"Well, Mrs. Denham and Abigail are very kind, and I'll do all I can. Miss Marian said she would help, too."

"I'll check on them from time to time," Bates said.

"I'll get some money and pay you, Doctor."

"Never mind that," Bates snorted. "Just be sure that he takes the medicine I left."

Joel waited until the doctor drove off, then went into the house to relate the doctor's report to the two women. They listened carefully, and then it was Esther who said, "The poor dears. We'll have to do what we can for them. She's just a child."

"Yes, and she's very thin. We'll have to fatten her up."

"I didn't know this would be such a long imposition on your hospitality," Joel said. "I've dumped these folks on you and I feel responsible."

"We don't feel that way at all," Abigail said instantly. "Aunt Esther and I have been praying about it, and we feel that God had you on that road that day to find them, and He put us on your heart, so now they're on our hearts. We'll have to be obedient to the Lord and take care of them."

Joel stared at the two women and muttered, "That's mighty fine of you. I admire you for it."

After Joel left the house, he went back to the foundry and related the full story to Micah. It was hot in the forge, and Micah was stripped down to a shirt with the sleeves torn off. He had powerful forearms and large, hard biceps, and his chest swelled deeply. He put down the blacksmith's hammer he was using to forge a piece of steel and looked at Joel.

"I think it's times like this when Christians really are at a place of judgment. It would be so easy to let somebody else do it, but you folks opened your hearts to help this poor couple and did what Jesus would have done."

"Why, I haven't done anything, really," Joel said.

"Don't be ridiculous," Micah retorted rather sharply, glancing at his young friend.

"But I'm not a Christian, Mr. Bradford."

Micah examined the young man even more closely, and a thought came to him. He smiled and said, "You will be one day, but until then God has used you—perhaps to show you what it's like to be a Christian, to help others as you've helped the Tyrones."

During the next few weeks Joel thought often of what Micah Bradford had said. He became a regular visitor with the Tyrones, who improved to some degree under the kind ministrations of Mrs. Denham and Abigail. Joel fixed up their room more comfortably, and Mrs. Denham and Abigail saw that they had good food, bringing them to the table in the house three times a day.

Ezra's health seemed to improve as the warm weather came on. He was still too weak to get around a great deal, but Joel would sit with him often outside in the shade watching as people went by. He found that Ezra Tyrone had led a fascinating life. He had served in the militia as a young man in the French and Indian War. Afterward, he had joined a traveling group of actors. He had the mobile features of an actor and a resonant round-shaped voice that could raise the dead when he chose to use it.

Joel loved to listen to his stories about the theater, and Ezra had said to him more than once, "You'd make a fine actor, Joel."

Joel was astonished. "Me? I'm no actor!"

Ezra laughed. "Of course you are. You can mimic anybody, and not just their voice. I've seen you mimic the tradesmen that come here from time to time. You can even walk like them, and your sister, Phoebe, tells me you've always been like that."

"Well, I'm not likely to become an actor, Ezra."

"No, I hope not. It's not a good life." Ezra dropped his head and then lifted his face, and there was pain etched across it. "I've led a miserable life most of my years, Joel, and I've ruined my health."

"Have you been married long, Ezra?" Joel had not heard the story of how the two had met. They were so different, and now he asked the question gently and was prepared for a rebuke.

Ezra looked at him thoughtfully and said, "I'm surprised you haven't asked before, Joel. We're a strange match, aren't we? Here I am an old man and Leah's a young woman. Now she's having a baby, and we don't have a shilling between us. Well, it's a long story. She was an orphan and was badly mistreated. As a matter of fact, the man she was working for abused her and beat her. I showed her some kindness and she fell in love with me, old man that I am, so I took her away and married her. Things went well for a while. I found some work, but then I started getting sick about a year ago. Not long ago we found out that she was expecting a child." A flicker of doubt filled his fine eyes, and he said simply, "I don't know how it's all going to turn out. I can't live long, and what will happen to her and the child then?"

Joel Bradford was speechless. He was not prepared to handle matters such as this, and all he could do was reach out and put his hand on Ezra's thin shoulder. "It'll be all right. God will do something."

Ezra looked up with surprise. "You're a believer, are you, Joel?"

"Well, no, sir. I'm not a Christian, but I've seen God do some things," he said thoughtfully. "I know He's real, and just looking at people like the Bradfords—well, you can't doubt them, and they're Christians." He smiled encouragingly, squeezed the man's thin shoulder again, and said, "God will take care of you, and your wife and the baby."

Ezra examined the young man's face and smiled. He had a kind face, though it was drawn and filled with unspoken fears. "I trust you're right, Joel."

4

A Call From His Excellency

BY THE TIME THE FIRST WEEK in June arrived, Ezra Tyrone had improved significantly. He was still thin and had a hacking cough most of the time, but as Dr. Bates had suggested, that symptom was incurable. The aging actor, however, was able to get outside and even do a little work around the house. He was outside hoeing in the small garden that Abigail had started with the help of a neighbor who had broken it up for her. The sun was beaming down and he would glance to the west occasionally, where the main part of Boston rose up. He was wearing a pair of gray knee pants and a well-worn shirt that had once been maroon but was now faded to an indiscriminate color of old wine. As he moved down the road slowly, he was thinking, as usual, of his wife and of the indistinct future that lay ahead for them. When he had been alone he had given little thought to how he would survive, but now with a wife and a child on the way, a burden seemed to have settled over him.

A sound caught his attention, and looking up, he saw Joel Bradford driving a wagon pulled by two matched bays. It was loaded with supplies of some kind. Ezra smiled as Joel stopped the team and leaped to the ground agilely after tying the lines. He came up with a smile on his face, which was customary.

"Good morning, Ezra. It's a beautiful day."

"That it is, Joel. Whither are you bound?"

"I've just been to Pineville and picked up some more timber from the sawmill there." He studied the garden and shook his head. "I don't know much about gardening. We didn't do much of that right in the center of London."

"I grew up on a farm. It was a good life. Many times I wish I had never left there," Ezra said.

Catching a tone of sadness in Ezra's voice, Joel understood at once that he was worried about money and the future. "I'm hoping that a job of some kind will come up," Joel said. "The work in the foundry would be too heavy for you, but there are lots of shops. Maybe you could become a clerk in one of those."

A smile creased Ezra's wide lips. He had a mobile face that could move from one emotion to another easily. "I could never count straight," he confessed, shrugging his thin shoulders. "I'd lose more money from an employer than I'd be worth. I don't know what I'm fit for, Joel. I've never been a success at much of anything."

"There must be something around here you can do. I know that if a man wants to work, there's got to be work of some kind."

"The only work I know is acting." The wide lips closed firmly, and sticking the hoe into the ground, Tyrone leaned on it and, after a moment's hesitation, said slowly, "Well, lad, I have been thinking of something."

"You have? What is it, Ezra?"

"Nothing permanent, but I've been thinking about Boston. It's full of people who have very little to do. The whole city is cut off by the British blockade, nothing is coming from overseas, and although times are hard with the war and all, there's still a little money to be spent for entertainment."

"Entertainment?" Joel narrowed his eyes and asked quickly, "Are you thinking about doing some sort of acting? A play perhaps?"

"That was my thought, but it would be too much for one man."

"A play. Well, why not?" Joel's understanding was quick, as always, and he said, "What sort of play would you do?"

"Well, the play is no problem. What people want to hear and see in a play is something that agrees with what they're doing, and what these people are doing now"—he smiled faintly—"is having a nice little revolution against King George III. So a play ought to show the king as a rascal, all the British soldiers as scoundrels, and every man jack who's born an American as a hero." He laughed then and said, "They're not interested in anything sad like Othello or Hamlet."

"Who are they?"

"Oh, just fellows in a couple of plays written by an Englishman over a hundred years ago. As a matter of fact," Ezra confessed, "I wrote a play myself before we left our last place. It's called *The Continental Hero*. It's all about a young fellow who has difficulties at home. He's not very successful, but he joins George Washington's Continental Army and saves the general and all of the army by his boldness and courage."

"Sounds good," Joel grinned. "Does he have a sweetheart?"

"Of course he does!" exclaimed Ezra. "What sort of a play would it be without a romance?" He grew animated as he spoke about his play, and finally he said, "I've been thinking if I could get just a few folks to help and a building—someplace to put it on in town—it might catch the public eye!"

"How many people would you need, Ezra?"

"Oh, not more than four or five. Some could play two roles with a quick change backstage." He studied the young man carefully. "I began thinking about it last night after you were mimicking Mr. Blevins down at the foundry. I only met him once, but you've caught him in every point. You could play the young soldier, the hero of the piece."

"Me? Why, I'm no actor!"

"Yes, you are. You're acting all the time, and the only thing that would be different would be learning lines, and that wouldn't be hard. You are very quick, my boy."

For a time Joel protested, but as Ezra continued to speak, the young man grew interested. He had never even *seen* a play, much less performed in one, but as the idea grew he thought, *It might be fun, and it could help Ezra and Leah out with some money*.

Finally Joel said, "Well, if you think it might work, I'll do all I can, and I think Phoebe would help, too, and even Miss Abigail."

His enthusiasm encouraged Ezra, and the two sat down under the apple tree and talked excitedly about the play. Finally Joel asked, "Who would play the villain?"

"That's me, and a more villainous rascal you will never see. I'll be General William Howe. Of course I'm not as bulky as the general himself, but an actor has to overcome these physical limitations. I'll have to make several copies of the play first—I only have my original, which I've been carrying with me just in case I found a use for it someday." He looked at young Bradford and said wistfully, "If I could just make enough money to take care of Leah and the child, I think I could die a happy man."

"We'll do it, Ezra. Don't worry about it." Leaping to his feet, Joel said, "You start making some copies and I'll go talk to Mr. Daniel. He knows everybody, and I'm sure he'll be glad to help. I bet he could even find a place for us and perhaps have some posters printed that I can stick up around town."

"That's wonderful, Joel!" Ezra exclaimed. He rose to his feet with a light of pleasure in his eyes. "Oh, to be treading the boards again and to have a couple of guineas in my pocket! I must go tell Leah. She can help with the costumes."

🔔   🔔   🔔

The play written by Ezra Tyrone was soon the object of conversation, at least in the Bradford household and at Esther and Abigail's home. Joel's enthusiasm was contagious, and soon the cast was complete. Abigail had agreed to play the female lead opposite Joel, and Joel had also pressured Patrick Mears into taking a part. Patrick had insisted he knew nothing about acting—only horses—but he eventually gave in at Joel's insistence.

Joel had little difficulty in persuading Phoebe to act in the play. He was somewhat taken aback when Silas Bickerson also volunteered to be one of the actors. Since there was no money involved, Joel couldn't very well turn him down. He simply shrugged and accepted the bulky man as gracefully as he could.

For the next two weeks, Ezra and Joel and the cast were caught in a blur of activity getting ready for opening night, for Daniel had given Joel time off from his work at the foundry. Daniel had procured an empty building and made himself responsible for converting it into a theater. This amounted to very little except putting up a curtain, which Marian offered to make from some old fabric pieces she found in their attic, and collecting enough assorted chairs and benches for the spectators. Daniel also had some fliers printed that were written by Ezra himself and were rather spectacular:

> Direct from an overseas engagement, Mr. Ezra Tyrone will star in the production of *The Continental Hero*. Accompanying Mr. Tyrone will be a group of stellar actors and actresses from Boston. *The Continental Hero* is a play that exposes the villainy of King George III and the courage of a young American patriot and his struggles against the tyrant. Performances will begin at seven o'clock each evening. One shilling. Come early to get a seat.

One new acquaintance Joel and Phoebe made while preparing for the play was Katherine Yancy, a young woman of twenty-one and a close friend of Abigail Howland. Katherine had become very interested in the play—so interested, in fact, that she volunteered to help with the costumes. She was an attractive young woman with gray-green eyes and a wealth of dark brown hair. She had a squarish face and a straight nose, and her eyes crinkled when she laughed.

"She's had an interesting and tragic experience, Phoebe," Marian said as the two women were working on sewing the curtain together. "As a matter of fact, I suppose it's the sort of thing that's happening all over the Colonies."

"What's that, Miss Marian?"

"Well, as you know, my husband has a sister, Lyna Lee. She married a man named Leslie Gordon, who is a colonel in the British army. They have a son named Clive, who is a physician—a very fine one, I must say.

"Katherine's father was captured in battle and was in a prison ship up in Halifax waiting to die. She went to help him, and while she was there, she encountered Clive Gordon. He fell in love with her and came up with a scheme to set her father free, which he did. He's doing very well now. You'll meet him if you haven't already."

"How romantic!" Phoebe exclaimed. She looked up from her needlework and her eyes were glowing. "Are they going to get married?"

"I doubt it," Marian said. "After all, the Gordons are loyal Tories, and Katherine's an ardent patriot. It's a sad situation. I don't see any end to it."

Phoebe repeated this story to Joel that evening as they met for the first rehearsal. "It's so sad. Katherine Yancy is such a nice young woman, but I don't suppose she and Clive will ever get married."

"If I were him, I'd kidnap her and carry her away."

"And what would you do with her, Mr. Joel Bradford?" Phoebe demanded. She put her hands on her hips and glared at him. "Would you keep her locked up and shove her food under the door?"

Joel laughed and came over and put his arms around Phoebe and swung her around. He laughed at her protest, saying, "I don't know what I'd do. I don't think that far ahead. Do you know your lines yet?"

"I . . . I hope so."

They were in the building that had been procured by Daniel Bradford, and at that moment a voice called out, "Well, are we ready for the play?" Silas Bickerson was all smiles as he came over and bowed slightly to the two. "I'm looking forward to acting with you, Miss Phoebe," he said. He stepped closer and seemed ready to reach out and touch her when Ezra Tyrone stepped out from behind the curtain.

"Well, I hope the others hurry." Ezra was obviously excited about the play, and soon Sam and Keturah entered, accompanied by Abigail Howland.

"Now the cast is all here. Suppose we just walk through the whole thing. Don't worry if you don't remember your lines. This is just a first rehearsal."

It was good that he said that because none of the cast knew their lines—except for Joel. He not only knew his own part—the most comprehensive in the play—but he also knew the lines of everyone else. Every time one of the cast faltered, he immediately fed them the needed line, which amazed Ezra considerably.

"Why, Joel, you've got the whole play memorized! You have a prodigious memory."

"Oh, Joel could always memorize anything." Phoebe smiled proudly. "I believe he could memorize the entire Bible if he set his mind to it."

Joel smiled with embarrassment but made no answer. After the rehearsal was over, Ezra said, "I really believe we can open in a week."

"I'll put the posters all over Boston," Joel volunteered. He had enjoyed the rehearsal but afterward was aggravated that Silas Bickerson insisted he and Phoebe ride home in his carriage. It was a fine carriage, for he owned the largest livery stable in Boston. He was also a horse trader of famed proportion, and despite the poor economy of the times, he was prospering. He outmaneuvered Joel this time, and Phoebe found herself seated beside the large man as he drove through the streets of Boston. He spoke in an awkward, flowery fashion of Phoebe's abilities as an actress, which embarrassed her considerably. When the fancy carriage pulled up in front of the Bradford home, Silas practically invited himself inside when Marian greeted him courteously. After he left, however, she pursed her lips and studied Phoebe. "Well, it seems you have a suitor, Phoebe," she said.

"Oh no, ma'am, nothing like that."

"Indeed, I think you do."

"Well, it's not what I want," Phoebe insisted.

"He's a very persevering man and quite prosperous from what I hear," Marian ventured. "He might be a good prospect for a husband."

"Oh no, indeed, Mrs. Bradford, I don't think of him like that at all!"

"I should think not!" Joel growled. "He couldn't remember a single one of his lines."

"Well," Marian laughed, "that's hardly grounds for excluding him as a possible husband. He would be a good provider, I'm sure."

"No, ma'am, not at all!" Phoebe said with alarm.

"Why, the man's an oaf. He couldn't even walk across the stage without tripping on his own feet. He may be strong as an ox, but he has no grace about him whatsoever." Joel spoke for some time about the limitations of Silas Bickerson.

Finally Marian said, "I think you're jealous of your sister. You don't think any man would be good enough for her."

"Indeed you're right, ma'am," Joel agreed, "so let's have no more talk about prospective husbands."

T   T   T

Joel looked up with surprise as Micah came dashing down the steps from the office and rushed by the forge where he was working. "Something wrong, Micah?" he called out as Micah headed for the front door.

Stopping abruptly, Micah turned, his face tense with excitement as he spoke rapidly. "The British have landed some sort of force up at Roxberry. The militia's been called out to meet them."

"The militia!" Joel exclaimed, and then at once excitement flared in his eyes. "Let me go with you."

"Why, you're not a member of the militia!"

"But I can shoot a musket. You taught me how, remember?" This was true enough, for Micah had given him several lessons in loading and firing a musket and found him to be a very good shot.

For one second Micah Bradford hesitated, then nodded briefly. "All right. If that's what you want, we can always use an extra man. I don't think General Arnold will care."

"Who's that?" Joel said, ripping off his apron and throwing it on the floor.

"General Benedict Arnold. He'll be in charge of the militia. Come along, they'll be forming up and leaving right away."

The two rushed to the town square carrying their muskets, powder, and shot. Joel kept pace with Micah, asking more questions than could be answered. When they finally reached the village square, a large body of men, nearly two hundred or so, it seemed to Joel, were already milling around.

"That's General Arnold coming there," Micah said, pointing to a short but muscular individual. General Benedict Arnold had a swarthy face, which was now set with dead determination. "He's the best general we have on the field, so Father says. He fights like a wildcat and he insists his men do so, too."

General Arnold reached the center of the milling group of men and called out, "All right, Sergeants, get your men in position for a rapid march! Be sure they have plenty of ammunition!" He grinned briefly, and his white teeth stood out against the darkness of his skin, and his eyes seemed to glow with excitement. "We'll give those Lobsterbacks something to think about! They are attacking our stores at Roxberry. It'll be too late to stop them there, but we'll set up an ambush and be waiting for them as they make their way back to the ship. All right, let's give a cheer for General Washington and for the liberty of every American!"

An enthusiastic cheer went up, and then following Micah's quiet direction, Joel fell in with the lines of men. At once Arnold, who had mounted a steel gray stallion, said, "All right, forward, and every man do his duty!"

𝕋   𝕋   𝕋

A force of over a thousand British and Hessian troops had hit the unprotected village of Roxberry, where only a few scattered militia had been assigned. Quickly the British drove the Americans out and then proceeded to destroy the supplies as quickly and efficiently as possible. They destroyed seventeen hundred barrels of pork, fifty barrels of preserved beef, seven hundred barrels of flour, thirty barrels of fat, and a number of hogshead of rum and wine. In addition, sixteen hundred bushels of grain were burned. The worst blow of all was the loss of a large supply of tents and ten new wagons intended for Washington's men at Valley Forge.

A burly Hessian lieutenant named Ludwig urged the men on to an all-consuming rampage of destruction. "Burn every house you can!" he screamed, his beefy red face cruel with the pleasure of the attack. "If anyone stands in your way, shoot them down!"

The Hessians were German troops, most of them speaking little or no English. They had been hired from Hesse, a province in Germany, by George III when efforts to enlist Englishmen in the unpopular war against the Colonists had not produced enough troops. None of the Hessians had any concept that there were many Colonists still loyal to King George. To them everyone was simply a rebel, and they burned and pilfered everything in their path.

Dolly and Peter James were two of those who had remained loyal to the Crown. It had been difficult for them, for many of the residents around Boston were strong patriots. Mr. and Mrs. James had endured much grief from overenthusiastic patriots, but they had remained firm. When Mrs. James came out and saw the British approaching, she was not at all alarmed. Her husband had gone to a nearby glen to cut some wood, and she was confident that she could explain their loyalty to the king to the officers. She was a middle-aged woman, not in the best of health, with hair already turning gray. Moving out to the front of her small house, she faced the squad of soldiers led by Lieutenant Ludwig.

"Oh, sir," she said, "I'm glad to see you."

Ludwig laughed. "You're the only one who is. Get out of the way, old woman. We're going to burn your house!"

Dolly James stiffened with surprise, and shock ran across her face. "But, sir, we are loyal to the king!"

"*Ja*, I've heard that before! Shut up, old woman, and back away if you don't want to get hurt!" Lieutenant Ludwig motioned his soldiers toward the house and said, "Go in and take what you want, then burn it down!"

Ludwig led the way, grinning at Mrs. James, saying, "I'll find your gold, old woman, but you can save yourself some trouble by telling me where it is."

Dolly James began to protest, but Ludwig grabbed her by the hair and dragged her inside the house. "Tell me where the gold is!" He slapped her across the face, and she reeled back against the wall, her mouth bleeding and her eyes incredulous.

"We've always been loyal to the king!" she began crying out. "You can ask anyone—"

But none of her pleas helped. The Hessians fell to destroying her home, stripping and tearing the curtains to pieces, then breaking the glass in the bureau table with their bayonets. They stuffed the silver from her dining room in their pockets and ran their bayonets through the paintings of her ancestors, all the time laughing and speaking in German.

Lieutenant Ludwig kept slapping her in the face and finally ripped the buckle from her belt and her silver sleeve buttons, insulting her rudely in the most abusive way. He dragged her around the house to the different rooms, threatening her with death if she did not tell him where she had the gold hidden. He finally found the store of gold in the bedroom in a drawer. Stuffing it into a bag, he said, "You'd better get out if you don't want to burn!"

"Please don't burn the house, please!"

Rudely he shoved her away, and when she fell he motioned to two of the Hessians. "Get her out of there!" he snarled in German. Then picking up a lamp, he threw it across the room. It shattered and the oil caught fire immediately, the flames running across the floor and igniting the curtains.

The soldiers dragged the woman outside and threw her down in front of the house. Lieutenant Ludwig came out carrying the gold in his left hand and pulled his sword. He put the edge of it against her neck and snarled, "I ought to cut your head off, you rebel!"

But he contented himself with slapping her with the flat of it, then screamed to his men, "Now burn all you can. In twenty minutes we've got to get back to the ship! We can't be cut off here!"

The pillage continued, until thirty minutes later the Hessians marched out of Roxberry, leaving it a burning ruin.

Mrs. James, her face bleeding, rushed back into the house several times trying to rescue her family heirlooms, including some of the portraits on the walls and a collection of letters. The house was quickly going up in flames when her husband came running up, his face pale at the sight.

"Dolly, are you all right?"

"Yes, but they burned our house, Peter." She was weeping now.

"Didn't you tell them we were loyal to the king?"

"They didn't care. They wouldn't even listen when I tried to tell them! Look, they burned the Hewitts' house, and I've heard that they've killed some people, including old Mr. Toliver, as faithful a man to the king as ever lived."

Peter James had been a faithful loyalist standing against the Revolution and suffering much loss for his stand. Now, as he stood looking at the bleeding face of his wife and the burning house that he had built with his own hands many years ago and where he had raised his children, his loyalty to the British Crown came to a bitter end. "If this is England, I'll have no part of it!" There was utter conviction in his voice, and his eyelids shaded his dark brown eyes. "I'll fight them to the death from now on!"

He refused to let his wife go back into the burning house, but he himself made several trips. When he came staggering out for the fourth time, blinded by the smoke, his wife grabbed him and said, "Look, the militia, they're here!"

Wiping his burning eyes, Peter James stumbled across the road to meet the officer who was getting off a gray horse.

"How long ago did this happen?" the officer asked.

"Not fifteen minutes," Peter said in a daze as he stared at the man.

"Where did they come from? We need to cut them off."

The neighbors were gathering, and one of them said, "Don't listen to him, General, he's a loyalist."

"Not anymore!" Peter said. "You see what they did to my wife and my house? If you'll have me, General, I can shoot a good musket. I'll kill as many of them as you get me within sight of!"

"Good for you! The country needs men who've come to their

senses." General Arnold beamed at the man. Though he knew the Hessians had brought tragedy to the people here, there would be no more loyalists in Roxberry. The British had committed a grievous error in burning and killing indiscriminately those who had been faithful to the king, along with those who were in rebellion against the Crown. "All of you who want to get revenge, follow me! Where can we cut them off before they can get back to the sea?"

"I know this country," Peter James said. "There's a valley they have to go through. We can get on both sides of it and cut them to pieces. It's right down close to their ship."

"Lead the way, then," General Arnold grinned. He turned to Micah, who was an acting sergeant in the militia, and said under his breath, "I'm sorry for what these people have suffered, but the British have made patriots out of a whole township. Everyone who's burned out will have uncles, aunts, brothers, children. They may have been loyal to the king up until now, but no more. These British have no sense."

"I believe you're right, General. Do you think we can get there before they return to their ship?"

"We've got to." Arnold glanced around at the men of Roxberry, who were boiling out of their houses carrying muskets, their faces grim and hard with anticipation.

"All right, lead the way! Let's strike a blow for liberty!" Arnold shouted.

The forces moved out at once. Arnold estimated there were no more than four hundred in his force against a thousand British, from what information he could get from the survivors of the raid. He also knew there were more reinforcements on the ship. He drove the men hard until finally Peter James led them through some rough terrain, coming at last to the sea. He paused then and swept his arm around. "You see, they had to go through this cleft, and they have to come back this way. There's the ship with the boats waiting to take them back out, but they've got to come through here."

Arnold at once became a marvel of efficiency. He mounted the single six-pound cannon he had managed to bring and said, "I'll fire it myself. Sergeant Bradford, you take half the force to the other side of that ravine. I'll keep half here. Hold your fire until they get to that chestnut tree and then let them have it with everything you've got. We'll have them caught in a crossfire."

"Yes, General." Micah began yelling orders and Joel was right by his side. They crossed the open field, mounted up into the hills on the side, and following Micah's strict commands, they hid themselves in the dense bushes that lined the banks.

"Are you nervous, Joel?" Micah asked, crouched behind a log.

"Yes, I guess I am. I never shot at anybody before."

"There's still time for you to change your mind," Micah said in a kindly fashion. "After all, it's not really your fight." He saw that the young man did not waver and smiled grimly. "All right, then. We'll have time to get in two volleys. The first one will catch them off guard, and as soon as you fire, load up. They may charge us, but we can get in those two shots. Besides, General Arnold will be peppering them with that cannon, and the other half of the militia will be firing from the other side."

Peter James had come to be with Micah's group. He ran his hand up and down the side of his musket. "My wife told me that a lieutenant, a beefy red-faced man, slapped her face and burned my house. I intend to get that man!"

Ten minutes later a cry came up, "Here they come! Get ready!"

Joel crouched behind the log, his eyes alive as the flash of green uniforms showed itself from the gap to the east. He was breathing harder than usual and his lips were dry. His musket was primed and loaded, and as the Hessians marched with machinelike precision into the open space headed toward the chestnut tree, he found it more and more difficult to breathe.

"Take your time. Breathe deep, take a good rest, and pick one man," Micah said, "and don't hurry. Plenty of time."

A major was out in front and behind him Lieutenant Ludwig. Peter James saw the red-faced man, beefy and bulky, exactly as Dolly had described him.

"Slap my wife, will you! Burn my house? You'll pay for it now!" James was an expert shot and carried a rifle instead of the usual musket. It was a deadly weapon, one that could hit a deer at a hundred yards. The distance here was no more than that, and he put the bead carefully on the face of Lieutenant Ludwig. When he heard the scream and the sound of the cannon going off, he pulled the trigger. The rifle beat against his shoulder and the muzzle kicked up, but he saw Lieutenant Ludwig fall, dead before he hit the ground.

Joel fired also but was not sure whether he hit his man or not. Screams rent the air, for the patriots were screaming like mountain lions. Cries of alarms came from the Germans below as the major tried to rally the men. Many Hessians fell at that first volley and the major, seeing that he was caught in a crossfire, led the men to an outcropping that hid them from the fire of the hidden marksmen.

"Come on, we've got to get on the other side of them," Micah yelled.

For a while there was a great deal of maneuvering. The German major was a good soldier and he did the best he could, but it was only the arrival of more soldiers from the ship that saved them. They evidently heard the cannon fire and the sound of musketry and sent in boat after boat with more troops.

General Arnold saw that he was about to be flanked and began yelling, "All right, we've given them their own! Now we'll have an orderly withdrawal!"

The militia rallied and General Arnold led them away. There was no danger of the troops following, for the dead and wounded littered the shoreline. Arnold called a halt and rode up and down addressing the men. He stopped right beside where Micah stood with Joel and smiled down. "You did well, sir."

"So did my kinsman. He's just over from England. This is Joel Bradford, General."

"Oh, a new recruit. Well, I'm glad to see you're on the right side. His Excellency has spoken of the Bradfords. Congratulations to you both."

"Thank you, sir," Joel whispered. He watched as Benedict Arnold went up and down the lines congratulating the men warmly. "He's a great general, isn't he?"

"All the men admire him. They'd follow him anywhere. Like I said, he's the best we've got."

The lines formed soon and headed back toward Boston. When they arrived, Joel found Phoebe nearly wild with fear. He laughed at her and said, "It was easy. We drove them off. If we'd had more men, we'd have gotten them all. Phoebe, I've got to join the army!"

"No, please don't do that. Not yet, Joel."

"I can't stay on the outside of this. This is going to be my country and I've got to fight for it!"

🛡   🛡   🛡

"Mr. Bradford—Mr. Bradford!" Joel burst into Daniel Bradford's office where his employer was seated at a desk, with his bookkeeper, Albert Blevins, standing at his side pointing down at some figures. "He's come! He's right outside!"

Looking up with some amusement, Daniel demanded, "Who's come, Joel?"

"General Washington! That's what Micah said."

For a moment Daniel Bradford did not move, then he leaped from his chair and dashed to the window, almost knocking Blevins down in his haste.

"By heavens, it is the general and some of his staff!" Whirling quickly, he ran downstairs. By the time he got outside he found several of his employees gathered in a small group to look with awed expression at the four men who had drawn up outside the foundry.

"General Washington, how wonderful to see you!" Daniel came forward with a smile and started to bow, but the general put out his hand.

"Good to see you, Mr. Bradford." Washington was a very tall man, six feet three, and wide in the shoulders and hips. He had strong, sloping shoulders, and a thick torso with long arms. His hair was brown and his eyes a very light blue, and his cheeks were pitted with smallpox scars.

His face was stern as a rule, but now it was relaxed, and he said quickly, "I'm on my way to Philadelphia, but I'm going to stay in Boston for several days."

"I'm very happy, sir. Would you come in and take some refreshment?"

"I believe we will," Washington nodded. "We came here because General Knox is interested in seeing those cannons you promised us."

Henry Knox, over six feet and weighing fully two hundred and fifty pounds, came forward. His uniform was spotless, for this ex-bookseller who had become the ordnance expert of the Continental Army loved fine clothes. His right hand was wrapped in a handkerchief, for he had lost several fingers in a hunting accident. His face was round and rosy as he beamed, saying, "Ah, Daniel, it's good to see you again." The two had been good friends before the Revolution, for Daniel had often visited Knox's bookstore. Now the two men greeted each other warmly. "I'm here to see the cannons. They must be good ones for His Excellency."

"They're the best we can do, General. We'll be glad to show you everything, but first come up to my office."

Washington moved quickly, following Daniel up the stairs, and Daniel whispered to Micah, "Come along, you too, Joel," and the three went upstairs, followed by the staff of General Washington.

When they were inside, the general said, "I believe you know General Benedict Arnold."

"We have never met," Daniel said, "but your reputation precedes you, General."

Arnold greeted Daniel warmly; then his eyes went to Micah and Joel. "I believe I have met your two kinsmen. They did good service at

Roxberry last week. You're a fighting family, the kind we need more of in this country."

Joel's face flushed and turned red with pleasure. He could hardly breathe he was so excited with seeing General George Washington, of whom he had heard much, even in England.

"May I introduce Mr. Edmund Dante."

"An honor, Mr. Dante," Daniel said, bowing slightly. It seemed to him, as the man answered his greeting, he did not go with the other three, for he was dressed in drab civilian clothes, gray and black, and had no color whatsoever about him. He was somewhere over forty, very swarthy, and rather small. He had a stoop in his back and a list to the right. The only outstanding thing about him were his eyes, which were large, deep-set, intensely black, and seemed almost to burn.

"Your servant, sir," he said quickly.

Daniel waited for Washington to make some remark about the status of Mr. Dante, but the general said only, "We're going to be in Boston several days. I trust we will get to talk more about the cannon."

"Oh, indeed. We are happy to hear it, Your Excellency!" Daniel said quickly. A thought came to him and he grinned at Joel. "My young kinsman, Mr. Joel Bradford, is starring in a play that I understand has very patriotic highlights. Perhaps if you could spare the time from official business, you and your staff could attend."

"A play. Well, I would like it very much," Washington said, "and these gentlemen, too, I'm sure."

General Arnold smiled. "If your acting is as good as your fighting ability, Mr. Bradford, it will be a fine play indeed."

Joel was electrified with excitement, and as soon as the general and the staff had left, he said to Daniel, "I'm going to put notices all over town that the general and his staff will be there. It'll pack the house."

"I expect it will," Daniel grinned. "Why don't you take off now and go to it."

"Yes, sir!"

Joel raced from the foundry and did not stop all day until he had plastered businesses with handwritten notices and had informed many more by word of mouth. When he arrived home he went at once to Ezra and gave him the great news.

Ezra listened with an incredulous look on his face, then rubbed his hands together and grinned. "Excellent. I must put in some more speeches praising General Washington and insulting General Howe."

"It'll be great, Ezra. It'll pack the house. We'll make plenty of money."

Ezra nodded slowly. "I could use some," he said quietly. "Thank you very much, Joel, for all you've done for me."

"Why, it's nothing, Ezra. We actors have to stick together, don't we?"

5

THE PLAY'S THE THING

GETTING READY FOR THE PRODUCTION of *The Continental Hero* almost became a way of life for Daniel Bradford's family. At first Daniel thought nothing of it, but after a time he quite ran out of patience with it. One morning he complained to Marian, "I can never get any work done with Sam and Micah caught up in that crazy play!" He shook his head and looked across the table at her. They were having an early breakfast of porridge with cream, eggs, butter and spices added, bacon, spiced bread with butter, and wigs, small cakes of lightly spiced and sweetened bread dough. He picked up a cup of scalding black coffee and drank it down, then shook his head again. "And I think it's some sort of a disease. Even Rachel and Jeanne have lost their minds. You'd think grown people would have better sense."

"Did you have better sense when you were Sam's age?" Marian asked.

A rash grin suddenly creased Daniel's lips and he said, "No, I think I was told several times that I was studying for the gallows." He reached across the table, picked up her hand, and squeezed it. "I guess I'm getting to be an old grouch."

"You're not any such thing," Marian said. She put her other hand out and enclosed his large one between hers and held it tightly. She felt especially attractive this morning, for she was wearing a new dress she had bought to please Daniel—one that fully complemented her best features. In her heart she knew that she'd never really tried to please Leo, her first husband, in this way, but things were different now. She said suddenly, and without meaning to, "I feel like a bride for the first time, Daniel." Color swept across her face, and she laughed nervously and tried to pull her hand back. "What a foolish thing for me to say."

"Not foolish at all. I feel like I'm about nineteen years old and still

73

on a honeymoon." He reached out and stroked the softness of her hands, then shook his head, and a mischievous light brightened his eyes. "We'll continue this discussion tonight at a more suitable time. I'd say that bedtime would be appropriate."

"You're awful, Daniel Bradford!" Marian said, blushing.

"No, I'm not awful. You would never have fallen in love with an awful fellow." Daniel rose, wiped his lips with a napkin, then put it back on the table. "Well, I'm going to try to get a day's work done if I can round up enough help. I wouldn't be surprised if Micah had recruited Albert Blevins to be in the play." The thought of the dour bookkeeper with the cadaverous face acting amused him, and he came over and kissed her. "They should have recruited you. You're the most beautiful leading lady I ever saw."

He held her for a moment, and she put her arms around his neck. She felt a oneness and a unity in their love that she had never known before. It was difficult for her to explain how she felt. Her loveless marriage with Leo Rochester had not soured her, but it had grieved and saddened her and quenched her spirit greatly. Now as she clung to Daniel she whispered, "I love you more than I ever thought I could love a man, Daniel."

Huskily Daniel replied, "That's good to hear. I never thought I'd have you as my wife, Marian, and now that I do, I think I can face anything." He kissed her thoroughly until she pulled away protesting, and he winked, saying, "I'll see you tonight."

By the time he got to the foundry, Daniel discovered that he had indeed been right. Albert Blevins met him with a caustic expression. "Well, Micah dropped by and said that he would be busy."

"With the play, I suppose," Daniel nodded, taking off his coat and hanging it on a peg. He turned to face Blevins and grinned. "But I suppose Sam is downstairs hard at work."

"Sam? We haven't seen him for a week." Disgust scored the tall bookkeeper's features and he scowled fiercely. "You'd think he was six years old instead of seventeen! The lad hasn't got a lick of sense in his head!"

"Aw, Sam's all right. He's just full of high spirits. Now let's see if we can keep this place going until the play's over."

"How long is it going to run?" Blevins demanded.

"As long as people keep paying to see it, I think. The Tyrones are in pretty bad shape. Ezra is really too ill to do much work. I'm glad that General Washington and his staff will be there. At least they'll have a full house for one night."

On opening night the hastily improvised theater was packed to capacity long before the curtain was due to open. Sam kept running to the curtain, pulling it apart, and staring out. Then he'd go back and give a report to the other actors and actresses waiting nervously for the play to begin. "It's going to be great, Ezra!" he said. "All the seats are filled up except those reserved for the general and his staff. They've got ribbons tied around those."

Ezra Tyrone was dressed fit to kill for his role. The costume consisted of a suit that had once belonged to Daniel Bradford. Since Bradford was six feet one and weighed over one hundred and eighty-five pounds and Ezra was no more than five nine and weighed less than one hundred and thirty-five, it had taken the combined sewing expertise of Marian Frazier Bradford and Phoebe Bradford to cut it down and make the necessary alterations. Still, they had worked hard, and now Ezra stood there in all his glory ready to take his place on stage. The suit was a deep royal blue coat, close-fitting and waisted with the flared skirt reaching to just below the knees. The coat had no collar, was cut rather low in front, and fastened with buttons from the neck to waist level. The sleeves were close-fitting with deep cuffs ending well above the wrist. The waistcoat was a dark yellow in color, tight-fitting to the waist, and was buttoned to the top, where a white ruffled shirt was exposed. The breeches were white and gathered onto a waistband with the leg narrowing downward, finishing just below the knee in a knee band over the white silk stocking. His shoes were made of black leather, had blocked square toes, square high heels, and were fastened by straps and buckles over the instep.

Ezra's face was wreathed in smiles as he moved around to his cast, encouraging them all. His wife, Leah, followed him, for she had helped a great deal with the makeup and the costumes.

"Well now. That is encouraging to have a full house on opening night," Ezra said, rubbing his hands together. He stood beside Abigail Howland, who was calmer than the rest. She was wearing a burgundy silk dress with light blue and pink embroidery. There was a beauty in this young woman that shone forth. "Well, do you think you know all your lines, Miss Howland?"

"I doubt it, Mr. Tyrone."

"Well, you don't need to worry about it. I think Joel's in every scene with you, and he's got every line that you speak memorized. I'm sure he'll prompt you if you falter."

"He does have a phenomenal memory, doesn't he?" The two looked over to where Joel was standing beside Keturah Burns, who was flanked on the other side now by Sam. "I think Sam's got a very strong attachment for that young woman, hasn't he?" Ezra said.

"I believe so," Abigail agreed. "Sam's not the greatest in the world at covering his emotions, but they're both very young."

Suddenly a man appeared from the side of the stage, and Ezra noticed Abigail's face growing quite pale. "Who's that?" he asked.

"That's Matthew Bradford," Abigail said quietly. "Mr. Daniel Bradford's oldest son."

Ezra shot a quick look at the young woman. He had a sharp mind and a quick ear and had heard that there had once been an engagement between these two. He had also heard that it had been broken off, although he did not know the reason why. "He's a fine-looking young man, Miss Howland. He doesn't resemble his father much."

Abigail did not have time to explain to Ezra that Matthew was not Daniel Bradford's natural son. Matthew had come over at them and bowed slightly. He was wearing a dark gray suit with a white ruffled shirt and black boots.

"Good evening, Miss Howland," he said quietly.

"Good evening, Matthew," she said, deliberately using his first name. She saw that this caused a flush to appear in his cheeks, but he merely turned to Ezra.

"I'm anticipating a fine play this evening, Mr. Tyrone. My name is Matthew Bradford. I'm very happy that my cousin Joel found you on the road. He told me the whole story."

"If it had not been for your kinsman, sir, I fear it would have gone ill with us." Ezra would have said more, but Matthew turned and bowed stiffly to Abigail.

"I trust you'll do well, Miss Howland."

"Thank you, sir."

Ezra would have responded, but Sam had left Keturah's side to go again and look out the curtain. "He's here!" he cried with excitement. "It's General Washington and his staff!"

"Get away from that curtain, Sam!" Joel hissed. "They'll see you!"

Sam grinned rashly. "I want him to see me. You need to catch the attention of important people."

"Well, you can do that with your good acting," Phoebe said. "Now come away, Sam."

It was almost time for the play to begin. A quick glance through the curtain assured Ezra that the hall was packed. Every chair was filled, and there were even people standing around the door. He turned now and said, "All right, get off the stage. We're ready to begin. Don't stare at the audience. Throw yourself into this as if it were real life."

In truth, the amateurs were pretty stiffened by fear, all except Abigail, who had acted in several amateur pieces before. And Joel Bradford seemed to be more excited than frightened. Now that the curtain was about to open, Sam stood there with his mouth open. His face grew so pale that his freckles stood out.

"What's the matter with you, Sam?" Phoebe asked quickly. "Are you sick?"

"N-no. I . . . I . . ." He could not say more and swallowed suddenly. "Well, maybe I am a little bit."

"It's too late for that," Phoebe whispered fiercely. "Now get ready. You have to go out in the first scene."

The curtain was strung on a wire, and Micah pulled one side while Joel Bradford pulled another. As the curtain parted, a hearty round of applause went up from the audience.

Sam seemed frozen in place. In the first scene he was to go out on the stage and answer a knock at the door. The knock came and Sam did not move. Quickly, Joel stepped up beside him and placed his hand behind his back. "Here you go," he said gleefully. "Wake up." He struck Sam a hard slap on the back and propelled him out on the stage. A laugh went up as Sam suddenly emerged as if shot out of a cannon. His arms were wheeling as he caught his balance, and he turned suddenly and stared at the audience—exactly what Ezra told him not to do. The footlights, which consisted of lanterns just below the level of the stage, half blinded him, but he could see his father seated in the front row beside Marian. General Washington sat up front also in his buff and blue uniform, seated beside Generals Knox and Arnold. Sam suddenly came to himself and said loudly, "Guess I'd better answer the door." He rapidly turned on his heels and headed toward it.

The play itself was terribly overdone, but that did not seem to displease the spectators. Joel, as the young townsman who enlists in the army out of love of liberty, had several lofty speeches that he gave with great exuberance. Those who had been to rehearsal knew he was aping the manner of Ezra Tyrone and doing it well. He seemed to have a natural aptitude for it, and General Washington was highly amused. Halfway through the first act, he leaned to his right and said, "Mr. Bradford, that kinsman of yours is a fine actor. He must have great experience."

"No, sir, I believe this is his first. He is good, isn't he?" Daniel said.

"Very good indeed!"

The rest of the cast were not so fortunate. Perhaps the worst was Silas Bickerson. He almost destroyed whatever illusion there was by his poor acting. Fortunately, he only appeared in a few scenes. The rest of the cast performed fairly well. There was one warm, tender, romantic scene between the young soldier who was going out to fight for his country and the young woman he was leaving, portrayed by Abigail Howland. It was a love scene and Joel put his heart into it. When he had said his flowery lines about going out to die for liberty, he embraced Abigail and kissed her soundly, then left. Abigail, in truth, was amused by the young man. Although she wasn't much older, she felt almost motherly toward him.

When the play finally ended, a rousing, thundering applause brought the actors back out on the stage. They were shoved into place by Ezra Tyrone, who said, "Go on out and take your bows like I showed you."

With some awkwardness they did so and managed to make several bows as the audience continued to applaud them.

Immediately after the play, General Washington said, "I think we should go congratulate the cast. I didn't know that I was such a noble person." Washington was not a man who laughed loudly, but he had a keen sense of humor that close friends such as General Knox could appreciate.

"He didn't gild the lily, I think, General, but he made up for it by insulting General Howe in an admirable way, I thought."

The general, followed by his staff, and Daniel and Marian made their way up the stage. Washington went at once to Joel Bradford and put his hand out. Joel, for once, was almost speechless. The general's hand was very large and enclosed his completely, and his grip was crushing.

"I appreciate very much your sentiments, Mr. Bradford," Washington said.

"Why, thank you, General. The credit, of course, belongs to Mr. Tyrone. He wrote the play."

"A very fine play indeed. Very patriotic, Mr. Tyrone."

"Thank you, General. Thank you very much!"

Joel was filled with excitement, for the play had gone well despite the few missed lines and Sam's abrupt entrance. He listened as Ezra called out to the audience as they filed out, "The same time tomorrow, ladies and gentlemen. Come back and we will give you an even better performance, and bring your friends and relatives with you."

Joel was smiling at Ezra's enthusiasm when a voice at his side said, "Mr. Bradford—"

Turning quickly, Joel saw the civilian who had arrived with General Washington and his staff.

"Mr. Dante," Joel said quickly. "I hope you enjoyed the play."

"Very much so. So much, indeed, that I would like to invite you out to have a meal, a celebration supper."

"Well, I must see to my sister, Mr. Dante."

"Of course, bring her along, by all means."

Joel did not hesitate. He was curious about Dante, who did not fit in at all with Washington's military entourage. He said quickly, "I'll get Phoebe and we will be glad to dine with you."

Thirty minutes later the three were sitting in the inn where Dante was evidently staying. "Innkeeper, we will have the very best you can provide."

"Yes, indeed, Mr. Dante. How does fresh roast mutton sound to you?"

"That sounds fine, and could we please have some of that good bread your wife makes in such an excellent fashion?"

Before long, the innkeeper returned and set plates heaping with steaming mutton and thick slices of bread lathered in butter before them. Both Joel and Phoebe ate with the eagerness and hunger of youth. Dante ate less and told little about himself. He was, however, adroit at drawing out others, and by the end of the meal, without seeming to pry, he had learned most of the history of the young pair.

"So you will not return to England, I take it?" he said.

"No sir, Mr. Dante!" Joel said, shaking his head firmly. "This is a good country here. We had nothing there. I'm very grateful to Mr. Bradford for bringing us here."

At that moment Silas Bickerson suddenly entered the inn. When he saw them, he came right over and said, "Well, I'd wondered where you had gotten away to." He stood there waiting for an invitation, but since it was not their place to issue one, Joel and Phoebe remained silent. In truth, both were dreading having to share their fine meal with Silas Bickerson.

Whatever Edmund Dante did with General Washington, he proved himself a skillful tactician at that moment. Somehow he greeted Mr. Bickerson graciously and said good-bye almost in the same sentence. It was so smoothly done that Bickerson did not know for a moment what had happened; then he realized that he had been dismissed. His face flushed and he turned stiffly and left, slamming the door behind him.

"A rather hotheaded sort of fellow. A good friend of yours?" Dante asked.

"No!" Joel said emphatically. He glanced at his sister in such a way that Dante turned to look at Phoebe and saw that her face was flushed. His dark eyes studied her, and he thought, *She doesn't like the fellow, and her brother doesn't like him, either. That's just as well.* Finally, when the meal was over, Dante said amiably, "I enjoyed the play very much. In fact, I will probably come and see another performance."

"Thank you very much for the excellent dinner, Mr. Dante," Joel said as he rose. "We'll look forward to seeing you again."

Dante waited until the two had left, then said, "Bartender, I'll have another glass of wine." He sat there drinking wine until Washington came in, followed by Knox and Arnold. Getting to his feet, he followed the three into a private dining room.

Washington seemed preoccupied. He had been amused during the play, but now the weight of command fell upon him. After the innkeeper had brought the meal and left, shutting the door behind him, he looked around and sighed heavily. "Well, gentlemen, what are we going to do?"

The question was indeed a pressing one. The winter encampment had strengthened the Continental Army so that Washington now had at least enough men to try to counter the British general, William Howe. Howe had spent the winter in New York, mostly occupied with the charms of Mrs. Loring, the wife of his commissary. It was commonly known that Loring provided his wife to General Howe. In return, Howe saw that Loring was well provided with ample funds, most of which remained in his own pocket.

But now that winter had broken and spring had finally come, Washington and everyone else who studied the subject understood that it was time for Howe to make a move—but which way? Trying to anticipate Howe's military strategy kept George Washington occupied night and day. Knox knew his chief very well. He studied the tall man who slouched back in his chair now, away from the public eye, and said, "One bit of good news was that new shipment that just arrived. I just got a count of it." He pulled a paper from his pocket with his good hand and read aloud, "Twelve thousand muskets, one thousand barrels of powder, blankets, and quite a few other supplies."

"Where did they come from?" Benedict Arnold inquired.

"They came from France," Washington said. "Have you ever heard of a man called Beaumarchais?"

"No, I don't believe so."

"His real name is Pierre Augustin Caron. Quite a romantic fellow."

"He certainly is," Knox grinned. "He's a composer, an actor, a poet, and a jewelry maker, but most of all he is interested in our cause for liberty."

"The French can help us, I believe," Arnold said. His swarthy face was highlighted by the candles on the table. He was a strong man, intelligent and, in the opinion of many, the best general on either side of the Revolution. He grinned suddenly and said rather cynically, "It's not that they like us so much, but they hate England. Anything they can do to wear England down, they will do it."

"I can't question their motives," Washington said, shaking his head. "We can use all the supplies and cannons we can get, but the question is, what is Howe going to do?"

"He will try to draw us out into a battle," Washington said calmly.

"Then let us fight him!" Arnold exclaimed.

"No, sir. As much as I would like it, we dare not trust our resources so recklessly." Washington's face was still and he added, "The army, sir, is the Revolution. We cannot risk it. We must wait until the enemy is worn down and we ourselves have built up a more formidable adversary."

"I think, sir," Knox said, "that Howe will attempt to take Philadelphia, our capital. That would be a logical move."

"I believe you are correct, General. He has eighteen thousand disciplined and splendidly equipped regulars. We have nine thousand largely untrained troops. I'm sure he will feel confident that he can capture the city easily, so all our efforts must be to prevent them."

"I wish we knew more about what he was doing there," Knox said, shaking his head in despair. He looked over at Edmund Dante, who had said nothing during the entire discussion. "What can you tell us, sir, of events in New York?"

Dante looked at the three generals and said softly, "It is getting more and more difficult for my people to gain information."

"How is that, sir?"

Dante looked at Washington and answered quickly, "It is always difficult for spies to get their information back to their superiors. We have lost three of our best agents in the past month."

Edmund Dante was an intelligence officer. He never wore a uniform and never carried a weapon, but it was his occupation and task to discover what the British were doing and to inform General Washington and his staff as quickly as possible through his spies.

"Can you not get more men in place?" Washington asked. "It is terrible to have to endure this blindness as to the enemy's movements."

Edmund Dante was not a man who revealed all the details of his missions, even to General Washington. All he did now was to nod and say quietly, "I intend to increase my staff at once, sir."

The three officers studied Dante carefully. He was a terse man with information, but all three understood that he was making some kind of commitment. Washington only nodded with approval, saying, "You have done a fine job, and we are greatly in your debt, Mr. Dante."

⊤   ⊤   ⊤

The play enjoyed another full house the following evening, although the general and his staff were not there, having left for Philadelphia. In ordinary times an amateur play would have attracted few viewers, but there was a paucity of entertainment in the city of Boston. So for the next two weeks attendance boomed.

After the final performance, Micah spoke to Daniel about the success of the play, saying, "I'm very pleased for Ezra Tyrone. He seems a worthy man, though very unfortunate."

Daniel nodded and said, "He's not well, and I'm glad this play has managed to generate a little income for him—though what he will do next I'm sure I don't know." He looked over at Micah and asked suddenly, "What about you, son?"

"About me? What about me, Father?"

"When are you and Sarah getting married?"

The question seemed to confuse Micah, and he answered rather slowly, "Well . . . I'm not sure. Things are so up in the air. I may go into the army."

"There was an English poet once who said *carpe diem*."

"I guess I've forgotten my Latin."

"It means 'seize the day,' " Daniel said. "The first line is, 'Gather ye rosebuds while ye may.' I guess that's what Marian and I decided to do, although I'm not telling you what you should do, you understand."

Micah was much slower to make decisions than his brother Dake. He said now, "If we were to marry and I were to get killed in the war, I'd leave a widow, perhaps a child. It's not something to be quickly decided."

"Of course not." Daniel leaned back and said, "What do you make of this fellow Dante?"

Quickly Micah looked up. "I don't know. He didn't leave with the general. He's a closemouthed fellow, isn't he?"

"Yes, he is. Washington trusts him completely, which is recommendation enough. He's spending a great deal of time with Joel. Did you know that?"

"I knew they had had several meals together."

"Rather strange," Daniel shrugged, "but I suppose he'll be moving on soon." He rose and said, "Well, let's see if we can make some more cannons for General Knox."

6

A Doctor Comes to Boston

"I DON'T BELIEVE YOU'VE MET my nephew." Daniel Bradford looked up as Joel entered the room with an armload of wood. "Drop that wood over there and I'll introduce you properly." Daniel waited until Joel put the wood in the box, then said, "This is Dr. Clive Gordon. He's the son of my only sister, Lyna, who lives in New York with her husband, Colonel Leslie Gordon."

"Clive, this is your cousin, Joel Bradford."

"I'm happy to meet you, Mr. Bradford." Clive Gordon bowed gracefully. He was an extremely tall man of twenty-four, lean with long arms and legs. His hands were long and sensitive, and he had reddish hair that went well with a pair of cornflower blue eyes. "Uncle Daniel has told me about how you came from England. Welcome to America."

"Thank you, Dr. Gordon," Joel said. He was somewhat puzzled and his brow wrinkled. "Your father is in the Continental Army?"

"Oh no, indeed." Clive smiled slightly and turned to catch the astonished look on his uncle's face. "My father's a colonel in the British army."

"So we're more or less on opposite sides politically," Joel said.

"Makes for an unfortunate situation, if you ask me, but we don't let it get in our way," Daniel Bradford said, smiling at his tall nephew. "I wish you could have been here a few days earlier. Your cousin and his sister turned out to be proficient actors."

"Is that so? I do love a good play," Clive said.

Joel listened with some embarrassment as Daniel explained the play, stressing the fact that General Washington and some of his staff had

85

been there the first night. "General Howe would not have enjoyed it," he said, laughing as he remembered lines from the play.

"Well, he might. He's a good-natured man," Clive said. He thought for a moment, then added, "I don't think his heart's in this war. He's doing a better job than General Gage, I suppose, but I must inform you, Joel. I'm not in sympathy with British politics insofar as the Colonies are concerned."

"You're in sympathy with the cause, sir?" Joel asked with some surprise.

"Indeed I am, and so is my father. So are many influential people in England, including the prime minister, Lord North. I wish they'd sit down and see what they are throwing away. England will lose this war eventually, and they'll lose the most valuable possession they have."

Joel listened carefully as Clive Gordon spoke, and finally when the subject was changed, he asked quickly, "Dr. Gordon, since we are kinsmen, might I ask a favor?"

"Why certainly. What is it?"

"Mr. Ezra Tyrone has become quite a good friend. He's the gentleman who wrote the play and put it on. He's in very poor health and his wife is expecting. They have very little money and I was wondering— well, would it be possible for you to see them? I would be glad to pay the fee."

"No, don't speak of money, Joel," Clive said. "I'd be glad to pay your friends a visit."

Joel thanked Clive profusely and persuaded Daniel to lend him a carriage. Twenty minutes later the two were getting out in front of the home of Esther Denham. "This is the place, Doctor," Joel said eagerly. "If you'll come upstairs, they have a room up over the stable."

They ascended the stairs and found Ezra and his wife, Leah, somewhat startled to see them. When Joel announced that Mr. Gordon was a physician, Ezra grinned slightly. "Well, we can't pay your fees, Doctor."

"There'll be no charge. Suppose I look you both over while I'm here?"

Leah led Joel into the small room that had been made into a combination kitchen and dining room to separate it from the rest of the quarters. As she fixed him a cup of tea, Joel saw the worry in her eyes.

"I hope he'll be able to help Ezra. He's getting worse, I fear," Leah said as she poured the tea.

"I'm sure he will. From what my uncle tells me, he's a fine doctor."

Soon Ezra came out and motioned for the door. "The doctor would like to see you, Leah." He sat down as Leah left and poured himself a cup of tea.

"Did he give you any encouragement, Ezra?" Joel asked.

"Oh, doctors do that. They don't tell you much, and you can't believe what they do say. It's not me I'm worried about, but Leah. She's very small to bear a child."

The two men sat there for a time, and then Leah appeared at the door, saying, "Let me fix the doctor some tea." It was very crowded in the dining area, but the three men sat around the table as Leah poured more tea and served cakes.

"What do you think, Dr. Gordon?" Ezra asked eagerly.

"As far as I can tell, your wife is in very good condition. She's rather small, of course, but that's no problem. It's you I'm worried about. You need to be down south. This isn't a good climate for you."

"I've been down south. There's nothing for us there."

Joel and Clive stayed only long enough to drink tea and have cakes, and then they left. As they got into the carriage, Clive said, "I have a few items I need to buy if you don't mind taking me there, Joel."

"Of course."

The two men drove downtown quickly and Clive visited a store, buying a few items. Joel accompanied him, and when they turned to leave, he suddenly was confronted by Edmund Dante.

"Why, good day, Mr. Bradford."

"Oh, Mr. Dante, good to see you!"

"Doing a little shopping?"

Clive had turned to come and stand beside Joel, and Joel introduced him to Dante. "This is my distant cousin, Mr. Clive Gordon, from New York."

"From New York? I'm happy to know you, sir."

"Happy to know you, Mr. Dante," Clive said, shaking Dante's hand.

"Have you just come from your home?"

"Yes, I have."

"I suppose things are quite busy there with being occupied by the British army."

"Well, I suppose so."

Joel said, "Dr. Gordon's father is a colonel for General Howe."

"Do you tell me that?" Dante's eyes narrowed and he smiled. "A very able man. You are acquainted with him?"

"Oh yes, in a small way," Clive nodded.

"Would you gentlemen come with me and have something to drink?"

Somehow Dante had a way of getting what he wanted, and soon the three men were sitting in Dante's inn engaged in conversation. They had more than drink, for he had ordered a light meal. Joel noticed that he seemed very interested in Clive Gordon. He had learned that Dante knew how to get information when he wanted it, so now he sat there wondering about Dante's interest in his cousin.

Finally Clive rose and said, "Well, I have a call to make if you gentlemen will excuse me."

"Of course," Mr. Dante said. He bowed slightly, and as the two men left, he muttered to himself, "So Joel Bradford has a relative in New York whose father is a colonel under General Howe." A smile turned the corners of his lips upward, and he nodded as if coming to some kind of decision. He sat back down and said, "Innkeeper, let's have another bottle of wine."

🔔   🔔   🔔

Joel followed Clive's directions and pulled up in front of a cottage that lay close to the sea. It was obviously the home of a family of fishermen. "Is this the place, Dr. Gordon?"

"Yes, this is the Yancy house."

Clive stepped down and smiled at Joel. "Thank you for being my coachman today, Joel. I will be seeing you."

"Will you be staying in town long?"

"I'm not sure. In any case, it's been a pleasure meeting you."

Taking Joel's good-bye, Clive moved along the walk and knocked on the door. It opened almost at once and Katherine Yancy stood before him.

"Why . . . Clive! Come in," she said.

"Thank you, Katherine." Stepping inside, Clive was met almost at once by Susan and Amos Yancy, Katherine's parents. He was welcomed royally, for they were both convinced that Clive had preserved Amos's life from certain death.

When he said he had to leave, they insisted he must stay for supper. Smiling, Clive finally surrendered and actually welcomed the chance to enjoy a meal with them and visit.

It was a simple but pleasant meal consisting of beefsteak pie, sweet potatoes and apples, buttermilk biscuits, and a freshly baked berry pie, all served on dishes brought over from England. The dining room was small and attached to the kitchen. The walls were painted a light green, and a large area rug was spread out under the table. The table was made of oak, small and well used, and covered with a fine linen cloth.

Clive leaned back finally and shook his head. "No more, Mrs. Yancy."

"Why, you haven't eaten enough to keep a bird alive!" Susan Yancy exclaimed.

"Plenty for me."

"Well, go into the parlor, then. Katherine and I will clean up while you and Amos talk."

It was a very pleasant evening indeed. The Yancys were very fond of the doctor, and he had come to admire them for the courage they showed during the hardships that had fallen on them because of the war. He was, however, somewhat relieved when they went to bed rather early and left Katherine sitting beside him on the horsehair couch. It was too warm for a fire, so the windows were open, letting in a light breeze. Finally Clive said, "Come and show me your garden. It's rather close in here."

"Of course." Katherine led him outside, and soon they were wandering among the roses and other flowers that gave forth a sweet fragrance.

"What have you been doing, Clive?" Katherine asked.

"Well, nothing really."

"You haven't thought of joining the army as a surgeon?"

"Oh, General Howe has invited me to do so, but I can't make up my mind what I should do." He turned to Katherine, reached out, and took her hand. "You know why I came. I love you and I want to marry you."

Katherine Yancy was a sensitive young woman. She was also passionately in love with Clive Gordon. Nothing would have been easier than for her to say yes, but she had learned wisdom along the way. It would be wonderful—for a while. She faltered then and shook her head. "But we're too different, Clive."

"We're not different at all," he insisted.

"I mean politically. This war has separated us."

"It doesn't have to be that way."

Katherine looked up at him and said quietly, "One of us will have to change—and I cannot."

Clive Gordon then knew that sooner or later he would have to make a decision. "I don't believe in this war," he said gloomily. "I keep hoping that it will be over, and I think one day soon it will be."

"Then we'll just have to wait."

Clive reached forward and pulled her into his arms. Her lips made a small change and became soft. She made a little gesture with her shoulders and smiled at him. She possessed a fire of independence that made her lovely in his sight. It brought out the richness and headlong qualities of a spirit otherwise hidden beneath a cool reserve. He pulled her close and the pressure of his extreme emotion held him there. He kissed her and found a sweet response in her lips. There was a mystery about her, and finally she drew back.

"We will have to wait, Clive," she whispered.

☦   ☦   ☦

Joel sat in the church on the solid straight-backed church pew, suddenly aware that Edmund Dante was smiling at him from down the row. He returned the smile and nodded, but was thinking, *What's he doing here? It seems like everywhere I go he's there.*

Joel had no more time to think, for right then the service began. It was an experience that shook Joel. He had been to church several times, but something about the preaching of Pastor Asa Carrington was different from any preacher he had ever heard before. Carrington was not a tall man, but he was strongly built. He had hair black as a crow's wing and eyes fully as dark. His voice could be gentle and soft, but at times it sounded like a trumpet. He began preaching after the song service, and something about the sermon riveted young Joel Bradford.

Carrington read his text: " 'It is appointed unto man once to die, but after this the judgment.' " For some time he brought up biblical passages concerning death and the inevitable end of man. Joel Bradford had given little thought to death, but the eloquence and conviction Reverend Carrington poured into his words began to work on Joel's heart. He sat and listened attentively as the preacher said, "Where death leaves me, judgment finds me. As I die, so shall I live eternally. It is forever, forever, forever! I read in God's Word that the angel shall plant one foot upon the earth and the other upon the sea and shall swear by him that liveth and was dead, that time shall be no longer, but if a soul should die in a thousand years it would die in time. If a million years could elapse and then the soul could be extinguished, there would be such a thing as time. Talk to me of years and there is time, but the angel said time shall be no longer. One day," Carrington thundered out, "you will meet God. There is a passage in Revelation that says, 'I saw death on a pale horse and hell followed him. There was death on the pale horse.' Yes, death is after me and it is after you!"

Suddenly Carrington raised his hands to heaven and cried out, "Ah, run, run, run, but run as thou wilt, the rider on the white horse shall overtake you! You may escape him for seventy years, but at last you will be his. Death is riding. I hear his horse, I hear the snortings, I feel his hot breath. He comes, he comes, and then you will die!"

Joel Bradford's hands began to tremble and a sudden fear gripped his heart. It was unusual, for he was not a young man given to fears. The preacher continued asking, "Will it be heaven or hell? I pray God deliver you from hell, poor helpless one. Come to Jesus and all is secure. Storms may blow, but you cannot be overwhelmed. Come into the cleft of the rock and you shall be hidden until the vengeance is overcast."

Joel sat there until Carrington dismissed the congregation, then he took out his handkerchief and wiped his brow. He was suddenly startled when a voice said, "A rather striking sermon, eh, Mr. Bradford?"

Looking up, Joel saw that Dante had come to stand beside him.

"Yes, I . . . I suppose it was," Joel said.

"It troubled you, I see."

"I think it did. I've never thought much about death, but it will come to all of us."

"Indeed it will." Dante was moving slowly out along with Joel. When they were outside, he turned to him and said, "I wonder if I could meet with you later. Perhaps this afternoon."

"Why, I suppose so. What would you like to speak of?"

"It might be better if I would wait until then. You know my inn. Come when you can. I will be there all day."

"Very well. I'll see you later then, Mr. Dante."

Phoebe came up and said, "I was surprised to see Mr. Dante in church. Did he invite us to supper again?"

"Not this time." Joel was thinking hard but said nothing to Phoebe about his meeting for later that day. *He's a strange man. I wonder what he can want with me?*

🛡   🛡   🛡

Dante's room in the inn was larger than most. It was about ten by ten with dark wooden floors marked by many years of hard use. The walls had recently been redone in light tan paper with brown images of trees and animals throughout. The room had two small windows covered with dark brown curtains, and many pictures of animals and scenery in heavy, dark wooden frames hung on the walls. It had a large tester bed made of oak that was covered by a handmade quilt in blues, browns, and greens, and a washstand and wardrobe stood along the far wall. Two horsehair-covered chairs flanked a small table with an oil lamp on it, and a dark blue area rug had been placed beneath the table.

Dante sat down and leaned forward. "I will be brief. I've heard that you have had thoughts of joining the army. Is that so?"

"Why, yes, I have," Joel responded, wondering how in the world Dante could have found this out. He had spoken to few about this, and now he asked directly, "How did you hear about this, Mr. Dante?"

"Your sister, Phoebe. She did not realize she told me, but I got it out of her."

Joel suddenly grew half angry. "Why are you following me, Mr. Dante? You're connected with General Washington, I know. What is it you do?"

"I, sir, am a spy."

Joe's eyes flew open and he could not think for a moment. He thought, perhaps, he had misunderstood and repeated the words. "You are a . . . a spy?"

"An intelligence agent, if you would prefer a more eloquent term. You will understand that I am putting myself in your power, for very few people know this. I serve the cause as well as I can in this way."

Joel was fascinated. "A spy. I have never met an intelligence agent before."

"You may have and not known it. It is the chief business of an agent to keep himself unrecognized." Dante smiled suddenly and leaned forward. "You are wondering why I've told you this?"

"Well . . . yes, sir, I am."

"If you are serious in your desire to help in the cause for liberty, I would like to know about it."

"Why, I'm very serious, sir. I'm a newcomer, of course, but I love this country. I will never go back to England again."

"And if England wins the war, then America will be like England. Is that correct?"

"I suppose so." Joel turned his head slightly to one side and studied Dante. "What is it you want, Mr. Dante?"

"I want you to become an agent."

If Dante had said, I want you to fly to the moon, Joel Bradford could not have been more surprised. "An agent? Why that's . . . that's insane!"

"Why should you say that?"

"Because . . . I have no training."

Dante laughed. "Training? Do you think there is a course in college, special studies in how to be an agent of intelligence? Certainly not! My staff comes from various walks of life. One of them is a farmer. No one ever suspects him, but he has a mind and memory like a steel trap. I know that you also have a prodigious memory. I've been talking to Mr. Tyrone. He said you memorized the play almost instantly."

"Well, I suppose I have a fair memory."

"And you are a fine actor."

Joel laughed. "Why, I've been in one play."

"You must understand I talked to Ezra Tyrone, although he never recognized what I was doing. He says you are a natural mimic, that you can assume any role. What could be finer for an intelligence agent than to be able to do that?"

"But I don't—"

"Why, you could go anywhere. A little disguise, a new voice, new mannerisms, and there you are."

"I can't do it, sir."

"It's possible you cannot, but I will tell you this, young man." Dante leaned forward and tapped Joel on the knee. "You can do much more for the cause of liberty by serving in this way than you could in a line of battle. Other men can do that. Very few can do what I'm asking you to do."

For over an hour the conversation went on. Joel attempted to evade the request, but every time he made any sort of objection Edmund Dante had an answer.

Finally Dante said, "I made up my mind when I met your cousin, Mr. Gordon. That would be a perfect door of opportunity."

"You mean I would have to deceive my family, the Gordons?"

"Certainly. Would that bother you?"

Joel said indignantly, "Would it bother me to deceive my family? Of course it would!"

"Then you are not the man for me. I'm disappointed in you, sir."

Joel somehow felt disappointed in himself. "Understand, Mr. Dante, I would like to do what I can to see this country set free, but what you are asking is impossible."

"Difficult—but not impossible." Dante began to speak earnestly. "You could tell no one of your true feelings. You would have to convince even the Bradfords here that you had changed loyalties. We would have to see to it that you left Boston, or it would be better if you were run out for being a Tory."

"But that's very hard, sir."

"It's hard for the men who are facing bayonets or death from a musket ball or a cannon, but if liberty is to be obtained for these Colonies, then it will take valiant acts of sacrifice."

"Could I tell Phoebe?"

"Her least of all. She would not betray you intentionally, but an enemy agent with talent would have it out of her in no time. No, you would be a man alone. You and I would know you were serving the

Continental Army without a uniform. It could be of tremendous help to General Washington and to the cause."

Dante knew men and he knew he had pressed his case as far as he could. Rising, he said, "Go think about it. It's a big decision. Say nothing to anyone. If you decide to help us, I will be in your debt. If you decide not to, no one will ever know."

"Yes, sir, I will think about it."

After Bradford had left, Dante shook his head with regret. "I wish I were a praying man," he muttered. "If I were, I'd pray that God would change that young man's mind. I must have him! I must!"

7

VALLEY OF DECISION

FOR DAYS AFTER EDMUND DANTE had spoken to Joel about becoming an intelligence agent, Joel went around almost in a daze. Phoebe grew quite concerned about him and said once to Marian, "I don't know what's the matter with Joel, Miss Marian. It's like he's gone deaf, but I know he can hear perfectly well. He's troubled about something. I can tell that much."

"Well, young men have problems sometimes," Marian said gently. "I'm sure he'll share it with you when he's ready."

Shaking her head doubtfully, Phoebe said, "I don't think so. It's the first time he's ever shut himself up away from me. We've always been so close. It bothers me, Miss Marian—indeed it does!"

Joel was not only troubled by the decision that he was facing concerning his future role in the Revolution, but he could not get over the feeling that somehow God was putting him in a corner. Ever since the church service, Joel felt as if he was being pursued, and this frightened him considerably. He knew so little about God and realized he was ignorant, but the sermon on death that the pastor had preached had stuck in his memory so that he could not get it out of his mind. At night sometimes he would wake up and hear almost the entire sermon as if it were being preached again. He slept so poorly that one afternoon at the foundry, even Micah noticed something.

"Joel, you'd better go home. You're going to smash your finger or something. You act like you're half asleep. What's wrong with you? Are you sick?"

"No, sir, I'm not sick."

"Well, I think you'd better take the rest of the day off. Go take a walk. Do something. You won't be any good to us until you come out of that stupor you're in."

Joel left the foundry and walked for hours. Twilight came and still he continued to walk. When he finally snapped out of it, he looked up with surprise to see that he was not three blocks from Edmund Dante's inn. He stood there uncertainly. The streets were nearly empty at this time. Only a few tradesmen headed toward their homes after closing up. Joel began to walk slowly, his mind fluttering almost like a wild bird trapped in a cage. *I don't know what to do! I've never had to make a decision this hard, and I can't talk to anyone about it. If I could just talk to Phoebe! But Mr. Dante says I can't tell anyone.* He continued to walk, and when he reached the inn almost in desperation, he squared his shoulders and said audibly, "All right, I'll give it a try."

Entering the inn he moved across to where the innkeeper was cleaning off a table. "Is Mr. Dante in, do you know?"

"Yes, he came in an hour ago. He said he'd be down for supper. Go on up if you like. The second door on the right at the top of the stairs."

Moving to the stairs, Joel went up and every step seemed to get more difficult. By the time he reached the second floor and peered down the gloomy corridor lit only by a small candle in a glass cylinder, he had almost changed his mind. "What's wrong with me?" he muttered. "I can't make up my mind to do anything." Reluctantly he moved to the door the innkeeper had indicated and knocked on it. There was a silence inside for a moment, and then the door opened just a crack. "Hello, Mr. Dante."

"Ah, Joel, come in, my boy."

As Joel stepped inside, he saw that Dante had a pistol in his hand. He stared at it and then glanced up to meet the man's eyes.

"You never know who's going to come through a door," Dante said, shrugging his shoulders. He placed the pistol down on a washstand beside the bed, then turned to face Joel. He stood straight, and there was an intense look in his dark eyes. "Have you come to a decision yet, young man?"

"It's not easy, Mr. Dante. I want to do something for this country."

"You have a good spirit, Joel, and of course it would be the honorable duty, and the dramatic thing, if you were to join the army. Put on a uniform—assuming they had one for you, which isn't likely—and go marching out to the sound of fife and drum."

"I don't care about that, sir."

"You don't?" Lifting his eyebrows, Dante stared intently at the young man, then shook his head. "That's unusual. Most young fellows are interested in getting into the heat of battle. What have you decided, then?"

Joel felt he was at a crucial fork in the road. If he turned one way, his life would take a certain direction—but if he turned the other way, it would go completely differently. Finally he blurted out, "I'll help you if I can, Mr. Dante, but I still think you're making a mistake."

A satisfied light illuminated Edmund Dante's dark eyes. "Don't you worry about that, my boy," he said with a trace of exultation in his voice.

He was more excited than Joel had seen him, and now he took him by the arm and squeezed it hard. He had a strong grip and Joel had to flex his muscles to keep from collapsing.

"You'll do fine, but we have a great many plans to make. Sit down. I'll go down and have the innkeeper bring up supper for both of us."

A wave of relief washed over Joel now that he had made his decision. As he waited for Dante to come back, he walked over to the window and looked into the darkness that had fallen on the streets. A few lanterns were lit on some of the businesses, but it was a dark night with not a cloud in the sky. A feeling of despondency settled on him, and suddenly he wondered again if he was doing the right thing. *I hope*, he thought, *I feel better about this after a time.*

Dante came back and soon the innkeeper brought their meal. After the innkeeper had left, Dante said, "Eat hearty, we've got a lot to do."

"How do I go about being a spy?"

"You listen to me, and you mind everything I say," Dante said, punctuating each word with a probing stab of the fork he had in his left hand. "You've got to learn how to avoid suspicion, and we don't have much time. We start tonight."

"How long will it take?"

"It depends on how quickly you absorb it. I would say a week perhaps, and you've got to be doing some other things while you're listening to me."

"What sort of things?"

"You've got to begin showing a new spirit about this Revolution." Dante placed a bite of mutton between his teeth and chewed on it thoughtfully. "Not all at once, but tonight when you go home start saying things like, 'I thought the Revolution might work, but I see now it won't.' Say this in front of your family, and especially in front of strangers. Tomorrow make it a little stronger. Every day you complain more, and by the end of the week, you'll have lost whatever reputation you might have had as a patriot. People are suspicious, and talk like this will get you in trouble, which is exactly what I want." He grinned at this thought and speared another piece of mutton. "You're soon going to be a very unpopular man in Boston, Joel Bradford, very unpopular indeed."

🕈 　 🕈 　 🕈

Edmund Dante proved to be a true prophet. By the time five days had passed, Joel noticed that he was greeted with scowls wherever he went, whereas before he had gotten smiles from everyone. Phoebe was hurt and terribly concerned by his attitude. Joel had worked hard to convince everyone that he had no use for the Revolution and had gotten into one serious argument with one of the workers at the foundry. It would have come to blows, for the young man, whose name was James Townley, had lost a brother in the Revolution. It had not been a private scene either, for Joel had chosen a time at lunch hour, when all the hands were eating together, to cast aspersions on the Revolution. "What does Washington know? He's an Englishman, and so am I. All of you are subjects of the king."

"That's not the way you talked when you came here!" Townley snapped. "If you don't like it here, then go back to England!"

Joel had answered in kind, and Townley had gotten up and started toward Joel with his fist flexed. Micah quickly leaped between the two and stopped the trouble. Afterward, he said to Joel, "I don't know what's changed you so, Joel, but I'll tell you this. You're not making any friends for yourself."

Joel had thrown himself into his part, and now he glared at Micah, although he liked him very much. Frowning, he said, "You're wrong, Micah, and your family's wrong. You ought to be fighting for the king."

Micah Bradford stared at the young man. He did not know how to account for the change, but he did not like what he saw. He had talked with his father about it, and with Marian, and they had all been gravely concerned. He finally said, "Townley may be right. It's going to be uncomfortable for you here. You might think about returning to England, Joel. It'll be your choice."

That evening Joel spent hours listening to Dante as he went over the methods of passing information. Finally, when they were done and he was about to leave, Joel told Dante of the argument that had happened in front of the men at the foundry that day. "It was almost a fight and Micah told me to go back to England." Now that he was not acting a part, he showed grief and shook his head. "I like Micah. It's hard to see that he's disappointed in me, and so is his father." He looked up with pain in his eyes. "As a matter of fact," he said, "everyone is disappointed in me now."

"Do you want to quit?" Dante asked almost harshly. "Thomas Paine said something about 'sunshine soldiers, and summer patriots'—those who are for the cause as long as everything's right and well, and there's no trouble." He stared at Joel, then said, "I don't have time for men like that. You think I don't know what it costs?" His voice grew softer then, and he added, "If you do this, you'll be helping General Washington and the cause for freedom from England's tyranny. You'll be helping your own family, because one day what you do will count."

"No, sir, I'm not going to quit."

"Good. Do again tomorrow just exactly what you did today and make it even more public."

Joel went home and slept badly that night, but he thought about what Dante had said: *"One day your family will know, and everyone will know that you've been a real soldier in this cause."*

The next evening Joel went to a gathering in front of the church. It was a fair and everyone had come. Joel watched, saying little until finally a group had gathered around Silas Bickerson. Bickerson was loudly proclaiming the stupidity of the English, and Joel took a deep breath and turned to say in a clear voice, "You don't know what you're talking about, Bickerson. The Continental Army hasn't won a single battle since the war started!"

Bickerson turned and stared at him. So did everyone else. "You know, you're ignorant, Bradford. I'm ashamed of you, and your family is, too, and you're dead wrong!"

"General Howe ran George Washington and the Continental Army out of New York across Jersey. Right now he's got his army holed up in Morristown, and as soon as he comes out, Howe will wipe up with him," Joel said. Looking at the people gathered around, he said loudly and boastfully, "If I were going to fight, I'd be wearing a red coat, not the rags they're wearing at Morristown."

A disgruntled murmur ran through the crowd, and Phoebe, who was standing beside Bickerson, looked at her brother with pleading in her eyes. She came over and said, "Please, Joel, don't say any more."

"I'll say anything I want to."

"You may regret it," Bickerson said. His eyes were half closed and there was a cruel look to his lips. "There have been others who talked like you did, but they don't do it anymore."

Joel laughed. He had discovered that he did have some skill as an actor. He felt like one now as he began to challenge Bickerson. He reeled off all the facts about the poor condition of Washington's army and the lack of support by the Congress. "Why, the Congress won't even vote to buy shoes for the soldiers. You think you can win a war like that?" He continued, and finally he saw anger on every face. At that moment he felt a touch on his arm and turned to see Daniel Bradford.

"I don't think I'd continue with this if I were you, Joel."

"You can't tell me what to say! Just because I work for you doesn't mean I can't think for myself." It hurt Joel to see the pain in the eyes of his kinsman. *I don't see how I can do this*, he thought grimly, but he had gone too far now with the ruse to back off. He jerked away from Daniel, saying, "You can have your Revolution! You're all idiots!"

He turned and left, but he felt miserable as he walked away. He heard the gabble of voices behind him and knew he was the subject of some very bad conversation. Moving on down the street he thought about how hard it had been to say the things he had said, and yet he had done it. *Maybe Mr. Dante's right. Maybe I will make a good agent. I hate to disappoint my people, though.*

For some time he walked, going all the way down to the harbor, where he stood watching the sea for a while. It was a cloudless night, but the moon was not up, so only a few stars glinted overhead. He thought about Phoebe and what she must think about him now. He longed to be able to confide in her, but he sighed, knowing it would only endanger her if she knew the truth. Finally he started back toward the house. His feet grew heavy, for he knew what he would find there. He passed down the main street and turned off to go to the Bradford house. When he heard some steps behind, he glanced over his shoulders and saw several men following him. Suddenly he grew alert. They were coming faster, and one of them called out, "All right, Bradford, hold it right there!"

Several of the men were carrying short clubs, and Joel felt a wave of fear close in around him. When he turned and ran, the men cried out and went after him. He was a fast runner, but he could not elude some of the pursuers. He took a right turn and then found himself in a blind alley. A fence barred his way. He made a wild jump and caught the top of it, but as he tried to pull himself over, strong hands gripped his ankle and yanked him back. He fell to the ground and began to strike out to fend off the men who were striking at him and cursing him.

"Since you don't like it here, we'll see if we can't make things a little bit better for you!"

Joel did not recognize the voice, and even as the words were spoken, a club took him over the ear, and he dropped into a black pit of unconsciousness.

☖   ☖   ☖

Reaching out from time to time to dip his quill in the bottle of ink, Edmund Dante wrote steadily. It was a letter to General Washington, and he was very careful with the details of his report. It was unusual for him to put his thoughts in writing, but he knew that this time it would have to be done. When he was almost finished, he added, "We have a new recruit. I will not say his name here, but when I see you face-to-face, I will give you a full report."

He had just reached out to dip his quill in the ink bottle when he heard shouts outside his window. Lifting his head, he turned his ear and tried to identify the sounds. There was laughter and jeering, and he got up quickly and went to the window. Several men were coming down the street bearing lanterns. He could not see clearly, but when they passed under one of the brighter lights he saw with a shock that the individual they were leading had been tarred and feathered! "It's Bradford," he whispered. He wanted to rush out and help the boy, but it was too late. He watched as they tied him up to a post. He could see the black tar that covered him. One of his tormentors brought a sack full of feathers and dumped it over his head. Clenching his fist and staring down at the sight, Edmund Dante knew it was in his heart to go get his pistol and leap into the fray, but he could not do such a thing. He could not even show an interest, for that would be evidence to everyone that Joel had some connection with him.

For a long time he watched as the crowd came, jeering and laughing. Finally he heard one voice say, "We'll leave you hangin' there until morning, then maybe you'll go back to England where you belong, Bradford."

☖   ☖   ☖

Joel Bradford could not open his eyes. The tar completely covered them. It had been hot and had scorched his skin, and now his hands were pinioned behind the post as he sat helpless and unable to move. The tar had an acrid taste, and the feathers had gotten into his mouth and into his nose, making it difficult for him to breathe. They had stripped off his shirt so that the tar clung to his chest and his arms.

He gritted his teeth, for he wanted to cry out, but he refused to let himself do it. He had not cried out when they applied the tar, nor when they had slapped his face, or punched him, or struck him with their clubs. He had never had anything so degrading happen to him, and the humiliation burned in him like a white iron.

Time passed and most of the jeering stopped. He still could not see, but it grew silent. From time to time he would hear a pair of footsteps. Usually they would stop, and Joel knew he was a spectacle for some curious passerby. They had hung some sort of sign around his chest. He could not see it, of course, but his tormentors had read it to him: "This is what happens to traitors."

Finally he heard footsteps stop very close to him.

He lifted his head and tried vainly to open his eyes, but he could not. His lips were covered with the tar, and he tried to spit out some of it, but it was a sorry effort.

"Well, Joel, I'm sorry to see you in this condition."

Joel had heard that voice before. "Who is it?" he croaked, speaking around his bruised lips coated with tar and feathers.

"Matthew Bradford."

Joel felt a hand touch his wrist, and then there was another movement and the ropes fell off. He fell to one side, unable to sit up, and then he felt the hands support him.

"Come along, we'll have to try to get you cleaned up from all of this."

Joel struggled to his feet blindly. He felt Matthew Bradford's hands on his arms as he staggered along, unable to see anything. He blindly turned toward Matthew and whispered, "Why are you helping me?"

"Because you need it. Now let's move along before those who did this return and tar and feather me as well."

Joel felt Matthew's strong hands on his arm again as he was led to a carriage. The entire street was silent now except for the occasional snort from the horses.

"Here, let me help you in," Matthew said.

Joel climbed in and fell on the seat, then he felt the carriage sag as Matthew climbed in beside him.

"I'll take you home and we'll get all that mess off of you."

🌱   🌱   🌱

Joel sat in a chair and squinted out of burning eyes. He could barely see, but he could make out three figures. Matthew had stripped down to a light linsey shirt that was stained with the tar. Beside him stood Keturah Burns, and on the other side was Rachel Bradford. They had worked steadily for an hour, cleaning off the tar with some sort of oil, and now the floor around his chair was littered with it. They were all stained and Joel wanted to thank them, but he knew he could not.

"I'm obliged to you," he said, his throat still raw and his lips swollen, "but I have to tell you, I'm not going to stay in this place. I may even enlist in the British army. What kind of people would do this?"

"You should have known better than to state your views so blatantly, Joel!" Rachel said sharply.

"A man's free to say what he thinks. That's the trouble with this Revolution. The bunch that's running it are just as bad as the people they want to throw out. Let me out of here!"

"I'll take you home, Joel," Matthew said quietly.

Joel could not help turning to the women and saying gruffly, "I'm not ungrateful, but we have nothing to say to each other. I'm leaving this place. Thanks for what you've done and good-bye."

In the carriage Matthew did not say anything, which made Joel wonder. Finally he said, "I still don't know why you helped me."

"I told you, you needed it. Besides, we're kin."

"Well—" Joel could not think of a rejoinder and sat there silently as the carriage rolled along. When Matthew pulled up in front of the house, Joel said, "I'll be leaving here, Mr. Bradford. You've always tried to help me and do the right thing by me, but you won't like what I'm going to do next."

"You're going to go over to the British, I take it?"

"That's right. I'm going to New York."

"Well, a man makes his own way, Joel. I haven't fully decided where I stand myself. Good luck to you."

Joel stepped out of the carriage and watched as Matthew drove off. He whispered, "I wish I could tell you the truth."

He looked at the house and knew that Phoebe would be waiting for him. He squared his shoulders, went inside, and knew that he could give her no comfort. There was none to give.

🔔   🔔   🔔

"It was a hard thing, my boy," Dante said as he looked at Joel. The poor lad had had to cut his hair short because all the tar would not come out. He had waited for three days before contacting Joel, and now there was a harder look in Joel's eyes than Dante had seen there before. They were standing at the dock in front of a ship. It was night and Dante had arranged to meet him here secretly. Joel had his passage and some money, and now the two men stood in the shadows.

"It just about killed me, Mr. Dante. I can't lie to you about that."

"Understandable," Dante nodded. He suddenly said, "If they knew what you were doing, they'd love you for it. But now I'm the only one who knows, and all I can say is God bless you, my boy. One day it will be different. They will know that you are not what they think you are."

"I told Phoebe she couldn't come with me, as you told me, but I don't see why."

"You can't be burdened with her. She's well settled where she is. The Bradfords love her and they'll take good care of her."

"It's hard turning my back on them," Joel said. "They're the only family I have now." He looked out at the ship. "I wonder if I'm doing the right thing."

Dante did not answer. He knew the heartache the young man felt, but he knew there was no way to make it any easier. He clapped Joel on the shoulder and said, "There will be one who will be very grateful."

"Who's that?"

"General Washington. I'll be telling him about you, and he's depending on you. Good-bye now."

"Good-bye, Mr. Dante."

"Remember your instructions, Joel. Information is no good unless we can get it to the right place. You know your contacts."

"Yes, sir, I remember them all." They had written nothing down, and Joel's phenomenal memory had served him well. "Will I see you in New York?"

"Very possibly, but do not contact me directly. Never do that."

"I understand. Good-bye, sir."

Joel waited until the man had faded into the darkness, then he turned and walked down to the ship. He felt as though life had been cut off short. He did not know what he would find in the days to come, yet deep inside he realized he must do something to win liberty for all. As he stepped on board the ship and was greeted by a sailor, he gave his name and was taken to a cabin. When he sat down inside on the bed, he put his head down and hot tears rushed to his eyes. He pressed his fists against his lips and fought against the weakness. He had endured everything without tears, but now he could not seem to stop them. "Well," he said aloud, "I guess if no one sees a man, it's all right to cry."

PART TWO

—

NEW YORK

Spring 1777

8

A Timely Rescue

THE REVEREND ABIRAM HOOKS took his place behind the pulpit, opened his Bible, then lifted his massive head to gaze out over his congregation. He was a bulky man in every respect, and his black robe maximized this impression. His fingers were large and thick, and his face was blunt, accented by a pair of extremely direct hazel eyes that moved over the faces of those in front of him with all the focused attention of a man aiming a cannon. Reverend Hooks looked more like a pugilist or a soldier than he did a minister. In fact, some members of his congregation had intimated that such a vocation might have been more suitable than the ministry. His words, as a rule, were as blunt as his features, and his gray hair was thick and wiry so that it gave him the impression of a stern judge. He wore a wig that covered it, but none of the congregation were readying themselves for a gentle sermon.

In a way this was unfair, for Reverend Hooks was a kind man, despite his rather fierce appearance as he stood there in the pulpit looking out over his flock. He had a large family of eight children, and the liberties they took with him in private would have shocked the congregation, for Reverend Hooks allowed none in public. His eyes moved over the congregation steadily. Hooks had formed the habit of selecting a few prime suspects, candidates for the gospel. He located one such victim, a tall man sitting near the rear dressed in foppish attire with a bored look on his face.

So, you're bored to be in the house of God, are you? Hooks thought grimly. *Well, we'll see about that!* For a moment he almost forgot his choice of a sermon, which was "Love Thy Neighbor" and had a momentary impulse of changing it to "Turn or Burn!" But he had long since learned to stick with his subject and, indeed, he had prepared what he felt was a good sermon. He had read it to his wife the evening before, and she had smiled, saying, "That's very good, Abiram—very good indeed!"

Valuing his wife's judgment greatly, Reverend Hooks quickly shifted his gaze and allowed his eyes to pause on the young woman who sat only three rows back over to his right. She was not a newcomer, for she had been a faithful member of his church ever since he had assumed the pastorate. He had learned to admire Heather Reed, although he felt she expressed her feelings too bluntly, at least for a woman. And besides, he found it convenient at times to see an attractive, intelligent face as he preached his sermon. Now he noted her abundant auburn hair, the steady blue-green eyes that were fastened on him and, not for the first time, thought, *She's too strong for a feminine beauty. Men like their women to be delicate.* She had a squarish face, strong lips that were full in the center, and her cheekbones were accented, which gave her appearance another impression of strength. He noticed again that she was wearing black as always. *For her brother*, he thought.

His eyes went to Timothy Reed, Heather's father, who sat beside his wife, Virginia. Reed was a small man, no more than five five, a member of the Continental Congress, a fiery speaker, and one who always overstated things. He had married late in life, Hooks knew, and had found a rare beauty in Virginia Custis Reed. She was related to Martha Custis Washington, and the Reeds were now mourning their son, Justin, who at the age of fourteen had been killed by the British during the Battle of New York. He had not been a soldier, of course, but a victim of shellfire. He had died in his mother's arms, and all of the Reeds, who had been staunch patriots, now were consumed with the desire to see the British defeated.

"My subject this morning is a common one," Hooks said, his voice filling the large auditorium. "Love your neighbors." The announcement of his subject aroused no enthusiasm, he saw, in his hearers, and grimly he thought, *They're not ready to hear about love. Most of them are totally dedicated to hating their neighbors—those who are Tories. Maybe when this war is over we can get back to love again, but for now they're going to hear what the Word of God says about such things!*

Heather Reed listened attentively as Abiram Hooks preached his sermon. It was a good one, as usual, for Hooks was a fine preacher. Heather was a dedicated Christian young woman and an astute judge of sermons, having heard them all of her life, mostly from this very church. From time to time she glanced at her parents and saw that her mother's face was set and fixed. *She's thinking about Justin*, Heather thought, and sadness came to her as memories of her lively brother, now dead and in his grave, came to her. Her jaw tightened, and for a moment a wave of absolute hatred for the British filled her thoughts. Then with an act of will she forced herself to listen to the words of the minister.

"Jesus said," Reverend Hooks intoned, "that anyone can love their family, or their good neighbors. Even the Pharisees did that. But you will remember that Jesus also insisted, 'I say unto you love your enemies, pray for those who despitefully use you.' This is what set Jesus apart from all other teachers and, perhaps, from all other men who ever lived. And it is only by the grace of God," Hooks said, his voice falling to a lower pitch, "that we are able to do this. When someone hurts us or our family, our natural instinct is to strike out. Our Lord Jesus faced this same temptation, for He was a man, as human as any of us, though at the same time He was God."

A silence had fallen over the church as Hooks continued to speak, for most of the congregation had relatives who were fighting for the cause of liberty against the British. It was true enough that New York was probably the most loyalist city in all of the Colonies. Still, in the Congregational church there were few loyalists. Those who favored the British cause were mostly Episcopalians. Now the air was almost thick with tension as Hooks came to the conclusion of his sermon.

"I realize this has not been a popular message," he said quietly. "Some of you have lost brothers, or husbands, fathers, or sons. Many of you have relatives who are fighting against the British. I would only remind you of this. Hatred destroys not its object but the one who hates. It is corrosive, and it will eat away at you until you lose your sense of godliness. It brings you down to the lowest common denominator of human existence. Anyone can hate, but Jesus—who of all men had a right to hate those who destroyed Him—chose to love them instead. 'He came unto his own and his own received him not.' But He did not hate those who rejected Him. He looked down from the cross and said, 'Father, forgive them for they know not what they do.' "

Closing the Bible, Hooks bowed his head and prayed a fervent prayer that love would be the key note of the church and of the good people under his charge. Finally he concluded the prayer, and as the people filed out, he moved to the front of the church to shake hands with those who passed by.

Heather had reached the end of her pew when suddenly she bumped into someone. Her mind was elsewhere and she looked up, startled to see a tall, fine-looking man, one she had seen before.

"I beg your pardon." The man bowed slightly and stepped back to allow Heather to pass.

"Certainly," Heather murmured and moved on out to shake hands with the pastor. Hooks held her hand for a moment, smiled, and said, "Not a popular sermon, I fear, Miss Reed."

"No, it's rebuked me, Pastor, but that is well." She looked up at him fearlessly, then summoned a smile. "You can never be accused of pandering to the whims of your congregation, sir. A fine sermon indeed!"

Heather waited until her parents stepped outside, and her mother said, "We're going over to see the Henrys, Heather. Perhaps you would like to come with us, but I doubt it."

The Henrys were an elderly couple, and ordinarily Heather would have enjoyed spending some time with them. Nevertheless, she shook her head, saying, "I have things to do at home. Tell them I'll call on them later in the week."

The congregation lingered around the church, but Heather hurried on. It was a fairly long walk to the Reed house, and she covered the ground quickly, taking long strides. She walked actively, as she did everything else. As she moved through the streets of New York, she glanced occasionally at the burned-out homes that had been destroyed by the great fire immediately following the British invasion. Many of the houses were unharmed, but others were nothing but blackened shells. She felt greatly saddened at the sight of so many homes in ruins that had once belonged to her friends, and she wondered where they had taken refuge.

Suddenly a shadow loomed in her path, and she turned to find a British sergeant who had planted himself firmly in front of her. He was a big, broad man with a rash smile and a red Irish face. He wore the scarlet coat of the British regular, and there was a cockiness in his manner.

"Well, what have we here? Been to church, have we, now?"

"Move out of my way, please," Heather said. She was not alarmed, for it was not uncommon for the British soldiers to speak to women on the streets. She waited for him to move but saw that he did not intend to. "Did you hear what I said? Get out of my way!"

"Well now, I like a lass with spirit. Red hair and green eyes! Might be you have some Irish in you, now? Just like back in the old country. Come along, darlin', I'll have the pleasure of your company."

Heather felt her arm seized by the man's massive grip, and anger flared through her. She tried to pull away but his grip was like iron. "Let go of me!" When he did not but continued to grin down at her, Heather suddenly doubled up her right fist and, swinging hard, hit the soldier in the eye. It was a hard, solid blow and drew a gasp from him.

He dropped her arm and held his hand over his eye, and suddenly an ugly look swept across his face.

"You think you're better than a British soldier, do you? You're nothing but a worthless rebel!" He reached out and grabbed Heather by the arm and started to shake her when suddenly a voice cut through from behind them.

"Turn that lady loose!"

Heather turned quickly to see the man with whom she had collided in church. He was very tall, over six three, she judged. He was lean with long arms and legs, and now there was an angry look on his tapered face.

"Turn that woman loose and be on your way, Sergeant!"

"Who do you think you are to be giving commands to the king's men?" The sergeant loosed Heather and stepped forward, his fists doubled up. He had obviously been drinking and now was ready for a fight. "I'll just see if I can mess up that pretty suit you're wearing."

"Sergeant, I'm perfectly willing to have you try, but even assuming that you are able to whip me, you'll have difficulty explaining your behavior to your commanding officer."

"That's none of your business! Your business is to take a beating!"

"My name is Clive Gordon. My father is Colonel Leslie Gordon."

This information struck the sergeant with all the force of a fist. He actually took a step backward, and a harried look crossed his face. He knew that his commander, Colonel Gordon, had given strict orders against harassing any civilians in the street, and now he saw the resemblance between his commanding officer and this young man. Swallowing hard, he nodded and muttered, "No offense, sir, no offense."

"Get on your way, Sergeant!"

"Yes, sir, right away!"

Clive Gordon turned to the young woman and smiled down at her. "I'm sorry you have to endure such things."

"Thank you very much, Mr. Gordon. I'm afraid I lost my temper and said some things I shouldn't."

Clive Gordon laughed, his white teeth showing against his tanned skin. "I would have said worse, I'm afraid. I've seen you in church, but I don't believe we have met."

"I'm Heather Reed, and I'm very much indebted to you, sir."

"Are you on your way home, Miss Reed?"

"Why, yes, I am."

"Let me accompany you. There may be others like the sergeant."

Heather hesitated. "I'm not sympathetic to the British, and your father's in the army."

"Well, I'm certain that you won't hit me in the eye as you did the sergeant."

Clive Gordon offered his arm, and Heather suddenly found it difficult to hate such a gentleman. "Very well," she said taking his arm, "although I usually don't need protection."

The two strolled along, and she asked almost at once, "You're not in the army like your father?"

"No, I'm a physician."

"A physician, is it? Well, that's better than being a soldier trying to destroy a country." Heather looked up at him directly as she said this. She wanted no mistaking the fact that she was totally opposed to the British position in America. She searched his face for some anger or intemperance, but he merely shook his head and said nothing. "You're not offended by such talk of your people?"

"I don't agree with what is happening in America. As a matter of fact, my father is opposed to the Revolution as well."

This information took Heather aback. "I'm surprised to hear you say that. Why doesn't he resign his commission?"

"Being a soldier is all he knows. He has served the Crown faithfully for his entire military career. He does all he can to mitigate the circumstances. As for myself, I wish there were no such thing as a Revolution." He hesitated for a moment, then said, "I'm very attached to a young woman who lives in Boston, but she won't have me for the same reason you wouldn't, I suppose. She's very much a patriot."

Heather Reed was an outspoken young woman. Her hand was on his arm and she pulled at it. As he looked down with some surprise, she said with asperity, "If you love the young woman, why then marry her!"

Clive laughed suddenly. "That's coming right out with it—and that's exactly what I'd like to do. But she feels as you do—that we're too far apart." He walked a few paces in silence, then said, "For strangers we're talking quite freely about personal things, but I might add, Miss Reed, that I am a physician. Medicine is not political."

Heather was rather taken with young Clive Gordon. She saw at once that, besides being a handsome young man, he had sense, and there was a gentleness and a tactfulness in him that she admired. Perhaps it was because she lacked some of these qualities herself. Finally she said, "I know you think me hard, but I have cause, Mr. Gordon. My . . . my only brother, Justin, was killed when the British invaded New York. He was only fourteen years old, and I—" She could not go on as tears came to her eyes. She dashed them away and shut her lips, unable to say more.

"I'm dreadfully sorry, Miss Reed, for your terrible loss," Clive said quietly. "There's nothing to say at a time like this, but I am truly sorry."

The two walked on until they stopped in front of the Reed house. Heather turned and offered him a slight smile. "Thank you, sir, for your most gentlemanly conduct."

Bowing slightly, Clive said, "I live with my father and mother for the moment. If I can ever be of any service to you, please don't hesitate to send word. Colonel Gordon, my father, lives on the east side on Seventh Street. Anyone can show you the way."

He bowed and left at once, and Heather stared after him thoughtfully. Something began to stir in her, and she turned to go into the house, thinking of the strangeness of the encounter.

Her parents came home later that afternoon, and she told them what had happened.

"I'm surprised that you even spoke to him, Heather," Timothy Reed said severely. "I wish every British officer in this country were blown up by gunpowder!"

Heather knew her father well. Though the grief of losing a son had nearly destroyed him, she knew deep inside he had one of the kindest of hearts. "Mr. Gordon was actually very kind, and as I said, he's not in favor of what the English are doing here. But that's not what I wanted to talk to you about. It's about Mrs. Cartwright. Since he's a physician he might be helpful to her."

Mrs. Cartwright was a widow in poor circumstances. Her husband had been killed at the battle of Bunker Hill, and she had been left with one son, Jamey, who was ten years old and very sick.

"The boy's not getting any better," Virginia Reed said quickly. "I was by there today. He needs to see a doctor badly, but she has no money."

"If Doctor Smith hadn't left to go to Boston, I would have insisted that he go see Jamey," Mr. Reed said, shaking his head. "Now I just don't know. It's hard to get a doctor these days."

"I was thinking that perhaps I might go to this young man, Dr. Gordon," Heather said. "He offered to do anything he could."

"Go to a British officer?" Reed snapped. "Certainly not!"

"He's not an officer. It's his father who's the colonel," Heather said. She began to speak quickly, and being a very impulsive young woman, she soon had persuaded her parents. She concluded by saying, "I'm going to do it, then. All he can do is say no, and somehow I don't think he will. He told me medicine is not political."

"You can't go now. It's starting to rain."

"Just a slight drizzle. It won't come to more than that," Heather said as she put on her coat and bonnet.

As she left the house like a whirlwind, Timothy Reed said to his wife, "I don't know where she gets this wild, abrupt mannerism. It's not fitting for a woman."

Virginia smiled up at her husband. She knew exactly where that strain came from, for Heather was very like Timothy Reed in this respect. "She'll be all right, Timothy, and Jamey does need to see a doctor very badly. . . ."

🐦   🐦   🐦

The rain was coming down now in long, slanting lines, and Joel Bradford's face was plastered with it. He pulled his black hat down closer over his features, but it was soaked. The water drained off the brim like a miniature waterfall. It had been raining only slightly when he had gotten off the coach and begun to inquire the way to Colonel Gordon's house, but the dark clouds had turned into black blossoms and had begun to shed water in torrents almost at once. Now his clothes were sodden through, and the canvas suitcase that he carried was also waterlogged. He feared that all his clothes inside were just as wet.

The trip from Boston had been difficult for Joel. He could not keep from thinking of the humiliation he had gone through. Even now as he moved along the street, water running like a miniature river, flashes of the ugly ordeal came to him. He thought of the kindness of Matthew Bradford, but then anger swept over him as searing memories returned of how he had sat helpless, covered with tar and dotted with white feathers as people laughed and jeered at him. He could not forget the humiliation, and nothing that Edmund Dante could say would ever erase it from his memory. He regretted bitterly, at times, his decision to leave the safety and security of the Bradford family, and especially that of his sister. But it was too late now! He tried to shake off the bitterness that filled his heart as he made his way down the streets, but with little success.

After several wrong turns and being misled as far as the directions to the colonel's house, he finally stopped a British soldier and asked, "I'm looking for the home of Colonel Leslie Gordon."

"Why, it's right down there. That big brownstone on the right. See it?"

"Yes, thank you very much."

Trudging on down the street, his shoes making splashes, Joel kept his head down. He was almost at the doorway of the house, which was right on the street, when a figure appeared before him. Quickly, thinking he would dodge inside the short walk that led to the door, he lunged forward, but the individual he met performed exactly the same maneuver.

"Oh—!" Joel collided with a small person, which he instantly recognized was a woman. The force of the collision sent her backward, and she fell full length in the street.

"You clumsy oaf!" she cried out.

Joel wiped the rain from his face but leaped forward at once to help the woman up. "I'm awfully sorry! I thought you'd go the other way!"

"Look at me. I'm soaked to the skin!"

Joel got a quick look at the young woman's face, which was as drenched as his own. He saw a pair of green eyes snapping and flashing at him from a face framed with damp red hair. Her expression was filled with anger, and he stammered, "I . . . I'm very sorry. I truly thought you were going the other way."

"I'm trying to get into Colonel Gordon's house." Heather shook her sodden clothes, picked up her reticule, and turned down the short walkway. When she reached the door and knocked loudly, she turned and saw that the young man who had knocked her down was standing beside her. "Go away," she said.

At that moment the door opened and a woman stood before them. She had hair the color of dark honey and a pair of gray-green eyes that studied them carefully. "Yes, what is it?" she said.

"I'm looking for Mr. Clive Gordon," the woman said.

"Please, come in. I'm Clive's mother, Mrs. Gordon." Lyna Lee stepped back, and when the two came in, she said, "Why, you're soaked to the skin, my dear, and you, too, sir."

Turning, she called, "Grace, come here at once!"

A young woman appeared in the hallway who looked much like her mother. She was about nineteen, and surprise came to her face at the sight of the couple who were dripping water on the carpet.

"Grace, take this young woman up to your room. She is absolutely soaked. What is your name, my dear?"

"Why, I'm Heather Reed."

"Take Miss Reed upstairs and get her something dry to wear. You're about the same size."

Heather tried to protest, but Grace simply came and smiled at her. "Come along. You'll catch your death soaking wet like that."

As the two young women moved upstairs, Mrs. Gordon turned to the young man. "And now, sir, you're as wet as your companion."

"Well actually, Mrs. Gordon, she's not my companion," Joel said with some embarrassment. "We just happened to get here at the same time."

"Oh, you're not together?"

"Well, no, not actually." Joel started to explain when a young man came in. He was about seventeen with dark brown hair and a square brown face. He stood to one side grinning at the newcomer, which embarrassed Joel all the more.

"This is my son David, sir. But you're sopping wet, too."

"That doesn't matter," Joel said. "My name is Joel Bradford."

Instantly Lyna Gordon's gaze narrowed. "Are you any relation to the Bradfords of Boston?"

"Yes, ma'am, I'm a cousin. A rather distant one of your brother, Daniel Bradford."

"Why, in that case, you're my relation as well." She saw the look of surprise and that he was speechless. "Come in by the fire. We'll have to get you some dry clothes, but first you can explain our kinship."

"Let me get him some dry clothes, Mother," David said.

"That would be good, David."

"This way, cousin." David grinned and led Joel to a room on the second floor. "Here, strip out of those wet things. We can outfit you, I'm sure."

"I don't want to be that much trouble."

"No trouble at all." David was going through an armoire and soon came up with a pair of trousers, a shirt, a coat, and some socks. Glancing at Joel's feet, David shook his head. "My feet are smaller than yours, but at least you can have dry socks."

Joel dressed quickly and was glad for the warm clothes, then David said, "Come down. My mother will want to hear about this kinship of ours. We don't have many kin, you know."

Joel followed the young man downstairs and soon was standing in a small parlor in front of a fire. He said awkwardly to Mrs. Gordon, "Your brother heard of my sister and me not long ago." He explained the relationship and added, "Mr. Matthew Bradford was kind enough to bring us to America. My sister, Phoebe, is a maid now for Mrs. Bradford, and I've been working in his foundry. And I met your son, Dr. Gordon. He was quite helpful to a couple that was having hard times there."

"How do you happen to be in New York?" David asked.

Joel thought quickly and said, "I had difficulties over politics. I am not sympathetic to the Revolution." He felt miserable for telling a lie, and he saw interest quicken on the faces of his two hearers. He went on to explain how he had been tarred and feathered and practically run out of town. "It was Matthew Bradford who cleaned me up and gave me the money for the trip. He also suggested I call here since I know no one else in New York."

"Why, then, you don't have a place to stay," Lyna said.

"I might have that at least. Mr. Matthew has a friend named Jan Vandermeer. He suggested I call on him."

"Oh, the artist fellow!" David said. "Yes, Matthew stayed with him while he was here in New York."

The conversation went on better than Joel had hoped, and he drew an inward sigh of relief. *At least I've come this far*, he thought, *but I hate deceiving people, especially family, even if they are distant relatives.*

Upstairs, Grace Gordon had seen to it that Heather had been provided with dry clothes. As Heather buttoned up the last button on the warm, dry dress, Grace said, "I've seen you in church. I go to the Congregational church."

"Yes, I've seen you there too."

"My family doesn't go, but I like Reverend Hooks very much." Grace hesitated, then said, "Most of the members of the church have little liking for British officers."

"I think that is true." This disturbed Heather, for the kindness of this girl and her mother was evident. "I'm sorry to be so much trouble," she said, "but I really need to see your brother."

"Come downstairs. We'll fix tea while we wait for Clive to come home."

They descended the stairs and had no sooner reached the main floor when the door opened and Clive Gordon stepped in. He was dripping wet, but as he took off his hat, he looked with surprise at the young woman. "Why, Miss Reed!" he exclaimed.

Heather felt awkward and said quickly, "I am quite embarrassed coming like this, but you said if I had any requests, I might."

"Why, of course. Allow me to get out of this wet coat and we'll go in where it's warm." Taking off his coat, Clive hung it on a peg, then said, "Grace, you've met Miss Reed?"

"Yes, she came in quite soaked, along with another gentleman who's with Mother."

They moved to the library, and as soon as Clive entered, he said, "Why, Joel, it's you!"

"Yes, Dr. Gordon, the bad penny turns up." Joel was glad to see Clive Gordon again.

The two men shook hands, and Lyna said, "I didn't know we had relatives in Boston, aside from Daniel's family. He's been telling us how you managed to help the Tyrones."

"I did what I could. How are they, Joel?"

"Not too well, sir. Mrs. Tyrone seems to be doing all right, but Ezra just can't seem to get well."

There was an awkward silence then, and Heather wished she had never come. Almost at once, Clive said, "If you wish to speak with me, we could go into the library."

"Thank you very much."

Joel watched as the young woman followed Clive to the library. He cleared his throat and said, "I'm sorry about our little accident, Miss Reed."

Heather turned and looked at Joel and shook her head slightly. "That's all right, sir. Don't bother yourself about it."

When they were inside the library, Heather said at once, "I feel terrible, Dr. Gordon, coming to you, but I have a need you might be willing to help me with."

Gordon listened quietly as Heather spoke. When he heard the nature of her mission, he said, "Why, that's no problem at all. I would be glad to see the lad. Now come back and visit with us awhile. I want you to get to know my mother, and my brother and sister. My father isn't home, unfortunately." And then he suddenly remembered her stand against British officers and smiled. "But you, perhaps, wouldn't like to meet him, since he's a British officer."

Heather could not help smiling. She was an impulsive girl and often said exactly what was on her mind. "If, sir, he is anything like his son and his daughter and his wife, I would not be at all adverse to meeting the colonel."

They returned to the parlor, where they sat down to tea. Heather wanted to leave, but she was curious about this family. She listened as Joel related his experience in Boston to Clive Gordon. Studying the young man's face, she thought, *You're on the wrong side, young man.*

Finally Heather rose to leave and Clive accompanied her to the door. "If you'll give me the address of your friends, I'll call on them."

"Why don't you come to our house? You can meet my parents and I will accompany you."

"Very well, but let me get you a carriage. It's still raining a little."

Ten minutes later Heather was in a carriage. She sat there and looked out the window, thinking how strange it was that she, who was so adverse to anything in a British uniform, could find the family of a British officer so enchanting. And then she thought of the young man, Joel Bradford, and indignation filled her mind. *He knocked me flat*, she thought with a trace of anger, *and so he was tarred and feathered for being sympathetic to the British. Well, young man, I hope you learned a lesson.* She thought of his face, which was sensitive and handsome, but then put him out of her mind. *I hope I don't see him again*, she thought as the carriage bumped along over the wet streets.

9

Joel Meets a General

THE RAIN STOPPED SHORTLY AFTER Joel left the Gordons' home. He was carrying his wet clothes in a small package David had made, and had promised to return David's clothes at a later date. The sky was lowering and threatening with a promise of more rain to come, but Joel was not thinking of the weather. Over and over again in his mind he thought about the meeting with the Gordons. A keen sense of displeasure pierced him. He was an honest young man, this Joel Bradford, valuing his word, and the thought of having betrayed such kind people as these disturbed him greatly. He had listened as Edmund Dante had explained how it was necessary to create a facade that would be solid enough to deceive the agents of the British intelligence. At the time he had agreed. But deceiving the British was not as hard as lying outright to the only family he knew. Now as he moved along, staring at all the houses burned out completely and others in a state of half-completed repair, Joel could not reconcile what he was doing with his own conscience.

"I wish I didn't have to do it," he muttered, looking up at the white frame house that somehow had escaped the destruction that had razed the ones on either side of it. The white paint was charred, and the light blue that outlined the windows showed some damage, but as far as he could tell, it was the address he had been given. Still troubled over the affair of deceiving the Gordons, he walked up to the door and knocked. Almost at once the door swung open, and a short, heavyset woman with a wealth of brown hair done up over her head like a halo eyed him cautiously.

"Yes, what is it?" the woman said.

"I'm looking for Mr. Jan Vandermeer."

"Are you another artist?"

121

"No, madam, I am not."

A look of relief came to the woman's harried brown eyes, and she seemed to heave a sigh of relief. "That is good. If you are looking for a room, I have no more for crazy artists."

Joel almost spoke out, saying, *I'm rather crazy for what I'm doing, but I'm not an artist, madam.* Instead he subdued the remark and asked politely, "Is Mr. Vandermeer at home?"

"Yes, he's at home. Come, I will show you." She turned and, shutting the door behind Joel, led the way to some stairs at the back of the hall. "He is up there, and tell him to keep his voice down. He is disturbing the rest of my tenants."

"Certainly, madam."

Joel ascended the staircase, which ended in a landing with a door to his left. He knocked on it, and a voice said something that he could not discern. He knocked again and this time there was a rumbling that sounded like furniture being moved. The door swung open and he was confronted by a short, very round man in his early fifties. The man's blond hair was smeared with paint as well as with a few gray hairs, and his eyes were bright blue and very direct. He had on a smock smeared with every color of the rainbow and was holding a brush with vermilion paint dripping from it. It was pointed at Joel as if it were a saber.

"Yes, vat is it you vant?"

"My name is Joel Bradford. I'm looking for Mr. Vandermeer."

"Ach! So, you are a relative of Matthew Bradford, is it?"

"A distant relative, Mr. Vandermeer."

"Vell, don't stand there. Come in! Come in! Come in!" Vandermeer spoke in a staccato tone and waved the long paintbrush around in an excited fashion. As soon as Joel had stepped inside, he said, "Vell, come—sit down. Ve vill have something to drink."

He did not wait for Joel to protest but shepherded him across the large room that appeared to be a workroom, a sitting room, a study, a library, and any other sort of room required. It was filled with paintings on the walls, stacked in corners, and even covering up the furniture. Every one was done in brilliant colors, which almost blinded Joel. He soon found himself sitting at a table with a mug of beer in front of him. Across from him, Jan Vandermeer, who had tossed the brush on the table leaving a bright red smear, held his pewter mug high.

"Ve drink to art!" he said.

"To art!" Joel said, knowing almost nothing about the subject. The beer was warm and strong, and he was thirsty, so he drank it all down.

"Tell me," Vandermeer directed as he refilled the tankard, "how is my friend Matthew Bradford? He is vell, no?"

"Yes, very well indeed." Joel hesitated, then said, "He gave me your name, Mr. Vandermeer, and said I might have difficulty finding a place to stay in New York." He glanced around the cluttered room and said, "I see that you're pretty well filled up here."

"Filled up? No, not at all!" Everything Vandermeer said seemed to be spoken like a shot from a gun. His eyes were excited and he waved his arms around as if they were connected with his organs of speech. He now grinned broadly. "I am ver' much interested in my friend, Matthew. How is his love affair progressing?"

"Love affair?"

"Yah! You did not know Miss Abigail?"

"You mean Abigail Howland?"

"Yes, she is the one! He is ver' much in love with her, though he vill not admit it!"

"I don't know him quite well enough to know his personal concerns, although I have met Miss Howland—a very attractive young woman. Actually we were in a small amateur drama together in Boston."

"Is that so? Tell me about it!"

Vandermeer kept filling Joel's tankard to the brim and pumping him for information. Joel spat out information and filled himself up with the warm beer. As the time passed quickly, he related how he had come to be in America and found himself also telling everything about how he had been forced out of Boston.

"So you see, I'm a man without a country, Mr. Vandermeer."

"Yah, so am I a man without a country, but all artists are like that. Ve are at home wherever we go."

"How do you stand on this business of the Revolution?" Joel asked cautiously. He knew he had to be careful, for Dante had told him to trust no one. The rotund Dutchman seemed to be harmless enough, but Dante had said more than once, "The agents of the British are clever. They have no particular look or appearance that would help you discern their true function, so trust no one."

Vandermeer laughed loudly and drank thirstily again, then filled up his tankard for the fifth or sixth time. When Joel pushed his away, Vandermeer said, "Why, I am an artist, sir. Ve artists have no politics, except art."

Joel listened as Vandermeer talked about his art and about the fact that he cared practically nothing about the Revolution, or at least so he said. Finally Vandermeer said, "Come, I show you a place." Getting up, he knocked the chair over and let it lie where it fell, then shoved his way across the room until he came to a door on the west side. Opening it, he waved expansively, saying, "There, a cot, a place to sleep! What else does a man need?"

Stepping inside, Joel saw that it was a tiny room no more than eight by ten, but it did have a bed, a wardrobe, and a washstand. He turned and said, "I very much appreciate your offer, and I'll be glad to pay."

"Good! Do you haf' any money now?" Vandermeer grinned and said, "My landlady threatens to throw me out unless it's paid."

Joel smiled and plunged his hand into his pocket and pulled out his purse. The two settled the matter of rent, and he handed over enough coins to stave off Mrs. Johnson, the landlady.

"Come, let me go pay our rent, then ve vill go out and get something to eat. You haf' money for that?"

Cautiously Joel nodded. "Why yes, I suppose I do."

"Good! Ve vill eat vell! Tomorrow ve may be dead, but today ve have our appetites and ve vill enjoy life!"

Joel settled in at once with the rotund Dutchman and found that he liked him very well indeed. He spent the first two days acquainting himself with the city and soon discovered that Vandermeer seemed to know every street and a great many people. He was a great help to Joel, getting him oriented, and as he lay down to sleep on his narrow cot on the second night, Joel thought, *Well, I'm here. I feel like a fool or a pretender. Me a secret agent! But I've got to go through with it now.*

🔔   🔔   🔔

On Thursday morning, three days after his arrival in New York, Joel stopped by the Gordons'. It was his intention only to make a brief visit and return the clothes David had loaned him, but Lyna Lee Gordon had other plans.

"Come in," she said, "it's almost time for supper. I know it's late to give a proper invitation, but if you have no other plans, we'd be happy to have you join us."

"Why, I wouldn't want to impose."

"Nonsense! How could it be that? It will just be the family and one other guest."

Joel was once again displeased at having to use the hospitality of his family. He hesitated only for a moment, then he remembered that they could be the very means to gain the information that Dante demanded. He accepted graciously, and Mrs. Gordon led him to the library, where he found David sitting in a chair with his feet propped up in the window. He was reading a book, but as Joel was ushered in, he grinned.

"Hello, cousin!" Putting the book down, David rose and shook Joel's hand cordially. "Staying for supper?"

"Yes, I'm afraid I'm going to impose."

"Don't worry. Mother loves to cook, and you'll get to meet my future brother-in-law. You haven't met Stephen Morrison?"

"No, I haven't. He's Miss Grace's fiancé?"

"Yes, indeed." David sat back down in the chair and motioned toward a delicate Queen Anne style chair, saying, "Be careful with that. A big fellow like you could break it into pieces."

Gingerly Joel sat down and looked around the study. It was a warm, friendly room with several bookcases filled with books of all sizes and colors. "You all must be great readers."

"I suppose we are, especially me. I read everything I can get my hands on. What do you do? Do you like to read, Joel, if I may call you that?"

"Of course. Well, I'm not as well read as you are, unfortunately. My life in England didn't lend itself to such activities, but I intend to improve myself."

"Well, Father reads all the books of military history. They're in that bookcase over there."

"I'm not much interested in that," Joel said.

David made a pyramid of his hands. He had a square face, quick, active brown eyes, and there was a leanness and a strength in him that was pleasing. His quick intelligence showed through his speech, and his expression impressed Joel. Joel sat there listening as David went over the various sorts of books and finally said, "Thank you very much. I am interested in learning the geography of the country."

"Oh, that's easy! Father has maps of all sorts, as well as books."

Knowing he would have to master the lay of the land to be more effective as an agent, Joel said, "I would be gratified to have access to these."

"Why, of course. Let me show you some," David said, then got up and walked over to a desk covered with papers. He picked up a few and handed them to Joel and sat down again.

The two young men sat there talking. Joel studied the maps that David laid out for him and soon gained a rudimentary sense of the geography of New York.

"We're on an island, then," Joel observed. "That seems rather strange."

"I don't know why it should," David grinned. "England's an island, isn't it?"

"Yes, but this is such a small place." He looked up and asked curiously, "Were you here during the battle?"

"No, I was on the outside looking in, along with the rest of my family. It had to be won by General Howe before we could move in. It was quite a battle."

"General Howe defeated General Washington, so I understand."

"Oh yes. Washington made a great mistake. I'm not sure he's going to be the man who will win the Revolution. I don't think so anyway."

"Why do you say that?"

"Because he let himself get trapped on an island. All the British had to do was sail up the Hudson River with their ships of war. If Howe was any general at all," David added emphatically, "he should have taken the whole rebel army when he had the chance. Father says he made the biggest mistake an officer can make."

"I see. You know General Howe?"

"Oh, I've met him, of course."

"What do you think of him?"

A rash grin creased David's lips and his eyes sparkled. "I think he's more interested in Mrs. Loring than he is in winning the war against the rebels."

"Mrs. Loring? Who's that?"

"She's the wife of one of his commissioners, the man who handles all the stores." Seeing Joel's look of puzzlement, he shrugged and said, "Everyone knows about it. Mrs. Loring's an attractive woman, her husband gets all the business of the army, and General Howe gets Mrs. Loring."

"And everyone knows about this?"

"Oh yes, the general doesn't make any secret about it. In any case, Father says that the army will have to go out and settle this business now that spring has come."

At that moment a man entered and David rose at once, saying, "Oh, Stephen, I'd like for you to meet our guest, Mr. Joel Bradford. Joel, may I introduce Mr. Stephen Morrison, my sister's fiancé."

The two men shook hands and Morrison studied the face of Joel carefully. He was a lean man, almost too thin, indeed. He had brown hair, an oval face, and soulful brown eyes. His features were delicate, and there was something overdone about his dress. He was almost foppish in his attire.

"Stephen's a businessman *and* a poet," David said, then grinned. "I don't know how he reconciles the two. I always thought poets were very unbusinesslike."

"Not all of us, and you mustn't boast too much about my poetic abilities." Morrison looked somewhat embarrassed. There was a paleness about his face that spoke of a life indoors, and his hand was soft and seemed to lack strength when he shook hands.

"I've never known a poet before, sir. I'd like to read some of your poems."

"Well, I have written a few things you might enjoy. I'll see that you get a copy of one of my books."

The three men sat there visiting for a while until finally Grace came and said, "Supper is ready. Father's just come down." She was wearing a coral chemise gown, with a delicate pattern of flowers woven in. It was tied at the waist by a green ribbon and draped across the bodice with a muslin fichu. The front of the skirt was pleated, and the sleeves were close-fitting at the wrist with a chiffon frill.

Grace led the men out of the small library into the dining room, which was not large but well furnished. A large rectangular-shaped dining room table made of mahogany took its place in the center of the room and was surrounded by ten chairs covered in a yellow woolen moreen. Behind the master's chair was a mahogany and walnut sideboard, and to one side of the room was a large oak serving table covered with a white damask cloth. Crystal glasses and china were placed carefully in a pearwood and fruitwood inlaid china cupboard, and pictures hanging in heavy oak frames decorated the walls.

Leslie Gordon was still wearing his scarlet uniform and looked very dashing. His skin was tanned and he stood straight as a ramrod. "Well, good to have you again, Joel."

"I'm afraid I'm becoming quite an intruder, sir."

"Nonsense! Sit down there and make yourself at home."

Joel sat down and bowed his head as Colonel Gordon asked the blessing over the food, then as soon as he lifted his head, Gordon inquired, "You found a place to stay, I take it?"

"Yes, with Jan Vandermeer. He's a friend of my cousin Matthew."

"Oh yes, we met Vandermeer. Fine fellow, for an artist, that is."

"You shouldn't say that, Father," Grace said. "You make artists sound like second-class citizens."

"I didn't mean it that way," Gordon said. He cut a piece of the beef with his knife, speared it with his fork, and put it into his mouth before adding, "We have to have artists the same as we have to have soldiers."

"And poets, too," Grace said, glancing at Stephen with a slight smile.

"Of course, poets," Gordon agreed. "Have you written anything new I need to hear, Stephen? It seems to me," Gordon said thoughtfully, "that most poets are like preachers. Their greatest fear is that someone will understand what they are saying."

"Why, that's not fair, Leslie," Lyna spoke up at once. "I think you're prejudiced."

"Me? I'm not prejudiced," Gordon said with some surprise. There was a twinkle of humor in his eye, and he said, "I've even thought of giving up soldiering and becoming a poet myself."

This brought a loud laugh that went around the table, and David said, "You couldn't rhyme if you had to, Father. You'd better stick to shooting guns."

Joel enjoyed his meal immensely. Lyna and Grace had prepared an excellent meal of tender beef, potatoes in cream sauce, green beans with onions, freshly baked bread, cheese, fruit, and mugs of hot coffee. He studied the group carefully and was a little bit surprised at the engagement between Stephen Morrison and Grace Gordon. She was a beautiful girl filled with life and humor. Morrison, while handsome enough, seemed somewhat pale and washed out. He listened as Morrison spoke of his property in Carolina and finally asked, "Are you a farmer, then, Mr. Morrison?"

"I haven't been up until now," Morrison admitted. "My brother Jubal and I intended to divide the responsibility. He's in Boston. Did you by chance meet him?"

"Yes I did, as a matter of fact. Mr. Sam Bradford and he are caught up in some sort of venture concerning ships."

Morrison's face flushed and he said angrily, "Nonsense! As errant nonsense as I ever heard of! They're going to become privateers!"

Joel listened carefully, although he knew of the venture and had taken a liking to Jubal Morrison from the moment he had met him. Jubal was quite different from his brother, Joel noted. He filed this information about the property in Carolina in his mind, for Dante had informed him that they especially needed information on what the British were doing in that area.

Finally Lyna asked quietly, "Have you decided what you will do in New York, Joel?"

Joel had indeed concocted a plan. It had been Dante's suggestion to have a plausible vocation in case he was questioned. He now smiled and said, "I have thought of doing some writing for the British newspapers."

"What sort of writing?" David asked with interest. "Novels or things like that?"

"Oh no, I couldn't be a novelist. I don't have the imagination for it,"

Joel grinned. He grew more serious and added, "I had thought to write about what's happening over here concerning this Revolution. I have some connections in England with the newspapers, and I think I can get on as a correspondent. As a matter of fact, I've already had an offer of sorts from the largest newspaper in London."

"Well, I think that would be excellent!" Stephen Morrison exclaimed. "People in England need to know the truth about how things are over here."

"Well, perhaps I could help you some," Colonel Gordon said. He leaned back in his chair and sipped his tea, then added, "If you would like to see how the army performs, come with me tomorrow. You can meet General Howe and the other officers."

"Why, that's very generous of you, sir."

"You might interest them in another area," Grace said. "The general loves plays, and I understand you've done some acting."

"Oh, only in an amateurish sort of way."

"Nevertheless," Grace said, "if you ever do anything else, General Howe would certainly be supportive. He loves dramas and plays—anything to entertain his officers."

"He's vain, too," David grinned. "Like all generals—maybe like all soldiers." He laughed at the expression on his father's face and shook his head. "Give him a good press and he'll love you for it, Joel."

Feeling very much like Judas, Joel Bradford sat quietly and listened as the family planned his new venture.

If they only knew that I'm a Judas, they'd throw me out of the house. How can I betray my family like this?

Later, after Joel had returned to his room, Vandermeer asked him about the family and the dinner.

"They're very generous and hospitable people."

"Yes, they are, very much so!" Vandermeer said. "You're lucky to have a family like that. Myself, I have no family." A look of pain touched Vandermeer's blue eyes, and he said, "Family, how precious they are, and those of us who have none know it more than anyone else."

Vandermeer's remark cut into Joel like a knife, and he excused himself and went to bed. For a long time he tossed, struggling with his troubled conscience, but there was no help for it, and finally he resigned himself to being what he had to be in order to serve in the only way he could.

🏵   🏵   🏵

General William Howe was a corpulent man, over six feet with a prominent nose, brooding black eyes, and a dark complexion. He had served with Wolfe in the War of Austrian Succession and had lost one brother in the Seven Years' War. His other brother, Richard Howe, was the most famous admiral in the British navy. William Howe was an able man, a good soldier, but perhaps not as driving in his personality as many would have liked. He had taken over command of the British forces from General Thomas Gage, and now the war was his responsibility to win and no one else's. The opportunity to rise to greatness lay before him, and he had but to reach out and take it.

Joel had been escorted to the headquarters of General Howe, which was in one of the finest houses in New York. As they traveled in their carriage, Colonel Gordon gave him some insight into the nature of his commanding officer.

"I think, Joel, General Howe sees himself as a negotiator," Gordon remarked, glancing out the window moodily. "He thinks he can win the war by talk instead of by winning battles."

"I'm surprised that a man not committed to action would be appointed to command the king's forces over here."

"So am I. He was schooled in the careful and cautious warfare of the eighteenth century. They saw battles as the last resort of good generals, but that's not the case here. In England, wars were the sport of kings, but on this side of the Atlantic, it's a new world and a new kind of battle. I know General Gage didn't understand this, and now I'm becoming more convinced that General Howe is having difficulty changing his military strategy. He simply doesn't understand these Americans. He doesn't seem to grasp the kind of war that it will take to quench this Revolution. Every time we win a battle Washington fades away, and before you know it," Gordon added grimly, "there he is again with a *new* army! General Howe's biding his time, but he's got to take the offensive and fight. He has to learn that Washington and his army are where the battle lies."

When they arrived at headquarters, Joel was impressed with the luxury of the house. It was the finest he had ever been in. The dining room where he was escorted by Colonel Gordon was ornate. The room was large, about twenty by twenty-two, and dimly lit. The floor had wall-to-wall green carpet with a brown, heavy linen table rug under the dining table. The walls were covered with a bold green and gold mica diamond-shaped wallpaper. There were no windows in this room, but a set of French-type doors at the far end of the room that were covered with white lace curtains. The ceilings were high and domed, decorated with intricate patterns etched in gold paint. A large verde and marble chimney piece dominated one side wall and was covered with a dark mahogany fire screen and flanked by a set of three brass fire irons on each side. The large mahogany dining table was covered with the best French damask in white, and twelve Chippendale chairs of mahogany were covered with slipcovers of white chintz. Two round girandole mirrors with convex glasses and candle arms hung on the wall above a large sideboard with a glossy marble top, and a side serving table was decorated with a two-light candelabra and cut crystal glasses and dishes.

"General Howe, may I present a relative of my wife's, Mr. Joel Bradford. Mr. Bradford, General Howe."

"I'm happy to meet you, sir," Howe said in a genial fashion.

"It's my pleasure, General Howe," Joel said.

"May I introduce my officers."

Joel met the other six men who were there for the meal, but he paid attention to only one of them, a Major Lawrence Hartford. Hartford was a small, thin man with a set of very cold gray eyes. Dante had warned him of this officer, saying, "He's the head of the intelligence department for General Howe. Be careful of him if you ever meet him. He can see through a brick wall."

The officers all sat down, and soon General Howe turned his attention to Joel. "So you are going to be a correspondent for the London newspaper, Mr. Bradford?"

"Yes, General."

"Good, they need to be told the truth," Howe said emphatically. "The rebels manage to put enough lies in the London papers so that you'd think they owned a controlling interest in them."

"I'll do the best I can to rectify that, General Howe."

"Good." He added, with a look toward Leslie Gordon, "Take him around to see all of our works, Colonel."

"Yes indeed, General. I will do that."

"Interview the men, but," he said suddenly, "let me see what you write before you send it to the papers."

"Oh certainly, General. I'd be happy to do that."

After dinner Joel found himself paired off with Major Hartford. Hartford did it very efficiently, but Joel knew that he had been singled out. Hartford asked him question after question in a seemingly careless manner, but Joel knew the man was doing his best to pick his mind. He was greatly relieved that he had meticulously gone over all the details of his story with Dante and in his own mind until now he could answer any question with certainty.

"And so you were tarred and feathered for your loyalist views in Boston?"

"Yes, I'll never forgive them for it." A real anger came to Joel then and he faced the smaller man, adding, "No man knows what that's like until it happens to him."

"So I imagine you have no sympathy at all for these patriots as they are called."

"Certainly not!"

Hartford continued to control the conversation, but when it was over and the dinner broke up, Joel felt a tremble in his hands. *That man can see almost through your forehead*, he thought. *I'm glad Dante warned me about him.*

Thanking the general and Colonel Gordon, and arranging to meet him the next day to see the workings of the army, Joel went back to his room. Vandermeer was gone, so he at once set out to make an official report.

How to get information back had been a point he and Edmund Dante had struggled over. Dante had finally given him a code that he said would be safe. It consisted simply of a piece of paper with an irregular-shaped piece cut out of it. "I will have a piece identical to this," Dante had instructed him. "Put your message in here and then fill in around it with commonplace things. Then if the letter is taken, unless someone has the key, he will never notice it."

Joel sat down and put the paper with the cutout over a blank sheet. There he wrote the information he had obtained through the graces of General Howe. He filled the rest of the letter with meaningless information, then addressed it according to the directions Edmund Dante had given him. The letters would be mailed to an agent named Jonas Franklin, and then Franklin would turn them over to Dante.

When he was done, Joel looked over the letter carefully. He had done a good job, he saw, and no one reading it would be able to see the hidden information, for it was woven into the mundane contents of the letter. Finally he sat down and stared at the walls. He could not help thinking of how miserable Phoebe must be all alone in Boston. He wanted to write her a letter, but Dante had said it would be too dangerous. Nevertheless he knew he must do it. Sitting down again, he wrote her a letter simply saying that he had found a place to live and she could write him in care of Vandermeer and the address of the house where Vandermeer lived. He ended the letter by saying, "I'm sorry we must be separated, Phoebe. Perhaps in the future you can come and be with me. I do not think I will be able to return to Boston. I miss you very much and love you with all my heart. Your loving brother, Joel."

He prepared the two letters, took them out and mailed them, and then finally walked the streets of New York, wondering what a secret agent did to entertain himself. But he could think of nothing—and he found himself longing for someone to share with. After walking for over an hour, he went back to his room and went to bed. For a long time he lay there thinking of how his life had changed—and wondering what his future would be.

10

A Kiss in the Dark

AS THE DAYS PASSED AND THE WEATHER grew warmer, Joel Bradford spent his time learning the history of his adopted country and became quite an expert. He was a frequent guest at the house of Leslie Gordon but always was ashamed of how he was betraying the hospitality so freely offered. He also became a shrewd observer of the military strategy that had taken place in the war so far. He was fortunate to have access to the officers of General Howe's staff, many of whom had been in America from the very beginning. One of his sources, a burly major named Isaac Templeton, had been in the column that had heard the first shots of the war at Lexington. He related the incident to Joel in a speech liberally sprinkled with curses, and his face grew red as he said explosively, "These rebels hide behind trees and disappear into the bushes! They won't stand up like honest men and fight!"

Secretly Joel was amused by Templeton's temper, but he kept his face even, saying, "That is contemptible, Major. And were you at the Battle of Bunker Hill?"

"That I was." Major Templeton narrowed his eyes and his lips drew tight as he remembered that day. "That I was. It was a bloody afternoon, and I lost some good friends on that hill."

"But what about since then? You've beaten the rebels every time."

"Beat them!" Templeton loosed a string of epithets and ended with an explosive, "We beat them at Manhattan, we beat them at White Plains, we've beaten them at every occasion!"

"Except at Trenton," Joel offered. "I understand that was a defeat."

"Trenton! A mere skirmish, no more! Now that winter's over we can go out and clean up this pestilent group of cowardly fellows!"

"Do you think you have force enough for it?"

"Force enough!" Templeton stared across the table at the young man and began to rattle off a list of the troops that were available.

He was very exact and Joel paid close attention, knowing that he would put these figures into his next letter to Edmund Dante.

General Howe had plenty of men to go out at any time and give battle to George Washington's scrawny army, at least during the winter. If he had suspected that his "formidable enemy" had shrunk to only a thousand Continentals, he probably would have left his warm quarters long enough to wipe them out. However, the militia detachments gave Washington the semblance of an army at Morristown, and he managed to conceal his weakness and to create an impression of power by an activity that invoked the comment of an enemy officer. A Major Harrison Seybolt wrote of this:

> The rebels were scattered about the country and took up their quarters in the different towns our troops had withdrawn from. They were frequently very troublesome to us, and every foraging party that went out was pretty certain to have a skirmish with them.
>
> Beside which they made a practice of waylaying single persons or very small bodies on the road and killing them from behind trees or other cover in a most savagelike manner. Large detachments were often sent out to surprise them and sometimes succeeded, but in general their fears kept them so alert that when we showed any force they disappeared.

Justice Thomas Jones of New York, one of the leading loyalists of the area, spoke fervently against such warfare, if it may be called that. Jones wrote in a letter:

> The British were sufficient to have driven Washington out of Jersey with the greatest of ease, but nothing was done. Howe diverted himself in New York in feasting, gunning, and in the arms of Mrs. Loring. Not a stick of wood, a spear of grass, or a kernel of corn could the troops in New Jersey procure without fighting for it. Every foraging party was attacked, and though the losses were small, called nothing more than skirmishes, yet hundreds of them occurred in the course of the winter. The British lost men who were not easily replaced, while the rebel loss was soon repaired by drafts from the militia. It also aided the rebels in another way. It taught them the art of war. It inured them to hardships, and it emboldened them to look a British or a Hessian soldier in the face, whose very countenance would have made a hundred of them run after the Battle of New York.

T   T   T

Joel did learn through two secret meetings with Edmund Dante what the Continental Army was doing. He and Edmund had met at a tavern, and Dante was disguised so well as an older man that Joel did not recognize him. Joel had been sitting at a table in a corner waiting when a thin, gray-haired man dressed in a snuff-colored suit hobbled over and sat down beside him. Only after Dante spoke did Joel recognize, with a shock, that this man was his chief.

"Well, not a bad actor myself, am I, my boy?"

"Not at all, sir." Joel leaned forward, his eyes alight with excitement. "Can you tell me about my people back in Boston?"

"I can tell you a little, although I haven't been there for the past month. They were all well, and your sister especially misses you." Dante's eyes grew gentle, and he said, "I wish we could spare her her grief, but at the present I see of no way."

"What's going on? Are we winning or losing?" Joel demanded.

Dante leaned back and studied the young man, then in a low voice, he said, "General Washington has spent another winter of anguish and apprehension. It seems that the Congress is opposed to anything he suggests. Lack of money, of course, is a problem, and we've been struggling to get food, clothing, and equipment. Congress wants a spring offensive, but they don't want to furnish the equipment, the guns, or the powder to do it."

"That doesn't sound hopeful," Joel said, discouraged at the news.

"It's just the way politicians are. They're not out on the battlefield but in some warm, comfortable house in Philadelphia. What do they know about men whose feet are bare and bloody in the snow? But," Dante said quickly, "one good thing has happened. Congress at last agreed to long-term enlistments."

"What does that mean, sir?"

"It means that for the first time we can have an army not made primarily of militia who are always ill-trained and undependable. But, of course, it's hard to get men into the army by the former practice. Bounties, high wages, and short service have drained plenty of men of their patriotism." His lips grew thin, and he said, "There are those who make their living by feeding and entertaining them. These are the harpies that injure us much at this time. They keep the fellows drunk while the money holds out, then when it's all gone, they encourage them to enlist for the sake of bounty, then to drinking again. It's carried on daily and does an immense injury to the recruiting service, but I hope our new army will get together before long, and then Washington will be able to put a good face toward his enemies."

The two talked for long, and finally Dante said, preparing to leave, "Oh, I didn't tell you that smallpox has spread through the Continental camp. The general ordered the inoculation of the whole army."

"I had it when I was a child," Joel said at once.

"That's good. It didn't leave you marked."

"No, only a few marks around my shoulders."

"Well, we had the good fortune of having Dr. Benjamin Rush and Dr. Edward Archer. They had adopted the method of the English physician, Daniel Sutton."

"How was his procedure different, sir?"

"He employed a small puncture instead of the deep gash formerly required, but regardless of technique the men were afraid. But the general insisted, and his powers are now virtually dictatorial. He wrote a letter to Congress that stated desperate diseases require desperate remedies, so they granted him extraordinary powers. He used them at once, I must say." Dante grinned suddenly. "He lodged some of his convalescents in the houses in town over the squalls of the inhabitants." He got up then and drew his cloak about him. "If Howe had chosen to attack this winter, he would have enveloped the whole American army. I must be gone. Your reports have been good, thorough, and well thought out. I trust you will keep them coming. Have you encountered Major Lawrence Hartford?"

"Yes, I've met him often. As I've told you in my letters, Mr. Dante, I've become quite enamored at General Howe's table."

Dante frowned. "Don't use my name, and be careful of Hartford. He's a fox! Do nothing that would endanger yourself." He laid his hand on the young man's shoulder and said, "Others may not know what a sacrifice you're making at this time, or what a valuable contribution, but some of us know, and the general asked me to pass along his most grateful word."

Joel's face flushed at the thought of gratitude from General Washington! It strengthened his resolve and he stood up. "I'll do the best I can."

"Spend some time down by the harbor. Check out the ships. Get to know some of the sailors, not the officers necessarily. Most sailors know everything that's going on even before the officers do. We need to find out when Howe plans to leave New York. We especially need to know what route he's going to take." He frowned and said, "There are only two ways he can go. He can leave by water aboard the ships of war with all his troops, or he can come over land."

"Yes, sir, I will do that at once."

"Good! And now good-bye, my boy, and God keep you."

T T T

Joel kept his word to Edmund Dante. He haunted the waterfronts of New York, striking up conversations with many of the sailors. Since Dante had given him more money to spend if necessary, he spent it on taking the British sailors into the taverns and buying them rum. He could not drink the fiery stuff, so he contented himself with ale. He became quite clever at ferreting out information, which he passed along by letter to Dante.

And so the days passed and then the weeks, and still Howe made no move to leave New York. More than once Joel wondered if Howe had decided to stay forever and let Washington attack him, but Dante had said this was impossible. So he kept doggedly at his task. Soon Joel knew the names of all the military units stationed in New York, along with their commanding officers. They all had slightly different uniforms. The Hessians wore green, and the regulars wore red, but they all had minute differences. He mastered all of these, so that simply by seeing a group of men marching down the street, he could instantly identify their unit, such as the Sixty-first Foot, or the Scottish regiments called the Black Watch.

He found himself going to church out of motives he could not clearly identify. He was filled with shame because of his duplicity, for he was forced to share the services with Colonel Leslie Gordon and his wife, Lyna, not to mention Grace and David. Burning within him was always the knowledge that something about what he was doing was wrong. Over and over again he reasoned it out, sometimes lying awake for hours, but never successfully, and the burden of guilt lay heavily upon him.

Finally, after a brief struggle with himself, he rose on a Sunday morning and determined to ignore church. He had a meager breakfast with Jan Vandermeer and then left, mumbling something about taking a walk. Vandermeer stared at him, then said, "Valking is good for your health."

"I suppose so."

For hours, it seemed, he walked the streets of New York. He was familiar now with most of them and, as usual, found himself down at the waterfront. The white gulls overhead were immaculate, almost luminous, as they soared across the blue sky. They came down, swooping

139

to his head, but he had nothing to give them. Sometimes he liked to bring a stale loaf of bread and watch them come swooping down and arguing almost like humans at a feast. At times he had fed them by hand as they became emboldened, and once he had even put bread on his head, delighted how they would swoop down and snatch the morsels away. But he had nothing to give them this time, so after entertaining himself for a while, he moved slowly away from the wharf and wandered toward the center of the city.

Almost against his will, he found himself back in front of the church, and as he stood there looking, he heard a voice saying, "Well, Mr. Bradford, you come to services."

Turning quickly, Joel encountered the eyes of Heather Reed. She was alone and he took off his hat and bowed at once. "Good morning, Miss Reed. Your parents aren't with you today?"

"They are already here. I fear we are a little late. Shall we go in?"

Actually Joel had no intention of going in, but something in her steady gaze challenged him. He knew she despised him for his political opinion, and he more than once had longed to tell her the truth, that her cause was actually his. Now caught in her steady observation, he said quickly, "Yes, I think we should."

Moving inside the church they found the customary seats. Mr. and Mrs. Reed nodded pleasantly enough to the young man, somewhat surprised to see him. As Heather settled down, her mother said, "Where did you find him?"

"Wandering around in front of the church."

The two settled down, and once while they were singing out of the small hymnbook provided, Joel's hand touched Heather's. She glanced at him quickly to see if it was purposeful. He, however, gave her an innocent look and they continued to sing. Joel had a fine, clear tenor voice, and between hymns, Heather said approvingly, "You sing very well."

"So do you, Miss Reed. We make a good duo."

Reverend Abiram Hooks spoke eloquently and fervently from a text in Isaiah: "I will give thee a covenant of the people." He was almost through with the sermon, and Joel had hardly followed it. He was very conscious of Heather Reed, who sat beside him. From time to time he would steal a glance at her face, admiring the rich auburn hair and the sweep of her jaw, so strong and yet so utterly feminine. He longed, somehow, to say something to change her opinion of him, but he knew that her heart was totally in the Revolution, and she would have nothing to do with a man who was not committed to that same cause.

As Reverend Hooks came to the end of his sermon, he began to speak in a more gentle voice. It was as if he pleaded with his congregation to hear him. Holding his hands outstretched, he said, "I feel that we talk more about the offices and works of Jesus than we do about His person. Perhaps this is the reason few of us can understand the figures used in Solomon's Song concerning the person of Christ, because we seldom seek to see Him or desire to know Him as a person." He held his hands suddenly over his head in a gesture of prayer, and tears streamed down his cheeks. They looked strange, for he was a burly, masculine man, and yet somehow they did not show weakness, but strength.

"Will you not see Him who is white and ruddy? The chief among ten thousand and altogether lovely? Will you not note His feet that are like fine gold as they burn in a furnace? Will you see in Him the red and the white, the lily and the rose, the God and yet the man, the dying and yet the living, the perfect and yet bearing about in Him a body of death? Have you ever beheld the Lord with a nail print in His hands and the marks still on His side? Have you ever seen His loving smile? Have you not been delighted at His voice? Have you never," he said in a passionate whisper, "had love visits from Him? Has he never put His banner over you? Have you never walked with Him to the villages and sat under His shadow. . . ?"

Somehow as the pastor continued in this vein Joel felt his heart stirred. In truth he had intellectually given much thought to Jesus Christ, but this man was speaking of something far different. As he sat there a thought came to his mind. *If I could know Jesus like that, I think I would be satisfied. I think I could do anything for God.*

The pastor's voice went on for some time. "The woman loves her husband, she loves his house and his property. She loves him for all he has given her, for all the love he bestows. But what is it she really loves? *Him.* He is the object of her affections."

"That man knows something about married love."

Startled at the whisper, Joel swiveled his head abruptly to find Heather looking at him. Her eyes were half closed as she studied him thoughtfully, and her lips, firm yet rounded and gentle, were still. "Yes, he does," he murmured, "although I don't know it myself."

Finally the sermon was over, and after they were outside Mr. Reed shook Joel's hand. "A fine sermon."

"Yes indeed, sir."

"We would be pleased if you would have dinner with us."

The invitation caught Joel off guard. He glanced at Heather and saw that she was watching him carefully. He could not read her expression and yet somehow the thought came, *She probably doesn't want me in the house, but I'll go anyway.* "Yes, sir, that would be very fine."

When they got into the carriage, Reed inquired about Joel's activities. Joel answered easily, saying, "I've been quite busy. Being a writer is more difficult than I thought."

Heather listened as he explained that he was writing about the Revolution and the situation in general in the Colonies for London newspapers. She asked suddenly, "And are you telling the truth about the situation?"

"Why . . . I trust so, Miss Reed," Joel said, taken aback by her directness.

"Heather, that's no way to talk! You're too abrupt! You always were!" Timothy Reed exclaimed.

Virginia Reed suddenly reached over and put her hand on her husband's arm and laughed in a gentle fashion, saying, "I know who she gets it from, Timothy."

Looking at her critically, he winked at Joel and said, "From your side of the family, my dear. Don't be offended at my daughter. Women don't understand these political things."

Joel was certain that Heather Reed did understand political things, but he had no chance to answer, for Heather almost broke into her father's speech.

"The truth is that England has treated the Colonies shamefully. Is that what you're putting in your stories, Mr. Bradford?"

"Well, I must admit, not quite in that fashion."

"Of course not, but there are Englishmen such as Mr. Pitt and Mr. Burke who understand the problems over here. Have you read their accusations made in the very House of Lords, and in the House of Commons as well?"

As a matter of fact, Joel had read what these two outspoken leaders in England had said. They were both vehemently against the war and said so bluntly and eloquently, but their voices were not enough to stem the tide. So he said quickly, "They are very courageous men to voice their opinion. What I try to do is simply portray in my stories what is happening to the common people."

They reached the house without saying more and went in at once. The meal had already been prepared by the cook, and they sat down in a well-furnished dining room. The table was soon filled with heaping plates of roasted chicken and beef, sweet potatoes and apples, a potato pie with currants, raisin, and dates, freshly baked bread, and slipcoat cheese.

When they were halfway through, Mrs. Reed said, "Have you heard about the ball that's to take place tomorrow night?"

"Why no, I don't believe I have," Joel said.

"You wouldn't be interested in it." Heather smiled rather slyly. "There will be no English officers there, just a few of us patriots looking for a little fellowship."

"Why, I think I would enjoy it very much," Joel said, smiling at Heather.

"Would you indeed?" Heather said. "Then I will invite you to come. You might get tarred and feathered, of course, for your loyalist opinions."

He saw that she was teasing him and bowed his head almost gallantly. "I will risk it, Miss Reed."

⚔   ⚔   ⚔

The ball was a small affair, no more than thirty or forty people in attendance. It was held in the home of Mr. Ralph Jacobson, a wealthy shipper, who was practically out of business since the embargo. But he had money enough to spare, and his home was large enough for such an occasion. It took place in a rather small ballroom, but it had been done up quite tastefully. Chairs covered in burgundy, blue, and green damask outlined the room, and tables had been set up and covered with the finest white cloths, silver, crystal, and china.

A small group of musicians were playing valiantly on their violins and their flutes as Joel entered the room. He saw Heather turn and catch his smile. She excused herself from a couple and crossed the ballroom toward him.

"Come, I've alerted all of my friends that a Tory will be joining us tonight. They promised to hold off on the tar and feathers until after the ball is over."

Joel could not help but smile at her coy teasing. And the playfulness that continually surfaced in her he found quite delightful. He knew she was deathly serious about her views on things. Yet there was a joy of living in her that drew him. She still grieved over her brother's tragic death, which came to his attention from time to time. But now he saw she had put everything serious out of her mind and was intent on enjoying the evening with her friends.

"If I may have this dance," he said, "I think this Tory would be very happy."

"Why, of course, Mr. Bradford," Heather said and took his arm.

They began to move across the floor and he took this opportunity to admire her. She was wearing a sapphire blue dress made of the finest silk and laces. It had a tight-fitting bodice and a low neckline edged in delicate white lace, and the sleeves were elbow length, with three layers of wide lace at the edge. Her overskirt was full, worn over a hoop, edged in white lace, and the underskirt had insets of embroidered white flowers and large white lace frills.

Her skin was as fresh and clean and silky as anything he had ever seen. She was wearing some sort of mild perfume. The fragrance had a strange, intoxicating effect on him. As he held the small of her back and guided her around the dance floor, he was aware that she had a graceful and strong figure. She was rather small, so she had to look up to him, and that gave her gaze a provocative aspect.

"You dance very well, sir."

"Not as well as you, I fear. We didn't have much of a chance to dance like this back home."

"What was it like, your home in England?"

"Very poor indeed. Before my parents died it was bearable, but toward the last it was very difficult." He hesitated, then said, "I wound up in a debtors' prison along with my sister, Phoebe."

Heather had not known the hardships he had faced. She looked up at him with compassion, and her lips softened as she spoke. "How awful for both of you."

"If it had not been for Mr. Daniel Bradford, we would probably be there yet." He recounted how Matthew Bradford had come to the prison and paid their fine, securing their freedom. Then he told her how it was through the kindness of Daniel Bradford, who had paid for their passage, that they were able to come to America and begin a new life.

"He must be a fine man."

"He is indeed. As a matter of fact, all of my relatives over here are fine men and women."

"Then how can you go against such a fine family? They're all staunch patriots, are they not?"

"All except Mr. Matthew Bradford. I don't think he's found his way yet." He found it difficult to answer her questions, for he knew that he must not intimate the true nature of his feelings. He turned them aside, saying, "That young man over there is looking at me with daggers in his eyes. Am I to suspect that he's one of your admirers?"

Turning her head slightly, Heather smiled. "That's Mr. Joe Tanner.

I'm not sure you would call him an admirer. We have seen each other several times."

Mr. Tanner saw them looking and at once came and claimed the next dance. As they were dancing, he said, "What's gotten into you, Heather? You admit the man's a Tory. Why did you invite him here? Don't we see enough Tories during the day?"

"Don't be angry, Joe," Heather shrugged. "He's harmless enough."

Joe Tanner was a staunch patriot and said sharply, "No Tories are harmless! I'd like to run the whole lot of them back to England."

Heather calmed the man and then went to greet some of her other guests after the dance. Later in the evening she danced again with Joel. It was warm in the hall, and finally she said, "Would you care to see the gardens?"

"Very much."

When they stepped outside, the full moon shed its beams down upon them.

"The moon looks like a huge silver shilling, doesn't it?" Joel mentioned, looking up at the sky that was spangled with millions of stars.

"Yes, it does." Heather walked along the garden pathways, and the pleasant fragrance of the different flowers in bloom hung in the air. It was cooler outside and finally they stopped before a fish pond. The moon was mirrored in the water, and she reached down and picked up a stone and tossed it in. It shattered the image, and the moon turned to a shivering, quivering mass. "Now I've ruined the moon," she said.

"Just the picture of the moon. The moon itself is still there."

"What do you think about Grace's fiancé?"

The sudden question took Joel off guard. He thought for a moment, then said, "If he pleases her, then I'm satisfied."

"That's no answer!"

"Well . . . really, I don't think I have the right to judge the man."

"What do you mean? You've already judged him."

"What do you mean, Miss Reed?"

"I mean we judge everybody we meet, don't we?"

"I thought the Bible said, 'Judge not that you be not judged.' "

"Oh, that means harshly judging someone, condemning them. I simply mean what kind of man do you think he is?"

"Well," Joel said meditatively, "it's hard for me to say. He's somewhat different, being a poet and all. Artists are different altogether." He laughed suddenly, saying, "I've learned about artists a little bit from my friend Jan Vandermeer. He's different, all right."

Heather's mind, however, was still on Stephen Morrison. She had grown fond of Grace, and despite their differences in politics, they had become good friends. "I think she's making a serious mistake. She shouldn't marry him."

"Why do you say that? He seems a good enough fellow. He has money and a future."

Heather reached up and ran her hand over her hair. It was a graceful gesture, and her lifted arms threw her figure into bold relief. As if conscious of this, she suddenly hugged herself, then shook her head and bit her lip. "I'm always getting into trouble. My father says I'm too much like him, and that I make mistakes about judging people."

"I don't see anything wrong with Mr. Morrison," Joel said.

"Oh, there's nothing *wrong* with him. He's an honorable man, I'm sure, but he's just not very . . . vigorous."

"What would you have him do, grab a sword and jump on a horse and go slashing around the country?"

"I would prefer that to what he does presently. All he does is sit around and read poetry in a gentle voice. I think Grace needs a man with more strength."

"His brother's that kind of man. Have you met him?"

"Jubal Morrison? No. I've heard of him, of course, from Grace."

"Quite a dynamic fellow. He and my cousin Sam are outfitting a privateer."

"What did he look like?"

"Oh, he's a rough-looking fellow, rusty hair, blue eyes, very strong. He was raised in the south, I understand. In the Carolinas."

"I'd like to meet him. Maybe I could tell Grace to consider him instead of his brother."

Joel stared at her, then saw a piquant expression in her eyes. She was teasing him again, and he smiled at her suddenly. "You say a lot of things you don't really mean, Miss Reed."

"Well, now you've found out my little secret. I express opinions not my own."

"I see you like to disturb people. Well . . ." He looked at her for a moment and then thought of how he himself was playing a role and a soberness came to him. "Things are not what they seem," he said slowly. "Maybe Mr. Morrison is more dynamic than you think."

Heather Reed was a quick girl and read people rather well. She saw that something she had said had disturbed him, and she asked quietly, "Have I offended you, sir?"

Without thinking, he reached out and took her hand and held it for a moment. "No, of course not." He was very much aware of the strength

146

and the softness of her hand, and at that moment the moon came from behind a cloud and shed its silver light over her face. He was a lonely young man, but as she looked up at him, he knew it was not an invitation, only a quiet waiting, as if in anticipation, watching him from behind those green eyes. A recklessness came over Joel then. He had known a loneliness since he had been in New York, for he had revealed himself to no one. Knowing he was doing the wrong thing, he reached out and pulled her to him. To his surprise she did not pull away. He lowered his head and kissed her. She stood unmoving, her lips soft beneath his own, and suddenly he felt a rush of inexpressive things. *This is not right*, he thought, still waiting for her to pull away. But she did not rebuke him, and a shock ran through him as he felt her arms reach up around his neck. For what seemed an eternity, he held her tightly.

As for Heather, she had begun the embrace as an experiment. She had been kissed before, but something about Joel Bradford had captivated her from the first. There was more in him, she was certain, than met the eye, and she was drawn to his rough, rugged good looks. Now, however, as she received his embrace and gave her own, she felt stirred in a way that surprised her. She was an attractive woman, and she sensed the desires that revealed themselves in the strength of his arms and the demand of his lips. The thrill of something timeless, even thoughtless, brushed against them both, and it frightened her in a way. She had the power to stir him and found that she herself was feeling a wave of emotion she had not anticipated. Putting her hand on his chest, she stepped back, and the two stood there staring at each other. A faint color stained her cheeks, and she held him with a glance that was possessive and mixed with a trace of fear.

Joel stood watching her, unable to read her expression. Her silhouette in the moonlight held him for a moment. She was fresh and turbulent and strong, and he said finally, "I shouldn't have done that."

"No, and I shouldn't have let you."

"I ask your pardon—and yet the fault was not entirely mine."

Rashness stirred her lips. "You think I led you on?" she demanded.

"Not intentionally, perhaps, but there's something in you that can draw a man."

The two stood there for a moment, both strongly influenced by the embrace. "We'd better go inside," she said quietly.

As Joel Bradford followed her back to the ball, he knew he would not forget the kiss. Something had happened to him in the garden during that brief moment, and he was not certain if it was good, or if it was something that he would come to regret.

⚜   ⚜   ⚜

Phoebe examined the letter anxiously. It had come a half hour ago and she had already read it through three times. It was not a long letter, but somehow it made her more lonesome and more vulnerable than ever. Joel wrote of his daily activities, but she sensed a covert quality in his writing. He had always been so open with her, and now things had changed since he had left Boston.

Lowering the letter to her lap, she murmured, "I wish he were here—or that I were there."

Part of her unhappiness came from the fact that Silas Bickerson continued to pursue her undauntedly now that Joel was no longer there. She had done everything she knew to discourage his advances, aside from being absolutely rude. Uncourteous behavior was not in her, but she knew she would have to do something to dissuade him. Finally she arose and went about her work, but later that afternoon she left the house and went to the home of Katherine Yancy. The letter had mentioned Clive, and she knew that Katherine would be anxious to hear any news about him.

Katherine greeted her with a smile, and as soon as the two sat down, Phoebe said, "I just received a letter from Joel." She smiled gently and said, "He talks a bit about Clive. I thought you'd be interested."

Katherine Yancy was not a woman to deceive anyone. "I'd like very much to hear it," she said simply. She leaned forward, her lips half parted, as the other woman read that part of the letter. When Phoebe had finished and looked up, Katherine said, "Thank you for reading it to me."

"Does he never write you?"

"Yes, he does from time to time." She said no more, but there was something in her expression that revealed her longing for the tall, young physician.

"Have you ever thought that you might marry?"

"Yes." The single word expressed a longing and a frankness that was common with Katherine Yancy. She was a strong woman indeed, and during the rest of the visit, she revealed more of herself than she ever had to Phoebe.

After Phoebe left, Katherine went to visit the Tyrones and found them both in poor condition. She spoke to Abigail, who was very concerned about them. "They're not doing well at all," she murmured.

"No, I think they need more help."

"It's very difficult to get a doctor here."

The two women visited for a time, then Katherine left for home. She went about her work calmly enough, but a thought had been planted in her mind. By the time she had finished with her work, she had come to a decision and went to the small writing desk. Taking out a sheet of paper, she began to write rapidly:

Dear Clive,

Neither Ezra nor Leah are well. All of us are very concerned about them. Would it be possible for you to come and help them? It is difficult to find a doctor here willing to treat them.

She hesitated for a moment and then, after giving a more detailed account, she continued writing.

I miss you very much and ask you to come, not only to see them, but I long to see you.

She hesitated then, not knowing how to close the letter. She was a woman in love, this Katherine Yancy, and the barrier between her and Clive had been a burden to her spirit. Now she stared down at the words she had written and finally, slowly, carefully, wrote:

With all my love and affection,
Katherine Yancy

11

THINGS ARE NEVER WHAT THEY SEEM

THE WINTER OF 1776 HAD BEEN a trying time for Washington and his ragged army of Continentals. No one except George Washington himself could have held even this semblance of a force together. By sheer determination of will and that iron strain of character that lies in some men, George Washington daily rode among his scarecrow soldiers and encouraged them. It grieved him to see the poor condition of his troops, who at times had had no meat for days. He had an amazing ability to get the men to endure frightening hardships.

One cold day, Washington was riding among the troops, for he wanted them to see him sharing their misery. He came upon Private John Brantly and some of his companions drinking wine, which was probably stolen. Brantly was already a little tipsy, and looking up at the tall man, he said, "Here, General, have a drink with us."

Washington replied, "My boy, you have no time for drinking wine."

"Blast your proud soul!" Brantly answered. "You think you're above drinking with soldiers?"

Washington, who had started to ride away, turned his chestnut sorrel around and smiled. "All right, Private, I will drink with you." He put the jug to his mouth, took a swig, then handed it back to the startled soldier.

"Give it to the others," Brantly said, indicating Washington's aides, and there were beaming smiles from the soldiers as the jug was passed around.

Private Brantly took the jug back and stood for a moment, looking up with admiration at the tall form of his commander in chief. "Now," he cried out, "I'll spend the last drop of my blood for you!" The story, of course, went about the camp and strengthened the resolve of the men in their determination to stick with General George Washington to the very end. By early spring a rebirth, of sorts, came to the army. As the first of eight thousand Continentals began to arrive at Morristown, General Washington recovered from a brief illness. Soon the fears of the men were replaced by optimism, and social amenities revived the spirits of those who had been depressed. Soon some of the officers' wives came to add to the charm of Morristown—among them Martha Washington, who presided over the social life of the headquarters.

One welcome addition was Martha Dangerfield Bland, the twenty-five-year-old wife of Theodorick Bland of Virginia. Her face was marked by smallpox, which she had recently suffered, but she said in a letter: "I shall be pitied with them; however, every face almost keeps me in countenance. Here are few smooth faces and no beauties so that one does very well to pass."

To her sister-in-law, Fannie Randolph, in Virginia, Martha Bland wrote:

> I found Morristown a clever little village in a most beautiful valley at the foot of five mountains. There are some exceedingly pretty girls. Really I never met with such pleasant creatures.
>
> Now let me speak of our noble and agreeable commander (for he commands both sexes, one by his excellent skill in military matters, the other by his ability, politeness, and attention). We visited the Washingtons two or three times a week by invitation. He is generally busy in the forenoon, but from dinner to night he is free for all company. His worthy lady seems to be in perfect felicity while she is by the side of her "Old Man," as she calls him. General Washington puts off being a hero and takes on the air of a chatty, agreeable companion. He can be downright impudent sometimes. Such impudence, Fannie, as you and I like, and really I have wished for you often.

As spring brought the warm breezes and the even warmer sun, what had been a skeleton force grew slowly to over nine thousand men. Desertion still ran high, and discipline, perhaps, was all too lenient. Nonetheless, optimism prevailed among most of the experienced officers, and Washington himself was never more resolute than in the balmy spring days that followed the harsh winter they had all endured.

General Howe was certain to move soon, but neither Washington nor his aides could make a proper guess where he would strike. They studied the reports from intelligence that came in, some of which came directly from Joel Bradford in New York. It was one of his coded missives that prompted Washington to make a decision.

"Look at this, Greene," he said one day in early May. "According to Bradford's report, the fleet of transports in New York are being readied to make sail."

General Nathaniel Greene bent over and peered carefully at Washington, who was sitting at his desk. "That means that the English army will move by sea instead of by land."

Washington's face clouded. "Yes, and I don't like it, Nathaniel."

"Why not, sir?"

"Because our scouts and our spies can trace an army of men on land, but we have no way of tracking a fleet at sea. They could leave New York and sail out of sight of land. In that case, we have nothing to do but try to cover all their possible landings, which is impossible."

"This man, Bradford, is he reliable?"

"Yes indeed, his reports have been very accurate." He frowned again and shook his head. "I'll have Dante get word to Bradford to haunt the harbors. We need to know the instant the army moves, if they move by sea. In the meanwhile, we'll leave Morristown and move south to Middlebrook."

"Why is that, sir?"

"We'll take our position in the first range of the Watchung Mountains behind some heights. There we can see the country between Amboy and Brunswick. But most of all, we can see the road to Philadelphia. We've got to keep track of Howe's movements. We must not be caught off guard, Nathaniel!"

♟   ♟   ♟

Colonel Leslie Gordon sat upright in his chair, looking across the room at his commanding officer, General Howe, and desperately pondered if anything under heaven could ever stir him to action. He glanced over at Major Lawrence Hartford, the chief intelligence agent for the British forces, and wondered why the two of them had been summoned for a sudden, unplanned meeting. The message had come earlier from an aide to Gordon, which merely consisted of the words, "Sir, General Howe wishes to see you at once."

Now, sitting there studying Howe, Gordon felt a sense of desperation. He had believed from the beginning that the war against the Colonies was wrong. In his estimation, it could all have been settled by reasonable men. But King George III of England was not a reasonable man. He believed devoutly in the divine right of kings, and to him the Colonists were violating God's orders by daring to challenge the royal majesty of Great Britain.

General Howe was not wearing his best uniform, for he had apparently just awakened from sleeping. He had drawn on what amounted to his off-duty uniform, an older one almost tattered with use, but appeared comfortable. Howe was a big man, handsome and corpulent, and now a strange expression seemed to flicker in his brooding black eyes. He picked up a bottle of wine, filled three glasses, then waved toward his two officers. "Drink up, gentlemen." He drained his own while the other two sipped at theirs, for neither Gordon nor Major Hartford were much for strong spirits. "You're probably wondering why I called you here so urgently," Howe said. "Well, I must make a decision, and I want to get your ideas." He turned to the intelligence officer and demanded, "Major Hartford, what can you tell me about the position of the rebels?"

Hartford's thin, foxlike face sharpened. He ran his hand over his brown hair and shook his head with disgust. "There's nothing new to report, General. Washington is still camped at Morristown with his ragtag army."

"How many?"

"Almost impossible to say, sir." Hartford waved his hands in a futile gesture. "They come and go almost as they please, no order, no discipline. The whole troop of militia might come in on Monday and decide to leave on Thursday."

"Well, surely you must have some sort of estimate!" Howe snapped with irritation. He filled his glass, drank again, and said, "What would be your guess?"

"As best as we can ascertain, approximately ten thousand men."

"That's not a very large force, sir," Gordon said quickly. "We could send part of our forces around and catch them in a scissors movement." He had been in favor of attacking the rebels ever since the war began, but neither General Gage nor his replacement, General Howe, would listen to his advice.

"You must understand, Colonel, that we cannot risk our army. We must fight a delaying action. We will catch the rebels in one place where we can surround them totally, and then we will hit them hard from all sides."

Daringly Leslie Gordon said in a stringent voice, "Sir, that's exactly where we had them on Long Island."

Howe glared at Gordon but could not answer, for the charge was exactly true. He had received a reprimand from England about his refusal to strike and now he waved it off. General William Howe was a loyal officer of the king, but he had the reluctance of a professional who was schooled in the careful and cautious warfare of the eighteenth century. He thoroughly believed the theory of the day that battles were the last resort of a good general. He said as much now. "If we fight a pitched battle, we lose men and arms, highly expensive military commodities. We must be careful and move with caution."

"This is a different kind of war, sir," Gordon said. He knew he was arousing the anger of his commanding officer, but at this point, he cared not one whit. "In Europe, war is the sport of kings, in a way. They're rosewater wars, carefully regulated struggles." Gordon leaned forward, his face alight. He was a handsome man, tall and well formed, and now he had a mission to convince his chief that it was time to end this Revolution once and for all with an offensive strike. "Wars in Europe are fought with rules and precedence, traditions. There's a so-called proper conduct—most of all to preserve your army."

"Exactly right. That's why we must be careful!" Howe exclaimed.

"But it's different over here. This Revolution has brought on a new kind of conflict. It's an ideological war."

"Ideological? What do you mean by that?" Major Hartford snapped.

"I mean that in Europe, Major, there's a clear line between soldiers and civilians. There the civilians are, for the most part, let alone, while the armies fight. That's not the case over here. These people are no longer indifferent bystanders. They've got a spiritual purpose."

"What does that mean, Colonel?" Howe demanded.

"It means they have a zealous cause they believe in. They are a rabble in arms, as many have said, but to them their cause is noble." Gordon knew it was asking too much for William Howe to understand this. The general simply did not understand the kind of war he was fighting.

"Why should we relentlessly pursue a ragtag army obviously about to burst at the seams?" Howe lifted his mug again, then said, "Why risk precious soldiers to subdue a falling foe? Why, indeed, expose them to the rigors of warfare in a wilderness with a climate that is so harsh? No, sir," he said firmly. "We will wait for the moment when a slight push rather than a strong shove is all that will be needed to topple this army of strong men!"

At that moment Colonel Leslie Gordon gave up on William Howe. *He'll never fight*, he thought despairingly. He sat there while the two men discussed strategy, but he knew in his own heart the British cause was already lost.

Later he said to Lyna as he described the meeting, "They just don't understand, Lyna. It's true that Washington's men are untrained and slothful soldiers. They will surely run away when faced with trained troops, but there's one thing that Howe doesn't understand."

"What's that, Leslie?"

Leslie Gordon's face hardened. "These men may run away, but they will come back! That's something you can't expect of one of our regulars. If he runs away, he will *not* come back. He knows he would face the noose at the worst and certainly the lash. When we lose a man he's lost forever, but when Washington's men run away, they will gather and they will talk. They will be encouraged by their leaders, and they will come back for the next battle. General Howe will never understand this. It's obvious he's still living in another world."

🔔　　　🔔　　　🔔

Joel Bradford's instructions were clear. They arrived in a coded letter from Edmund Dante, and he studied the letter only momentarily before burning it. His quick memory had captured every detail.

"So I've got to find out when the ships will be leaving. That's the only way Washington will know which way the enemy is going to attack." His jaw tightened and he left his little cubicle of a room. When he came out he stepped over to look at a picture that Jan Vandermeer was painting. It was a street scene, but it was not one of the more beautiful scenes of New York. "Why did you paint such an ugly street, Jan?"

Vandermeer turned to look at him. Dabs of paint smeared his round face, and his blue eyes glowed with excitement, as usual. He always seemed to throw himself into whatever project he was painting. His life had become consumed by his passion for art. "Vell, because it's part of the vorld ve live in. Shall ve take only the pretty streets and ignore the ugly ones?" he said as he waved his brush in the air at Joel.

"I can see an ugly street anytime I want to. All I have to do is step out the door. When I want a picture to admire, I would like something a little more interesting than the ugliness of life I see on the dirty streets of New York."

Vandermeer, always ready for an argument, whirled and began jabbing at poor Joel with his brush smeared with yellow paint. "That is not the vay art is," he said loudly. He always spoke thunderously, as if his ears were half deaf, something that the landlord, Mrs. Johnson, complained about often. "Ve need to see life as it is. It is true that there are ugly people in the world, and there are beautiful people. They are all God's people."

156

"You believe God made some people ugly?"

"Certainly I believe that!"

"But you're not even a Christian, Jan."

"I vill be someday," Vandermeer said pugnaciously. "I am seeking God. When I understand enough about Him, then I vill go to Him and confess my sins, and He vill make me into a new man."

Joel was fascinated by Vandermeer's philosophy. He knew that the man was practically a drunkard and that his involvement with women was rumored to be atrocious. Still, he proclaimed to anyone who would listen that one day all this would be over.

"Why don't you become a Christian now?" Joel asked.

"You know the story of St. Augustine? When he was living in sin, he said, 'Oh, God, make me holy—but not *now!*' "

Joel shook his head in confusion. "I don't understand that."

"Well, are you a Christian?" Jan asked, pointing the brush at him again.

"Why . . . no, I'm not."

"Why not?"

The question caught Joel off guard, for Vandermeer had never been so direct. "Because I'm just not ready. There are things that have to be done."

"And you can't do them as a Christian? Then they're not worth doing, are they? You're exactly like I am, and like every other person who's not a Christian," Vandermeer said. His voice softened, and he put the wooden tip of the brush between his teeth and chewed it thoughtfully. "For all of us who do not know God, there is something ve vant more than God."

"I think you're right, Jan." Joel remembered the sermons he had heard in Boston and in New York. For a moment he wished he could confide in Vandermeer. However, he knew he could not, so he simply said, "I'm going out for a while."

Vandermeer stared at the door and wondered about the mission of this young man. He knew Joel was not working, and he doubted that the newspapers paid Bradford enough to live on. "Something is wrong with that young man, very deeply wrong," he muttered. "He is a fine young man in some ways, but he has a guilty secret. Someday I vill find out what it is; then, perhaps I can help him."

For the next three days Joel haunted the wharves. With General Howe about to make his move, Joel pumped the sailors more than ever for information. He watched supplies being loaded and tried to ascertain if they were supplies for a long voyage or for merely a short jaunt.

He gathered what information he could, but his surveillance came to an abrupt halt one day. He had been invited to share a meal with General Howe and his officers.

General Howe turned to him abruptly and said, "Mr. Bradford, there is something I must caution you about."

At once Bradford felt a cold chill run down his spine. "Yes, sir, what is it, General?"

He had no idea what the general would say, but looking around the room of officers, he sensed he was caught in a precarious position.

"Major Hartford tells me that you have been spending a great deal of time talking to the sailors down at the wharf."

"Why, that is so, General."

"And why is that, if I may ask?" Major Hartford demanded. He was standing beside Howe, and his eyes were direct and piercing.

"Why, I have been asked by my newspapers to try to get a clear view of how the men of His Majesty's Navy, as well as the army, feel about the struggles here in America." It was a quick lie that leaped to Joel's lips, and he saw that it did not convince Hartford.

General Howe shrugged and said, "I will ask you to work closely with Major Hartford."

After Howe turned and walked away, Hartford said, "I think it might be best if one of my men accompany you when you speak to anyone."

Boldly Joel said, "Are you suspicious of me, sir?"

"I am suspicious of everyone," Hartford replied coolly.

"I see. Well, of course, I will honor your request, Major. I would not want to be impertinent or in any way an impediment to the army."

"Come to me or my aide if you want to speak to any of the soldiers or any of the sailors. We will see that you have opportunity to do so."

Hartford tried to be amiable, but he was not convincing. He was a brilliant man, and Joel felt the cold fear of being exposed again. *This man will crucify me if he discovers I'm a spy. I've got to be careful.*

Joel did not ask Hartford's help. Instead, he disguised himself as an old sick beggar. It was simple enough. He easily obtained some ragged old clothes, including a hat that came far down over his face. He hobbled along on a crutch and was able to visit the wharf many times without raising any suspicion. He identified himself as no more than Old Thomas, and the sailors soon grew accustomed to him.

He found, to his surprise, that he was able to pick up more information this way than in a direct interview. The soldiers and sailors had been suspicious of any man well dressed in the company of the officers and were not completely honest with him. But they would say anything to an old beggar. For the most part, he just listened to their talk.

Early one afternoon he had been on the docks all day, sitting there as the sailors loitered around the shore, waiting for passage back to the ship. One of the workers named John was talking, and Joel moved closer as the man rattled off a series of speculations.

"I hear we'll be pulling out," one of the soldiers said, a tall, raw-boned man with a face caved in from the lack of teeth. "We're loadin' too quickly."

"I thought Howe would take his men by land," another soldier said, a short, chubby man younger than the other. "You always know what's gonna happen, don't ya, John?"

"I know when we're loadin' stores, which is more than you do, Frederick," the tall man said.

"You think the army will be comin' on board soon?"

"Watch what I'm tellin' ya. They'll be on in a few days."

Joel was so engrossed with what he was hearing that he was not aware that someone had come up to stand beside him.

"What's your name?"

Moving very painfully, Joel turned around—and stopped dead still. Before him stood Major Lawrence Hartford and one of his aides.

"What are you doing here on the dock?" he demanded.

"Just trying to beg a bit of money for a bit of food, sir." Joel's voice was whiny and sounded like a very old man. He had smeared his face with dirt and wore an old gray wig down in strands about his neck. He was stooped over now, and he let his hands tremble, as if he had delirium or palsy.

"You have nothing better to do than sit around like this?"

"Surely you don't suspect this old man, sir," the aide said quickly.

"Why not? Every American is a spy. We can't make a move without someone's running to Washington."

"Do you want me to arrest him, sir?"

"Yes, lock him up for a day. See if you can get something out of him," Hartford said, eying the old man with suspicion.

Joel did not protest as he was led away by Hartford's aide. He spent the afternoon and the night in a musty jail cell, but after a rather cursory set of questions, the aide gave up. "Let him go," he said the next morning. "He's nothing but an old beggar."

Joel hobbled out into the street, and the fear of discovery that had built up in him left as he hobbled away. He made his way back to the house, and as he entered, Vandermeer stared at him.

"What in heaven's name are you dressed up for, Joel?"

Caught in the act, Joel could only grin. "Doing a little undercover work. I thought I'd go out among the people and see how generous they were." He jingled some change in his pocket. "I made nearly a day's wages just holding my cup out." It was a feeble excuse, and he saw by the look on Vandermeer's face that the Dutchman did not believe him. "Well, it was just a thought, Jan. I thought if I disguised myself I could find out how people really feel about this war. These Americans aren't going to say much to a British newspaperman, are they, now?"

Vandermeer did not answer and Joel went at once to his room. He cleaned his face, and as he washed and shaved, he thought, *I've got to be more careful. Even Jan might betray me if he knew what I was really doing.*

12

Too Much Romance

AS SOON AS LYNA LEE BRADFORD saw the face of her oldest son, she knew that some sort of conflict was coming. He had entered the parlor where she and her husband, Leslie, were sitting, and both of them looked up without a great deal of interest. Now, however, Lyna rose at once and went to stand beside Clive, who stood before them, his face tense. "What is it, Clive? What's the matter?"

"I've got to talk to you—both of you."

At once Leslie rose and came to stand by his wife. He was not quite as quick as Lyna at reading their children, but now he saw the disturbed expression on Clive's face and repeated the question. "Is it some kind of trouble, son?"

Clive managed a smile. "You always could see through me, couldn't you? I never could hide anything from either one of you." Noting their anxiety, he said quickly, "Oh, it's nothing very terrible. As a matter of fact, I don't think it's bad news at all."

Instantly Lyna made a sudden judgment. "It's about Katherine, isn't it?"

Surprise washed across Clive's face. "Got it the first time, Mother." There was a rueful expression in his eyes, and he said, "I've been thinking about her so much, and I've come to a decision." He threw his shoulders back and looked at them as if he expected an argument. His voice, however, was firm as he said, "I can't lose the only woman I'll ever love. I'm going to ask her to marry me."

Leslie Gordon glanced at his wife in surprise, but he saw that Clive's announcement was something she had been expecting. He said tentatively, "I suppose you know the difficulties?"

"Because we're on the wrong side of this horrible war? I've tried to

161

think of some way to straddle the fence, but there really isn't any, is there?"

Lyna said quietly, "It won't make any difference in the way we feel about you, and you know very well that we think Katherine's a wonderful woman—very strong and godly as well." She put her arms up and pulled Clive down and kissed him, then stepped back, saying, "You always were a stubborn child, but in this case I think you're right."

Surprisingly Leslie Gordon nodded. "I think you're right, too, son. The love between a man and a woman is a precious thing. I haven't had much of this world's goods, but I have had a good wife." He reached over and pulled Lyna close and smiled down at her, then lifted his eyes to meet those of Clive. "Whatever you do we'll be behind you, son."

"Not everyone will feel that way, I'm afraid. She probably won't have me anyway." He was thinking, however, of the letter he had received from her. She said she had missed him and signed it with love. "I've got hopes, and I've got to go to her at once."

"When will you leave, and how soon will you marry?"

"As soon as she'll have me, but it'll be easier now that I have your blessing."

"Go to her, then, and may God give you good success," Lyna said. She kissed him again, and he turned and left the room.

"What do you really think of this, Leslie?" she asked quietly after Clive left.

"It'll mean trouble, I suppose, but if they truly love each other, it'll work out. I don't want to let it be a barrier between us and Katherine. She is a lovely young woman with a fine Christian character. We couldn't have asked for a better daughter-in-law." He grinned at Lyna suddenly and put his arms around her. "So now I'm going to be married to a potential grandmother. Somehow that makes me feel very old." He bent and kissed her, saying, "You don't feel like a grandmother. You don't kiss like one either."

"You flatterer!" Lyna laughed. She held herself against him for a moment and then laid her head on his chest. She did not speak, nor did he, but both of them knew that the road ahead for their family would never be the same.

T　　　　T　　　　T

David Gordon found his sister, Grace, in the kitchen setting out a pan of cookies from the fireplace. Deftly he reached out and picked up one of them just in time to catch a slap on his hands. He laughed and said, "A man that won't suffer a little for a good cookie doesn't amount to much."

"You leave those cookies alone, David. They're not for you!"

"Who are they for—Stephen?"

"Some of them." She put the cookies down and began packing them in a small basket, covering them with a white cloth. Grace turned to him and said, "Clive's leaving tomorrow morning. I'm worried about him."

"He'll be all right." David took another bite of the cookie, chewed it thoughtfully, and said, "These aren't as good as usual. I think they need more spice or something."

"Then you don't have to eat any more! What do you think about Clive and Katherine getting married?"

"Why, I suppose it'll be all right. I like Katherine a great deal."

"So do I, but they're so different."

David gave her an odd look and popped the rest of the cookie in his mouth. Between chews he answered, "You and Stephen are different, too."

Surprised by his remark, Grace looked over at her younger brother. She was wearing a blue dress with a white apron, and her dark honey-colored hair was pulled back, tied behind her head. "What do you mean we're different?" she asked quickly. Her gray-green eyes looked troubled at his question. "What do you mean by that?" she demanded.

"Why, I just mean you're different. He's a poet, I suppose, and you're not."

This is not what David meant and Grace well knew it. She had agreed to marry Stephen and they had set the date. Although she kept it well hidden, some sort of dissatisfaction or doubt still lingered within her. It made her feel disloyal to Stephen, and she had not said a word of her doubts to her mother or father. Although she was nineteen, two years older than her brother, they had grown up together and were very close. Now she went over and sat down on the chair, folded her hands, and looked down at them. "I don't know why you'd say a thing like that," she said quietly.

Sensitive to changes in people's moods, David went over to her at once, pulled up a chair, and sat down beside her. "To be truthful, I just don't think he's . . . well, strong enough for you, Grace."

"Strong? What do you mean by that?"

"Oh, I don't mean physically, although he's not physically very strong, is he? I mean the other kind of strong—the kind you are." He hesitated, and when she looked up at him, he said evenly, "You're one of the strongest women I know, Grace. I've always thought so, even when we were children. I could always come to you, and you would always help, no matter what it was. You have some sort of inner strength that most people don't have."

Confused, Grace shook her head. "I don't know what you mean by that. I'm no different from anyone else."

"Yes, you are." David had given a great deal of thought to his sister's marriage, and now he said, "I hate to see you make a mistake."

"You mean you think marrying Stephen is a mistake?" His words came almost as a blow to her, for they echoed the thin doubt that had been running through her mind. "I don't like to hear you say that!"

But David seemed to sense the struggle that was going on in Grace's heart. "You've had some doubts about this, haven't you? Otherwise you wouldn't be listening to me like this." He reached over and took her hand and held it for a moment. "Don't be in a hurry, Grace. Stephen's a good man, but . . . well, his brother, he's the kind you need."

"Why, Jubal's just a roughneck."

"Jubal's pretty rough, all right, but you're pretty rough yourself under that nice, pretty, smooth exterior of yours." He grinned as she glanced at him with indignation. "I can remember a few times when you piled into me just as if you were a boy, and gave good account of yourself, too."

"That was when I was a child!"

"No, it wasn't. And that fight's still there in you. You want more out of life than Stephen does."

"What are you talking about, David? You're not making any sense."

"But this is how I feel, Grace. Stephen is *safe*. I guess that's the way to put it. He's got money, he always wears the right kind of clothes, always says the proper thing, he's highly educated, but maybe that's what's wrong. He's too perfect."

"And I'm not! Is that it?" Grace said, the irritation evident in her voice.

"Don't be mad, Grace."

"I'm not angry, but I don't want to hear you talk about Stephen like this anymore." Grace rose suddenly. Agitation swept through her, but she kept a smooth demeanor as she said, "You're just too young to understand these things, David. I love Stephen and we're going to get married. And we're going to be very happy!"

David sat there as she swept out of the room. He was greatly disturbed, for he realized that Grace was not at all certain about her decision to marry Stephen Morrison. "I'm going to talk to Mother about this, but she probably already knows it. She knows everything about us."

He rose and went in search of his mother, and after a short talk with her, he felt even more frustrated.

Lyna Lee simply said to him, "Don't meddle with these things, David. She's nineteen years old and a grown woman, and Stephen is a good man."

"Well, I just don't feel right about it, that's all."

Lyna said nothing more to Leslie, but the next morning when he took Clive down to catch the coach for Boston, she waited until the pair were gone and then said to David, who was standing close beside her, "Remember, don't you say anything at all to Grace to disturb her."

David turned and studied his mother's face. At the age of forty-five, she was still a tremendously attractive woman. She was also very wise, and he whispered, "But you don't like it, do you, Mother? Tell me the truth. I won't say anything to Grace, but I'm not all wrong, am I?"

"I hope you're wrong, David. I pray to God that you are," Lyna said quietly.

As she turned and left David standing there, he knew in his heart that something was wrong. *I wish I could talk to Grace, but I'd better not*. He loafed around the house all morning and finally grew impatient. He had been studying under a tutor, but the tutor was ill and he had nothing to do.

"I think I'll go over and see our cousin, Joel," he announced to his mother.

"All right. Here, I have a cake that I baked. You can take some of it to them. Those two bachelors will probably fight over it."

Bearing the small basket, David left the house. He was in no hurry and had no real mission as far as Joel Bradford was concerned. He liked the young man, and during the brief time he had been in New York, they had become good acquaintances, if not firm friends.

As he moved along the street, he saw a young woman come out of a shop and called out at once, "Miss Reed, how are you today?"

"Oh, David! How are you?" Heather stopped to smile at the young man. "What are you up to?"

"I'm just going over to visit Joel and that artist fellow he lives with." A thought came to him, and he said, "Come along if you've nothing better to do."

Heather Reed was a woman of strong impulses who often made decisions quickly. Now she thought suddenly of the kiss she had shared with Joel Bradford at the ball. She had not seen him since, and a curious streak took her. "All right," she said. "I'll go with you. Is it far?"

"Not at all. Just a good walk. Come along."

She took his arm, and as they strolled along, David mentioned that Clive was leaving for Boston.

Heather gave him a quick look. "Is he going to stay there permanently?"

"I'm not sure." David did not want to discuss family business, so he said nothing that would reveal Clive's real purpose. Instead, they talked about unimportant things until they arrived at the boardinghouse. "This is where he lives," he said. "I don't know if they're here. Don't be shocked about Jan. He's an artist and quite outspoken."

As they walked up to the door, it was opened before David had a chance to knock. Mrs. Johnson, the landlady, stood there with a broom in her hands looking at them.

"Hello, Mrs. Johnson. We've come to visit Mr. Vandermeer and Mr. Bradford."

"Yes, they're both at home," she said and gave the young woman a harsh scrutiny. "I have rules here about women visitors," she said. "I want nothing but propriety here."

"Oh, you shall have it. This is Miss Reed, a prominent citizen," David said quickly. He gave Heather a secret wink, adding, "You are in favor of propriety, aren't you, Miss Reed?"

"Oh, one can't have too much propriety, I say. Why don't you come with us, Mrs. Johnson? Then you can hear things better that way. In case there's any lack of propriety, you will be right there to put a stop to it."

Mrs. Johnson knew she was being ridiculed. She sniffed and turned away without another word.

"Nosy old woman!" David grumbled. "Well, come on, they live on the second floor."

Climbing the stairs, Heather wondered if she was doing the right thing, but she was curious about Jan Vandermeer. She had heard of him from some of her friends. They called him the crazy artist. She justified her visit by saying, "I've never known an artist before. It should be an interesting experience."

The door opened at David's first knock and Joel stood there. Shock washed over his face as he saw Heather, and David simply brushed by him, saying, "We've come for a visit. Hello, Joel . . . Mr. Vandermeer. I have a lady here who would like to meet you."

Jan Vandermeer was sitting on top of the table eating a large sandwich in alternate bites along with a white onion in the other hand. He put both of them down at once, wiped his hands on the stained full shirt that came down to his knees, and moved over to the door. A pleasant smile spread over his round face, and he bowed as he came and stood before Heather.

"Allow me to introduce Miss Heather Reed, Jan," David said.

"Ah, Miss Reed, I am so happy you should come for a visit." Humor twinkled in his eyes, and he said, "Suppose I send these two barbarians away, and you and I can talk about the beauties of art?"

"None of that, Jan," David laughed. "We met Mrs. Johnson downstairs. She's very concerned about the virtues of propriety. So we must be careful to abide to all that is proper."

"Proper? I'm always proper!" Vandermeer snorted. "Here, come and sit down, Miss Reed. Would you care for some tea? Perhaps a sandwich? Ve have fresh cucumber sandwiches."

"Why, that would be very nice, Mr. Vandermeer," Heather said.

"Joel, you fix the tea. I will fix the sandwiches." Vandermeer at once created a small furor of activity, making a big production out of fixing the sandwiches and directing the making of the tea. He cleared off the table by the simple means of swiping everything away with one forearm, and then said, "Sit in this chair. I think it is the safest."

Amused at the Dutchman, Heather sat down and allowed him to exert his hospitality. She did not look at Joel, but she was well aware that he felt somehow uncomfortable with her unexpected presence. Surprising him in this way gave her a sense of impious satisfaction, and finally, when Vandermeer ran downstairs for a moment, she turned and said, "I haven't seen you since the ball, Mr. Bradford."

David saw Joel's face flush slightly and knew her question implied more than ordinary politeness.

"Why, no, I've been rather busy."

"It was a fine ball, wasn't it? And we should have more of them."

"I couldn't agree more," Joel said. He caught the hidden smile on the face of David Gordon and now saw Vandermeer's eyes also fixed on him with avid curiosity. He sat down, along with David, and the two ate sandwiches and drank tea, and Vandermeer, as might be expected, prattled on and on about art. He had strong opinions, and no one disagreed with any of his theories.

When there seemed to be a break in the conversation, Heather said, "How do you stand in the struggle for freedom in this country, Mr. Vandermeer?"

"I'm an artist, not a politician!"

"Still," she said, sipping at her cup, "you must have some ideas about the justice of it."

"You ask me what side I'm on? Yah, I'm on the side of—" He hesitated, then pronounced with a laugh, "I'm on the side of art!"

"That won't do," Heather said. "We all like art, music, and painting, but this is a matter of the freedom of people to live their lives as they choose."

"I live my life as I choose already, Miss Reed. I always have and vill continue to do so. In England, in Holland. I do exactly what I please."

Heather then launched into an argument proving that he did not do as he pleased, for he was under the laws of the land. At one point she grew so vehement in her opinion that finally she turned to David and said, "I'm sorry, David, I didn't mean to say ill things about your country."

"No offense, Miss Reed," David grinned. "I've heard much worse from some of the citizens of New York—some of your friends, no doubt. I know you feel strongly about this."

A thought came to him and without meaning to, he said, "It brings all kinds of problems, this Revolution." He turned to Joel and said, "Clive left for Boston today. He's going to see Katherine." As soon as he said this he bit his lip, for he had not meant to mention Clive, and he only hoped that the subject would drop. But it did not.

Joel asked at once with interest, "Is he going to ask Miss Yancy to marry him?"

David struggled for a moment, then saw that he was trapped. "I think he is going to talk to her," he said weakly.

"Who is this Miss Yancy your brother is going to see?" Vandermeer asked. He listened as David explained.

"She's a young woman who is strongly in favor of the Revolution. They have been in love for some time, but now it seems that Clive is going to simply ignore the difficulties."

"I don't think it will work," Heather said. "I don't know the young woman, but a husband and wife have to be one."

"Do you mean," Joel asked quickly, "that you don't think a man and a woman can ever disagree?"

"About small things yes, but this isn't a small thing."

"But my uncle, Daniel Bradford, my mother's brother, he's on the side of the Revolution, and my mother's married to an English officer. They still love each other."

"She's going her own way here in New York with her husband, and he's going his way in Boston with his family. They don't live together and have to face life together day to day."

"You have strong ideas about marriage, don't you, Miss Reed?" Vandermeer asked.

"Of course!" she said rather forcefully.

"Well, I have strong ideas myself, and I say that if a man and woman really love each other, they can overcome anything."

Despite herself, Heather smiled at the Dutchman. She found herself liking him. There was an openness about him that was rare. Perhaps it was the fact that he was an artist or, perhaps, just the fact that he was who he was. She said, "Are you married, Mr. Vandermeer?"

"No, alas not."

"Have you ever been married?"

"Me, Jan Vandermeer? Never!"

"There you are," David said with triumph. "You don't know anything about it, Jan."

"I am infallible in matters of the heart!" Jan Vandermeer snapped indignantly at David. He turned to Heather and said, "I have not been married, but I have been in love many times."

"If you were in love, why didn't you marry?" Heather asked.

Jan Vandermeer was seldom bested in an argument. Usually when he ran out of logic he could outshout his opponent, but there was a quiet intensity in this young woman and such steady honesty in her green eyes that he stuttered and stammered.

Finally she said, "You really didn't love them at all, I think, Mr. Vandermeer. If you ever do love a woman, you'll know that you have to give up some things to marry her."

"You are a very wise young woman, Miss Reed," Vandermeer said almost humbly. But his spirit rose again, and he said, "Perhaps ve had better talk about art. Maybe I know more about that than I do about romance."

"I think there's too much romance in the world and not enough love." Heather said this without thinking and flushed as she saw the men looking at her strangely. "What I mean by that is," she corrected herself hurriedly, "there are lots of romances—novels and dramas and such—but they never face up to the fact that life is very hard and that when two people tie themselves to each other, they had better be certain they are really one in every way."

Jan Vandermeer was watching Joel's face as Heather spoke. He saw something flicker in the young man's eyes. *Ah, this fellow is interested in Miss Reed. I will have to find out about it.*

Soon Heather stood, saying, "It's been a very nice visit, but I must go now."

"I too," David said.

The two said their good-byes, and when they were outside the room, Vandermeer said, "You have not known Miss Reed long, have you, Joel?"

"Why no. Just since I came to New York. About as long as I've known you."

"A very pretty young woman, is she not?"

"Very pretty indeed. And she comes from a fine family, too."

Vandermeer talked for some time, trying to draw Joel out, but he had discovered this was almost impossible. There was some sort of wall built around young Bradford that he could not penetrate, and when Joel left on one of his mysterious excursions, he went and stood before the canvas he was working on. He picked up a brush and dipped it into the paint but did not apply it. He turned and went to the window and stared out at the street below where Joel was just disappearing.

"He is a very strange young man, I say. Everybody in the world is caught up in the war, and somehow he is, too, although I cannot find out why. And he is interested in Miss Heather Reed, who is an ardent patriot, while he himself has been tarred and feathered by people of that persuasion." He carefully applied a dab of yellow paint, stared at it, then finally shook his head. "What sort of man is this I have let come into my house? He vill bear vatching. . . ."

As Joel made his way along the streets, he found himself unable to forget Heather's words about marriage. *She has strong feelings*, he thought, *but I knew that. She'd never change them for anybody, I don't believe.* He made his way down through the streets and could not stop thinking about Heather Reed. Nor could he forget how he had kissed her and how she had yielded to it. He had not forgotten that embrace, and now it came to him that he must forget about that moment. "This war might go on for years," he muttered. "I'll just have to put her out of my mind." Trying to forget her, he knew, would be more difficult than anything he had ever done. Somehow, she had stirred his heart more than any other woman he had ever known.

PART THREE

BLOOD ON THE BRANDYWINE

Summer 1777

13

A Troubled Woman

AS THE YEAR 1777 WORE ON, General William Howe became more and more frustrated. No matter how many battles he won against the rebel Americans, it apparently did little good. He had beaten the Americans at Long Island only to see them escape to Manhattan. After thrashing them thoroughly at that spot, they had retreated to White Plains. When he had driven them out of New York altogether, they had fled to New Jersey, and then after being driven out of New Jersey, they survived in Pennsylvania.

The British had captured so many American prisoners they could not accommodate them all. No matter how many they captured, or how many were killed, new American soldiers seemed to spring out of the ground. Howe was constantly hearing that the American Revolution was on the edge of collapse—yet wherever he turned, he still faced an American army in the field! It was a tattered, worn group of men wearing rags, some of them even without shoes, but the army with Washington at its head was still there. This sort of perseverance was completely outside the experience of the British, especially of General Howe. The more they tried to destroy the enemy, the more of a nation it became.

Howe himself was opposed to the Revolution and had been against encouraging the participation of their Indian allies along the frontiers—the Creeks and Cherokees in the south, and the Iroquois in the north. He was also appalled at the behavior of the Hessians along the seacoast, for he well understood that loyalist support in all of these areas dwindled with every new strike of the Indians and the Hessians. To Howe's disgust, the more the British did, the worse the situation became!

And if General Howe was discouraged and confused, so were his fellow Englishmen back in his homeland. War was fought at tremendous cost. After the Battle of Trenton, Howe had sent off a message demanding an additional twenty thousand troops to end the war. It was the familiar cry of generals, "I am winning the war! Send me more men!"

To make matters worse, France and Spain were waiting in the wings, rubbing their hands together, so to speak. Sixteen more ships of the line had to be commissioned because of the success of the American privateers. As the national debt rose at home in England, the speaker of the house lectured the king and the cabinet on the need for better financial arrangements.

But whatever was attempted by England's Parliament or by General William Howe, nothing seemed to change. As the days wore on, money continued to be poured into the effort to equip and send soldiers thousands of miles from home. Meanwhile, the Americans would fade back into the endless forest and mountains of the enormous continent, only to rise again like a phoenix from the ashes at the start of the next battle.

At this exact point in history, a new act began to unfold in the American Revolution. General John Burgoyne, debonair, handsome, and well connected, saw this time in history as his hour. He submitted to the government "THOUGHTS FOR CONDUCTING THE WAR," all written in capital letters, exactly the way Burgoyne spoke. He proposed a pinchers movement: He would lead a force down from Canada on the Lake Champlain-Hudson route to Albany. When Burgoyne's expedition was underway, General William Howe would proceed up the Hudson. The two would meet at Albany, the New England Colonies would be cut off, and the Revolution would collapse!

No one in the British Parliament, or anywhere else, for that matter, ever examined the plan too carefully. They were desperate, and because no other plan was offered, Burgoyne got his way. As always in these complicated maneuvers, one or more elements seemed to break down. In this case, it was a set of orders to General William Howe that caused the failure of Gentleman John Burgoyne. The orders to General William Howe from London were not clear. In his memoirs, he explained that the choice was left up to him as to the time and method of his part of the plan. This was a real weakness, because Burgoyne's plan called for split-second timing, and when Howe was left to make his own decisions, disaster for the British cause lay dead ahead.

Howe basically ignored Burgoyne and formed his own plan to lure Washington out of his hill fortress in Morristown into open battle on level ground. He knew he could destroy him and end the rebellion. By late May, Howe had eighteen thousand disciplined and well-equipped regulars, and Washington had managed to gather nine thousand largely untrained troops at Morristown.

Then began what amounted to a military minuet. Howe would march out and try to trap Washington. Washington would get word from his spies that the British were coming. He would shift his troops, so that when the British arrived they found no Continentals to attack. This occurred over and over. Finally Howe gave up and decided they needed another plan. Though no one knew where this new strategy would come from, something would have to be done. The Revolution was on the razor's edge. Sooner rather than later, Howe would have to make a move, and General George Washington would have to counter it.

♗ ♗ ♗

"Now then, Ezra, you must eat more of this good broth I've brought. I made it especially for you."

Katherine Yancy had arrived at the rooms of the Tyrones bearing a bowl of broth, some freshly baked bread, and some small cakes. She now sat down across from Ezra, who was propped up in bed, and she smiled, despite the fact that she was very concerned with Ezra Tyrone's poor appearance.

"It was good of you to come, Katherine." Leah Tyrone, large and swollen with child, tried to smile at her husband. "Here, let me feed you a little bit of this."

Ezra Tyrone opened his mouth obediently as his wife fed him the hot broth. He had eaten no more than half a dozen swallows when he shook his head and muttered, "No more, Leah. I can't get it down." Tyrone's face was shrunken so that his head looked almost like a skull. His eyes were sunken, and the flesh had shriveled, giving him a skeletal appearance. He had taken to his bed a week before, finding it impossible to stay up. During that time Marian Bradford and Katherine Yancy had made daily visits to bring food and to try to encourage the couple.

Now Katherine forced a smile. "Well, you can have it later, Ezra." She rose and moved over to the cabinet where she began examining the shelves for stores. Food had not been a big problem, for Marian had brought more than was necessary. The spring had brought warm weather, and now as she looked out the window and saw the white clouds rolling in a leisurely fashion across the bright blue sky, she felt a pang. Somehow she knew Ezra Tyrone would not survive to see another spring. *Perhaps not even fall. I've never seen a man go down so quickly.*

She remembered Clive Gordon's warning that Ezra could go very quickly, and now Katherine bit her lip nervously as she glanced over at the couple.

Leah was seated beside her husband holding his hand, a tremulous smile on her lips. She was so young and had known little happiness in life, and now she hung on to her husband's hand as if she could keep him from falling more deeply into his sickness by her strength of will. She whispered, "You'll be better soon, Ezra."

"That I will, lass," Ezra whispered. He knew better, for he realized that each day he was growing weaker. Now he looked at his wife's strained face and said, "You've been the sweetest thing ever to come into my life, Leah. I never knew what it was to have love until you came."

Tears filled Leah's eyes, and she held on to his hand tightly with both of hers. She tried to speak but her throat was tight, and when she bent over, hot tears fell on Ezra's hand.

"Now then, don't worry about me," he said wearily. "What will happen to you and the child when it comes? How can I take care of you?"

"We'll make out," Leah said in a strained voice. She had already spent many nights lying in bed wondering what would happen to her when he was gone, but she had never voiced them to Ezra. Now she dashed the tears away quickly. "We'll have us a fine boy. You'll see. What would you think to name him?"

"How about Melchizedek?" Little enough humor was left in Ezra Tyrone, but he was rewarded by a laugh from his wife as he sank back and whispered, "I'll think on it, wife."

Katherine did not remain long at the Tyrones. She was very concerned about both of them, so she prayed with Leah, as had become her habit. Leah had given her heart to the Lord, but Ezra felt himself to be too wicked. As Katherine finished her prayer, she said, "We'll keep on praying for Ezra. We'll see him come to Jesus."

"Do you believe it, Katherine?"

Looking down at the face so youthful and so vulnerable, Katherine said, "I've claimed Ezra for God. We'll see him enter into the glory of God. Mind what I say."

After saying good-bye to her friends, Katherine moved down the stairs. She stopped in long enough to give a report to Abigail, who had shared in the nursing, and to spend a few moments with Esther Denham. The three women all felt the burden of the sick man and his pregnant wife, and though they did not speak of it now, they were wondering how things would turn out for them. They comforted one another with the assurance that God in His mercy would take care of the Tyrones.

Finally Abigail walked out to the porch and accompanied Katherine to the front gate. "Have you heard anything from Clive?" she asked.

She knew that Katherine was in love with Clive Gordon, and he with her. Although her own life was incomplete and fragmented, Abigail was anxious to see this young woman find her way. This was new for Abigail Howland, for she had not cared about a single soul except herself for years. Now as she stood there speaking quietly with Katherine, she found this desire for another's well-being and happiness amazing. Suddenly she was filled with gratitude that she had found her way to God even though it had cost her the man she loved—Matthew Bradford.

"I did get a letter last week," Katherine admitted. She did not want to talk about Clive, not even to Abigail with whom she had become very close. She shrugged her shoulders and turned away, saying quickly, "I'll be back tomorrow, Abigail. Is there anything I could bring, do you think, for you or the Tyrones?"

"No, I think we have everything, thank you."

Katherine said good-bye and made her way along the street. She passed by a group of sparrows fighting and scrambling in the dust over a piece of bread and a thought came to her. *The poet said, if the birds in their nest agree, so should we. It doesn't look like those birds agree with anything except getting their own.* She passed by the sparrows, her steps going slowly, her thoughts on Clive Gordon. She was a deeply troubled woman, for she loved a man she knew she could never have. Her thoughts went to him and she seemed to see him in her mind's eye, six feet three, long and lean with reddish hair and cornflower blue eyes. She remembered how she had met him for the first time when she had been desperately trying to save her father and her uncle from dying as prisoners of war in a cold and filthy hold of a British hulk. It was a good memory, for if it had not been for Clive Gordon, she knew her father would have perished there. Unfortunately, her uncle had died there, the rescue coming too late, but now she thought of how her heart had been sick with grief when the tall young Englishman had come striding into her life.

"I never believed in romantic love very much, but it was romantic—no matter what anyone says." Katherine found herself whispering this aloud, and then as she turned to go down the street that led to the cottage she shared with her family, she thought of what life would be like if there were no Revolution, no war, just she and Clive. *He would come courting me, and bringing me flowers, and maybe even writing a love poem. I would find the prettiest dresses that I could find, and I would take great care with my hair, and all the young women would be jealous that I had such a fine-looking man, and a doctor at that! And we would go to balls, and we would be the most handsome couple there. He would take me outside in the garden, and there he would put his arms around me and steal a kiss, and I would let him do it. . . .*

Katherine suddenly shook her shoulders, and her lips went tight. "I've got to stop thinking like this," she muttered aloud. "It doesn't do any good. There are too many problems, and I'll have to go on with life without him."

She entered the house and spoke to her mother and father, telling them about how the Tyrones were doing. Then she threw herself into the work of the house. Her parents looked at each other, knowing that something was wrong. When she had gone to another room, Amos said, "Susan, she's terribly troubled about something."

"It's about that young Englishman, Clive Gordon," Susan Yancy said. A wave of pity went through her. "She can't have him, and that's breaking her heart."

☥   ☥   ☥

As Clive swung down from the sorrel stallion and glanced over at the Bradford house, he slipped into a reverie, stamping his feet on the ground to restore the circulation. He once again thought, *I'm a fool for doing this. Katherine's already told me she wouldn't have me until something changes.* He had thought this in one fashion or another on his trip all the way from New York to Boston. Still, there was something that drove him, and he knew he had to resolve the uncertainties and doubts that had been at war within him almost from the time he realized he was in love with Katherine Yancy. Now as he walked up to the Georgian-style house, he gave a casual glance, noting the hip roof and red brick chimney on each end that balanced it so well. It was a beautiful house, one he admired, but his thoughts were not on architecture. As he walked up the steps, he realized he had no plan and wondered what he would say to Daniel Bradford.

The door was opened by Cato, the butler. "Why, Mr. Gordon!" he said. A broad smile came to his lips.

When Clive had visited this house before, he had been impressed with the tall black man and with his wife, Hattie, who served as the cook. Now he found a smile and said, "Hello, Cato. Is the master in?"

"Yes, sir! He's in the study. You come in and I'll tell him you're here."

Entering the house, Gordon stood in the middle of the foyer glancing around at the paintings and the decorations that adorned the area. He had little time, however, to admire them, for a voice said, "Well, Clive, come in. I'm glad to see you."

"Hello, Uncle," Clive smiled. He had admired Daniel Bradford from the first time he had met him and now saw that no trace of worry was in the clear hazel eyes. "I suppose I'm disturbing you?"

"Not at all. Please come in. When did you get in from New York?"

"Just this moment."

"Well, you must be hungry. I'll have Hattie prepare something. I could eat a bite myself. It's almost dinnertime anyway."

Fifteen minutes later the two men were seated at a table in the small dining room just off the kitchen. Hattie stood looking over them. "There's plenty more of that fresh corn bread if you eat all that up."

"Well, if we eat all of this"—Daniel grinned at her and winked—"we'll be all right. I hope you have some more of that blackberry cobbler we had last night."

"Yes, sir, plenty of that!"

After Hattie left the room, Clive ate hungrily, listening as Daniel spoke of the foundry and the family. Finally he asked, "How's Lyna and your father?"

"Oh, they're fine."

There was something about the lackadaisical answer, or perhaps it was the contradictory tense look in Clive Gordon's eyes, that caused Daniel to give him a closer examination. "Is something wrong?" he asked. "You look worried."

"Uncle Daniel, I don't know what to do." Clive picked up a spoon and examined it thoughtfully, then put it down again. "I can't go on like this. I'm in love with Katherine Yancy, and she won't have me until this war is over—or until one of us changes our loyalties."

"Well, how much chance is there of that?"

With a startled look, Clive looked at his uncle. "Why, of her changing, none at all. She's a strong woman."

"Then I guess that leaves it up to you, Clive. How do you feel about it?"

Nervously Clive shook his head and stroked his jaw. "You know my father's never been in favor of this thing—the Revolution, I mean. I don't see any sense in it either, but a man can't change his loyalties as he changes his coat, can he?"

"He wouldn't be much of a man if he did—still, a man who doesn't change at times is pretty foolish."

"Are you telling me that I'm wrong and that I should throw myself into the Revolution? Grab a musket and go off to join Washington?"

"Don't be a fool, Clive. I didn't say anything like that! You're a grown man and a smart one, but I can't tell you what to do with your life. You've been here long enough that you must have some convictions about this war. I'd like to know what they are. You see," Daniel said quietly, "I've become quite fond of you, Clive, and of David, and of Grace. You're about the only kin I have except for Lyna."

"Well, that's kind of you to say that, Uncle Daniel, and, of course, we feel the same way about you."

"We had a hard time coming up," Daniel said thoughtfully, thinking of those early days in England when he and Lyna had struggled for survival. "Being in trouble together pulls people closer, don't you think?"

"I suppose it does." A thin smile turned the corners of his lips upward and he leaned back in his chair. "Well, I'm in trouble now and so is Katherine. We'll see if it pulls us closer together."

"Why did you come to Boston?"

"Why, to see Katherine, and to tell you that Grace is going to marry Stephen Morrison very soon."

"Well, I suppose congratulations are in order."

"Do you know Stephen Morrison?"

"No, but I know his brother, Jubal, quite well. Fine young man." He saw a troubled looked on Clive's face and asked, "What's the matter?"

"Oh nothing! I just wish Grace would put it off."

"You don't like the man she's going to marry?"

"I don't know him too well. He's a hard fellow to know, a poet and all that."

"I didn't know poets were hard to know, but then I've never known a poet."

"I'd like to meet Jubal Morrison."

"Well, that won't be hard. He's down at the shipyard working on this privateer he and my son, Sam, are going to win the war with. Come along, I'll ride down with you. . . ."

𝕋　　𝕋　　𝕋

"So Grace and Stephen are going to tie the knot." Jubal Morrison looked across at the tall young physician, his eyes questioning. Morrison was a husky man of twenty-five with rusty hair and blue-gray eyes. He had a squarish face with a scar beside the left eye, causing it to have a permanent squint. The two men were alone now, for after introducing them Daniel had gone back to the foundry.

180

"Yes, she asked me to give you this letter." Reaching into his inner pocket, Clive handed an envelope to Morrison and watched as he tore it open and read it.

"Well, I must say I'm a little surprised," Jubal said. A solemnity came to his face and he frowned. He looked up and said, "Do you know my brother well?"

"Not very well." Clive studied the other and said, "I don't know if I should say this, but I'm not much in favor of this marriage. "

"Why? Don't you like Stephen?"

"He seems to be a good man, but—" He stopped before saying what was on his mind and thrust his hands behind him. The two stood on the beach, listening to the moan of the waves coming in, as well as the sound of hammer and saw from the crew building the ships. A flight of sea birds flew overhead in a rigid formation, like soldiers on parade. Their white feathers gleamed in the brilliant summer sun, and they uttered muted cries as they sailed lower and touched the top of the waves as they glided effortlessly.

"I don't really know your brother very well, but I know my sister," Clive said soberly. A troubled look came into his eyes, and he shook his head almost in despair. "Grace is a lively girl, somewhat too lively, I think, at times. She likes to try things. She's innovative. I think she needs a man like that, and your brother is—"

"My brother is *not* like that," Jubal said quickly. "I'm not insulted. I agree with you. It would be a good marriage for him, for she's a fine woman, but I'm afraid you're right. They're not very well suited, but I fear there is nothing to do about it, though."

"No, of course not. We'll just hope for the best."

"She asked me to come to the wedding, and I suppose I will. I might get arrested for a spy."

Suddenly Clive laughed. "And I might get arrested here. If you'll look out for me while I'm in Boston, I'll speak for you when you come to New York."

"Done!" The two men suddenly laughed, and Jubal said, "Let's see more of each other. We're going to be brothers-in-law. I think that would be well."

"Fine, how about tomorrow?"

"Good! Do you have a place to stay yet?"

"No."

"Well, I'm staying at a private home. A Mrs. Stallings is my landlady. She's a widow. She has another room and she sets a good table."

"I don't know how long I'll be here, but that sounds better than an inn." He listened as Jubal Morrison gave him directions, then the two shook hands and he left. He made his way, however, not to the Stallings home, but to the Yancy place. Riding up to the front gate, he noted that the house, which was on the coast, had a clear view of the blue waters. Out past the house he saw a small cemetery, a private one no doubt, for it had no more than five or six graves. Dismounting, he tied his horse and started to advance to the porch when a voice came to him from his right. "Clive, what are you doing here?"

Turning quickly, Gordon saw Katherine, who had come from around the house. She was wearing a yellow dress with a white apron over it and a bonnet that shaded her eyes. She came to him at once and put her hands out, a glad look in her eyes. "I didn't expect you," she said. "Why didn't you tell me you were coming?"

Clive Gordon held her hands. They were strong and warm, and looking down into her face, he thought, *This is the woman for me*. He said aloud, "I didn't know I was coming myself."

"Well, come in."

"No, I want to talk to you. I suppose your parents are home?"

"Why, yes they are!" Katherine hesitated, then said, "Come out into the garden. It's quiet enough there."

The two made their way around the house and soon were standing in the midst of rows of peas and beans. Clive took in the healthy-looking squash and the small melon patch, with plump, small melons already beginning to form. They were sheltered from the house by a grapevine that was trained to follow a fence. It was, Clive thought, as close to getting her alone as he would have anytime soon. He turned to her and said, "I've come to tell you that I love you, Katherine."

"Why, Clive!" Katherine was surprised. She felt the strength of his hands on hers as he talked. Looking up at him, she admired his tall features and his lean strength. The look in his eyes was hard to avoid, and she quickly said, "You told me that when you left—but nothing has changed."

"Well, *something's* got to change, Katherine! We can't go on like this!"

"We have to. There's nothing else to do!"

"Marry me, Katherine. We'll leave here. We'll go to England."

"I can't leave here! This is my home! That's part of the problem," Katherine said. She tried to pull her hands away, but he held them tightly. "Let me go, Clive!"

"No, I won't!" He dropped her hands, put his arms around her, and pulled her close. Some restless, vague desires had stirred him and brought him all the way from New York. Now he bent his head and firmly kissed this woman he loved. He was at last living his dreams, and she was returning his kiss, not holding back. Then suddenly she pulled away and gazed at him. Her eyes had been troubled before, but now there was a warm light in them, and her face was changed in a manner he could not understand. She was a lovely form of beauty before him, and a fragrance and a melody seemed to swirl all around him. The loneliness that was always with him was suddenly insupportable, and he whispered, "Marry me, Katherine. We'll be happy."

Katherine longed to say yes, to give up the struggle that was in her. There was nothing between them now, no barrier except one that was political and that seemed far away and unimportant. She longed for him, and as she stood there, she saw that his eyes spoke of his longing. She whispered, "Oh, Clive, I wish I could . . . but I can't!"

Clive knew she was a strong woman, and there was no point in arguing with her. He smiled at her tenderly, then said, "When a man's alone, he's complete and he doesn't need anything, but when he sees the woman he loves, as I see you, he gives something to her and he never gets it back. If he's ever going to be whole again, he's got to have that woman at his side."

Listening to his words, Katherine struggled against the rising emotions that stirred in her heart. Her dark brown hair framed her face and the light sliding across it brought out a fine red tint. Her complexion was fair and smooth, though a summer darkness lay over her skin.

For a moment Katherine stood there, not knowing what else to say, and feeling her resolve slip away. She felt like a swimmer who had clung to a floating log for so long that her strength was almost gone. Now she felt herself slipping toward this man she loved. With a sudden burst of desperation, she put her hand on his chest and pushed him away. "Come along. We can't talk about this now."

"Later then?"

"Later." She had to get away to do something, to clear her mind. She said quickly, "Come and see Father and Mother, and then I want you to go see the Tyrones."

"How are they doing?"

"I can't say about Leah. I'm afraid Ezra's dying. He looks terrible. You've got to do something for him, Clive!"

⚜   ⚜   ⚜

Clive straightened up and said with a forced jovial tone, "Well, we're going to have to do something about you, Ezra."

Ezra Tyrone looked up at the tall form of Clive Gordon. He said in a raspy tone, "Not much you can do for me, I'm afraid."

"Oh, I'd not be too quick to say that."

"I've been around a long time. I feel my end has finally come." There was no plea for sympathy in Ezra Tyrone's voice, but he looked up at the doctor and said, "I don't worry about myself. It's Leah I'm worried about, and the baby that's to come."

"I'll be here to help when the baby comes," Clive assured him.

"But what will happen to them when I am gone?"

Addressing Ezra's concerns for his small family was beyond Clive Gordon's capabilities as a doctor. He saw death in the symptoms of the man that lay before him and knew there was little hope. For a moment he considered trying to give a comforting word of encouragement, but it was obvious that Ezra Tyrone knew the truth.

"It comes to all of us, Ezra," Clive said quietly. "I'll do what I can for you."

"And will you see to my wife and the baby?"

"I'll do everything I can," Clive promised.

Later, when he was outside on the way, taking Katherine back home, he said, "There's no hope. Ezra isn't going to make it."

"I think everyone knows that. He knows it himself."

"Is he a godly man?"

"No. I've witnessed to him and so has Marian, but he thinks he's been too evil for God to forgive him."

She turned her face to him and asked, "Will Leah be all right?"

"She's a small woman and the child is large. It'll be a hard birth, I'm afraid. I'm no expert in this, you understand."

"Will you be here, Clive?"

She put her hand on his arm and turned him around. She studied his face, seeing the strength that was in it, and at the same time was unable to avoid noting that his eyes were on her in the way that a man looks at the woman he loves. "I'm not asking you to stay for myself, but for them."

"I wish you'd ask me for yourself, although I'll stay for the Tyrones."

The sun was falling, for the afternoon had passed quickly, and now long shadows fell across the street from the row houses that lined it. They almost touched the pair that stood beside the white picket fence in front of a small white cottage. Inside the fence two small dogs came barking at the couple. They were not vicious, however, and came to a halt, their tongues hanging out and their tails wagging furiously.

Clive glanced at them, then dismissed them, saying, "I can't leave you, Katherine. I don't know what's going to happen to us, but somehow God in His heaven is going to give you to me."

Then Katherine Yancy, staring at him, felt a prophetic note in his words. They had been almost too low for her to hear, but she now looked up at him, and whispered, "Amen!"

14

JOEL GETS AN OFFER

THE HOT SUMMER SUN was already over the buildings that sheltered the far side of the street when Joel stepped out into the open air. Ordinarily the street would have been busy with the voices of peddlers selling their wares and the noise of carriages rumbling over the cobblestones, but this was the Sabbath, and what seemed to be a holy quietness lay over the city. Glancing around, he studied the dark smoke rising from chimneys, making lazy spirals against the blue sky. Somehow, this day was different, and for some reason it troubled him. He had returned to New York exhausted the night before, having spent several days working harder than usual to ascertain the strength of the British forces. He hated to send messages now to Edmund Dante saying nothing new, but that was all that was possible. Everyone knew the troops were moving—but for some reason no one knew where.

"I don't even think Howe knows where he's going," Joel muttered as he turned and moved slowly along the street. A carriage rattled along, carrying a group of British officers who looked as if they had spent the night carousing. Their faces were pale and two of them were so exhausted their chins rested on their chests. The other two kept themselves upright, and one of them turned a sour-looking face on Joel, then turned back.

Those officers are as tired of playing games as I am, Joel thought. *It's a good thing for General Washington that Howe doesn't listen to Colonel Gordon. If given the chance, Gordon would attack in a minute and it would all be over.* Shaking his head, Joel wondered, as did many others, what kept Howe from moving. Some had decided it was cowardice, others that it was the charms of Mrs. Loring, and still others thought he was just lazy and loved his pleasure more than he loved his military profession.

Church bells chimed, making a silver melody in the distance, and the sound seemed to strike at Joel. He lifted his head and listened carefully. He was not far from the church where Reverend Hooks preached, and the impulse seized him to go and investigate. Quickening his pace, he soon joined others who were headed toward the gray stone building with the towering spire. Sunlight caught the cross on the top of it, radiating brilliant flashes as Joel glanced up, and he wondered at his own motives as he ascended the steps. Passing through the door, he looked around and realized guiltily that he was looking for Heather Reed. He saw her seated by her parents, as usual, and almost turned and left. He knew she would have little welcome for him. He had seen her three times recently, and each time her demeanor toward him had been colder. He had no doubt this was due to the fact that she had read one of the articles that had been printed in a London newspaper. Joel had been shocked when it had actually happened. When he saw his name at the top and read the article—which had been written by Edmund Dante, not himself—he could scarcely believe it. The article was fierce and vitriolic, striking out against the Colonists as a confused group of rebellious subjects, traitors one and all. The whole tone of the article had glorified General Howe and the British forces in America in their attempt to squelch the Revolution. Joel hated the article, yet he knew there would be more to follow. Heather had mentioned it one time. She had said, "I read the article you wrote for the London newspaper." She had said no more, but the tone of her voice and the hard look in her ordinarily soft eyes had silenced Joel.

Straightening his back, Joel made his decision. *If she doesn't want me to sit by her, she can tell me to leave.* Making his way down the aisle, he paused by the side of the pew. When she looked up, surprise washed across her face. "May I join you, Miss Reed?"

"Certainly." Her voice was clipped, short, and offered no warmth or welcome. Nevertheless, Joel sat down and spoke quietly to Mr. and Mrs. Reed, who returned his greeting also with extremely formal looks. Joel had expected nothing more, and as the service began, he wondered, *Why do I let myself in for this? Am I so in love that I don't have sense enough to keep from getting hurt?*

During the song service Joel joined in the singing, and Heather, once again, was impressed at what a clear, strong voice he had. He held the small book steadily so that she could share it with him, and she saw that his hands were strong and capable. Once she shot a quick, curious glance at his face and studied him as his eyes were on the book. A pale scar ran down his right cheek to his chin, and she wondered where he got it. His thick blond hair was merely clubbed in the back and needed a good trimming.

Why does he come here? she thought, looking quickly back as he turned to face her. She was embarrassed and kept her eyes fixed on the book for the rest of the song service. When they sat down his shoulder brushed hers, and she wondered if it was intentional. He was attracted to her, she was certain of that. What actually troubled her more than this was the fact that she was finding herself spending far too much time thinking of this young man. He was handsome enough, and ordinarily she would have been interested in him, but his political views and the terrible article she had read had caused her to harden her heart. She sat back and kept her eyes fixed on the minister, Reverend Abiram Hooks, who rose, gave his robes a shake, then began to read from the Scripture.

Joel had become interested in the Scripture, especially since listening to the Reverend Hooks. He found himself liking the man's directness and his simplicity. Hooks had eyes that were like gun barrels when he would train them on people, and Joel well knew the pastor had singled him out for special attention. He had greeted Joel twice before and questioned him briefly as to his name and ferreted out that he was not married. He had welcomed Joel back, and the last time they had met, he had said without warning, "I see in your eyes that you do not know the Lord, but I will pray for you, young man, that He will find you quickly."

Joel had been shocked at the man's bold statement, but he had learned that despite the rather vitriolic tone of some of Hook's sermons, the man had a genuine shepherd's heart for his hearers. Compassion was a thing that could not be hid in a man, and Joel recognized it in Reverend Hooks.

Reverend Hooks preached on death, choosing for his subject the text from Hebrews, " 'It is appointed unto a man once to die, but after this the judgment.' " He began building a foundation by making it absolutely clear that no man, woman, or child was exempt from this summons.

Joel listened with an outward composure, but inwardly something about the way Hooks presented death frightened him. The minister continued his sermon by saying, "And death is forever. What I am when death comes for me, I must be forever. When my spirit goes, if God finds me hymning His praise, I shall hymn it in heaven. If He finds me breathing out curses, I shall follow up those curses in hell. Where death leaves me, judgment finds me. As I die, so shall I live eternally."

Somehow these words sent a chill through Joel Bradford. He had thought of death as every thinking man does, but it seemed far off, somewhere out in a dim and distant future. Now, however, it seemed very real, and he felt himself shrinking within himself as the preacher cried out, "It is forever, forever, forever!"

Finally the sermon came to an end, and the Reverend Hooks looked over the congregation and lifted both his hands. "Let each of you ask himself the question, 'Am I prepared to meet my Maker face-to-face?' Let each one ask himself, 'Am I prepared if I shall be called to die?' "

The church was deathly quiet, and yet Joel seemed to hear his own heart beating stronger and stronger until it sounded like the thumping of a distant drum. The pounding sounded along his veins and seemed to explode in his brain with a series of tiny concussions.

Finally the preacher said, "There is perhaps one in this building who has been here before. He has heard the Gospel of Jesus Christ, of His death on the cross, and it is my prayer that even now as he listens to this gospel again, he may yield his heart up. For whosoever believeth on the name of the Lord Jesus Christ shall be saved. Let everyone that heareth say come. Whosoever thirsts let him come and let him take the water of life freely."

Joel did not hear the rest of the closing words. His hands were trembling and his brow was damp with sweat. He took out a handkerchief, mopped it, and saw that Heather Reed was watching him carefully. He wondered, *Does she know what I'm feeling at this time, but then how could she know?*

When he stepped out of the pew and followed the Reeds out, he found Reverend Hooks waiting for him and wished he could slip by unnoticed. But Hooks reached out and took his hand, grasping it strongly. He said nothing for a moment, but then he said so quietly that those close could not hear, "God is speaking to your heart. See that you refuse not Him that speaketh, young man."

The pastor's solemn words shook Joel even more, for the man seemed to read his heart and his mind. He nodded, hurried on out, and to his surprise found the Reeds waiting for him.

"Perhaps you would care to join us for a light lunch," Mr. Reed said.

"Why . . . that would be most enjoyable, Mr. Reed!"

Joel never understood whether Mr. Reed had said this on his own, or whether Heather had asked him to. As they walked toward the Reeds' home Joel found himself in step with Heather. She was very quiet, and after a while, Joel said, "I'm afraid I have troubled you, Miss Reed."

"Of course not." Heather's tone was brief, but she turned and said, "I'm not in the best of moods today. We received bad news."

Surprised, Joel said, "I'm sorry to hear it! Is it something I might know?"

Ordinarily Heather would not have spoken what was so heavily upon her heart to this man, but there seemed to be no harm in it. "It's my sister. She is married to a man in Philadelphia and she's very close to her time."

Joel asked quietly, "Is there a problem, Heather?"

Heather turned and her eyes were troubled. "Yes, there is. She's lost two children, and she's afraid of losing this one. Her husband is afraid for her also." She bit her lip and shook her head. For several steps she did not speak, then she remarked almost as if to herself, "She wants me to come to Philadelphia and be with her when the child is born."

"And will you go?"

"I want to, but my parents think it's too dangerous to travel alone."

They reached the house, and the conversation during the meal was polite but tense. Afterward, Mr. Reed took Joel off to his study and, turning to him, said, "I read your article. Do you really feel what you have expressed, Mr. Bradford?"

With all his heart Joel wished he could say, *No, sir, I don't feel anything of the sort*, but he was constrained and could say only, "I know we do not agree on these things."

"I'm sorry to hear of it. I understand you're a relation of Mr. Daniel Bradford. I have met him. He's a fine man and a genuine patriot. I understand two of his sons are serving with General Washington."

"Yes, sir." Once again Joel longed to voice his own convictions, but he could not. After an uncomfortable silence, Reed said briefly, "You will understand then that I would not welcome a gentleman with your beliefs as a suitor for my daughter's hand. I don't mean to be unkind, sir, but that's the truth of it."

"I understand, Mr. Reed." Joel thought suddenly of how cold and indifferent Heather Reed had been toward him and shook his head. "I think you have nothing to fear, sir. Your daughter has no feelings for me, and I certainly have no intention of pursuing her."

"I am most grateful."

Soon Joel found himself leaving the house, and it was Heather who showed him to the door. "Your father," he said, "warned me away from you."

Heather hesitated. "It's rather strange. He likes you as a man, but your extreme political opinions made it necessary for him to speak out."

"You have a fine family." Joel hesitated. "I wish your sister well."

"You're not a praying man, are you, Mr. Bradford?"

Startled, Joel lifted his eyes. "Why . . . no, I'm not! Is it that evident, or do you think all loyalists and Tories are godless men?"

"No, I do not think so. Your relative, Major Gordon, is certainly a man of God, and I'm sure there're many others. No, it's not that. I was watching you in church. I could tell that the sermon made you very uncomfortable."

Joel dropped his eyes and shook his head. "Reverend Hooks is a very direct man. He does cause me to think about issues I've never considered before."

"I'm glad to hear it. I trust you will do more than think. If you're not prepared to meet God, then I would hope you would do something about it. Good day, sir."

Joel watched as she turned and left. He moved away from the house then, rather stunned, and when he got back to his room, Jan Vandermeer looked up from the couch where he sat reading a book written in German.

"Been to church?" he inquired.

"Yes."

"I vill go with you next Sunday. I am not a Christian, but I vill be one day."

Curiously Joel stared at the thick-bodied Dutchman. "What makes you think you will?"

"Because I know that God loves sinners, and I am a sinner. Therefore, God loves me."

"Maybe He will stop loving you."

Jan Vandermeer laughed loudly. "That shows your ignorance, my friend! God does not stop loving us! Of course, I may die before I have time. That is the risk I run." He put his book down and then said, "What about you? Are you a converted man?"

"No," Joel said briefly. "I'm not."

Something about his tone caught Vandermeer's attention. "I see!" he said slowly. "You are not converted, but maybe you vant to be a little bit?"

"I don't know, Jan. I just don't know." Wearily Joel turned and moved away into his room, aware that Jan was watching him carefully. He sat down heavily on his bed and put his head back against the wall and thought of the sermon. Then he thought of Heather Reed and for a long time did not move.

᛭   ᛭   ᛭

Major Lawrence Hartford was surprised when he heard Joel speaking to one of his younger officers about the Reed family. He had met Timothy Reed and knew him for a staunch patriot. He also knew the man had connections with others of the patriot belief, and therefore had a file on him. He listened as Joel spoke.

"Miss Reed told me that her sister is having a baby in Philadelphia, and she wants to go, but her parents are afraid for her to go alone."

Hartford had a memory that was practically perfect. For two days he went about his business, but somehow that statement would not leave him. Early one morning as he was having breakfast, as it often happened, an idea had fermented and suddenly bore forth fruit in his mind. He looked up quickly at his aide and said, "I want to see that young man, Joel Bradford."

"Yes, he lives down on the east side, I understand."

"Go find him and ask him to come and see me here."

"Yes, sir!"

Major Hartford filed the matter in his mind, but later that afternoon he looked up from his desk to see Joel Bradford. Putting his pen down, he said amiably, "Come in, Mr. Bradford."

"You wanted to see me, Major?"

"As a matter of fact, I did. Sit down. There, take that chair." Waiting until Bradford was seated, the major went directly to the point. "Do you know what I do, sir?"

"Certainly! It seems to be no secret that you're in charge of intelligence." Joel grinned, saying, "I thought that intelligence officers were supposed to be unknown, as far as what they do!"

"That is impossible! The men who work under me are unknown. But someone has to tie all the cords together. I have read your article," he added abruptly. "A very fine one."

"Oh, I think I could do better," Joel shrugged. He had been startled when the lieutenant had come to bring Hartford's message. His first thought was that somehow he had been found out, but now there was nothing but interest on the major's face. He waited to hear the purpose of his visit.

"I am assuming you are sympathetic to our side of this war."

"Why, certainly, Major. You must know that!"

"Good! I have something that you might help us with."

"I, Major? What could I possibly do?"

"You can go to Philadelphia and find out what the rebels are doing."

"Go to the capital? But what in the world would I do there? What excuse would I have?"

"The same excuse you have here. You are a journalist. You have shown the British side of the question. Now you can go and say that you want to talk to those who are on the other side." Hartford's thin lips creased with a smile. "I should think they would be anxious to present their cause to the British public."

Joel shook his head. "I'm not certain that would work, Major." He suddenly grinned, saying, "They tarred and feathered me in Boston for my views. They might very well do worse now that I've come out against the Revolution so strongly."

"I do not think they will. I think if you introduce yourself as a journalist and state honestly your purpose—" Here again he paused and touched his chin and smiled briefly. "As far as it helps them to know it. You might be able to learn a great many important facts for us there."

"They would be watching me constantly."

"Of course! That is only standard procedure. But we have our people there. We just need more. You could move around as a journalist. We need to know Washington's movements. We need to know if he is bringing his army to protect Philadelphia."

"Is General Howe thinking of attacking the capital?"

"General Howe would have to answer that. It is only one possibility," the major said smoothly. "I understand you have a perfectly good excuse for going to Philadelphia."

"Me? What can that be?"

"Miss Reed has a desire to go there and her family is afraid to send her."

Startled, Joel stared directly at Hartford. He was shaken out of his composure. "How . . . how did you know that, if I may ask, Major?"

"Why, I heard you tell it to my aide. Is it true?"

"Well," relieved, Joel nodded quickly, "well, yes, it is, but I never once thought—well, in fact, Major, Miss Reed doesn't care much for my company."

"I know. She's a fiery patriot. Her family is loyal to Washington also, but I think they would accept your offer to escort her to Philadelphia."

Joel thought rapidly, *I've got to do it to stay in the good graces of this man. If I don't, he'll be suspicious. In any case, I've found out all I can here.*

"Why, I'll be glad to make the offer, Major, but I can't speak for the Reeds."

"Excellent! Excellent! Here, I will let you talk with my aide. He will make arrangements for you to pass your information on. You must be very careful," he said. "You were right about one thing. If they find out you are a spy, they will hang you!"

Joel almost laughed aloud. He thought, *Both sides will be anxious to hang me. They'll have to flip a coin for it.*

He spent the next hour with Lieutenant Carter, Major Hartford's aide, and as he listened, he thought, *At least now I know something about their spy system I can pass on.* He had more than one name of their contacts in Philadelphia. If he turned them over to Dante, it would be the end of the British effectiveness there for some time.

As soon as he left the headquarters, Joel went at once to the Reed house and knocked on the door. When Heather came, he said, "Good afternoon, Miss Reed."

"Why, Mr. Bradford!" Heather was indeed surprised. "Will you come in?"

"I would like to make you an offer, Miss Reed."

"An offer?" A puzzled look came into Heather's eyes. "What sort of offer?"

Joel had prepared his speech all the way over here, and now he said easily, "I find I must make a trip to Philadelphia, and I remembered that you had a desire to go there to be with your sister."

"Why, yes, I would, but—"

"I understand your parents' concern, but if you would accept my offer with your parents' permission, I think I can guarantee your safe arrival."

Heather studied Joel Bradford's face and saw no trace of guile there, and finally she said, "Come in. I think it likely they will accept your kind offer."

Joel stepped inside, removed his hat, and followed her into the study. He had no doubt that they would accept his offer, and he longed somehow to find a way to open the heart of this lovely young woman who had so stolen his own, but he did not foresee anything like that ever happening. Even as she had opened the door he had seen the reserve on her face.

15

Howe Is Coming?

THE TRIP FROM NEW YORK to Philadelphia was hard and grueling. Fortunately, the summer had been dry, so there was no mud to contend with. Nevertheless, the coach that Joel and Heather shared with four other passengers rocked back and forth in the dry ruts, sometimes almost hub deep. The first day exhausted Heather, and when they stopped at an inn with a blue goose on the sign, she was so stiff that Joel had to catch her as her feet touched the ground. She swayed and grabbed wildly. He quickly took her hand and put his arm around her, murmuring, "It's been a hard day."

"Thank you," she answered. "I'm usually not so clumsy."

"No wonder, after that ride! Perhaps it will be better tomorrow."

The two entered the inn along with the other passengers, and Joel approached a tall woman with a hatchet face and cold gray eyes who appeared to be the innkeeper. "I need two rooms. One for myself and one for this lady."

"There's a room for the lady, but you'll have to share with these other men," the woman replied readily.

"That'll be fine."

Heather went upstairs at once. The room was small and ill-kept. She looked carefully at the shuck mattress to see if there were any signs of life. Breathing a sigh of relief when she found nothing crawling, she undressed down to her shift, poured tepid water into a basin, and washed her face. The water refreshed her slightly, but she lay down on the bed and fell asleep instantly. A sharp knock woke her up with a start.

"Supper, if you want it," a voice cried through the door.

Actually, Heather would rather have slept, but she knew the next day of travel would be just as hard. Quickly she dressed and went downstairs. She found the guests all seated at a big table, the meal already begun. Quickly her eyes went to Joel, who rose and pulled a chair back for her next to his.

"Better hurry," he smiled. "It's first come, first served."

The meal consisted of poorly cooked, greasy mutton, a pot of heavily spiced beans, and a liberal serving of limp greens.

"Not the worst I ever had," Joel murmured. He saw that she was picking at her food and said, "We'll just have to tough it out, Miss Reed. Things will be better when we reach Philadelphia."

She attempted a smile. "Since you're hauling me all over the country, I suppose you can call me Heather!"

"That's fine—and I'm Joel." The two finished off their meal with a pudding that was so heavy, neither could eat more than a bite or two. "Tastes like wallpaper paste," Joel remarked.

"Did you ever taste wallpaper paste?"

"No. It might taste better!" he said and caught the smile on her face.

When they had finished, Heather and Joel walked toward the stairway. Then by impulse she took his arm and murmured, "I can't face that room. Could we go for a walk?"

"Why, of course," he said and led her outside.

She had slept longer than she thought and a full moon was rising, casting its silver gleam over the street. The town was no more than a half-dozen houses scattered about with no apparent plan. The stage stop was the largest and the only one of more than one story.

"How long do you think it will take to get to Philadelphia?" she asked.

"Three days, according to the driver. One more night in an inn, and perhaps we'll be at your sister's house. I know it's not been easy, but it will soon be over."

They strolled along slowly, both more tired by the long ride than they would have been by a long day's work. After a while they reached a small cemetery outlined by the shadows of the surrounding trees. The silver moonlight streamed in, casting shadows from the gravemarkers standing like soldiers in a row. Without saying anything, Heather moved inside. There were no more than twelve or fifteen stones, none of them ornate. She leaned down and read one of them aloud: " 'Betsy Harkness. 1712–1732. Survived by her loving husband and two children.' "

For some reason the writing on the stone moved her and disturbed her, but she said nothing. She walked until finally they came to stand over a gravestone no larger than a brick that lay aslant. Heather tried to read the writing, but it had been obliterated by wind and rain and ice. "You can barely tell it's a grave," she said. Moved by some obscure motive, she picked up a stick and began to trace the outline of the grave, which was almost level now.

"Why did I do that?" she said. "Am I trying to turn back time?"

"I think we'd all like to do that, wouldn't we?" Joel murmured. He was studying her face in the moonlight. The silver beams accented her large eyes and made her face look stronger, casting her features into shadows.

Suddenly she turned and said, "Why did you decide to bring me to Philadelphia? You know I don't care for you."

"Well, it doesn't matter, does it? I mean, after all, you needed to see your sister. I know you're worried about her."

"Still, it's strange that you should offer. My family is very suspicious of you. I'm surprised they allowed me to travel with you."

"I'm surprised, too, but I suppose they're very concerned about your sister and the baby."

"They are. They want a grandchild more than anyone I ever saw. They talk about it all the time. They've already got names picked out, but my sister, Margaret, and her husband, John, will name it themselves. Do you have a large family?"

"Just my sister, Phoebe. She's in Boston. Our parents are gone." He hesitated, then said, "Of course, the Bradfords are distant relatives."

"I like Mrs. Gordon very much, and all the family," she said abruptly. "Is her brother anything like her?"

"Very much like her. They're both wonderful people. Not many would have done for a distant relative what Daniel Bradford did for us." He went ahead to relate the circumstances of his coming, and when he ended he turned away from her, stirred by the memory. He realized suddenly that he had not thought for some time of how miserable he and Phoebe had been in England. Finally he said, "When someone does something good for you, you're very grateful. You express it as well as you can, and you think about it every day. But as time goes on you don't think about it."

"You mean your uncle?"

"Yes. He's very disappointed in the way I've turned against his views on the Revolution."

"Does that bother you?"

"Of course it bothers me!" he said with some irritation. "Do you think I have no feelings at all?"

"I don't know anything about you, Joel," Heather said quietly, "except that you and I are a million miles apart on important things."

"No, just on the matter of the war. On other things we may be very close. For example," he said, "what do you think about marriage?"

Taken aback by his question, Heather looked at him with a startled expression. "About marriage? What about it?"

"Are you for it or against it?" he prodded.

"Why, that's crazy! I'm for it, of course! It's ordained of God."

"So you think a man and a woman are just being obedient to God when they get married? That's all there is to it?"

"I didn't say that!" Heather said quickly. She had a lively mind and a quick temper. Now as she looked at him, she was trying to understand the strange expression on his face. "Why are you asking these things?"

"I don't know. I've felt strangely about you ever since I met you. I've never met a woman like you."

"I'm no different than any other woman."

"You are for me." He reached out suddenly and took her hand. Surprised, she looked up at him, and he said, "I know you despise me for what I'm doing, but I don't despise you. As a matter of fact, I think you're the most beautiful woman I've ever seen."

Shock ran through Heather at his declaration. He was holding her hand, and her first impulse was to pull it away. She had formed a strong opinion about him in her mind and was determined to find nothing favorable about him. His politics and his views on the war she could not abide, but now there was a look on his face she had never noted before. Quickly then she pulled her hand away. "Please, don't do that again."

"I might," he smiled. "Would you be very angry if I told you I admired you very much?"

"It will do you no good."

"I know that. I just wanted you to know."

Heather was confused. "We'd better go back," she said. She turned and walked out of the small graveyard, and as they headed back toward the inn, she noticed they kicked up small puffs of dust. He was silent, and yet deep inside, a part of her wanted him to speak more of his thoughts. When they were almost to the inn, she turned to him and said, "Why are you talking to me like this, Joel?"

"I don't know. I've never talked to any other woman like this or said the personal things I've said to you. Maybe I'm falling in love with you."

"Don't joke!"

He remained silent for a time, then he said quietly, "We'd better go inside. Sleep as much as you can. It'll be a rough trip."

Dissatisfied with this answer, Heather said nothing else. She went upstairs at once, undressed, washed her face again, and went to bed. The window was open, and outside the large moon laid its silver beams over the landscape. It touched the roofs of the scattered houses and the trees, and even as she watched, a dog of some vague ancestry trotted across the street, intent on some errand. She watched him until he disappeared, then looked up at the sky which was studded with stars. They were brilliant pinpoints of light, and as always, she was amazed by them. Suddenly she realized she had forgotten to say her prayers. Slipping out of bed, she got on her knees and closed her eyes. Leaning against the roughness of the covering, she began to pray for her sister, for her parents, for her friends; then suddenly she found herself praying for Joel Bradford. She found herself quite intense in speaking to God about this young man and finally ended by saying, "Oh, God, you know his heart. He can never be for me, but he needs to find you, so I ask you in the name of Jesus to bring him into the family of God."

Quickly she climbed back onto the bed, lay on her back, and for a long time stared at the ceiling, thinking of the things Joel had said to her in the graveyard.

🏛   🏛   🏛

"This is Mr. Joel Bradford. Mr. Bradford, this is my brother-in-law, Mr. John Gilchrest." Heather watched as the two men greeted each other politely, then added, "Mr. Bradford was kind enough to escort me from New York."

"We're very grateful, sir." Gilchrest was a thin man of medium height and a pair of watchful gray eyes. "Will you come in?"

"No, I must find a place to stay, Mr. Gilchrest, but I would like to call later, if you don't mind."

Gilchrest looked at Heather, who nodded slightly, and he said quickly, "Well, of course, you'll be welcome anytime."

"Thank you, Joel," Heather said. She put out her hand suddenly, and when he took it and squeezed it, she managed a smile. "I wish you would call."

"I will do that. Good night. Good to have met you, sir."

Joel went directly to an inn the driver had recommended when the coach had arrived. He obtained a room with no trouble and then went down to eat. After such a long trip, he was extremely hungry and pleased to find the food very acceptable.

"Now," he muttered to himself, "there's nothing to do but wait for Dante." He had sent word of his coming and of his move to Philadelphia to Dante and felt certain he would be contacted sooner or later.

I wonder what Washington's doing now, he thought. *I wish I had more news to bring him about Howe, but I've done the best I can.*

He ate his meal, walked around the town until dark, and then finally went back to the inn. He hated waiting with nothing to do. As the inn grew quiet, Joel grew impatient. He wished that he could do something with himself, but now he knew that all he could do was wait for Dante to appear.

🔔　　🔔　　🔔

General George Washington had weathered the hard winter at Morristown. He had spent much of his time trying to understand the mind of General William Howe and predict his strategies. The Continental Army had been strengthened by new detachments, and counting the militia, the army was as strong a force as Washington had ever had under his command. He was never certain of the exact number of men he could count on, for the militia had a bad habit of coming and going as it pleased.

At a dinner in Philadelphia, the general had been pleased to meet a recruit who had interested him greatly. He was a young, tall, thin Frenchman with big shoulders and a pockmarked face. The new soldier was the Marquis de Lafayette, and the two men had liked each other on first sight. Lafayette had left home, wife, and daughter to throw all his energies into the cause of liberty. He was a pure idealist, and the light shone in his eyes as he had said to Washington, "Sir, I honor you and your cause, and I will lay down my life if necessary."

Washington had heard flowery speeches before, especially from foreigners who had come over to serve as mercenaries in the Revolution. He knew, however, that Lafayette had been slighted by Congress, who was also tired of these volunteers. Those who served in Congress were greatly surprised when Lafayette volunteered to serve without pay and asked for nothing more than to be in the service of General Washington.

Washington had been drawn to the smiling young man, perhaps because he had no son of his own. Lafayette had an unhappy family life and had, in effect, no relationship with his father. So perhaps it was only natural that the aging general and the youthful marquis found in each other what they were seeking. Washington invited him to the camp and asked him to ride with him the next day on his inspection of Philadelphia. The young Frenchman soon proved to be very popular with all of the staff, and Washington was eager for the rest of the country to understand and appreciate this young volunteer.

"My dear Marquis," he said late one evening after the two had dined together, "I intend to parade my army through the streets of Philadelphia. I would request that you accompany me at the head of the troops."

Lafayette was not a handsome man. His nose was large and thin, and his scant reddish brown hair flowed back from a sharply receding brow. He was also fairly awkward, except with a fencing foil. Now he smiled and bowed slightly. "I would be enchanted, Your Excellency, but I am not worthy."

"Of course you are. You've come all the way from France to fight our battles for us. Before long, you will be ready for a command. I will ask you to serve in this battle against General Howe."

"You think there will be battle, sir?" Lafayette inquired, leaning forward, his eyes burning with a desire for action in the field.

"There is no question about it. Howe has no other choice now but to attack us. The press back in England is beginning to get more and more restive," Washington said.

Lafayette laughed aloud. "Do soldiers fight according to the whims of the newspapers?"

"British generals do. Perhaps all generals."

"Not you, Your Excellency!"

"In any case, when the battle begins I will ask you to share part of my command with my staff. I know you will equip yourself marvelously well."

"I can promise only to do my best."

⚜   ⚜   ⚜

The march to the city by the Continental Army took place on Sunday morning, the twenty-fourth of August. General orders had gone out, clothes were washed, and arms burnished. To offset the shabbiness of their attire, the men were ordered to wear a green twig of some sort in their hats as an emblem of hope. They were also ordered to carry their arms well and that none should leave the ranks on march.

The drums and the fife were playing a quick march as the commander in chief rode in the forefront with the Marquis de Lafayette at his side. The parade itself began about seven o'clock. John Adams reported to his wife, Abigail:

> The rain ceased and the army marched through the town between seven and ten o'clock. The wagons went another road. Four regiments of light horse, four grand divisions of the army, and the artillery marched twelve deep, and yet took up above

two hours in passing by. General Washington and the other general officers, with their aides, were on horseback, including the Marquis de Lafayette.

We have not army well appointed between us and General Howe, and this army will be immediately joined by ten thousand militia, so that I feel as secure as if I were at home in my bed but not so happy. My happiness is nowhere to be found but there.

The army I find to be extremely well armed, pretty well clothed, and tolerably disciplined. There is such a mixture of the sublime and the beautiful together with the useful and military discipline that I wonder every officer we have is not charmed with it. Much remains to be done. Our soldiers have not quite the air of soldiers. They don't step exactly in time, they don't hold up their heads quite erect, nor turn out their toes so exactly as they ought. They don't all of them cock their hats and such as most do, and they don't all wear them the same way.

Though they may not have worn their hats exactly to suit John Adams, they were an army. And the citizens of Philadelphia stood cheering them as they marched by in formation led by their commander in chief.

Joel was one of the spectators at the parade that morning. He watched as the soldiers filed by, thrilled by the sound of the fife and the drums, and wished he were there marching with them. *I'd rather be doing that than sneaking around being a spy,* he thought balefully.

His reputation as a journalist had become known around the city by this time, and he made up his mind to present himself to one of Washington's officers. He located the camp without any trouble, and after some difficulty, he found himself in the presence of General Anthony Wayne, known as Mad Anthony Wayne. No one was quite sure why he was called "Mad," for there was not a more sensible officer in the army. Perhaps it was because of his fierce temper.

"What is your purpose, Mr. Bradford?" Wayne demanded.

"Well, sir, I am doing a series of articles on the Revolution for the newspapers in London. I have examined General Howe's forces in New York, and now, with your permission, sir, I would like to examine your own."

Suspicion leaped into the general's eyes. "You've been at New York?"

"Yes, sir, for some time."

"And now you want to look at our forces?"

"That is, with your permission."

"I could not grant such permission. That would be up to His Excellency. Do you know anyone who could recommend you?"

"Well, General, I'm a relative of Mr. Daniel Bradford of Boston. I understand he knows General Washington personally."

"I know Mr. Bradford. What relationship is he?"

"A cousin."

"Are you aware that his son is in my command?"

"Why, no, I was not, although I did know he had a son in the army. I have only met his son Micah."

Wayne said, "I will have to take this up with the general." His fingers drummed on the desk, and he said suddenly, "Perhaps you would like to meet your kinsman, Sergeant Dake Bradford."

"I would like it very much, General."

Anthony spat out an order and soon Joel found himself in the company of a young lieutenant. They marched down the rows of tents and finally the lieutenant stopped. "Sergeant Bradford!"

"Yes, sir!" A young man of nineteen, six feet tall and powerfully built, separated himself. He was wearing remnants of a uniform along with civilian clothes. He put an eye on the lieutenant and waited while the lieutenant spoke.

"This gentleman, sir, says he is your kinsman."

"Yes, we haven't met, Lieutenant, but I am Joel Bradford." Joel did not miss the sudden hard glint that leaped into Dake Bradford's eyes.

"Yes, I've heard about you," Dake said.

"Well, I'll leave you two to make your acquaintances," the lieutenant grinned, then turned and walked away.

Dake took his stance firmly. He had heard by letter of the young man and his sister who had been brought from England by the kindness of his father. He had also learned of how young Joel Bradford had turned against the Revolution and joined himself to the enemy. "What do you want with me?" he asked bluntly.

"Well, nothing really. I just—well, General Wayne thought we might—"

"I might as well speak right out," Dake interrupted. "I don't take kindly to what you have done! My father showed great kindness in bringing you over here, and now you've turned on the cause that's dear to his heart!"

Joel's face burned with anger and shame, and he could not answer. He saw there was little to be gained and said, "I can't argue with that, Sergeant." He hesitated and then said, "I wish you good fortune in the battle that's coming up."

"Do you now? Why would you do that? I'm on the opposite side from you!"

Joel could think of nothing to say to conclude the meeting. He finally said, "Look, I hardly knew a thing about this Revolution before I came, but I know one thing. Your name is Bradford. I'll never stop being grateful to your father for what he's done for me, and what he's still doing for my sister. I know you probably don't believe a word of this, but I think your father's a great man. Well, good-bye."

Dake watched as the young man strolled away, and he muttered, "What am I supposed to make out of that?"

When Joel reached his inn, he did not look carefully at the man sitting in a corner, but he heard his name called.

"Mr. Bradford!"

He turned and saw a bent, elderly man whose voice he recognized immediately. He went over and carefully said, "Good afternoon, sir." He knew better than to use any name and took a seat.

Dante murmured, "I got here as soon as I could. Are you established yet?"

"Yes, I just met General Wayne. He thinks I'm a spy for the British. I've met my cousin Dake, too. From the look in his eye he'd like to hang me. If Major Lawrence Hartford catches me, he will hang me for certain!"

"Slow down, boy. I know it's been hard, but I'll tell you you're doing more than your cousin Dake. He can only fire one musket, but the news you gather can save a hundred lives, maybe a thousand."

Looking around to see that no one was near, except the innkeeper who was all the way across the room polishing glasses, Joel said, "I've got to do something."

"You're getting nervous, are you?"

"I don't like this sort of thing, but I'd rather be moving about."

"That's good, because that's exactly what you're going to do." Leaning forward, Dante lowered his voice. "Howe disappeared with the fleet. At first nobody knew where he went, but we know now."

"Where is he?" Joel asked in a low voice.

"He's at Head of Elk. That means he's headed straight for Philadelphia, and Washington will go forward to meet him. There will be a battle, so I want you to go meet Howe."

"You mean to . . . talk to him?"

"No, disguise yourself. You mustn't be seen. From what you've said, Major Hartford is already suspicious of nearly everybody, so get out, find out what troops are coming, then get back to Washington with what you've learned. You won't be alone. There are others out there looking as well. What one man misses another may see."

The two sat there for a long time as Dante gave him his instructions. When Joel had the orders firmly memorized in his mind, he said, "I'll leave in the morning."

"No, leave tonight! Track Howe, my boy. Track him as if he were a prized animal. Find out how many troops are coming and where he's going. By now you know every one of his troops, something that none of the rest of us knows. You're familiar with every outfit, every regiment. You know what to do with your information? You haven't written it down."

"It's all in here," Joel tapped his head. His eyes were gleaming, and he said, "I'll do the best I can, sir. Maybe this battle will end it all."

16

A New Creation

AS SOON AS EDMUND DANTE said his brief good-bye and moved away from the table and disappeared, Joel's mind began working rapidly. He well understood the importance of not being seen. He would have to assume some sort of disguise and quickly ran over the possibilities. Among these he thought of disguising himself as a deranged young man, a role he had used more than once, but this did not seem wise. It might draw unnecessary attention. He tested the weight of the bag of coins Dante had thrust upon him, telling him to use it as seemed best.

"But what is the best?" he murmured. Abruptly he got up and left the inn and walked down the streets of Philadelphia. There was so little time! He had to do something and had to do it now. Suddenly the thought came to him, *If I were a praying man, I could ask God, and He could perhaps show me, but I can't do that.*

He had not gone more than two blocks, the thoughts fluttering in his mind like wild birds in a cage, when suddenly his eyes fell upon an unusual wagon. It was one he had seen more than once in England out on the country lanes. Now he stopped dead still and studied it as an idea began to form.

The vehicle he saw was obviously a gypsy vehicle. It was a small wagon with a covered top with all sorts of equipment hanging from the side—pots, pans, and a great variety of other wares for sale. The wagon was old and worn, and the canvas covering had more than one discolored patch sewn on it.

The horse was not in much better shape than the wagon. She was swayback and her head drooped. The poor mare looked as though she could not walk herself, much less pull a wagon loaded with items for sale!

As Joel stood observing the wagon, a small figure popped out from behind. He was an elderly man with a swarthy face and clothes that marked a gypsy—a garish yellow shirt, a crimson cloth around the forehead holding back the white hair, and a pair of blousy trousers with patches liberally sprinkled on them.

"You need your fortune told, sir?"

Instantly a thought came to Joel Bradford. It shocked him at first, but his mind was working rapidly with the intriguing possibility. "I don't need my fortune told, but maybe I need something else."

"Sure. Yes, sir, you need something sharpened. I have fine grindstone. I sharpen scissors, tools, scythes, swords, knives. You have a knife perhaps I could sharpen?"

Joel studied the man, who had bright brown eyes, one of which was half closed by a scar at the corner. He knew gypsies were adroit at bargaining, and yet the idea that had come to him seemed to grow and take a definite form in this thoughts.

"How much for your horse and wagon?" he asked suddenly and saw an avaricious light come into the gypsy's eyes.

"Oh, it's a fine wagon, as you can see! And my mare, there's none like her!"

"She's about to die, as anyone with an eye for horse flesh can see, and your wagon won't make ten miles. I'll give you thirty dollars silver for the whole rig."

The gypsy exploded, but he did not walk away. Joel had seen something in his eyes and knew he would be able to buy the wagon. *I must be a fool to think of such a thing*, he thought, *but it just might work.*

🛆   🛆   🛆

When Joel Bradford drove the gypsy wagon out of Philadelphia eight hours later, he felt as if everyone on the street was staring at him. He had disguised himself before, but never quite so daringly. He wondered if he had lost his mind completely.

He had bought the horse, the wagon, and the grindstone, as well as some of the pots and pans from the gypsy for fifty dollars cash. It was twice what the rickety outfit was worth, but the old gypsy had driven a hard bargain. Joel now had less than forty dollars left of the amount Dante had given him, but he thought it might be enough to accomplish his mission. As he rode along, he looked down at himself and smiled at the flashy colors of the fairly new shirt the gypsy had thrown in. It was some shade between purple and red. The pants fit him loosely, and he wore a pair of good black boots he had bought some time ago.

Carefully, without seeming to do so, he leaned over and picked up a small mirror from the seat beside him, saying at the same time, "Get up, Queenie!" Glancing around and seeing that no one was looking, Joel held the mirror on his lap and looked down into it. The sight of his face brought a shock to him. He had cut his hair short and dyed it black as well as his eyebrows. He knew he would have to keep very closely shaved, for his whiskers were fair with a reddish tinge. The reflection he saw was of a dark and dusky face, for he had taken walnut juice and stained himself thoroughly. He had gone further than necessary, staining his whole upper body so that no white flash of skin would show through and give him away. In his right ear a gold earring dangled. He had pierced it with an awl and knew it would be sore for some time, but the gold earring gave him an authentic look.

"Well, you *look* like a gypsy. Let's see if you can sound like one." He practiced an accent, remembering some of the European gypsies he had spoken with back in England. As he neared the outskirts of Philadelphia, he became more and more confident that he could pull off this daring feat.

He thought of the pastor's sermon on death he had heard not long ago, and a coldness came over him. Something about being hanged frightened him. It was not like being shot in a battle or dying of a sickness. Hanging at the end of a rope on a gallows somehow had an evil feeling attached to it, and yet he knew that he stood a good chance of perishing exactly that way if he got caught by the British.

"Well, they can't hang me but once," he said aloud as a gypsy might say it.

The wagon rumbled on and he spoke to Queenie, the mare, from time to time in an encouraging tone. He had no map, but Dante had given him instructions about Howe's movements. "He'll be coming from the Head of Elk. You can't miss him," Dante had said.

Now as Joel sat loosely in the seat of the rickety wagon, calling out every few minutes, "Pots, pans, and scissors sharpened!" just to get in practice, he thought of Phoebe and wondered what would happen if he were caught and hanged for being a spy. Once again something came to him, and he spoke it aloud. "If I knew God, I could ask Him to take care of her, but I'm in no position to ask any favors of God!"

☙   ☙   ☙

General William Howe's army disembarked on August 25, 1777. The British forces were in terrible shape, for they had endured a terrible voyage for thirty-two days, buffeted by winds that had caused much seasickness. The soldiers were in pitiful condition. They had also hit a period of calm weather when the men lay like live fish on a skillet, gasping in the heat. The suffering of these men was great, and some of them died on board. Others were unable to fight and could not join the army that marched to meet Washington's troops. Even the horses had suffered horribly. Many of them had perished and been thrown overboard. As soon as they landed, the three hundred that survived were turned loose in a cornfield, where they gorged themselves so terribly that half of them were felled by colic.

For all their discipline, the Redcoats and the Hessians were almost unmanageable on the march. They were filled with resentment and anger at their treatment on board the ships and then had been compelled to watch as two of their comrades were hanged and five others flogged as punishment for plundering. Roiled at their own mistreatment, they took every opportunity to plunder and loot as they moved inland.

Howe's army was divided into two grand divisions, one under Cornwallis, the other under Knyphausen. As they marched toward Philadelphia, they were uncertain as to the strength of Washington's forces. Estimates ranged all the way from ten thousand to twenty thousand.

On September the eleventh these two armies moved toward Brandywine Creek in Pennsylvania.

Joel had shadowed the forces of General William Howe since they had left the Head of Elk. He kept behind them on the road, sometimes getting information from farmers. He had traveled on one of the side roads so that he could parallel the forces. Many times he had tied his horse and gone on foot to see the colors of the regimental flags, or the uniforms, so he could identify the different troops. This was not difficult for him, for he had learned to recognize all these uniforms while Howe's forces were stationed in New York.

It was on a Thursday afternoon when he was trailing along behind the vanguard that he looked up with a start to see an officer in a red coat, accompanied by several other officers. He recognized Major Lawrence Hartford at once, and fear and apprehension swept over him. He had been able to convince most people that he was actually a gypsy, but he knew that Hartford was no ordinary man. It was his profession to see beneath disguises, and Joel ducked his head, pulling the slouched hat down over his face, hoping the group would go on by. To his dismay, the small group had pulled up as they neared the wagon.

"You there, fellow, what are you doing on this road?" Hartford called out.

Joel lifted his head quickly. There was no sense trying to hide his face. That would only make the major more suspicious. He smiled broadly, his teeth flashing against his dark skin, and pulled off his hat and bowed several times, the gold earring catching the sun's rays.

"Oh, General, me, I'm sharpen scissors! You need your sword sharpened?"

Major Hartford was exhausted, as were the other members of his company. They had been riding the side roads and going ahead as far as possible, trying to figure out what Washington would be doing. They had had little success, and, of course, everyone in this part of the country was a patriot, so they could not ferret out any useful information.

"You won't get anything from him, sir," one of the officers said impatiently. "He's a gypsy. They're all liars and worse!"

Hartford gave the officer an impatient glance and urged his horse closer to the wagon. Seated on a tall bay he looked down at Joel and said, "You know these parts, gypsy?"

"Oh yes, General, I know ver' well."

"Have you seen any soldiers?"

"Oh yes, many soldiers, all wearing red coats, but some green."

"I don't mean British soldiers!" Hartford snapped. "I mean have you seen any American soldiers?"

"Me? No!" He looked around nervously and opened his eyes wide. "They no like gypsies, Americans! I stay away! All I do is sharpen scissors and swords! I sharpen your sword, yes? Give you good price!"

Hartford glared at the dark face of the man seated in the wagon. He had a contempt for gypsies, and now he had half a mind to take his anger and irritation out on this one. But time was pressing, and he said, "Get your wagon off the road! If I see you again, I'll have you flogged! We need horses and wagons, and I may just take this one!"

"Please, General!" Joel folded his hands and wheedled in a high-pitched voice, "Please don't take my horse! It's all I have, General! Please! Please!"

"Oh, shut up!" Hartford said. He wheeled his horse around and said to his soldiers, "Come, we've got to sweep the east before we go back to report to the general."

As soon as the small company moved away, raising a cloud of dust, Joel passed a shaky hand across his beaded brow. He took a deep breath and then suddenly felt a thrill of accomplishment. "Well, Major Lawrence Hartford, you're not such an invincible intelligence officer after all!" He grinned then, thinking of how he would relate this incident to Edmund Dante. Flicking the reins, he said, "Get up, Queenie, we've got miles to go!"

🔔　　　🔔　　　🔔

The tall man who stood staring into the distance was not happy. George Washington had shifted his forces to meet the oncoming British. He was determined to keep them out of Philadelphia. He had taken up a defensive position along Brandywine Creek, a tributary of the Delaware River. He glanced back toward Philadelphia, some twenty miles west, and wondered if he would be able to stop the approaching forces of General William Howe.

He looked around and thought, *This situation's not a good one. That creek over there won't stop Howe's men, and there are eight fords within seven or eight miles that have to be covered.*

But he looked over at Lafayette and made himself smile. "Well, we shall soon hear the sound of musket balls, I think, my dear Marquis."

"I trust so." The marquis smiled back at the big man and said, "You have heard them before, General, but I have not. If I try to run, I pray you will shoot me, sir."

Washington laughed. He had become very attached to this young man in a short time. "I recall the first time when I was heading the militia in Virginia and we were attacked by the French. I said that musket balls make a rather charming sound as they pass by." He laughed at his own words and shook his head. "I have never heard the last of that. It's a remark of a vain, foolish man."

"No, it is the remark of a brave man, my General," Lafayette said.

Quickly Washington swept his arm toward the troops. "Do you see how we have arranged our forces?" He went over it again, not so much for Lafayette's information, but to reinforce it in his own mind. "We put our main force here under Nathaniel Greene and Anthony Wayne around Chad's Ford. We placed Sullivan's division on the right to cover all of those fords, but I'm expecting the main attack to come right here in the center. I've left General Sterling and General Stephen in backup positions for a reserve."

"And what do we do now, my General?"

"We watch and we wait."

What Washington did not know at that moment was that the British had all intentions of repeating the maneuvers that had won them the Battle of Long Island. Howe had commanded General Knyphausen to make a demonstration on the center while he himself would march to

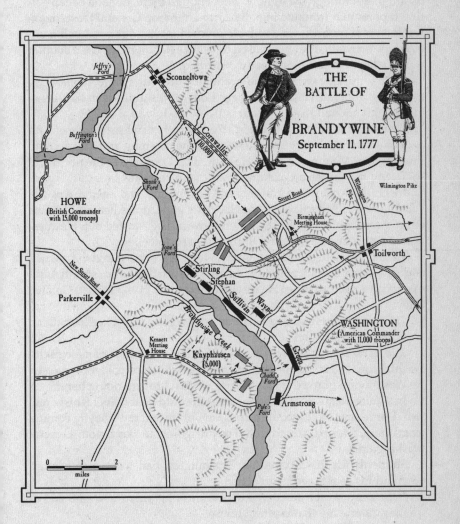

THE
BATTLE OF

BRANDYWINE
September 11, 1777

Jeffry's Ford

Sconneltown

Buffington's Ford

Cornwallis (10,000)

Skunk's Ford

Street Road

Wilmington Pike

Wilmington Pike

HOWE
(British Commander
with 15,000 troops)

Birmingham
Meeting House

Jone's Ford

Toilworth

New Street Road

Stirling

Stephan

Sullivan

Wayne

Parkerville

Brandywine Creek

WASHINGTON
(American Commander
with 11,000 troops)

Kennett
Meeting House

Knyphausen
(5,000)

Greene

Chadd's
Ford

Pyle's
Ford

Armstrong

0   1   2
miles

his left around the Continental right, fold up Washington's flank, and attack from the rear.

The plan almost worked. Knyphausen attacked the center, and Washington sent Lafayette out to command a force to help hold that position. But though the fight was hot enough there, he soon began getting reports that troubled him. By early afternoon General Washington received one report from a reliable officer that his right was being circled by Cornwallis, but he refused to believe it. Not much later, another report came that left him greatly disturbed.

Later a thickset farmer came trotting up on a little mare, demanding to see the general. Washington heard one of his aides turn him away but quickly moved to say, "What is it? What do you want?"

"My name is Chaney." Chaney's clothes were carelessly flung on and he looked agitated. "I heard the firing in the morning and I went up to Birmingham Meeting House." He turned and pointed to the north and said, "Sir, the British are coming from that direction!"

Instantly a cold chill came over Washington. The enemy was advancing on his right flank. If the Redcoats got around behind him, the entire cause for liberty for the Colonies would be snuffed out. He questioned the man carefully, still finding it hard to believe.

At that moment another altercation took place. Washington frowned and saw his officers trying to hold back a swarthy-faced, stoutly built man with a gold earring. He frowned and said, "Who is that, Colonel Riley?"

"Just a gypsy. He claims he wants to see you, Your Excellency."

"Come here, gypsy!"

The dark man approached and looked around, then came close to Washington. "Your Excellency," he whispered, "it's me, Joel Bradford."

Washington blinked with surprise. "What are you doing here?"

In a voice so low that only Washington could hear it, Joel whispered, "Mr. Dante sent me to scout the position of the enemy. They're coming from there, around your right. They're going to flank you, General Washington!"

Suddenly all the reports that Washington had heard made sense now and his mind raced into action.

"Bring my horse!" he roared to an aide at his side. "You," he said to Chaney, "show me that meeting house!"

The man jumped back on his horse, and Washington paused only long enough to lean over and say, "You've done well, Mr. Bradford, very well indeed!" and then he was gone.

Joel heard the general, who kept his horse right beside Chaney's, shouting all the time, "Go on, old man, go on!"

Joel felt that all the strength had drained from him. Suddenly he was aware that the aide-de-camp was staring at him. Turning to him, Joel asked, "Do you know where General Wayne's men are?"

The officer was not certain of the status of the dark-skinned gypsy, but he had seen Washington listen to him, then ride off. "General Wayne's down there. See, there's the creek. They're right on the other side."

"Thank you, sir."

Joel moved at once toward the creek that flowed sluggishly. The sun overhead was hot, and he hoped he would not lose the stain that disguised his face. But he was too tired to think about that much. All night long he had scoured the hills trying to decide what Howe would do, and when he had discovered him making a forced march around to capture Washington's right, he had galloped the weary horse at full speed to reach Washington to warn him.

Now he heard the sound of musket fire. It sounded like thousands of small sticks being broken, and now and again the boom of a cannon rent the air in the distance.

As he approached the battle front, the Continentals stared at him strangely as they passed him. They were retreating, he saw, and when an officer appeared, Joel ran over and said, "Sir, you know where Sergeant Dake Bradford is?"

"Bradford? We left him back there! He got hit and went down! He'll be a prisoner of the British for sure. What do you want him for?"

Without answering, Joel ran directly into the face of the enemy. He heard a musket ball whistle by his ear, flinched away, and dove into a thicket for cover. Steadily he moved forward, and soon he began to see red coats. He knew there would be no avoiding discovery, and when a British officer came by, he showed himself. The officer leaped at him with his sword in his hand.

"You! What are you doing here, gypsy?"

"I . . . am lost. I've lost my wife and baby!" Joel screwed his face up, and the officer, whose name was Menton, scowled at him.

"Get away from here!" he ordered. "You're going to get killed!" He turned and moved along the line of men who had taken up a position.

Quickly Joel moved in the direction from which the battle had flowed. For two hours he came across many Continental soldiers who were wounded, some unable to move, and, of course, many were dead. He found one soldier with his back against a tree with his foot almost shot away. "Do you know Sergeant Dake Bradford?"

"Dake?" the soldier grunted. He was pale and weak from loss of blood, but he stared at the gypsy and said, "He's over there. He went down beside that stone wall. There by those big oak trees."

"I hope you make it, soldier," Joel said, then turned and ran away toward the trees.

Fifteen minutes later he found Dake Bradford. He had almost given up, but he saw a pair of legs sticking out from under some bushes, and when he pulled the bushes aside, Joel saw the still face of Dake Bradford.

Quickly he examined the man's injuries. Dake had taken a wound in the leg that was still bleeding, and there was a crease along his temple where a musket ball had evidently narrowly missed.

"Dake, can you hear me?" Joel said, but there was no answer.

Joel looked around wildly and could not think what to do. Quickly his reasoning returned. "I've got to stop this bleeding in his leg." He saw a dead soldier and removed his shirt and tore it up for bandages. Dake awoke as Joel tightened a bandage around the wound on his leg.

His eyes blinked and he croaked, "Water! Give me a drink!"

Quickly Joel did what he could for the wounded man. He gave him a drink and was relieved when Dake seemed to regain some of his senses.

"Who are you?" Dake muttered.

Remembering that Dake could not see beneath his disguise, Joel said, "Just a friend. I've got to get you out of here, soldier."

Joel sat there as the sun was going down and knew that somehow he had to get this man away to safety. The British would be back to pick him up as a prisoner, and he had heard of the deplorable conditions in which prisoners of war were kept on both sides.

"I've got to do it," he said. "Soldier," he said, "I've got to go get my wagon. I'll come back for you. Don't move."

"Why . . . are you doing this?"

Joel thought of all that Daniel Bradford had done for him, and he said, "I owe you a debt, soldier." When Dake did not answer, he whispered, "Stay here. Crawl under these bushes. I'll be back shortly to help you."

He concealed Dake under the thick bushes and then stood up. He planned a way to get the wagon into the area, but it would take a miracle to get through the British lines undetected, for the British soldiers were everywhere.

"Well, God, I'm not a praying man, but this time I guess you'll have to help me whether I am or not. . . !"

17

A Small Miracle

JOEL MADE HIS WAY BACK to the American camp. With the battle raging all around him, this was no little task. Several times he was shot at by both sides. The British shot at him as he flitted from cover to cover to get back to the Brandywine. When he was halfway across the small stream, the Americans, thinking he was British, shot at him also, but he made it safely back.

Going at once to the headquarters, he saw the same officer he had seen before and said, "Sir, I must go back to my wagon."

"You're free to go, gypsy. But what did you say to General Washington that sent him off?"

"Oh, just a private matter."

The officer, a tall Virginian, grinned. He could not imagine what business George Washington would have with a poor gypsy, but he was accustomed to some of Washington's eccentricities. "Well, be on your way," he said. "If I were you, I'd get out of here. We're going to have to retreat. If the British catch you, they may treat you badly."

"Everybody treats gypsies badly!"

Joel turned and ran. He found his wagon and got in it at once. "Come on, Queenie, we've got some ground to cover!"

He turned the mare's head toward the southern fork of the Brandywine, and soon the sounds of the battle faded away. He could still faintly hear the musket fire and knew the worst of the fighting was taking place on Washington's right flank. Finally he came to a ford, and seeing no soldiers of any kind, he crossed quickly. Fortunately, the water did not come up to the hub of the axle, and soon he found his way on a road he had been on before. It took him nearly four hours to make a circle, but he knew this country well, having scouted it while watching for General Howe's movements. As he turned the wagon toward the north, the firing grew stronger. Before long, he was back where the main action had taken place earlier, and he breathed more easily when he saw no soldiers at all.

"They've all been sent to the north to sweep Washington's right," he said, "but they'll be back."

Forty-five minutes later he pulled the wagon up, jumped out, and did not pause to tie the mare. She was too tired to run away, and he could only hope she could still pull them out of danger. He ran quickly across the broken ground to the bush where he had left Dake. To his relief, when he pulled it back, Dake was still there. "Are you all right?"

Dake did not answer, and Joel quickly pulled him out into the open. Taking the canteen, he splashed water over the soldier's face.

Dake's eyes fluttered, and he studied the dark face before him. "You came back," he muttered.

"Yes, come. You must get in wagon." Joel had decided to keep his disguise in place. If Dake knew he was Joel Bradford, he would be suspicious of him, thinking he was still on the English side.

It took some doing, but finally Joel got the wounded man into the back of the wagon. He gave him another drink and then whispered, "You must be very quiet. We got to get away. The British come back soon."

"Get me out of here, gypsy," Dake whispered; then his eyes closed again.

Quickly Joel climbed up in the seat and spoke to the mare. "All right, Queenie. It's up to you now."

The mare shook her head wearily, but at the touch of the lines she began plodding forward.

"Just a little while and you can have all the rest you want," Joel muttered. He knew that at any moment they might come upon a group of English soldiers on patrol or being transferred to another part of the battle. If they did stop them and found an American soldier in his wagon, Joel already knew what his fate would be. But he looked up suddenly and said, "Well, God, could you please let me have one little miracle for Dake? I need to pay back a debt to his father, so get us out of this and I'd appreciate it."

At the same time that Joel was trying to cross enemy lines and save Dake Bradford, Major Hartford was taking in reports. The battle was going well. Washington's forces were being driven back, and he was smiling at the victory that seemed in their grasp. Suddenly, however, the smile disappeared, for he heard Roger Menton, one of the men who had brought in reports, say something that cut to Hartford like a knife.

"What did you say, Lieutenant?"

"Me, sir? About what?"

"What did you just tell the major you found in the woods?"

"Why, it was a strange thing, sir," Menton said. "We were advancing, and all of a sudden there was this gypsy right out in the middle of the fight. I couldn't believe it."

"What did he say?"

"Said he was separated from his wife and baby."

"What did he look like?"

"Why, like all gypsies—swarthy, a gold ring, a reddish shirt almost purple. . . ."

"Could you find him again?"

"Well, I could go where he was, sir, but that's been several hours ago."

"Take a patrol! Pick him up at once!"

"A gypsy? You want us to go after a gypsy?"

"This particular gypsy is not what he seems, I think. Now go and find him!"

As soon as Menton turned to go, Major Lawrence Hartford turned to his second in command. "Melton, I want this word to go out to all of our operatives. Be on the lookout for a gypsy."

"A gypsy?"

"Yes!"

"Well, what does he look like, sir?"

"You know very well what he looks like!" Hartford smiled at the astonished look on the officer's face. "He was the gypsy we stopped before the battle started. This gypsy was seen in too many places. I think if we washed him down, we'd find one of the American agents beneath that dusky face. Be off!"

18

"I Don't Know God"

THE BATTLE OF BRANDYWINE was a victory for the British. The patriots lost between twelve and thirteen hundred men—killed, wounded, and missing. General Howe's loss was much less, only eighty-nine killed, four hundred and eighty wounded, and six missing. As the battle came to an end, Joseph Townsend, a young Quaker, who had watched the fighting from behind cover in a field, described the aftermath:

> Awful was the scene to behold—such a number of fellow beings lying together severely wounded and some mortally—a few dead, but a small proportion of them considering the immense quantity of powder and ball that had been discharged. It was now time for the surgeons to exert themselves. Some of the doors of the meetinghouse were tore off and the wounded carried thereon into the house to be occupied for a hospital.
>
> The wounded officers were first attended to. After assisting in carrying two of them into the house, I was disposed to see an operation performed by one of the surgeons who was preparing to amputate a limb by having a brass clamp fitted above the knee joint. He had his knife in his hand, the blade of which was circular, and was about to make the incision. When he recollected that it might be necessary for the wounded man to take something to support him during the operation, he mentioned he wanted his attendants to give him a little wine or brandy to which he replied, "No, Doctor, it is not necessary. My spirits are up enough without it."

One of the losses of the Americans was Lafayette, who had taken a wound in the leg. But with an improvised bandage around it, the marquis had set up a guard and had helped to finish out the day's fighting.

Though beaten, the army was not despondent. Captain Enoch Anderson of the Delawares, who fought on the right, said in a letter: "I saw not a despairing look, nor did I hear a despairing word. We had our solacing words always ready for each other. 'Come, boys, we shall do better next time,' sounded throughout the little army."

The defeat called for a deep withdrawal, and on the morning of the twelfth, General Washington marched from the scenes of battle and encamped on the edge of Germantown, placing himself between the enemy and Philadelphia. He prepared to give battle, but a fierce rainstorm struck, and the Continentals lost forty rounds of ammunition apiece through the loss of powder. Howe maneuvered his army well, as he always did, and on the twenty-sixth day of the month, Howe, who had once more easily outwitted Washington, walked into Philadelphia unopposed.

🔔   🔔   🔔

The house had burned to the ground, leaving only one charred reminder of its existence, a chimney pointing to the sky, as if it were a lean finger. The fire had taken place some time ago, enough for the ashes to fade back into the earth, so that only the outlines of stone that had formed the foundation of the small cabin remained. But the barn had survived, and Joel Bradford sat inside it beside his wounded relative, Dake Bradford, wondering what to do next. *It is a miracle*, he thought, *that we got away without being captured. It's almost as if God led me to this barn for shelter.*

Joel's thoughts had turned to God often since he had gotten Dake Bradford safely away from the heated battle. Now he watched as the mare stamped and ate at the hay Joel had stolen for her from a haystack in a field they had passed. He had pulled the wagon into the barn, and the mare he kept inside as well, for British patrols were on the prowl everywhere. He did not know the outcome of the battle, but he felt sure that the British had won. There was no other explanation for the number of patrols that rode by. It proved that the Americans did not control the roads that led into Philadelphia.

Joel got up and moved across the barn, which smelled musty, and his feet stirred the remains of old grain, causing him to sneeze violently. He slapped the mare on the flanks, saying, "Queenie, I'll see if I can't get you some corn tonight. You earned it."

Opening the door a crack, the red sun cast a rosy glow over the landscape as it sank on the horizon to the west. The house evidently had been a lone one, and as he stood there thinking, he had no idea on how to find help for Dake. But as he stepped outside cautiously and scanned the line of trees that bordered the north, he knew he had to get medical help.

For a long time he stood there, undecided, uncertain, and finally turned and went back in. Kneeling down beside Dake, who lay on a blanket over a rude mattress formed of hay, Joel asked, "How are you doing, soldier?"

"Not . . . too good." Dake did not even open his eyes, and his lips were pale, pressed firmly together.

Joel sat down and began to bathe the soldier's face, noting that he had a fever.

"I'm afraid you're getting some infection in that leg. You're going to lose it if we don't get you to a doctor soon."

Dake opened his eyes. The fever that gripped him distorted his vision, but he saw the dark face of the man who had pulled him off of the battlefield. Once again he muttered, "Why are you doing this for me?"

"I've already told you," Joel said. "I owe it to you."

Dake had made no sense of the gypsy's strange answer, but his mind was wondering. He sat up for a while as Joel cooked a meal from the supplies. He was not a great cook, but he managed to make a stew out of the meat that was left over and got Dake to eat a little bit of it. After a few spoonfuls, Dake shook his head.

"No more."

Joel took it and put it aside. Sitting down across from the wounded man, he fished into his pocket and found a candle. It took some trouble to light it, for he lit it from the fire that he had made and carefully guarded to keep it from spreading. Setting it on a low beam, he said, "You're not doing well."

"Better than if you had left me on that field. I'd have bled to death by now, or else I'd be a prisoner. I'd a heap sight rather be dead than a prisoner of the Lobsterbacks."

Joel did not acknowledge this remark. His mind was going to and fro like a hound dog searching for his scent. Finally he said, "We've got to get you into a town somewhere and find a doctor. Otherwise, at the very least, you'll lose that foot. We need help."

"What's it like out there?" Dake asked. "You see any Lobsterbacks?"

"They're everywhere." Joel still kept the accent of the gypsy, and he continued to sit there quietly. Finally he said, "We've got to do something."

Dake was woozy, but the food had warmed him and had made his mind somewhat clearer. "Are you a man of God?" he asked suddenly.

"Me?" Joel blurted out. "Why, no!"

"That's too bad. I think I'm going to die if somebody doesn't pray for me."

Joel swallowed hard. Hearing Dake talk about death somehow caused a fear to grip him. He shook his head and said, "You pray for yourself. I don't know God."

"Too bad," Dake said. "I bet if my wife were here, or my pa, they'd pray me through this, or my sister. You got a family?"

"One sister."

"Is she a Christian?"

"No, neither of us."

"Too bad. You'd better think about it, gypsy. One day you might be lying somewhere dying like me. If I die I'll go right to the Lord. I'd hate to leave my wife, that's all. Haven't been married long, no children—never thought it would end like this."

"You maybe not die."

"I think I will, unless God rears back and does a miracle."

Dake did not speak further, for his strength was gone. Joel noticed that he would be perfectly conscious at times, and suddenly a wave of weakness would come over him, causing him to almost fall over with exhaustion and pain.

Sitting there watching the flickering fire play its feeble light on the warm face of the man he had risked his life to save, Joel's mind was filled with thoughts about his life and what he was doing. He sat there until he grew stiff, and still after shifting, he remained there tossing small branches into the fire. Finally he began to remember some of the sermons he had heard in Boston and in New York. One of the preachers had said, "God sees you, and knows you, and loves you. Anytime you have a need, He is aware of it, and He has said, 'Call upon me and I will answer thee and show thee great and mighty things thou knowest not.' "

Suddenly in that musty barn, sitting before the flickering fire with the dying man, that Scripture seemed to leap out at Joel. He said it aloud, " 'Call upon me and I will answer thee and show thee great and mighty things thou knowest not.' "

For nearly an hour Joel sat there pondering that Scripture, wondering why it had come to his mind so strongly. Finally something came to him, and he whispered, "God, you know I don't have any right to pray, and I know it, too, but I'm going to pray. The preacher said to call on you and you'd show me great things. Well, Lord, I need to see a great thing. I'm not asking for myself, but I'm asking for this man here. Dake Bradford is a man of God, and he desperately needs your help right now. God, please show me some way to get him where we can get help. Lord, if you'll do that, I will never forget it."

For a long time Joel sat there. He was not sleepy, and it seemed as though the prayer he had just prayed echoed around the barn. An owl flew in suddenly, carrying a mouse in his beak. Seeing Joel, it swooped, angled himself, and sailed back out of the crevice through which it had entered. Joel hardly paid any attention, for his thoughts were focused on God. For the first time in his life, Joel Bradford seemed to hear in his mind what he knew was a word from God.

🦃   🦃   🦃

Heather Reed had not been happy at her sister's house. Her sister was not the problem, for Heather had quickly learned that she was better off physically than she had ever been. It was not this that troubled her, but something she could not put her finger on.

Now as darkness was beginning to fall, she took off her apron and said, "I'm going outside, Margaret, just for a little walk."

"All right," Margaret said and smiled at her. "I'm glad you came. It makes me feel better, Heather, just to have you here."

"You'll be fine. The doctor says he's never seen a healthier woman or a healthier baby."

Stepping outside, Heather moved quietly down the walk. The house was surrounded by a white picket fence and stood alone, for both Margaret and her husband had wanted to live on the outskirts of the town. Now as Heather walked along the lane that led to the next house a quarter mile down the road, she thought of how dreary her life had become. Living in New York under the British occupation had been unbearable. Now that they had come to invade Philadelphia, it seemed there was no place safe from the Hessians' constant plundering and cruel ways on patriots and loyalists alike.

Suddenly a sound attracted her attention, and she whirled to see a wagon coming down the road in the lengthening shadows.

She moved over to one side, scarcely paying heed, but as it came closer, even though the dark was almost complete now, she saw that it was a gypsy wagon. She was afraid of gypsies, having heard stories, and then chided herself, *You're a grown woman now! Don't be afraid of old wives' tales!* Still she moved off warily and was startled when the driver pulled the horse up with a curt word as it stopped beside her. The driver was a formless shadow, but when he leaped to the ground and came closer, Heather became truly afraid. He was a tall man, at least six feet, and well muscled, she saw, through the garish clothes he wore. She could see the whites of his eyes in his dark face, although he wore a black slouch hat pulled down. She started even more when he spoke.

"I look for a lady."

"A lady? What do you mean you look for a lady?"

Joel had already decided he could not risk discarding the gypsy outfit. Heather would never believe him if he had come himself. She would have been suspicious and believed it to be a trap. After he had heard God speak to him, Joel had bundled Dake into the wagon, saying, "We go now and find you help." He had made his way into Philadelphia from the scene of battle and had miraculously not seen a single British patrol. As he had approached the outskirts of the city, hardly hoping to find Heather without trouble, his heart had gladdened when he saw her in the gathering darkness. Another strange thought crossed his mind: *Could God have led me to her?*

"I look for Heather Reed."

Instantly Heather grew suspicious and even more frightened. "What do you want with her?"

"Man in wagon is wounded. Needs help. He's American. If British capture him, they put him in prison."

"What's that to me?" she said cautiously, but she came closer and stared into his face. It was a swarthy face, and the man had short dark hair and a clipped-off gold earring. Even though the hat was pulled down low, she could see that his eyes were half closed as if in suspicion.

"His name is Bradford. His foot hurt bad. Need doctor."

"But why bring him to me?"

Joel had already prepared a story. He had written a letter addressed to Dake in which he had said, "I have just brought Miss Heather Reed to Philadelphia. If you can, go by and see her. Her father knows you very well."

Joel had added other details in the letter and then signed it with his own name. He handed it to her and watched her scan it.

"Do you know what this says?"

"No, can no read. Soldier say bring to Heather Reed."

Heather said suddenly, "Let me see him."

"He not conscious."

Heather moved to the rear of the wagon, and when the gypsy pulled the canvas back, she crawled up in it. Even in the darkness she could tell that the man was badly wounded.

Getting out of the wagon, she said, "What do you expect me to do?"

"Hide soldier. Get doctor."

"Why, I can't do that!"

"Then he dies." Joel then took a chance. "He prayed for help from his God. God maybe gave him your name. You a Christian?"

"Why, yes, I am."

"He Christian too." Joel stood there waiting. There was nothing else he could do. He found himself holding his breath, afraid she would send them on their way, and then what would he do?

But Heather Reed was a quick-thinking and impulsive young woman. She had heard her father speak of Daniel Bradford and of his two sons serving in the army. She also knew that what the gypsy had said was true. If the British found him, he would die in a British prison. *I've got to do something, and I can't tell my sister or John.* Something inside her stirred and a rebellion came to her. She was tired of the British. She had learned to despise them for what they had done to some of the people in Philadelphia and at other places. The memory of her brother's needless death still grieved her heart deeply, and almost without thinking, she said, "Come, we'll put him in the barn."

A sense of relief washed over Joel Bradford, and he almost spoke out the truth about himself at her sudden display of concern. Catching himself, he said, "You show."

Ten minutes later Dake was settled in the barn. He woke up during the transfer and looked at the young woman who was helping. "Who are you?" he muttered.

"I'm Heather Reed. I'm a friend. We've got to get you help, Mr. Bradford."

"Do I know you?"

"No, but my father knows your father. He admires him very much. He's often spoken of you and your brother Micah."

"Well," Dake said as he lay back in the blankets, "you find friends in strange places. Miss Reed, I've been praying that God would get me out of this mess, and it looks like He has done just that."

"I'll have to find some help. I don't know how I'll do it, but I will," she said.

Heather stood up and saw the gypsy standing close beside her. "What will you do?" she demanded.

"I stay and help."

"You'll have to hide that wagon and that mare in the woods. My brother-in-law never comes out here, but he might. I'll go see about a doctor. There's bound to be one patriot who'll tend to an American soldier."

"You good woman."

"How'd you find him?"

"Found him in woods after battle."

"All right. You wait here. Don't shoot anybody if they come in here!" she warned.

"No, I no shoot."

"All right. I'll be back as soon as I can. There's a doctor who lives down the way. He's treated my sister and he's sympathetic to the cause. I'll have to sound him out, but you stay here until I come back."

"I stay right here."

Joel stood there watching her through a crack in the door as she left. *What a woman! It'd take a real man to keep up with her.* Kneeling down beside Dake, he said, "You be all right. She bring doctor soon."

"How'd you know to bring me here?" Dake asked.

Joel hesitated for a while, then he said simply, "I pray, and God told me."

Dake looked up at the swarthy face and grinned. "Well, gypsy, for one who's not a man of God, I think you did right well!"

PART FOUR

THE GYPSY

Fall 1777

19

THE HIDING PLACE

HEATHER WALKED BRISKLY down the street, turning in at the brick walk that led to Dr. Smith's home. It was an unpretentious cottage, for the doctor and his wife had no children and lived alone. Moving quickly, her mind ran over the speech she would have to make. She was not as certain of the doctor's loyalties as she had indicated to the gypsy. Many Philadelphians had loyalist leanings despite their protestations of allegiance to the cause of liberty for the Colonies. Now as she stepped up on the low brick stoop and knocked on the door, she was assailed with doubt.

What if that gypsy's not what he says and that wounded soldier isn't Bradford? And even if he is, isn't this a foolish thing to be getting myself into?

The door opened slowly and Heather had no more time to think. She had never met the doctor's wife, but she assumed that the tall gray-haired woman who stood before her was Mrs. Smith.

"I'm Heather Reed," she said quickly. "I'd like to see Dr. Smith, if I may."

"Why, my husband isn't home. He's away on a trip to Claremont."

Heather was confused. "Will he be back right away, Mrs. Smith? It's rather important."

"I'm afraid not. He won't be back until next Thursday. His brother died and he went to attend the funeral." Mrs. Smith said quickly, "He's asked me to refer all his patients to Dr. Williamson. His office is off the square downtown. I'm sure he'll be able to help you."

"Well . . . thank you, Mrs. Smith." Heather nodded, turned away, and quickly walked back toward the gate. As she stepped back on the street and turned toward home, she thought, *Now what can I do? I've heard about Dr. Williamson. He's a firm Tory! I wouldn't dare go to him!* All the way back to the house she was thinking furiously. If she had been in New

York, she would have known several doctors. Here she was a stranger, and a mistake could perhaps be fatal.

By the time she arrived back at the barn, she had exhausted every possibility and was filled with a sense of helplessness. She went around the house, following the brick pathway, passing through the garden, and arrived at the carriage house. When she stepped inside she could hardly see, for the carriage house was cast in gloomy shadows. There was no candle nor lantern. The silence was oppressive, and advancing into the darkness, she whispered, "Are you here?"

When no answer came, fear and confusion swept over her. Moving to her right, she went to the side of the injured man and knelt beside him. His eyes were open, she saw, and she asked, "Where's the gypsy?"

"He left." Dake's voice was thin and reedy, and he asked, "Could I have a drink of water?"

"Of course."

She groped around in the dark, and finding the pitcher of water she had brought earlier, Heather filled a pewter cup. She moved back, reached under his shoulders, and helped him to a sitting position. He gave an involuntary grunt of pain, and she asked, "Is it bad?"

"I've had worse." Dake gulped the water down thirstily, then when he had finished it, he asked for more. He drained it twice and then sighed, "That's good. Thanks."

Helping the wounded man lie back down again, Heather had never felt more helpless in her life. Just how bad his foot was she didn't know, for she had not seen the wound, but the gypsy had said it was serious. She knew that the bandage around Bradford's head needed to be changed, and her mind raced from one possibility to another. She thought suddenly of the gypsy with a tinge of bitterness. *He just brought him here and dumped him! Just like what I've heard about gypsies!*

But there was a strength in Heather Reed that belied her feminine appearance. Once she made up her mind about something, she would not let anything interfere and would go at it with all her strength. One of her favorite Bible verses was, " 'Whatsoever thy hand findeth to do, do it with all thy might.' " *Well, Heather, don't just sit here, get busy!* She said briskly, "I'm going into the house, Mr. Bradford. I'll get some medicine and we'll clean that wound up."

"I guess you can call me Dake. Everybody else does."

"All right, Dake." Heather smiled. The man had courage, which did not surprise her. Her father had often spoken well of Daniel Bradford, and how he served the cause fearlessly in the best way he could. It pleased her that she could help his son. "You just lie here and try to get some sleep."

"Don't reckon on goin' anyplace."

Leaving the carriage house, Heather walked briskly and stepped inside the door of the house. Moving softly, she went down the hall, then paused outside her sister's room, listening carefully at the door. When she heard no sound, she nodded with grim satisfaction. *At least she's asleep and John's gone.*

She returned to the kitchen and began to search for anything that could be used for medicine. She was not even aware of what she was searching for. She only knew that laudanum would give the wounded man relief from his pain. She could not find any, however, and in despair gathered up cloth for bandages and then determined to go to the apothecary and get a supply of medicines. Perhaps the man there could suggest something if she could put it in such a way that would not arouse suspicion.

She left at once, and after stopping by the carriage house to check on Dake, she found him asleep. He moaned once as she studied his face, uttering an involuntary gasp of pain, so she quickly left.

Twenty minutes later she was standing inside a small apothecary shop. She did not know the owner and wondered how to approach him. He was a short, round individual with thinning sandy hair and a triple chin that quivered when he spoke.

"Yes, ma'am, what can I do for you?"

Heather glanced around the shop. The shelves around the wall were filled with various sizes of bottles, jars, and other supplies of his trade.

"I want to stock up my medicine chest," she said. "I live a little far from here, and when an accident occurs, I want to be ready for it."

"Well, now, that's a big order, ma'am," the apothecary said, smiling at her. "Can you be more specific?"

"Oh, you know how it is on a farm. People get hurt, they get cuts, and things like that. Just give me whatever would be good to take care of injuries, something for pain. I'm sure you know better than I." She smiled at him and added, "I'll just put myself in your hands."

"Well now, ma'am, I wish all my customers were that wise and trusting. Most of them try these old wives' tales. You'd be surprised how many high-class folks go to these herb ladies and try to heal themselves with weeds and strange concoctions."

"Oh no, I wouldn't want to do that! I will need a stock of bandages. I'm sure you know what to give me."

Flattered, the apothecary moved around his shop gathering various bottles, vials, and containers, which he placed on the counter. Then in great detail, he explained what each of them were for. Heather carefully marked those that were for cuts and also the elixirs the man recommended. He put far too many out, including remedies for stomachache and other minor maladies, but at last he finished.

"There, that ought to do you for almost anything that might happen, ma'am."

"Thank you very much. Could you put it in some sort of bag for me?"

"Certainly I could!" The apothecary placed all of the supplies in a bag, then named his fee.

Heather was glad she had silver and not Continental money, for already it was difficult to get merchants to accept it, since the value of it changed constantly. As she picked up the bag, she said, "Thank you very much, sir."

"I hope you won't be needing any of that, but in case you do, you're well supplied."

Quickly Heather left the shop and made her way back to her sister's home. She went straight to the carriage house. She looked around, half fearful of seeing British soldiers, but saw no one. Her sister's small house was hidden by tall hedges, and she was grateful for the privacy it provided them. Stepping inside the door, a voice close beside her startled her.

"You've come back."

Heather jerked with sudden fear, for the gypsy had materialized out of the shadows. He still wore his slouch hat pulled half over his face so that she could not see him clearly. She said sharply, "Don't sneak up on me like that!"

"Sorry."

"I've been to the apothecary," she said hurriedly. "I've got everything he recommended. We've got to change those bandages."

"You know how to fix bad wound?"

Heather shook her head. "No, just minor things, but it has to be done. I'll go get some hot water."

She returned to the house and put a kettle on to boil and waited impatiently for it. While it heated, she checked on her sister again and breathed a sigh of relief when she heard nothing.

Finally, when the water was heated, she picked up a basin and carried it out to the carriage house. The gypsy was waiting for her as she stepped through the door. He looked at her curiously from under the brim of his floppy hat, but he said nothing.

"We've got to find some covers," Heather said. "Let me go back and get some." She returned to the house, pulled two quilts off the rack at the foot of her bed, and brought them back to the barn. "Here, put him on this one. We can pull the other one over him." The two of them helped Dake up over to the makeshift bed. She also brought a lantern back, and the gypsy rigged it on a hook on a beam while she fixed Dake's bed. The yellow light spread itself over the barn, and she looked down at Dake's pale face as he lay back. "We're going to have to look at these wounds. I don't know much about it, but I'll do the best I can."

"You go right at it, ma'am."

Putting off the worst wound in the foot for last, Heather removed the bandage stiff with dried blood from around Dake's head. When she saw the wound it gave her a start. The musket ball had plowed a clear path right along his temple, leaving a ragged, bloody gap an inch above his ear.

"If that had been another inch toward your head, you'd be dead," she said.

"I think God looked out for me," Dake said simply.

Heather managed a smile. "I'm glad you look at it that way. Here, I'm going to clean this off. It's going to hurt." Carefully she began to soak the wound. The hair was stiff with blood, and she wanted to get it as clean as possible. It took some time to get the dried blood out, and the wound began to bleed again. She began to tear some of the bandages into smaller pieces, and she looked at the gypsy, who was kneeling silently on the other side of Dake. "Hold this in place while I tie a bandage on," she said, for it seemed natural for her to give orders to him. As he lifted his head, she saw that he had blue-gray eyes that were very direct.

"All right," he grunted and held the piece of cloth in place.

Carefully Heather wound a strip of white cloth around Dake's head, tied a neat knot, and nodded firmly. "That ought to be all right in a few days."

"The foot won't, though," Dake said. "It's pretty bad."

Reluctantly Heather turned toward the foot. "Shift that lantern," she commanded, "so I can see what I'm doing."

Without speaking, the gypsy moved the lantern so that the yellow light fell down over the bloody bandages on Dake's right foot. With hands not quite steady, Heather gently began to remove them.

"Let me do that," the gypsy muttered.

He moved down to her right, and she watched as he removed the bloody bandages. His hands, she saw, were very dark and strong. The man had a strength about him scarcely concealed by the colorful, loose blouse that he wore.

Finally the foot was laid bare, and when Heather looked at it, she started involuntarily. She had seen very few wounds in her life, but she instantly knew that this was a bad one!

She did not want to say so in front of the wounded man, so she said only, "We'll need to clean it out."

As they cleaned the wound, she whispered, "I don't know anything about this, but it looks like two or three wounds. How could someone get shot in the foot several times?"

"I think maybe shell go off," Joel whispered. He was sure this was what had happened. He had heard the soldiers talk of battle and of wounds, and the fragments had torn the flesh in at least three places. Shaking his head, he said, "Probably metal still in them wounds. Need to come out."

"Come out? How can we do that?"

"Don't know. Doctor could dig them out, but we got no doctor."

For one rash moment Heather considered digging into the wounds, but she knew she could not. That would take a skilled hand. Instead, she merely washed the foot, bandaged it, and turned back to Dake, saying, "Well, we've got that cleaned up. You'll be better soon."

Dake looked into her face. There was a grimness in her expression, and he muttered, "A shell went off. It's a wonder it didn't do worse than it did." He knew better than either of these two what would happen if a bullet or shell fragments were left in human flesh. Gangrene would set in soon if it was not tended to by a doctor who could remove the metal. He said nothing, however, except, "Thank you, Miss Reed."

"Here, I brought something to make you sleep better and take away the pain." She pulled the bottle of laudanum out, along with a spoon, but had no idea how much to give him. "I don't know how much of this I should let you have," she said.

Dake suddenly grinned, reached out, and took the bottle. "Just this much." He removed the cap, tilted the bottle up, and took a healthy swallow. Making a face, he handed it back to her. "That's what the doctor would order." He lay back and murmured, "Thanks again, both of you."

Heather looked at him for a moment, then whispered, "I've got to get back in the house. I'll try to think of some way to get a doctor."

"I think that would be good," Joel muttered. "I stay here."

"If the British come, what will you do?"

Joel merely shook his head and did not answer. Heather left, went back inside the house, and Joel sat down beside Dake. "Hurtin' pretty bad?" he said.

"Not too bad."

"You sleep soon. Don't worry."

Dake turned and stared at the dark face of the man beside him. "I'm a little bit surprised at you. You're a mysterious fellow."

Joel put his back against the wall and pulled his hat down over his face. "Yes," he muttered, "very mysterious. You sleep now."

☦　　　☦　　　☦

Time passed slowly for Heather. She forced herself to be cheerful, at least outwardly, so that Margaret would not suspect anything. John was there only briefly. He left the next morning, saying to Heather, "I'll just be down at the office. You send me word if Margaret needs anything."

"All right, John, I will."

As soon as he was out of sight, Heather went to sit for a while with Margaret, who talked happily about the child that was to come. Once she reached over and took Heather's hand and squeezed it.

"I'm so glad you're here," she said. "I just feel that everything's going right this time. We'll soon have our baby. It won't be like the last time."

"That's right," Heather said, patting her hand reassuringly. "We'll just pray this child into the world strong and healthy."

The two talked for some time, and then finally Margaret said, "I think I'll lie down and read for a while."

"That will be good. I have a few things to do, but I'll be back soon."

Heather went to the kitchen, fixed hot porridge, fried some bacon, and took out some fresh bread. Putting it on a tray, she covered it with a white cloth and went stealthily out of the house. As she entered the carriage house, she saw Dake sitting up, his back against a beam, and his face was flushed. "Here," she said, "I've brought some breakfast."

"Not very hungry," Dake muttered.

"You've got to eat something to keep your strength up."

"Here, you." She stopped abruptly and said, "What's your name?"

The answer was somewhat delayed. "Stephen." It had been Joel's uncle's name, and it was the only name that would come to him quickly.

"All right, Stephen, you sit down and eat too."

"All right. Smells good."

Joel ate hungrily but noted that Dake could only force a few bites of the porridge down. He did drink several cups of the hot tea, but there was a slowness in his movement.

Heather noticed Bradford's face also and reached out and put her hand on his forehead. Holding it there for a moment, she said, "You've got a bad fever!"

"Yes. It got worse last night."

As cheerfully as she could, Heather said, "Well, you'll just have to sweat it out. I'll bring some more covers in from the house."

Heather rose and, motioning, waited until the gypsy had come to the door of the carriage house. Whispering, she said, "It's not good, is it?"

"Me—I think not." Actually Joel was more worried than he had allowed Heather to see. Looking back at Dake, he frowned, then turned to Heather and said, "What about another doctor?"

"There are other doctors here, but I don't know any of them. Any of them who are sympathetic to the British would be sure to report a wounded man like this."

The two of them stood there uncertainly, and finally Heather asked, "Why are you doing this for this man? I didn't know gypsies were so compassionate."

Joel looked out from under the brim of his slouch hat. He was always concerned that she would recognize him and was amazed that she had not. Still, he had discovered that people see what they want to see. He said slowly, "I cannot say." His eyes half closed as he studied her. "Why you help him?"

"I'd help any man that would fight for liberty. You understand that?"

"I think so."

Heather had a sudden desire to see the gypsy's face, for he always kept his hat on with the brim pulled down, but she rebuked herself, *What difference does it make?* "Try to keep him quiet. My sister's husband will be home in the afternoon, but I'll bring more food out after they've gone to bed."

As she moved toward the house, a sense of desperation filled her. "We've got to do *something!*" She tended to Margaret's needs, and for the rest of the day moved about the house as she did the necessary work, but her mind was always on the two men out in the carriage house.

🜨   🜨   🜨

When General Howe and his army marched into the city of Philadelphia after the Battle of Brandywine, the Tories who had endured some hardship from patriots rejoiced. Most of them did not doubt the outcome of the rebellion in any event. Few of them could imagine that

Washington's poor, tattered, ragtag army could continue to evade another crushing defeat by Howe's splendidly trained and equipped troops. Those loyal to the Crown had endured the insolence and the harassment of patriots by saying little and lying low. But now with the British among them—the brilliant and aristocratic officers, the sturdy-looking soldiers—it seemed that things had taken a turn at last. Many believed that soon it would be business as usual with King George. Order would be restored and he would be as much sovereign over America as he was over England.

The British army settled in and made itself as comfortable as it could. The officers, for the most part, fared considerably well. The common soldiers were not so fortunate. The Hessians hated Philadelphia and made no secret of their despisal. They plundered from Tory and patriot alike, for they were unable to discriminate between the two. To them they were all American rebels, and their officers could never make them understand that there were still people loyal to King George.

At once the British settled down to making life pleasant for themselves. The officers were much lionized by the Tory ladies and their pretty daughters. Soon a constant round of parties was taking place in the homes of some of the wealthy Tories. Horse races on the commons were soon occupying the time of the unwelcome visitors. A theater company sprang up, and the officers were soon producing their own drama to the delight of the Tories of the city.

Heather knew little of all of the social events being held, for she kept close to the house, seeing to the needs of the two men hidden in the barn. The British soldiers proceeded to systematically pillage the vegetable garden. Once she ran outside when a sergeant with three blunt-faced Hessians invaded her sister's garden. "Get out of here!" she cried, shaking the broom she held in her hands at them.

The sergeant simply laughed and waved her aside. "Soldiers have to eat," he grunted. He came closer and would have put out his hand, but she slapped it away.

"Leave me alone!" she said, stepping back. "Take what you have to and get out!" Actually she was thinking, *What if one of them decides to go into the carriage house?* She held her breath, but when the soldiers had filled their arms with vegetables and departed with rude remarks toward her, she went at once and opened the door. She found both men awake and said breathlessly, "I was afraid they might come in here."

Joel nodded. "So was I."

Going over to Dake, who was sitting up, Heather said, "It's time to change the bandages."

"I don't see that it'll help much." Dake's voice was weak, and his breathing labored. He had lost weight and his skin was more pale than ever.

She bandaged the wounds and noticed a slight difference in the color around the wounds, but she could not tell why. It was not good; she knew that.

She left, but late that night she came back to bring more hot food. She tried to get Dake to eat more, but he could not. He lay back, and after taking the laudanum, he soon slipped into a heavy sleep.

She sat down for a while on a stool and stared down at the pale face of the sick man. She was very much aware that Stephen was watching her intently. Finally she looked up and asked curiously, "What's it like to be a gypsy?"

Her blunt question caused Joel to smile. "Not much fun in it," he said. He did not know, of course, as much as he pretended, but he had seen the poor gypsies of England, who were at the bottom of the social scale. Then he added, "Anytime there's any trouble, the gypsies get blamed for it." A look of mischief came to him then, and he said, "What's it like to be a fine lady?"

Heather suddenly laughed. The strain of the last few days had been great on her. The concern for Dake Bradford, and the fear of being discovered for harboring a soldier weighed heavily on her. But the question seemed to amuse her. "I don't know," she said. "I'm not a fine lady."

"Me, I think so."

"Well, you don't know much about fine ladies, then." She hesitated, then leaned forward, studying the golden earring and the beads around his strong neck. "Where's your family?"

"Only one sister left now." This was telling her more than he wanted to, but the answer just popped out. "Mother, father dead."

"I'm sorry."

"Not your fault."

"It must be sad to be so alone in the world. Where is your sister? Is she married?"

"No, not married. No good for a woman to travel around the country. She works for a fine family." He did not say where and hoped she would not ask.

Finally, Heather looked up and sighed heavily. "I suppose gypsies don't take part in wars. They don't really have a country, do they?"

"No country."

"I still can't understand why you're doing this for Dake." A thought came to her, and she said, "Are you kind to everyone?"

Joel suddenly felt the pressure of her question. "No," he said. "Stephen not always kind."

She thought of his answer for a moment. The yellow flickering flame of the candle lighted the lower part of his face. Something about his direct gaze made her uncomfortable.

"You no have a man, Miss Reed?"

Even more uncomfortable now, Heather glanced at him, but his eyes seemed to have an unfathomable depth to them. "No," she said. "I don't have a man."

"Why not?"

Heather, once again, was amused by his questioning. "I never found one I liked well enough."

"Maybe you will someday."

"Maybe." Heather put her hand down on Dake's brow and then looked across at Stephen. "We've got to have a doctor. I don't know how."

"I think he will die if he does not get better help." Joel had already foreseen this and now said, "We cannot stay here forever. Sooner or later someone will find us."

Heather had worried about what to do until her mind was weary. She passed a hand over her brow and shook her head. "I think it will take God to solve all of this," she said wearily. She looked up and started to ask a question, but then stopped. Rising, she said, "I'll try to think of something. Good night."

For a long time that night she lay in bed staring at the ceiling. Outside the stars were bright. It was a beautiful fall night, cool and pleasant, but there was no rest for Heather Reed. She had thrown herself into the cause of saving the wounded American soldier. Finally she drifted off to sleep, but it was a troubled sleep, full of strange dreams.

20

A Dream in the Night

"LOOK, IT'S THOSE BRITISH soldiers. They're coming here!"

Heather, who had been stirring oatmeal for breakfast for herself and Margaret, looked up with a startled expression. "Where?" she asked. Putting the pan down, she came and stood beside Margaret, who was looking out the side window. She saw six British soldiers wearing scarlet coats shove through the gate and make their way toward the vegetable garden.

"They're going to take everything!" Margaret cried. She was a highly nervous woman and put her hand over her stomach. "I'm afraid! What if they come in the house?"

"They won't! I'll go outside and stop them!" Heather said as anger welled up inside her. Putting down the pan, she slipped on a coat and walked out into the yard.

This was a different group from the first ones who had come to raid the garden. There was no sergeant with them, she saw quickly. They were all privates, which would make it worse to try to reason with them.

"Take what you want out of the garden and then leave! There's a sick woman in the house."

"Ja, ve vill take vat ve vant," one of the men said. He was a tall, bulky man with a thick German accent. He grinned and winked broadly at his companions. "Maybe ve vant more than vegetables."

Coarse laughter went up from his companions, and they came to form a half circle around Heather. They made obscene jokes, and finally one of them turned and put his hand on Heather's shoulder. Swinging with all her strength, she slapped him across the face. The laughter broke off and the soldier fixed an icy stare on her. "Maybe I fix you!" he said.

"Maybe you'll get put in the guard house! We're loyal to the king here! When your lieutenant finds out about it, you'll all be punished!"

One of the soldiers was a small man with a thin, intelligent face. "Let her alone," he said quickly.

"Why should ve obey you?" the one who had been slapped demanded.

"Because I've got more sense than all the rest of you put together. Now go back into the house, miss, and don't come back until ve're gone."

A streak of fear rose in Heather, and one look at the small man and the warning look in his expression convinced her not to challenge them again. She turned without a word and went back into the house. Going to the window she stood and looked out with Margaret at her side.

"What did they say?" Margaret whispered.

"They're just brutes like cattle! More like criminals really."

The two women watched as the men gathered up armfuls of vegetables, and then Heather breathed a sigh of relief as they started for the front gate. But then suddenly one of them said something and pointed toward the carriage house. Her heart seemed to stop, and her hand flew up to her lips to stop what she had started to say, for Margaret was standing beside her.

"Look, they're going into the old carriage house! There's nothing there for them, though."

Time seemed to stand still for Heather as all of them went inside. She waited for a shout, for a shot, for something—but nothing happened. *What can it be?* she thought, her mind running over every possibility. *There's no hope. They'll be coming in here to arrest me next!*

Suddenly the door swung open again and the six came out. One of them was carrying a bucket, the other a blanket. All of them had something in addition to their vegetables, but the gypsy and Dake were not with them!

With her mouth dry and her hands trembling, Heather watched as they left the yard laughing loudly, speaking in German.

"I'm so glad they didn't come in here," Margaret whispered. "I don't know what I would have done if they had."

"You stay here, Margaret. I'm going out to check the carriage house."

"But there's nothing there," Margaret said.

"I know, but I just want to see."

Quickly leaving the house, Heather ran to the carriage house. She opened the door and stepped inside, then looked down at the place where Dake's bed had been. It was gone!

Almost timidly, Heather called out, "Dake—Stephen!"

"Up here."

The voice was faint and Heather looked up at the loft. She saw a dark face peering down at her, and he grinned suddenly.

"We're all right. Luckily for us, they didn't think to come up here."

A sense of relief washed over Heather, and she paused for a moment to get control of her voice. "How did you ever think of that, Stephen?"

"When they come into the yard without an officer or a sergeant, I thought they might come poking around in here, so I managed to get Dake up here. It not easy up that steep ladder."

"Are you going to stay up there?" she asked.

"I don't know." It had taken all of Joel's strength to get Dake up and cover him with the hay. They had lain there while the soldiers laughed and rummaged around downstairs. He expected any minute to be found, and he knew what awaited him if that happened. Now he said, "I think we just stay up here in case some of them come back."

"All right. I'll bring water and food as soon as my sister lies down."

"All right."

When she returned to the house she found a letter waiting for her. Margaret held it out, saying, "It came by the post. John had it, but he forgot to give it to you before you went to bed last night."

Opening the envelope, Heather quickly scanned the contents of the letter, recognizing the graceful script. She looked up and said, "It's from Grace Gordon. She wants me to attend her wedding in New York." She had told Margaret all about Grace, and now she read the last line. "She says here that her brother Clive is in Boston."

"He's the doctor, isn't he?"

"Yes, he's in love with a young woman there in Boston, so Grace tells me." She put the letter away, saying, "I can't go to that wedding. I need to stay with you until the baby comes."

All afternoon Heather worried about Dake. She knew now that it was just a matter of time until the pair were apprehended. The city was filling up with British soldiers. They were everywhere now—on the streets, breaking into houses, taking what they wanted, and the British officers really did not care. With the Hessians roaming all over, they wouldn't be so fortunate the next time. It was what she expected of the hated British, and she grew more concerned for their safety, especially for Margaret.

When John came home that night, she must have showed some sign of agitation, for he asked her at supper, "You seem nervous tonight, Heather. Is something wrong?"

"Oh no, just nervous about those soldiers coming."

Her brother-in-law shook his head. "They're getting worse. They force themselves into wherever they please, and the authorities don't care. I may have to move Margaret out of the city, but I hate to at this time."

"I think it will be all right, dear," Margaret said. "Maybe they won't come back."

"I don't like to leave you two here all alone. Maybe I'd better stay," John said, looking at Heather.

"We'll be all right, John. Dr. Smith said the baby won't be along for another two or three weeks. Later you will want to stay more closely at home."

John seemed content with her answer as he rose from the table. As usual he spent the evening in the library reading to Margaret. The two were a happy couple, and Heather sat there looking at her sister's face, thinking, *She's happy. She loves her husband and she's going to have a baby. I'm glad I came to help.*

After the pair had gone to bed, Heather quietly stole out to the carriage house and found Dake already unconscious.

"I no give him medicine. He just weak," Joel said. The two were standing looking down at the still figure.

"He's going to die," Heather said suddenly. "That foot's infected."

"I'm afraid maybe he lose it," Joel said.

"Maybe we'd better turn him in," she said. "He might be better off with the authorities. At least the British army would have a doctor of some kind."

"He already say he'd rather die."

"From what I hear of the prison hospitals, I don't much blame him, but we've got to do *something!*" She gave him a straight look and said, "Will you help me take him away from Philadelphia? If we get out to a village somewhere, maybe we can find a village doctor who can treat him."

Joel had already thought of this. "They would hang all of us."

"No, God won't let that happen."

"It is too dangerous," Joel said. "I take him alone. I'm sorry I brought this trouble on you, Miss Reed."

She looked up quickly, for his voice had sounded different. She stared at him so long that Joel knew that he had made a mistake and forgotten to put on his accent. He said in a more guttural tone, "We leave tonight. Get away from you."

"No, let me pray about it."

Joel gave her an odd look. It seemed that he was being brought up against praying people, and his own bleak spiritual condition suddenly came to him. "You think God hears?" he asked quietly.

"Of course God hears! The Bible says that we are to pray and He will hear. My favorite Scripture has been, 'Call upon me and I will answer thee and show thee great and mighty things thou knowest not.' " She said this firmly, although her heart was not as steady as she would have liked. Finally she shook her head, saying, "Let me pray. I'll think of something."

Before she went to bed that night, she read the Scriptures for a long time. She was not one of those who believed in simply opening the Bible and letting whatever was on the page speak to her. She had tried that, of course, as most Christians do at one time or another, but it did not seem to be right. Her pastor had said, "God speaks through His Word, but through study of it, not in just taking a lucky dip."

Nevertheless, she read until the candle beside her guttered down and her eyes were weary. Finally she closed her Bible, knelt down on her knees beside the bed, and prayed for what seemed to be a long time. "Oh, God, I can't pray, but please help that poor man who needs you so badly! Anything, Lord, that I can do, I give myself to it. In the name of Jesus save him." She got up, fell into bed, and felt herself slipping off into slumber at once. She did not remember going to sleep, but when she awoke the next morning, it seemed that she had dreamed all night long.

She awoke before dawn, jerking as a particularly vivid dream came to her remembrance. She lay there instantly awake and thought of the dream. She dreamed a great deal, but usually her dreams were more fragmented. What she had seen was a single scene, but it had been so clear and vivid that she knew it was not meaningless as so many of her dreams were.

As she lay there considering it, a thought came to her. *Can this be God speaking?* She had never had a dream she had actually acted upon, but now Heather was desperate. The longer she lay there, the more she became convinced that the dream was real and sent from God. Getting out of bed, she stood straight beside her bed and said, "God, I don't know if this is from you or not, but I'm going to act as if it were. If it is, then bless it. If it's not, then keep me from harm."

Swiftly she dressed, glancing at the clock on the mantel and noting that it was four-thirty in the morning. It was still dark outside as she made her way out of the house. Moving as quietly as she could, she made her way back to the carriage house in the silky darkness. She opened the door slowly and whispered, "Stephen!"

"Yes!" There was a rustling in the hay, and then he came to stand beside her. He left the lamp on, turned down low, and said, "What's wrong?"

"We're going to leave here!"

"Leave? How can we do that?"

Heather hesitated. She felt like a fool telling her dream, but she knew she had to do it. She began to speak. "I had this dream and I think it's from God." She related the dream and then revealed the plan that had come when she had awakened. When she had finished, she asked, "Will you help me, Stephen?"

"This dream, you think it's from God?"

"Yes, I think it is."

His face was impassive for a moment, then he nodded slowly. "Well, if you have heard something from God, it's better than anything else that I can see. We will follow your dream."

21

WHAT'S IN A HAND?

"HOW DO I LOOK?"

Heather stood up and felt a sense of embarrassment. Ever since she told her dream to the gypsy, she had felt like a fool. Now as she stood before him dressed in clothing such as she had never worn before, she felt more uncertain than ever about this plan.

Joel was looking at her with a strange expression in his eyes. He was thinking of the dream she had related to him. In the dream she had seen a pair of gypsies driving a wagon down the road. It was, she had told him, a man and a woman, but the wagon had been the same one in the dream as he had driven when he had first come upon her that dark night when he entered the city with Dake. He thought of how she had said, "It's simple, Stephen. I'll disguise myself as a gypsy woman. We'll make up Dake to look like an old man, and if anyone stops us, we're just a couple of gypsies with their ailing father."

It had sounded completely preposterous, but now, looking at Heather, Joel said, "This just might work."

"Do you really think I look like a gypsy?"

Sensing the doubt in her voice, Joel grinned. "You look more like a gypsy than my poor dead mother." He walked around her slowly, admiring his handiwork. They had spent a great deal of time coming up with a disguise. They had watered down some walnut juice until it had tinted her skin with a very light shading. She darkened her eyebrows and eyelids with the mixture, then put on a black wig she had purchased from the local wigmaker. She had not pierced her ears but had obtained a pair of gold earrings that could be fastened on in the ordinary fashion. She wore a full black alpaca skirt and a brilliant red blouse. From her wrist jangled a series of bracelets, and she had four rings, two on each hand.

"Actually, you pretty gypsy," Joel murmured.

"Really? Do you think so, Stephen?"

"Very pretty!" Joel said. The dark skin and the darkening of her eyebrows and eyelids had changed her appearance, but her green eyes might give her away if they weren't careful. "If we are stopped, you must not look at anyone. Gypsies not have such pretty green eyes." Still, as she turned around for his inspection, he smiled and said, "We are good-looking gypsy couple."

Suddenly it all seemed possible to Heather. She came closer and, without thinking about it, put her hand on his arm. "Do you really believe this can work?"

"I think so. We stay off the main roads until we get away from Philadelphia. Then we meet this Dr. Clive you speak of."

"I sent the messenger this morning. I paid him a good number of silver coins. He's very reliable and has a fast horse. Clive will get the message and meet us at Greenwood."

"Where is Greenwood?"

"It's a small village halfway between here and Boston." Her green eyes suddenly flashed, and she smiled. "It's got to work, Stephen. We can't stay here anymore. It's too dangerous!" she said.

"All right, I trust you. If this plan come from God, it will work."

Heather removed her hand from his arm, aware of the strong muscles. "Well, we'll just have to go on my faith, then."

"What will your sister think when you disappear?"

"I left her a note. I told her not to worry about me, that I had something I had to do."

"She will worry."

"I suppose so, but there's nothing I can do. I can't tell her why I'm leaving. Come, we need to get started. We can be down the road by daylight."

When they went to get Dake, he stared at them strangely, especially at Heather. He had been told all that would happen, and they had spent some time making him up to look like an old man. Heather had powdered his hair white and darkened his skin with the walnut juice dye. Now, sick as he was, he smiled, "Well, I'd never know you, Miss Reed. You make a fine-looking gypsy."

"I hope so. Come, we've got to get you into the wagon. We'll make you as comfortable as we can, Dake."

It was a long process, for his injured foot was extremely painful now. Finally they got him inside on the bed Heather had made out of a number of quilts. She pulled the cover over him, for it was growing cold outside. "We're going to leave now, Dake," she said. "We'll find you a doctor. Do you remember Clive Gordon?"

"I ought to, since he's my cousin. We fought over a young woman once, but I was the one who won her heart. I find it strange that Clive would be coming to help me."

His voice was blurred, and the laudanum they had given him was taking effect even now. Pulling the covers over him, Heather said, "Let's go, Stephen."

"All right, we go now."

As they pulled out of the carriage house and then out of the driveway, Heather cast an anxious glance at the house. She knew the note would not satisfy Margaret, but it was all she could think of. *I'll get back to her as quickly as I can*, she thought, but still she did not feel right about leaving so secretly.

Sitting beside Stephen as he drove down the road headed toward Greenwood, Heather felt a strange feeling. She had never in her life acted on a word from God, not directly. She had always tried to be obedient to His commandments, but never had she thrown herself into a dangerous situation like this in an act of faith. She knew that if they were apprehended, it was entirely possible they would all hang, but strangely the thought did not trouble her. They rumbled along the cobblestone streets for over an hour, and then just as dawn broke, Joel saw something in the darkness and heard the sound of horses approaching.

"I think maybe it's a patrol," he said quietly. "Let me do all the talking. Don't look up. Them green eyes don't look like gypsy woman."

It was a patrol of cavalry headed by a young officer. He cried out a command, and they rode up beside the wagon and looked down at the pair of gypsies. "Who are you?" the officer demanded.

"My name's Stephen. My wife, Maria."

"Anyone else with you?"

"My father, old man. He very sick."

"I'll have to have a look."

"Yes, sir." Jumping to the ground, Joel went to the back of the wagon and drew back the canvas. The officer dismounted, holding the reins of his lively horse firmly. He came and peered in and studied the face of the man lying in the bed of quilts.

"What's wrong with him?"

"He old and sick."

"No plague or anything like that?" the officer said. He turned to face Joel squarely. "Let's see your pass."

"Pass? I no have pass. Gypsies no have passes." The lieutenant stared at Joel hard, and Joel thought for one minute that the man meant to arrest him or make an issue of it.

Finally he shrugged and said, "All right." He swung up in his saddle and called out, "Forward!" and the patrol of cavalry thundered on into the interior of Philadelphia.

Joel clambered into the seat of the wagon and picked up the lines. "That was close," he said.

"Were you afraid, Stephen?"

"No, I wasn't—were you?"

Heather thought about his question, considering her state of mind for a moment, then said, "No, I really wasn't. It's strange, isn't it?"

"Yes." He flicked the reins and the horse picked up the pace to a fast walk down the road. "I hope that's the last patrol we meet. The next one may not be so nice."

They drove all day and saw soldiers constantly, but no one stopped them. That night they camped by a small creek. Joel had pulled off the main road, and looking around, he said, "I don't think any soldiers be here. We'll cook up something. How far to Greenwood?"

"We'll get there tomorrow."

Joel nodded. "That good. Dake is bad."

Joel cooked up a quick meal of bacon and eggs. That, along with fresh bread, made their supper. Heather had had time only to throw a few supplies into a sack before their hasty departure. They ate hungrily, although Dake could do no more than eat some of the eggs.

As they sat around the fire afterward Heather grew quiet. She studied the face of the gypsy across from her. He had pushed his hat back and his black hair fell over his brow. It was a strong face, and now in the darkness the flickering light threw its glow over the planes of his cheeks. The gold earring in his ear gave a twinkling reflection, and suddenly she said, "I've heard that gypsies tell fortunes."

"You believe in fortune-telling?"

"No, not really."

"What do you believe in?"

"Why, I've told you," she said. "I'm a Christian. I believe in God." She smiled ruefully. "It was a dream I believed was from God that got us out here beside this creek where we may be captured and hanged."

"That is true. But they can only hang us once."

Heather smiled at his reply, then asked curiously, "But you believe in fortunes?"

An impish impulse came to Joel. Perhaps it was the fact that they were out of Philadelphia and away from the British troops. He had been under tremendous strain cooped up in the barn, and now, looking over at Heather in her gypsy dress with her gold earring shimmering, he suddenly got up and moved beside her. She looked up startled, and he reached down without saying anything and looked at her palm.

Heather tried to pull her hand back, protesting, "No, don't do that, Stephen!"

He released her hand at once but sat down beside her. "The fortune is not in the hand. It is in the eyes," he said. He threw himself into his role and began to speak. Still retaining his accent, he said, "I can look at your face and tell you many things."

"You've been looking at my face," Heather said pertly, "and I'm not sure I want to hear what you have to say!"

"But you may never have a chance for a real gypsy to tell your fortune, not from the hand but from the eyes."

Heather laughed. She was feeling a release from the tension as well and said, "All right, tell me about myself."

"You strong woman," he said. "Your parents brought you into the world and taught you to be strong."

"That doesn't take any skill to know that. I've told you about my parents, so you could know that."

"But you are unlucky in love."

Swiftly Heather looked to him and said, "Why do you say that?"

"We gypsies know things like that," Joel said smoothly. "I look in eyes and I see a lovely woman, but an unhappy one."

"That's not true."

"Ah, perhaps you do not even know it yet, but a woman without a man, what is she? She is only half of something that was made to be different. God made man but He see it not good for man to be alone." He reached out suddenly and touched her cheek, saying, "You have smooth cheeks and very beautiful, but it is not good for a woman to be alone, either."

Heather was shocked at the touch of his hand on her cheek. She wondered why she did not reach out and knock it away, but his face was still half hidden from her, and she let his hand remain there. For one thing she could not refute his argument. She had known unhappiness. Finally she did push his hand away, saying, "That's not part of telling fortunes."

"Only with very beautiful young women. Never with old ugly women."

"You crazy gypsy!" she laughed. "I don't believe a word you're saying!"

"That probably good. Young woman should not believe everything a man says. It might get her in big trouble."

"You're a strange fellow, Stephen. Have you ever been married?"

"No."

"Then I'll tell your fortune." Impulsively she reached out and took his hand and looked at it.

"Ah, I see you have a strong life line. You have a big loneliness, I see."

She spoke lightly, but Joel was only conscious of her hands holding his. Finally she released it and laughed, "We both have lost our minds, Stephen!"

Joel suddenly rose and went back to his place, pulled his hat down over his eyes, and said, "I think you will have good fortune, Heather Reed. You are a good woman and love God. Good things will happen to you."

Heather was suddenly struck by a different tremor in his voice. Before he had been only teasing, she knew, and now he was serious. "It's kind of you to say that, Stephen, and I'll pray God for good fortune for you, too."

"I—need such prayers."

Heather smiled at his reply, then asked curiously, "Would you like to know more about God? I'm no preacher, but I love God."

"Tell me," he said.

Heather began to speak. It was easy sitting there, for the tension of the past few days had flowed out of her. She told about how she had found God when she was only a girl of fourteen. She spoke of how she had grown to love Him more as she read His Word and learned more about Him. At one point she hesitated, then said, "If you would only call on God, that's all He asks—that you turn from your sin and believe in Jesus and His death."

She continued to speak, and Joel sat there quietly, looking at her intently. His silence encouraged her, and she spoke for a long time. Finally, when she grew quiet, he said, "It is a good thing to believe in your God. I see you love Jesus. This man"—he pointed at Dake—"he is a man of God, too. You know what he ask me when I found him? He said, 'Are you a man of prayer?' and I said no." He looked up suddenly at her and shook his head. "But I prayed that I could get him away from the battlefield, and I did. Do you think that was God?"

"I think it was, Stephen," Heather said gently. "You had a good and kind impulse, and God used you to help one of His servants in need.

Why, even your coming to me was miraculous. I can't really believe it's happened yet."

"It was good thing. I never forget you."

Heather again caught a note in his voice that struck at something in her. "I'll never forget you either, Stephen. I think tomorrow we'll get to Greenwood. Clive will be there, and he will help Dake. What will you do then?"

"Go on being what I am."

"No, you mustn't do that." Heather's voice was suddenly intense. She found herself caring about this man, and she said eagerly, "You could change. All of us need to change, Stephen."

Joel did not answer. He felt a sense of hopelessness and looked down at the ground. For weeks he had struggled with his own heart, and now a dark despair seemed to descend on him. "How does a man change?" he whispered, asking the question of himself as well of Heather.

"Why, none of us can change ourselves, Stephen," Heather answered. Leaning forward she studied the dark face. "We are all weak and helpless. But God can make us different."

"But—how?" Anguish tinged Joel's voice.

As he looked up at the woman across from him, his eyes were filled with a despair that she knew a compassion such as she had never known for anyone.

"I can't tell you exactly how. I think it may be different for all of us. I've told you I was saved when I was fourteen. I wasn't in a church, but I'd heard the pastor preach on salvation. He'd said, 'Whosoever shall call upon the name of the Lord shall be saved.' And the next day I was out in the garden cutting roses, and I was very troubled." Heather's face grew soft as memories came to her, and she smiled slightly. "I remember I had just cut a beautiful pink rose, and suddenly I dropped it and closed my eyes. I said out loud, 'God, I want to be saved. I've done a lot of bad things, but Reverend Thompson said that Jesus can make us pure. Well, I'm calling on you, so please make me one of your children.' "

Joel studied her face for a moment, then asked, "And . . . that was all?"

"It was the beginning, Stephen," Heather nodded. "I felt a peace, and all my fears left me at once. I ran in and told my mother, and she took me by to see Reverend Thompson. He talked to me for a long time, and finally he said he was happy to see me become a part of the family of God." She drew a deep breath, then said, "The Christian life has a beginning, Stephen, and mine began when I turned to God and called on Him, asking him to save me. Since then I've followed as best as I could the teaching of Jesus."

"It sounds too easy."

"My father always says that it's easier becoming a child of God than it is being the child of God you become." Seeing the despair in his eyes, Heather said quietly, "Stephen, don't try to reason God out. None of us can do that. Just come as a child. If you want to have God in your life, all you have to do is turn from your sins and *ask* Him to save you."

A silence fell then, and Heather saw the struggle going on in the dark eyes. Quickly she said, "I think you need God now. Let me pray for you, and as I pray, just tell God you need Him and that you want Him." She half expected that Stephen would rebuff her, but he dropped his head and she closed her eyes and began to pray.

Joel heard the words of Heather, and they moved him. *She really cares for me—for a poor gypsy!* He was somehow aware that she was close to tears, and he felt an urge to run away—but he could not. Struggling with his soul, he felt his own sins as they lay heavily on his spirit. Fear came, but even in the midst of the fear, he knew that God was speaking to him in a way he'd never known. He heard no voice, but deep in his spirit he cried out for relief. Finally he groaned, and without intending to speak, he whispered, "Oh, God—I am such a sinner!"

Suddenly hot tears came to his eyes and he could not move. Heather's voice seemed far away, and he knew he must call out. *Lord . . . I know that Jesus died for sinners . . . and that's what I am. I can't help myself, so I ask you to save me! Jesus died for me, so save me in His name . . . !*

Heather prayed for what seemed to be a very long time. She finally looked up and saw tears running down the dark face of the man before her. "Did you call on the Lord?" she asked.

Joel took a deep breath, then took a red bandanna from his pocket. Wiping the tears away, he whispered, "I haven't cried since I was a boy!" He replaced the bandanna, then noted that his hands were trembling. He could not speak for a time, then he looked directly at Heather. She was watching him, her lips halfparted, and he said quietly, "I called on God."

"I'm glad!" Heather had the impulse to reach out and touch him, but instead she said, "Never forget this night, Stephen! When things get bad—remember this place. Remember that you obeyed God."

"I won't forget."

The two stood very still, and there were many things that Heather wanted to say, questions she wanted to ask, but somehow she sensed that Stephen needed to be alone with his own thoughts. "We'll talk about this tomorrow," she said. "I'm glad for you!"

Joel watched as Heather turned away, then went to roll up in his blankets. He looked up at the stars that glittered overhead, and a great stillness came to him. As he lay there he was aware that something had changed—that he was different. As the fiery stars wheeled overhead doing their great dance, he finally whispered, "Oh, God—let this be real! I want to love you and serve you all my life. . . ."

✠   ✠   ✠

Early the next morning before dawn, Joel had awakened and fixed a quick meal. Before the sun cast its first rays across the land, they were on their way again. Now as the sun began to rise in the sky Joel drove back to the main road. He had no sooner done so when a troop of infantry suddenly appeared, coming over the rise.

"More soldiers," he said. "Too late to run."

The troop was led by a captain atop a bay stallion. He pulled his horse over and questioned them, asking for a pass. When Joel repeated the same act that had been successful before, the captain asked, "Have you seen any American soldiers, gypsy?"

"No see soldiers. Only British men."

The lieutenant stared at the gypsy and then at Heather. "Did you come from Philadelphia?"

"Yes, sir."

"Where are you going?"

"To next village. We sell something there. You want me to sharpen your sword or your knife? I have good grindstones," Joel said.

"No, none of that. Go on your way." He spurred his horse and caught up with the head of the column that had continued marching down the road.

"Well, we got out of that all right," Joel said with relief.

The lieutenant, whose name was Smedley, forgot about the gypsies, but at noon when he reached Boston and dismissed the men, he went to his quarters. Later he went to have dinner with the members of General Howe's staff.

"Anything to report, Smedley?" Howe asked during the meal.

"No big troop movements that I could see, sir. Of course they'd stay out of my sight. They wouldn't be likely to attack a whole brigade."

"Keep your eyes open, Lieutenant." The speaker was Major Lawrence Hartford, who was sitting across from Smedley. He grew irritated sometimes at regular officers who saw nothing except what the enemy wanted them to see. "Nothing at all unusual to report?" he asked with some irritation.

Smedley did not like the major but had to be respectful. "Nothing, sir. Only civilians." He remembered the gypsies and said quickly, "Oh yes, we passed some wandering gypsies selling their wares."

Instantly Hartford was alert. "Gypsies? Where was this? What did they look like?" He listened carefully as Smedley told him more. "It was a man and a woman? Describe the man."

"Well, he was like any other gypsy. Dark skinned, gold earring, and gaudy clothes." Smedley shrugged and went on. "A well set up fellow. His wagon had about everything a man jack could ever need. His eyes were light colored for a gypsy, though. Kind of blue-gray."

Instantly something clicked in the mind of Major Hartford. He stood up and walked away from the table without a word.

"What's the matter with the major?" Howe said with surprise.

"I don't know, sir. Haven't a clue," said another officer seated to his right.

Howe was aware that Hartford was a strange man and merely shrugged it off. "I suppose he knows what he's doing."

Hartford had gone at once to a sergeant he had used before. "I need a small group of four men. We are moving at once!" he snapped.

"Yes, sir!"

"Have them well mounted! We're going to make a quick trip! Snap to it now!" As the sergeant turned quickly away, Hartford murmured, "It's him, that gypsy! I'll get him this time!" A sense of satisfaction came to him. For some reason, Hartford felt that he was about to have a breakthrough. He had captured several of the spies and agents who served Washington, but exposing and apprehending this gypsy seemed right.

"I'll get him," he said, "and then we'll see. . . !"

22

"What Sort of Man Do You Want?"

THE SKY HAD BARELY BEGUN to reveal a fine crimson line across the horizon as Heather and Joel settled on the wagon seat and left camp. Peering into the predawn, Joel was barely able to make out the ruts and had to trust the mare's instinct. He was troubled about Dake Bradford. Unless they found help soon, Dake would be in a critical condition. Keeping his thoughts to himself, Joel concentrated on guiding the mare until they reached the main road. As they turned toward the north, he said quietly, "Dake is not good."

"No, he isn't," Heather agreed. She had changed the bandage on the wounded man's foot by the light of a candle, and although she was not a doctor, she saw that the foot was in terrible condition. Right then the front left wheel of the wagon struck a pothole, careening the vehicle wildly and throwing Heather against her companion. She caught at him involuntarily, noting the strength of muscle beneath the thin colorful shirt and drew back, saying with some embarrassment, "I'm sorry."

"It's all right. Rough road."

Settling herself back and holding on with one hand to the seat in case the wagon lurched again, Heather looked involuntarily back to where Dake lay on the bed she had made for him. Lowering her voice, she whispered, "We've got to get him out of here! We've got to get help for him!"

"Maybe today," Joel answered.

For the next hour they both remained silent. Heather drew a thin coat around her shoulders and watched as the sky lit up toward the east. She had always liked the morning hours and had risen early to

261

catch the colors of the horizon, but there was no pleasure in it now, for their situation was desperate. She finally began speaking to Stephen, more to break the fear that rose in her from time to time than for any other reason.

"Tell me about when you were a boy," she said.

"When I was a boy? Why you want to know that?"

"I'm just curious. As I've told you, I've never known gypsies."

Actually Joel would liked to have told about his youthful days, but he didn't want to invent a story, so he merely said, "Very hard. Hungry days. No work." *This was true enough*, he thought grimly. But in order to change the subject, he said, "Tell me about you as a girl."

"Why, I was like other girls, I suppose," Heather said.

"What are girls like?"

Heather suddenly laughed. "What a question! You might as well ask what boys are like. Girls are what they are, Stephen. Some are sweet and gentle, others are sharp and rough. Some are pretty, some are plain."

"What about you? Tell me."

Once again, to keep the fears away, Heather began to speak of herself. She was not a young woman to give her confidences easily, but somehow as she sat on the wagon bed beside this strange, dark-featured young man, she felt it would be like whispering her secrets down a well. If she had formulated her thoughts at all, she would have said, *Telling things to this gypsy is not the same thing as revealing them to someone else. After this is over, maybe soon, I'll never see him again, so I can say anything to him.*

"When I was a girl," she said, "I did what all girls do. I played with my dolls, and I learned how to sew and how to cook a little bit." She went on describing her childhood, and finally she said almost dreamily, "But of course there is a fine line between being a girl and a woman. Women are different from children."

"They are bigger," Joel said wryly. He turned to face her, and his teeth were gleaming against his dark skin.

"Why, of course they're bigger!" she said, returning his smile. "But that's not the only thing. They're different in other ways, too."

"How different?"

"Why, they think of different things," Heather said. She sat on the seat as the wagon lurched over the ruts, the hooves of the horse making a muffled rhythm against the earth. The wind blew from the east, and her auburn hair, which was only loosely tied, brushed across her cheek. She pushed it back and said, "There comes a time, of course, when a young woman has to think of what she'll do with her life. She has to marry—that's about all there is for a woman to do." A streak of rebelliousness touched her tone and revealed itself in the glint of her green eyes. "Men can do anything they want, but women can't! They have to get married, so," she said, with a shrug of her shoulders, "that's what I began thinking about. All girls do that."

"What sort of a fellow would you like to marry?" Joel asked. He kept his head forward facing the road, but he shifted just enough so that he could see the outline of her features. He admired the strong lines and planes of her face, which he found very pleasing. The smoothness of her cheeks was evident in the glow of the reddish gleams of sunrise, and he admired the way her head smoothly joined her strong but graceful neck. Her lips, he saw, were firm, and as he watched her, he saw that her eyes had grown dreamy as she answered.

"A strong man," she said. "Every woman, I would think, wants a strong man."

"Not all. Some women want weak men, then they can be the boss."

"Then they're fools!" A touch of impatience tinged her voice and she shook her head, sending her hair fanning around her cheeks in a slight motion. "I've always wanted a man who was strong. Not so much physically, although, of course, one likes to see that in a man, too. Strong in other ways."

"Tell me."

"Why, there are certain qualities I would like to see," she said. "I never thought about it before, but there were several men I knew who had traits I admired, individual qualities, that is. For instance, James Dangerfield won all the foot races. He was strong and fast, could throw the iron bar at the contest farther than anyone else. I never admired bulky strength such as our blacksmith, but James was graceful and strong at the same time. But," she admitted with a shrug, "he was one of the most boring men I ever talked to."

"He could throw the bar if you married him and amuse you, maybe."

"Don't be silly! A woman can't spend her life watching a man throw bars around! She's got to talk to him!" She thought for a moment, then said, "Mr. Roger Henry, now there was an interesting man. He had been everywhere, done everything, and I loved to hear him talk. He came to our home often."

"You wanted to marry him perhaps?"

"Don't be silly! He was happily married and had five children, but he was an interesting man who knew how to carry on an engaging conversation."

"So, maybe you could marry two fellows. One could throw the bar and one could talk."

Somehow talking lightly with Stephen the gypsy took away her immediate fears for the future. Heather smiled and said, "Why do you want to know what kind of man I want?"

"Maybe I find you one," Joel said. "You tell me exactly what you want. I go find you a good husband."

"And what would you get out of that?"

"You could pay me a fee. Gypsies do things like that. They have matchmakers. Maybe I do the same for you, Miss Reed."

"All right. Find me one who can throw the bar farther than anyone else, and one that talks well—but he also has to know the Lord. I couldn't marry a man otherwise."

"I could have told you that. And he must believe in your war."

"Exactly!"

A silence settled down on the two for a moment; then suddenly Heather laughed. "I'm a fool for telling you all these things. I'm not likely to find all the qualities that I like in one man, but that's all right. When people get married they have to adjust to each other's shortcomings. So I suppose," she said and turned to him, "you'll just have to let me pick my own man, Stephen. When I find one I love, he may not have all of these qualities. But if we love each other, we can make it work."

"I think that very good."

The wagon rolled on, and from time to time the two would sit in silence. Then after a while they would strike up a conversation, often about the war. Twice before noon they stopped the wagon, and Heather climbed in the back and gave Dake a drink and bathed his face. He still had a fever, and she could tell that the pain in his foot was getting worse.

"We'll be there soon, Dake," she whispered, "and it'll be all right."

Dake's eyes were sunk back in his head, and the pain came in waves. He had his mind about him enough to say through clenched teeth, "I'm glad you're here, you and that gypsy. He's a funny fellow—but a good man."

"Yes, he is. I never knew a gypsy before. He's not what I expected."

When she got out and climbed back into the seat, she bit her lips, saying, "He's worse, Stephen. Can you go faster?"

"All right. Make a bumpier ride, but perhaps we do better to hurry."

⚜   ⚜   ⚜

"There it is up ahead," Major Hartford said. "It looks like the one we've been looking for. Be ready for trouble, Sergeant. He knows he'll be hanged if we catch him, but don't shoot to kill. I want to see him dangling from a gallows."

"Yes, sir!"

Hartford had brought his small squad, only four men, for he had confidence that would be enough to handle one spy. Drawing his pistol, he said with a grim smile, "All right, let's take them!" He spurred his horse and the party moved forward. Hartford held his pistol pointed in the air, his finger on the trigger. He was, however, determined to take the spy alive. As his horse pulled near the wagon, his mind worked agilely. He actually did not know that this was the exact wagon. If it was, there might be more than one man, and they might be well armed and dangerous. Still, when he drew closer he saw, with some relief, only a man and a woman.

Joel had heard the horses approaching and knew that it was a patrol coming. Glancing back, he saw one officer and a small group of soldiers.

"Another patrol," he said grimly. "I didn't think they'd be this far away from Philadelphia."

Even as he spoke he recognized Major Lawrence Hartford and knew instantly that this was no ordinary patrol. He turned to Heather and said quietly, "I think this is going to be bad."

Something about the tone of his voice was different, and Heather stared at him. "What is it, Stephen?"

He did not answer but turned to face the soldier who had now pulled up beside them and had thrown a large, cocked pistol straight into his face.

"Pull up! Pull up!" Hartford shouted and saw that his men had formed a circle around the wagon. A sense of satisfaction filled him, and he thought with exultation, *I've got him now!* When the wagon stopped, he said, "You two get out of the wagon!"

Without a word Joel stepped to the ground and Heather followed him. Her heart was beating fast, for she knew from Stephen's attitude that this was not just another patrol.

Swinging out of his saddle, Major Hartford rapped out orders to his men. "Keep your eye on them! He's a slippery devil!" He tied his horse to the wheel of the wagon and advanced to stand before Joel. His eyes ran quickly over the dark face and his hand shot out, grabbing Joel's hat and throwing it to the ground.

"Well, we meet again!"

Joel knew then that all was lost. His disguise might fool Heather and others, but this man's profession was to recognize disguises and ferret out spies. He knew at that moment he was no better than a dead man, and for one brief instant he felt pride because he knew he would be able to face whatever came and overcome the fear that rose in him. "Good afternoon, Major. I didn't expect to see you."

Admiration tinged Hartford's eyes. He always valued courage and was certain this man knew what faced him. "You're a cool one, that's for sure—and to think you almost got away with it."

"What is it? What's he talking about, Stephen?" Heather asked.

"Who is this woman?" Hartford demanded. "One of your camp followers?"

"No, Major. She had nothing to do with this. I talked her into it."

"Do you expect me to believe that?" Hartford moved over to where Heather was standing. His hand shot out and he pulled the neck of her gown away, exposing the fair skin that had not been stained. "She's a spy just like you are!"

"No, I'm not a spy!" Heather protested. "I'm just trying to save a man's life!"

"What man?" Hartford demanded.

"A wounded soldier. He's in the wagon."

"Keep your eye on them! Watch these two, Sergeant!"

Hartford moved to the back of the wagon, still holding his pistol on half cock. Drawing the canvas back he looked inside, his eyes trying to adjust to the gloom. "Who are you? What's your name?"

Dake had awakened. He managed to sit up, and now he stared at the British officer, noting his insignia. "Well, you've got me," he said. "I thought I'd make it, but it looks like I won't."

"Who are you?" Hartford snapped.

"Sergeant Dake Bradford, serving under General Nathaniel Greene."

Hartford studied the man and then looked down at the foot that was heavily bandaged. He did not speak but nodded briefly, then threw the canvas back in place. Coming back to stand in front of the pair, he said, "All right, let's have your version of this, Bradford."

Heather started at the major's words. "Bradford!" she exclaimed. She stared at Joel wildly, and the truth began to creep up on her. She narrowed her eyes and then something rose in her. "Who are you?" she whispered.

"Why, this is Mr. Joel Bradford, the famous spy," Hartford grinned.

"That . . . is that you . . . Joel?"

"I'm afraid it is, Heather."

"But what are you doing?"

266

"What he's doing is serving as a spy against His Majesty's army, an offense that will bring him to the gallows very shortly."

Heather was completely stunned. Her mind began to spin, and her eyes were locked with those of Joel. She was trying to think how all this could be, and she could only whisper, "Joel, I can't believe it's really you!"

Joel immediately turned to the officer. "She didn't know a thing about my being a spy. The soldier inside is kin to me. I found him in the woods after the battle, and I was trying to get him home safely. Do what you want to with me, Major Hartford, but this young woman has done no more than to try to help a wounded ally. I don't think your honor would permit you to take action against her."

Major Hartford stared at Joel. "I have to admire your gall, Bradford," he said. A smile turned the corners of his thin lips up. "But I'm inclined to think that in this case you're right. I believe you're telling the truth."

"It *is* the truth," Joel said firmly. "You admire courage, and this young woman has plenty of it. Let her go. It will be the act of a gentleman."

The major stood watching the two, and more and more he was impressed with the calm courage he saw in Joel Bradford. He had seen many men executed. Some of them had died well, some had not. He had the idea that this one would be one who did. He said finally, "I'll have to take your kinsman in, of course, as a prisoner of war, but I'm going to take it on myself to let the young lady go. Obviously she's quite taken with the cause, but if I hanged all the women in this world who were sympathetic to Washington and his ragtags, there wouldn't be enough rope."

He turned and said, "Sergeant, take this woman back to that village and leave her there."

"Yes, sir!"

"You'll say your good-byes now. You won't be meeting again," Major Hartford said.

A chill ran through Heather as she stood there. Her legs suddenly became weak, so that she was not certain of them. Joel stood directly across from her, and she whispered, "I can't believe it. Why didn't you tell me?"

"I couldn't. An agent can't tell people things like that."

The world around the two seemed to have grown smaller. They were both oblivious to the waiting soldiers and to the major who had stepped back a few paces and was staring off toward the horizon, although he could still hear. Heather could hear the sound of a bird far off singing some sort of a merry song, and it lent a macabre atmosphere to the scene. She suddenly reached out and his hand caught at hers, "Joel, I . . . I can't believe this!"

Her face, Joel saw, was very pale and he knew she was shocked to the core. "I love this young country, and I was persuaded that I could serve it better in this way than by carrying a musket in battle as Dake did. I wanted to tell you, but I couldn't." He hesitated and then said, "I wanted to tell you one more thing."

"What is it?" Heather asked, her eyes locked with his.

"Since I've known you, I've been different." He found it difficult to put his feelings into words, for he knew he had only a few moments. Finally he said, "Two things I'll tell you, for we won't meet again." He felt her gasp and squeezed her hand tightly. "The first is, I've met God these last few days, and it's been your doing. I never knew what a Christian was really like, and somehow God used you, Heather, to lead me to himself."

"Oh, Joel, I'm so glad," Heather whispered, a look of complete astonishment on her face.

"The other thing," Joel said, and he put his arms around her and held her close for a moment. Her eyes were startled, and he said, "For a long time I've known that I love you. I've never loved a woman before, and it will come to nothing now. But sometimes think of me and remember that one man loved you with all of his heart." He bent his head then and kissed her. It was a brief kiss, and he held her tightly for that one moment.

Her heart seemed to stop and then it began to beat rapidly. She felt her arms go around his neck, and she clung to him as a small child clings to someone in times of trouble. She could not put her thoughts together, and the world seemed to be turning around. When he stepped back his face was set in a look of determination.

"Good-bye, Heather. Tell my uncle that I did the best I could to serve this country."

"All right, that's enough! Take her away!" Hartford ordered.

The sergeant grabbed her arm then and led her away to his horse. He helped her mount up into the saddle and then swung up beside her. She turned as he spoke to the horse and saw Joel watching her. He did not move, nor wave, but his eyes leaped out at her, and she cried out, "Joel—!" and then the soldier put his arm around her, swung her back into position, and as she turned, the world seemed to close down for her.

"Well, a very romantic scene, Bradford. Like something out of a novel."

"Better than that, Major." Joel's voice was steady, and he ran his hands through his hair with a strange gesture and then shook his head. "I'm sorry most of all for Dake going to a prison. He needs medical care right away."

"We'll get him to one of our doctors. I'll do that much for you. Get back in the wagon. Corporal, you get in the wagon beside this man. Shoot him if he tries to escape." His face was sober then, and he said, "I'd like to hear some of your experiences." He saw the expression on Joel's face. "Oh, I'm not asking you to give up your associates. I know you'd never do a thing like that."

"That's right, I wouldn't."

"But we can be gentlemen about this. If I were in your place, I think you would treat me with some generosity, Bradford."

"I'm glad I made that sort of impression on you, Major."

"General Howe will be quite surprised when he learns of you. I'm looking forward to seeing his face when we tell him how much of his military intelligence he revealed to an agent of General Washington. Well, come along, we'd best get started. It's a long way back to New York."

As Joel climbed in the wagon, he thought of how he was about to lose the family he had just discovered and the woman he loved. A shroud of hopelessness settled on him. The guards surrounded him, and the corporal sat beside him with a loaded musket. He knew there was no chance of escape. The shadows of the gallows lay ahead of him, but as he spoke to the horse and they moved along, he thought of Heather's face. Suddenly he thought, *I'm glad I was able to tell her that I loved her and I'm glad she knows the truth.*

The corporal who sat beside him was a powerfully built man, and he kept a watchful eye on his prisoner. The shadow of death, he knew, already lay on this man, and he said, "Tough luck. Goes that way sometimes."

Joel managed a smile as he turned to his captor. "Yes, it does go that way sometimes, but when a man knows God he doesn't have to think too much about it."

The answer took the corporal off guard. He settled down in his seat and shook his head. He himself was not a man of God, but somehow the courage and the faith in the eyes of the prisoner silenced him.

23

A New American

CLIVE ARRIVED AT THE *Red Lion Inn* in Greenwood at midday. He obtained a room easily, for the inn was practically empty, but his accommodations were too confining, so he went for a walk outside. He read repeatedly the brief message he had received from Heather Reed, as if he could find something new to make out of it, but there was nothing. It was merely a plea for him to come and meet her there and help his cousin Dake Bradford, who had been wounded.

Walking back and forth on the road in front of the *Red Lion*, Clive tried to imagine how such a thing had come about. *He must have been wounded in a battle*, he thought. *But why didn't they get him to a doctor close by?* Filled with questions and apprehension, Clive grew restless. He remained outside for some time, then he went back inside the inn to drink some of the thin ale served by the barkeep, a small, wiry white-haired man with muddy brown eyes. Clive sat at a table in the far corner so as to avoid the questions of the barkeep.

Several times he got up from the table to step outside and scan the street. After looking for the fourth or fifth time—he had lost count—he finally saw a buggy approaching. Greenwood had little enough traffic, and he had watched every arrival carefully. Now, as the vehicle drew closer, he muttered, "Well, here she is, but where's Dake?"

Moving up to the wagon, he said, "Hello, Miss Reed," and then immediately asked, "What's this all about?"

Heather's face was pale and her lips were drawn together in a tight line. "It's trouble, Clive," she said. "It's Dake . . . and Joel." She added the last with effort and shook her head. "Get in the buggy. I have to tell you some things."

Quickly Clive swung into the seat, and Heather slapp and began to tell him all that had happened in the past related all the events clearly, although her voice was tense and tight. Finally she said, "The British officer didn't think I was a spy. He had one of his men take me to a village down the road. I rented this buggy and came to meet you."

"So Joel Bradford isn't what he always seemed to be."

"No he isn't, and he's going to die. They'll hang him for sure, Clive!"

"That's what they'll do, all right." He was staring down at her. She had explained her disguise as a gypsy, and although his thoughts were mostly on Dake, he asked suddenly, "Why did you help him do all this, Heather?"

"Because it was all I could do. Soldiers can go out and fight, but here was something I could do. I wanted to do it so much, Clive."

She had used his first name almost unconsciously, and when her face turned toward him, Clive saw the look of pain and sorrow, and something like fear reflected on it. She had a vulnerable air about her, despite the strength he had noted there before. "You didn't like Joel Bradford much, did you?"

"No, and I let him know about it, and all the time he was—" Heather broke off and bit her lip. She had thought about Joel constantly since learning his identity, and now she whispered, "They're going to hang him, Clive. And Dake's being sent to a prison. There's nothing I can do about it."

"Where did they take him?"

"To New York. The major wanted to have him executed there as an example to other spies."

"Well, he won't get far today," Clive said slowly, "and we know which road they'll be on."

Catching an unusual nuance in Clive's voice, Heather sensed something was in the tall young man's mind that she could not understand. Quickly she asked, "What are you thinking?"

"I'm thinking Dake and Joel are Bradfords. We're a very close family, Heather. Remember I told you how Dake and I both fell in love with the same woman, and a fine woman she is, too." Memories came to him then of the young Jeanne Corbeau he and Dake had battled fiercely for. She had been the most beautiful young woman he had ever seen, until he'd met Katherine Yancy. He sat quietly in the seat, thinking of how much he liked Dake Bradford, and finally he looked at her and said quietly, "He's a kinsman of mine, Dake is—and that means something. And Joel is a true patriot. We just didn't know it."

Heather saw a look of determination on his strong face. Though she did not know him well, she had heard a lot about him from his sister, and now she said, "Isn't there something you can do? Maybe we could get help."

Clive did not answer for a moment. Then the muscles in his jaw tightened and he turned to stare at her. There was a flat expression in his light blue eyes, as if somehow a curtain had fallen over them. He had a sensitive English face, and now the long leanness of his strength seemed to tense. "Joel's a Bradford and a kinsman, too. I'll not let them hang him." He suddenly reached over and took the lines and swung the startled horse around. "I'm going to stop and get a few things from the inn. I want you to wait there."

"What are you going to do?"

Clive Gordon suddenly grinned rashly. "I'm going to get Dake and Joel back," he said.

Heather stared at Gordon and a startled expression swept across her face. Inadvertently she reached out and grabbed his arm and held to it tightly. "Let me go with you. I can help!"

"No, I can handle this alone." He thought for a moment, then said, "Did you say he was wounded badly?"

"Yes, and he needs your help, Clive."

"All right. Come along, then. You can drive the wagon when I get him away."

"How are you going to do that? What's your plan?"

"I don't have any plan. I'm just going to trust God. If you have a prayer left in you, you'd better say it now, Heather!"

🏵   🏵   🏵

"Well, Dr. Gordon, what brings you out here?"

Major Lawrence Hartford rose from his place beside the fire where one of his men was cooking up some beef they had obtained along the way. Always alert, Hartford watched as the tall young man swung out of the saddle. "You didn't bring a message from your father, did you, or from General Howe?"

"As a matter of fact, I did."

Immediately the major became alert. "How did he happen to send you, Mr. Gordon?"

"Come over here and I'll explain it to you. It's very confidential," Clive said. He had put on a cloak, and now he reached under it as if to pull out a message. Glancing at the soldiers and at Joel, who was staring at him from his place across the fire, he lowered his voice to a whisper. "They didn't want me to carry anything in writing."

Hartford was accustomed to this sort of thing, although he was still suspicious of the unusual circumstances. He glanced around at his small group and nodded. "All right." He followed Gordon until they were thirty yards away from the fire, then said, "This is far enough. They can't hear us."

Gordon had told the truth when he had said he had no plan. They had traveled hard, he and Heather, stopping to ask if a group of Redcoats had passed recently. When they approached the camp, he had said, "You stay here. I'll see what I can work out." Now as he stood there, he realized that attempting a rescue single-handedly was, perhaps, the most foolish thing he could have done. But he had crossed a bridge somewhere in his mind. He knew somehow that Katherine Yancy was connected with it, and yet nothing was settled between them. With one single motion he reached under his cloak, pulled out the flintlock pistol, and pulled the hammer back. It made a loud clicking in the silence, and then he pressed the muzzle against Hartford's stomach. He saw the officer's eyes widen and heard the involuntary gasp.

"I don't want to kill you, Major, but I will if I have to."

"What are you doing? Have you lost your mind?"

"I'm afraid you would say so. What I intend to do is take your prisoner away."

Hartford's eyes narrowed. "You're some relation to Dake, if I remember. Your mother's brother is a Bradford."

"That's right, and that's his son in the wagon. He's badly wounded, and I'm going to care for him and take him home."

Understanding came at once to Hartford. "The girl got to you, didn't she?"

"That's right."

"You can't do it." The major's voice was flat. "I'd never live it down if I let you take a prisoner away from me."

"Major, you'd never live *anything* down if I pull this trigger. I understand that I wouldn't have a chance. You've got armed men there, so we'd both be dead. What's the use of that?"

Major Lawrence Hartford was a man of quick understanding. It was a necessary attribute of his trade. He had no real interest in Dake Bradford anyway, merely one more prisoner to die in a camp or in one of the prison hulks. "All right," he said, "he's not worth dying for. You can take him."

"I'm taking Joel Bradford, too. He's a kinsman as well."

Anger flared in the major's eyes. "That's a different story! I can't let a spy go! He's my responsibility!"

"Make up your mind, Major! Either I leave with both men or else we both die here!"

Something about the expression on Clive Gordon's face stopped the words that came to Hartford's lips. He stood there weighing his chances, the hard barrel pressing in his stomach, and he knew Gordon would do exactly as he said. "You mean it, don't you?"

"Yes I do!"

"You'll be a castoff from your own people and branded as a traitor!"

"That's not your concern, Major Hartford. Your only question is this. Do you want to die for these two men?"

Hartford answered at once, "No, I won't die for them!"

"A wise decision, Major," Clive said.

"What will you do after this? You know I'll report you to General Howe."

Clive grinned briefly. "I'll be a new American," he said. "All right, here's the way we're going to do this. . . ." Clive's mind worked more rapidly than it ever had in his life. A plan almost fully formed came to him, and he said, "Call your sergeant over here and tell him that I brought a message that they're needed back at headquarters—that you'll take the prisoners in alone."

"He'll never believe that."

"You forget, Major, I'm the son of a British officer. I've been around British soldiers all my life. I know as well as you do, whether they believe you or not they'll obey you. At least I hope so, for all of our sakes. Now, call the sergeant." For one moment Clive thought that Major Hartford would refuse.

The major shrugged slightly and said in a spare tone, "It's not a cause worth dying for." Lifting his voice and turning, he said, "Sergeant, come over here!"

Clive tensed as the tall sergeant came over and stood before his commanding officer. His finger was on the trigger. He wondered if he would have the nerve to kill a man in cold blood and prayed fervently that he would never find out. It went well, though the sergeant showed surprise on his blunt face at the order.

"Yes, sir, any more orders?"

"Tell General Howe I'll return soon and give him a full report."

"Yes, sir!" The sergeant turned and began to bawl out orders.

Within five minutes Clive and the major were watching as they rode out. As soon as they disappeared, Clive let the hammer down carefully and thrust the pistol back under his belt. "Now, what am I to do with you, Major?"

"You might let me go. I'll be glad to give you my parole."

"I have your word that you'll make no attempt to recapture either of the prisoners?"

"You have my word, sir."

Actually Clive was relieved. He knew they would have to move fast, and there was no time to spend guarding Hartford as a prisoner. "I accept your word, Major. You can go now."

Joel Bradford had come up to hear the last of this. "You're leaving, are you, Major?"

"Yes, Mr. Bradford. It appears that blood ties are very strong in this part of the world. Your kinsman here has saved you from a hanging—unless I can get my hands on you again."

"I sincerely hope that won't happen."

"It probably won't. In any case," he shrugged, "I've always felt that fate has a hand in these things, and who is a lowly British soldier to argue against fate?" He stepped to his horse, swung into the saddle, and turned his head to one side with a curious look. "I should be angry at both of you, but somehow I'm not. I'll give General Howe your best wishes, Mr. Bradford." He turned the horse's head, sank the spurs into the startled animal's side, and galloped away at a furious rate.

"You think he'll give us away?" Joel said doubtfully.

"I think not, but we won't give him a chance. Come along, I'll need to take a look at Dake."

"I assume that Heather found you?"

"I'll tell you all about it later, but first I've got to see that foot." He hesitated, a strange look coming into his eye. "I've got bad news for you, Joel."

"Is it Phoebe?" Joel quickly asked, fear coming into his eyes.

"No, she's fine. It's Leah—"

Seeing the hesitancy in Clive Gordon's eyes, Joel suddenly knew the truth. "Is she dead?" he asked quietly.

"Yes. She died in childbirth. I'm sorry, Joel. I know you were very fond of her."

"Yes, I was—very fond."

Clive put his hand on Joel's shoulder. "The child is well—a fine boy."

"Leah would have liked that." Joel found that his eyes were burning and he turned abruptly and walked away.

🛡   🛡   🛡

Twilight had come and gone, and now as the last vestiges of light lit up the sky, Heather gave a start as she saw the wagon turn from around the bend. A great sense of relief came over her, and she strained her eyes in the gathering darkness. As the wagon neared she ran forward and called out, "You got them, Clive!"

"Yes, I did. Come along, we've got to find shelter for the night."

"I've been talking to the innkeeper. I think he's dependable."

"Did you tell him anything?" Clive asked.

"No, but he gave me the names of some of the people around here. There's a woman whose husband is in the army. I think we could find a welcome there, at least for one night."

"All right. Lead the way."

Joel leaped down suddenly and came over to stand beside the wagon. "I'll ride with you, if you don't mind."

"Get in," Heather said. The buggy settled as he stepped inside, and she spoke to the horses. As they moved out she turned to him after a silence and said, "I don't know how to talk to you. It's all so strange."

"We never did have much to say to each other."

Heather flushed slightly. "I said awful things to you, Joel. I keep remembering them."

"You can't be blamed." He turned to her and studied her face in the fading light. All he could see was her profile dimly, and he did not speak for a time. He knew now that he loved this woman and always would, but a war stood between them and a great many other things. He had no idea about what would happen to him.

Finally she broke the silence by asking, "Will you go back to being a secret agent again?"

"I don't think so. Now that Major Hartford knows about me it would be a pretty dangerous occupation. I expect," he said finally, "I will go into the army. That's what I wanted to do in the first place."

Heather said nothing. She had thought of little else but Joel Bradford ever since she had learned his true identity. As the horse moved along through the darkness, she did not speak until they got to the house the innkeeper had mentioned to her, then she said simply, "The woman's name is Mrs. Denton. I'll go in and talk to her."

Thirty minutes later Dake was in a bedroom lying on a mattress, and Clive was examining the foot. He was slow and methodical, very careful, and finally he looked up and saw Dake watching him.

"Pretty bad, isn't it?" Dake remarked.

"It's not good, Dake."

"Can you save the foot?"

"I think so, but it'll never be as good as it was before. You won't be running any foot races."

"I was never one for races anyway."

"You won't be doing much soldiering, either."

"Don't know about that," Dake said. His face was gaunt and the sickness had drained him, but still his eyes flared with a fighting light as he said, "They still make horses, don't they? Maybe I can be a cavalryman or fire a gun off in the artillery."

Clive came over and sat down beside him. "You had a close call."

"I did," Dake nodded and lay there quietly. "If it hadn't been for Joel, I don't think I would have made it. If I had lived, I would have wound up in a prison. From what I've heard, I'd rather be dead."

"He's quite a fine young fellow. Your father will be glad to hear that he's loyal."

"Yes, he will. Where is he, by the way?"

A smile came to Clive. "I expect he's out talking to that young woman. They've got a lot of things to discuss, from what I understand."

At that very moment Heather and Joel were standing outside the house. The moon had come up now, large and round and silver. Looking up at it as they stood beside a white picket fence, Heather tried hard to carry on a conversation, but it was difficult. She was a young woman who did not like to be wrong, and she had been dreadfully wrong about Joel Bradford. She had treated him shamefully, and now she was trying to find some way to reach a common meeting ground again. Finally she said, "What will you do now?"

"Well, I imagine the first thing I'll do is go back to Boston and see Phoebe."

"That's your sister. She'll be happy that you're all right."

"She'll never know how close she came to losing a brother."

At his remark a shiver went through Heather. "Don't say that!" she said sharply. "I don't even like to talk about it!"

Surprised by her reaction, Joel turned to her. "Did it mean that much to you, Heather?"

"Of course it did!" She was an honest girl, and now she turned to him and said simply, "You're not the man I thought you were. Even when things were at their worst, Joel, and I believed the worst about you, there was—" She hesitated and finally faced him squarely. "There was something about you that drew me to you."

Joel stood stock-still, shocked by this straightforward remark. He looked at her face and saw that she was watching him almost expectantly. Her expression was not composed, and he knew she was still not over the shock of all that had happened. "Nevertheless," he said quietly, "it's too early to speak of some things maybe, but I'll say what's been in my heart for some time. I love you, Heather, and I think you care for me, too." He did not wait for her to answer but put his arms around her and pulled her close. She looked up, her lips slightly parted, and said, "I . . . don't know how I feel right now about things, but you're the kind of man, I think, that I could learn to love."

He smiled then and touched her cheek. It was smooth and satiny, and there was a smell of lavender about her that he had noticed before. "I'll have to be as strong as that young iron-tosser you were talking about, and as smooth a talker as that old man if I'm going to keep your interest alive."

Suddenly she reached up and put her hand on his neck. "No," she whispered. "Just be who you are, Joel."

"I love you, Heather Reed, and if it takes me ten years, I'll prove it to you. And someday you'll love me, too."

Heather Reed then knew with an abruptness that comes to a woman unexpectedly, and from nowhere, except her own heart, that he was right. She put her hand on his chest, and her voice had a half-humorous, half-serious tone to it as she said, "You'll have to come courting, Joel. I'll be anxious to see what kind of a courting man you are."

Joel took her one hand. In a gesture that was far more chivalrous than any he had ever performed, he pulled it to his lips, kissed it, and held it there for a moment. When he lowered it, he said, "We'll have time for me to come courting. But one thing I know in my heart. I'll never let you go, Heather."

Heather listened as if she heard some pleasant music from far away, an old familiar strain somehow familiar and yet new.

"I'll be waiting," she said, and then the two turned and walked back into the house.

24

A Man Sent From God

KATHERINE YANCY OPENED THE DOOR and then stood as still as a statue. Her mouth was slightly open, and her eyes reflected the shock at seeing the tall man who stood there smiling at her.

"Clive!" she gasped quickly and reached out to take his arm. Drawing him in, she demanded, "What are you doing here? I thought you had gone back to New York."

Clive Gordon looked pleased with himself. "No," he said. "I didn't get that far."

"Where did you go?"

Clive had been thinking of what he would say when this moment came. The house was quiet, and he suspected that Katherine's parents were in bed. "Invite me into the parlor and I'll tell you all about it."

"Come along. Mother and Father are already asleep." She led him down the short hall, then through the double doors that led into the parlor. As soon as they were inside, she turned to him and carefully studied him. "You look . . . odd!" she said. "Somehow you look like the cat that swallowed a canary!"

"I have something better than that. At least I hope you'll think so." Clive reached out, put his arms around her, and before she could protest or respond, he pulled her close and kissed her.

"You mustn't do that!" she protested when he released her.

"I'm sorry. I'm afraid it'll be happening a lot," he said, smiling.

"Clive we've gone over all this!"

"No, you'll have to marry me now, Katherine." He held her still, and her breath was warm and sweet. He saw her lips open to protest, and he closed them with another kiss. This time he lingered longer and felt her yield herself to him. When he lifted his head, he said, "You'll have to marry me now because I'm a rebel."

Her shock was so great he could not help but laugh. "Come, I'll tell you about it."

The two sat down on the horsehair couch, and Clive began to tell her about his rescue of Joel and Dake. "It was quite a scene when we got together with Daniel and Marian. They'd been worried sick over Dake, of course, and then there was Joel. They had pretty much written him off as a traitor to their cause."

"What did they say? Tell me all about it! Don't leave out anything!"

"All right, just as long as you sit right here." He put his arm around her, and she laughed and yielded herself to him. She sensed a peace and security surround her as she leaned against him. She felt a freedom she had never felt before, and finally, when he finished, she said, "But what about you, Clive?"

"I made my choice. This is a good land, Katherine. I love America, and I'm going to do my best to become the best American I can. That means," he said slowly, "I'll be serving somewhere. Probably with the army as a physician." He looked down at her. He was so tall that she had to look up. "But I want you to marry me now before I leave. I want us to have some time together. It may be years before we have anything like a normal life. Will you marry me, Katherine?"

Katherine Yancy was not a woman to waste time or words. "Yes," she said simply, and this time it was she who pulled his head down and kissed him. Her heart filled with a happiness she never knew possible, and she knew she would love this man as long as they lived. Suddenly she pulled away and jumped up. "Clive, I almost forgot! You've got to go see Ezra Tyrone. He's very ill!"

"All right, but I'm surprised he hasn't passed on before this. He's lived longer than I expected."

"Come along. Marian and Daniel will be there. They've hardly left his side."

"What about the baby?"

"Marian's taking care of him most of the time." She hurried quickly to get a coat, and the two left at once.

🜚　　🜚　　🜚

Ezra Tyrone's frail body contained only a spark of life, but that spark was reflected in his eyes. He was lying half propped up against a pillow and looking at the child Marian held in her arms. He reached out and touched the fresh cheek of the child and murmured, "A fine boy."

"Yes, he is," Marian said. "The finest I've ever seen, Ezra."

"We always . . . wanted a son, me and Leah."

Not knowing how to answer, Marian looked at Daniel, who was sitting beside her, his arm around her. They had been there when Clive had arrived. After a brief examination Clive had shaken his head, saying, "He can last only a few hours. Katherine and I will stay with him."

Now Daniel reached over and took the frail hand of the sick man and said, "Ezra, is there anything I can do for you?"

Silence fell over the room as the dying man struggled to find words. "I hate to leave, but God is taking me." His glance shifted slowly to Marian, and he smiled. "You taught me how to believe God—it's a good thing, Marian. It came almost too late for me."

"You'll be with Leah soon," Marian said, her eyes dim with tears. She dashed them away and held the infant closer. Looking down into the round face, she said, "I can see both of you in him. You are leaving part of yourself and part of Leah."

Marian sat quietly for what seemed like a long time. Ezra's mind seemed to come and go. He would open his eyes and look at his son for a moment, then he would drift off again. This went on for what seemed like hours. Finally Ezra opened his eyes, and his voice was somehow stronger. "Lift me up, Daniel," he whispered.

"Here." Daniel reached down with his strong arms and pulled the dying man up.

"Let me hold the boy."

At once Marian put the child in Ezra's feeble arms, supporting them at the same time. She glanced at Daniel, and the two of them watched as the man in the bed drank in the features of the baby for a long time.

He looked up and whispered hoarsely, "I'd like to name him Enoch."

"A good name," Daniel nodded.

"Your wife read me about him. He walked with God and was so close to God that God took him. I think he'll be a man who will walk with God."

That was the last time Ezra spoke. He finally surrendered the baby, reached out and touched his cheek, then lay back and closed his eyes. It was only thirty minutes later that his going took place, so gently that it was almost impossible to tell when he went. But finally Daniel leaned over and held his hand close to his lips, then he turned to Marian and said simply, "He's gone, Marian."

"He's with Leah now."

"Yes, and he got to see his son before he left."

Stiffly Marian got to her feet and walked over to the window. Daniel lay the body down flat, composed the arms, then came over to stand beside her.

"What are you thinking?" he asked, for she was strangely silent.

Marian turned and her eyes were damp with tears. She held the baby close and, in a gesture as old as womankind, leaned over and kissed the silken hair. "You have your sons, Daniel, but this one is mine."

Daniel Bradford knew a joy then, for he had known the longing of his wife's heart for a child. She had been denied one of her own, but now in some way God had answered, and he put his arm around her gently, with the child between them. He looked down into the tiny red face and said, "He's yours—and he's ours. God has entrusted him to us, Marian, and we'll raise him as one of our own."

Marian Bradford could not speak, her heart was so full of love for this tiny infant now left in her care. After years of longing for a child, this warm little one lay within her arms. She stroked the silky hair back and whispered, "He's a child sent from God."

Daniel held her tightly, leaned over, and kissed her cheek. "We have a son now. We'll see what God makes of him."

The house was quiet, the room was still, and Marian looked up at her husband and nodded. "Yes, we do have a son. God is good!"